# NOCTURNAL ASCENDANCY

Deirdre Jonker

Publisher: Inspiring Publishers,
P.O. Box 159, Calwell, ACT Australia 2905
Email: publishaspg@gmail.com
http://www.inspiringpublishers.com

 A catalogue record for this book is available from the National Library of Australia

National Library of Australia The Prepublication Data Service

Author:   Deirdre Jonker
Title:      Nocturnal Ascendancy
Genre:    Fiction

Paperback ISBN: 978-1-923087-48-4
ePub2 ISBN: 978-1-923087-47-7

# Prologue

"Welcome to my world again, Arabella Ambrose," Gabriel said, smiling at Arabella. "How are you feeling?" Arabella looked around, her emotions swirling as if she were a newborn baby. She examined her hands, noticing the absence of her wedding ring.

"Oh right," said Gabriel. He reached into his pocket, pulling out a metal band, and handed it to her. Arabella slid the ring onto her left ring finger, studying it closely.

"Mom, how wonderful to have you back in our lives," Ginger said with a smile. Arabella turned to Ginger, embracing her tightly. Amy cast a glance at Gabriel, seeing a hint of relief in his eyes. Then, Arabella drew Amy into a warm hug.

"The feeling is mutual, my loves," Arabella murmured. Tears welled up in Amy's eyes as she clung to her mother. After a moment, Arabella released them both, looking them over.

"You both are so beautiful. Once I adjust to this new chapter of my life, I do have questions and concerns about how this all came to be," Arabella said, her gaze shifting back to the castle. "Am I a second wife or will Katrina leave?" she asked. Amy and Ginger exchanged a glance before turning their attention to Gabriel, who remained silent. "Where will I sleep, Gabriel?" Arabella asked.

"You'll be with me, my beloved," Gabriel said, his smile tender. "Just like old times." Arabella's face lit up in response. "The girls have their own rooms, and Hildegard, now older, serves as our housekeeper." Gabriel gestured for them to head inside, and as

Arabella looped her arm through his, they made their way to the castle. She took in every detail, noticing even the floating dust particles and the diverse scents of various shape-shifters, including Hildegard's. After a moment, she gently extricated herself from Gabriel's hold and began exploring the ground floor, her steps firm and grounded.

Lucien, Daniel, Vladimir, and Amelia approached Arabella, embracing her warmly. "Welcome back," said Amelia, squeezing a little tighter. "It has been hard being one of the very few females in this coven." Arabella planted a kiss on Amelia's cheek, examining her.

"You haven't changed a bit, Amelia," said Arabella with a chuckle. Amelia smiled and took a step back so Daniel could hug her. "You all have not changed. How does Gabriel keep you all so beautiful?" Arabella said in a cheery tone.

Meanwhile, Gabriel stood a distance away, observing the reunion. Glancing at his watch, he noted the time: three in the morning. He moved to the living quarter and settled on a sofa. Ginger and Amy stayed close to Arabella. "So, where is Katrina?" Arabella asked, scanning the room. Soon, Katrina descended the stairs, a forced smile playing on her lips. Arabella watched intently as Katrina approached her with open arms.

"So glad to have you back, dear Arabella," said Katrina as she hugged Arabella gently. "I never knew any of the potions or spell books would work, but Gabriel managed to bring you back after all these years."

Arabella chuckled. "Yes, I guess he had to figure out some things in his life," Arabella said, stepping back. "Where do you sleep, dear Katrina?" Arabella asked, glancing at Amelia.

"In my own bed," Katrina said. "After your passing, Gabriel felt it best to keep some distance between us." Arabella nodded.

"Well, I think I want to see what the second floor of the castle looks like. Girls, would you care to join me?" Arabella asked as she looked at both Amy and Ginger. They both smiled and nodded. Arabella took both their hands in hers, and together, they walked up the stairs.

Gabriel remained in the living area, feeling anxious and overwhelmed. Lucien and Vladimir entered, keeping a respectful distance from him. Gabriel looked up. "How are you holding up, Gabriel?" Lucien asked, crossing his arms. Gabriel motioned for them to sit. Both men approached the sofa opposite Gabriel and took their seats.

"It's astounding how the spell worked, brothers," Gabriel whispered. "I never imagined any of this was possible." Vladimir smiled, while Lucien who kept his focus on Gabriel.

"How are you feeling, Gabriel? You seem a bit tense about this new situation," Lucien remarked, glancing at Vladimir. "It might be a bit of a change, but it does not have to be that big of a problem, right?" said Lucien. Gabriel leaned back, lost in thought.

"I don't know how to handle this situation. For being master of all covens, I am starting to feel very weak and weary about it all. Should I have placed my daughters up for adoption for eighteen years? Should I have awoken Arabella from the dead? Should I have kept Katrina in my life?" He stood, walking to a window to overlook the courtyard. "I fear things may worsen, especially with Larry's plans against my children and me." Gabriel sighed, placing his hands on the back of his head as he took a deep breath.

Lucien rose. "Gabe, we're with you. Amelia, Vladimir, and I— we won't let anything happen to you or Amy and Ginger." Vladimir approached Gabriel, resting a reassuring hand on his shoulder. Gabriel turned, his face softened by gratitude.

"I am so glad to have such a wonderful family. You all know how to alleviate my worries," Gabriel said, smiling. Perhaps I just have to get used to this new situation with Arabella and..." Gabriel gulped. "Katrina." Lucien simply shrugged.

While Gabriel and his brothers conversed downstairs, Arabella and her daughters explored the second floor. "How are you girls feeling, my dears?" Arabella asked as they walked into Amy's bedroom. Ginger exchanged glances with Amy. "We're still getting used to this new situation, Mother," Ginger began, her eyes shifting back to Amy. "There's so much we don't understand. How did you and Gabriel even meet? He told us something awful about your family being massacred?" Arabella rolled her eyes, prompting a quick response from Ginger. "Forgive me, Mother," she said, a hint of fear in her voice.

Arabella sighed. "Is that all he said?" Arabella asked with a hint of sharpness in her tone. Amy looked over at Arabella and chuckled nervously. "Not really, except that he loved you." Arabella looked at some of Amy's adoptive parents' pictures. "Emma and Athan took good care of us while we were infants," said Amy as she placed her thumbnail in her mouth. Arabella scoffed and shook her head. "Mother?" Amy asked.

Arabella turned to face Amy with a smile. "Gabriel should have never done any of this to you two. Yes, he murdered my family. He charmed me into marrying him, and then he manages to get me pregnant. You two would have done much better with Alistair and Darcia. They could have taught you your true identity and even help you with Gabriel's adjustment as well. Now, my beloved Amy, you are carrying triplets. I believe it is time for a family reunion from everyone all over the world," Arabella said. Could you girls show me where my closet is with all of my clothes?" Amy and Ginger led Arabella down to the basement area.

# New Beginnings

Arabella rifled through her closet, noting the various dresses designed for different weather conditions. Taking a step back, she examined herself looking at herself in contemporary clothes. "Women wear pants these days, don't they?" she said, her gaze fixed sternly on the array of dresses. Ginger cleared her throat.

"Yes, Mother," Ginger said sheepishly.

Arabella nodded and closet the closet. "I think it's time for a fashion update. Don't you agree, my beloved daughters?" she mused. "After that, I'd like to involve everyone in addressing my questions and concerns."

Amy took Ginger's hand in hers and held it tightly. Arabella proceeded to the living quarters where she found Ginger, Vladimir, Daniel, Amelia, and Lucien assembled. "Husband, would you assist me with what modern folks refer to as 'shopping'?" Gabriel met her gaze, a hint of concern evident.

"Where is Hildegard? Can she drive?" Arabella asked, tension lacing her voice. Gabriel cleared his throat.

"I kept your clothes down in the living area, my beloved. Aren't they to your liking?" he asked. Arabella's lips curled into a gentle smile.

"I believe a family reunion is in order, perhaps involving the members of each coven to discuss some matters. What do you think?" Gabriel's brow furrowed. "Well?"

"Why, Arabella?" Gabriel's voice rose, a touch of anger bleeding through. "I brought you back to life and our children are safe and sound." Arabella sighed, settling beside Amelia on the opposite sofa.

"Perhaps I am still getting used to this new life of mine," she admitted. "And I am not feeling entirely okay with everything."

Gabriel sent a telepathic message to Lucien, his expression softening. *Please bring Arabella some blood for her to drink. She might be thirsty.* Lucien promptly made his way to the dining area, retrieving a chilled bottle of blood.

Arabella's gaze darted between Gabriel and the exit. "What's going on? Where did he go? Lucien?" she questioned sharply. Lucien soon returned, placing a filled glass before her. "What is this? You think I will quiet down after a cup of blood?" Gabriel's eyes stayed fixed on the cup. Arabella shook her head and leaned against the sofa. "How are Darcia and Alistair, anyway? From what I saw the last time, Gabe, is that you almost had them executed for supposedly putting our Amy in harm's way, even though they were quite loving and supportive of her through her tumultuous journey."

Gabriel finally met Arabella's eyes. "Lucien, would you fetch a glass for me as well?" he asked. Lucien, obliging, retrieved glasses for everyone present. Gabriel filled his to the brim, downing the contents in one gulp. A momentary sigh of relief escaped him.

"My love, I don't know how any of this happened nineteen years ago. I never knew shape-shifters, immortals, and humans could produce offspring together. I was blindsided by it all. Initially, I was wary of Alistair and Darcia due to their backgrounds. I truly didn't anticipate them returning to me after they were born. All I yearned for was to live eternally beside you. But then you became pregnant. Fear and anger overwhelmed me. Yet, our children came back, and I witnessed our Ginger claim her first victim. Amy, under Alistair and Darcia's guidance, had her own initiation," Gabriel said, glancing lovingly at his daughters.

Just then, Caleb burst into the living quarters, his face reflecting shock. "So it is true. Arabella is back from the dead?" Caleb looked over at Amy and Ginger.

Arabella, upon laying eyes on Caleb, snarled defensively. "Gabriel, what's going on? Am I to leave his home?" Gabriel raised his hand to hush Arabella.

"No one is going anywhere. Arabella, meet Caleb, my adopted son. And no, he is not Katrina's son. I never had any children with her, my love." Gabriel clarified, pulling Caleb into a reassuring embrace.

Arabella's unease was palpable. "My sweet girls," she beckoned. "How about stepping out with me?" Amy and Ginger both smiled and nodded.

Gabriel, however, intervened. "Perhaps you can save your moments for tomorrow evening?" he proposed, glancing at his wristwatch. "The sun will be rising in a few hours. I believe you all might appreciate some rest come dawn?" Amy and Ginger both smiled, remembering how they have become light sensitive.

"Very well," Arabella conceded. "I guess we can wait till tomorrow. I might want to see what our bed looks like again. Do I still have my evening gowns?" Gabriel, grinning, directed her towards the sleeping chambers. Unlocking the multiple barriers, he gestured for Arabella to proceed. Her eyes roamed the familiar space, almost as if seeing it anew. As Gabriel secured the door, Arabella caressed the foot of the bed. "Where does Katrina sleep?" she inquired, her gaze settling on her pristine Victorian nightgowns within the wardrobe.

"In that room…" Gabriel said, pointing at a closed door. "Is where she sleeps."

Arabella, striving for composure, selected a silk white gown adorned with frontal buttons. As she transitioned into her nightwear, reflections in the dusty mirror caught her eye. Gabriel, retrieving a brush, tenderly removed the knots from her hair. Memories flooded back; those of Gabriel lovingly grooming her tresses before sealing the moment with a kiss.

Arabella felt a surge of mirth and looked away. Gabriel chuckled, moving her hair over her left shoulder and gently kissed it. "You always knew how to lift my spirits, Gabriel," Arabella said with a chuckle. "No matter how livid I became, you always found a way to soothe the ache." Gabriel smiled, continuing to brush her hair.

"A husband should always care for his wife, and I was always eager to alleviate any pain you felt," Gabriel whispered. "You were always the light in my life, Arabella." With newfound strength, Arabella playfully pinned Gabriel to his back. "This strength is a new addition, my love," Gabriel commented with a laugh. "I reminisce about our days when I'd carry you around the courtyard, showcasing the myriad flora and fauna outside our residence." Absorbed in the memory, Arabella smiled. "I truly never wished any harm upon you or your kin. Can you ever forgive the misdeeds of my past, my cherished wife?" Memories of her youth and kin flashed before Arabella, as vivid as lightning.

"Forgive me," Gabriel said.

Arabella gently extricated herself and sat on the edge of the bed. "My love, I am sorry for bringing up the past. Please come back to me," Gabriel begged. Arabella, however, shook her head. "I may not have been the best husband, but I just hope that someday you can love me, flaws and all."

Arabella rolled her eyes and felt herself getting frustrated. "I think I want to just slumber for now, my love," said Arabella as she tried to control herself. She settled into the bed, her back to Gabriel. He, too, sought refuge in sleep's embrace.

By eight in the evening, Arabella emerged from her restful slumber. She got out of bed and noticed that Gabriel was gone. She felt disoriented and afraid till she came back to her senses and remembered what had happened. She was awake and alive in her own way. She grabbed her clothes from her night table, put them on, and walked up to the first floor of the castle. It was quiet, but she heard the faint murmurings of Amelia and Daniel. Approaching them, she noted their drinks in hand. "Good evening, Arabella," Amelia greeted. "Fancy a drink?" Declining with a shake of her head, Arabella was informed, "Gabriel is dining with Amy and Ginger." She proceeded in their direction.

"Good evening, my beloved wife," Gabriel said cheerfully. "Care for something to drink? You look like you may need several glasses." Arabella shook her head. "I want you to remain healthy, my love. At least let me take care of you."

Amy and Ginger, having emptied their glasses, embraced their mother. "We're glad to have you back," Amy said. "I hadn't fully metamorphosed the last time we met, but a shopping excursion with Darcia – on an overcast day, no less – had kept me oblivious to our sun sensitivity in this era. However, from distant human conversations, my heightened senses discerned a modern solution: online shopping."

Arabella chuckled. "What is that? What does 'online' mean and how can people shop without being there?" Amy couldn't help but laugh, until Ginger nudged her with a serious glance. "Sorry, but we are in the twenty-first century, and traditional in-store shopping is becoming more outdated. Last time when Darcia and I went shopping for my suit, the mall was practically empty. Perhaps it was near closing time, but I remember how it just felt so bare," said Amy. Arabella nodded and looked at Ginger who gave her a faint smile.

"Were you with Darcia, too?" Arabella asked, her gaze fixed on Ginger.

Ginger shook her head. "Where were you? Why was Amy alone on her journey to meet the other family members? Gabriel did not want to make it obvious about our true identity, so he had Amy go by herself while I remained in Oregon."

Arabella shifted her gaze to Gabriel, a mixture of confusion and curiosity in her eyes. Gabriel, setting down his glass, said, "To clarify, I never intended any harm. In hindsight, I realize the plan was fraught with uncertainty. My hope was that they'd be more inclined to believe a lie over the truth. Introducing myself in this era, under the cover of night, could easily have spiraled out of control."

Arabella took a seat, crossing her arms in contemplation. Sensing her needs, Gabriel said, "Please drink up, my love. I need you to keep up your strength." He set a filled goblet of blood before her.

After an initial sip turned into a long gulp, Arabella remarked, "This tastes quite different from my first experience with that human outside."

Gabriel chuckled. "I get my source from blood bank orders. Hildegard places orders and accepts them at the front door and places them in our cooling area."

Eager for more, Arabella motioned for a refill. As she polished off several goblets, Gabriel watched with growing amusement. Arabella's giddiness spread, sparking laughter from Gabriel, Amy, and Ginger.

"I'm invigorated," Arabella admitted, her spirits visibly lifted. "I feel so much more buoyant and joyful." Gabriel smirked at Amy and Ginger, "Nothing like a hearty meal to lift one's spirits, right girls?" The girls responded with mirth. "Speaking of adapting, Arabella, perhaps we can have Hildegard explore this 'online shopping' you're curious about? That's the term, isn't it, Amy?"

Amy nodded. "Indeed. It involves using electronic devices, browsing, and making selections until a delivery arrives at your door." Arabella chuckled at the marvels of the modern world.

"It's astounding how times have evolved," Arabella mused. "From online shopping and wearing pants to this new way of sustenance, it's a lot to wrap my head around." Sensing her fatigue, she added, "I think I'll need time to fully adjust to this new lifestyle."

Gabriel sat down next to Arabella and placed his hand on hers. "Considering you've only been back with us for two days after such a long absence, you're adjusting remarkably well. Take all the time you need." Arabella, reassured, clasped Gabriel's hand.

"Speaking of Darcia and Alistair, when will we see them again, my love? Are they planning to visit soon?" Gabriel leaned back in his chair. "Whenever you are ready to see them again, my love. I really do have some questions for them, as well," said Arabella, placing her glass on the table and closing her eyes.

Back at the motel, Alistair and Darcia were in their rooms when they heard their boys talking amongst themselves. Alistair and Darcia walked over to their room. "What's going on?" Alistair asked as he waited for Darcia to enter before he closed the door. Raymond looked at everyone and smiled.

"Arabella has been resurrected," he announced. Darcia and Alistair exchanged surprised glances.

"Are you certain?" Alistair pressed. Darcia, suppressing a chuckle, queried, "Has Gabriel truly undone the spell to bring her back?" Raymond affirmed with a nod.

"How shall we do this?" Darcia asked. "Shall we show up as a surprise to their castle or should we just wait for Gabriel to invite us over?" Alistair shook his head and chuckled. "Amy and Ginger might be in for a shock. First their father lies to them, we take care of them, and their dead mother shows up as a ghost and now in actual form. I feel for them."

"Don't forget about Amy's future children, as well," Bryan said as he got up from his bed. "How that even happened is beyond me." Darcia nodded in agreement. "What about that Larry guy and don't even forget about Caleb," Bryan said with disgust. "None of this makes sense." Alistair smiled, feeling Bryan's frustration.

"To my mind, we've fulfilled our part by reuniting Gabriel with his daughters. Yet, I'm curious about Arabella's return. Perhaps a spontaneous visit is in order?" Darcia retorted, "After our close shave with death? I won't risk another visit unless Gabriel gives his blessing." The others concurred. "Moreover," she continued, "having completed our task, shouldn't we just return to our peaceful lives, pre-drama?"

Joshua's eyes sparkled with mischief. "How about indulging in an evening snack? Word has it there's a local celebration." Darcia signaled her approval, and Alistair conceded, "A bit of family revelry might do us some good." Turning to Joshua, he inquired, "Where's this human gathering?" Joshua, beaming, led them to a park where about fifteen people celebrated a colleague's promotion, their evening marked by wine and merriment.

From a distance, the seven observed the gathering. "There are fifteen of them and only seven of us. That means two for each of us and one of us gets three," Bryan noted.

"I propose Darcia gets the extra one," Alistair interjected. "During our trial with Gabriel, she proved to be the braver of us two." Darcia, beaming, leaned in to kiss Alistair. "You just made me fall in love with you all over again," she confessed. "Let's join their party." As they approached the party-goers, they bared their teeth, swiftly dispersing the humans until none remained. Sated, they strolled back to their motel and settled down, watching the sunrise through their curtains, succumbing to a profound sleep.

Meanwhile, at the castle, Arabella felt a peculiar sensation throughout her body. Distressed, she questioned, "My love, what's happening to me?" Gabriel swiftly enveloped her in his embrace. "Your body is adjusting to the new diet," he soothed. "It's not uncommon." Arabella's restlessness persisted as her breathing grew rapid. "Focus on my voice," Gabriel urged, employing his powers to help calm her. Arabella's anxiety subsided.

Regaining her composure, Arabella met Gabriel's gaze as he cradled her face. "All will be well," he murmured. With a grateful nod, Arabella replied, "Thank you, Gabriel," and leaned against the headboard. As Gabriel mirrored her, drawing her into his embrace, Arabella mused, "I think we should invite Darcia and Alistair for a family reunion. They deserve our gratitude for caring for Amy and Ginger. They've always struck me as a good couple."

Gabriel, with a smile, tightened his hold on Arabella. "They were good to our Amy," he affirmed. "Perhaps in a week or so?" Arabella's strength ebbed as she yielded to sleep within Gabriel's comforting arms. He remained awake, vigilant over her for several hours.

Morning ushered in serenity within the castle. Amy woke while sunlight still spilled through the curtains. Reflecting on her human past, she recalled how, at times, the sun's intensity weighed on her. Emma and Athan would simply apply sunscreen to protect her. She pondered Arabella's evident disdain for her human parents. While Emma and Athan weren't perfect, they offered unwavering love and support throughout her high school years. Retrieving her diary, which chronicled her travels to Australia, Croatia, Italy, and Romania, Amy was transported to those moments, reliving her myriad emotions.

"I wonder what Bryan and the other boys are up to," Amy mused. "They were such goofballs, yet supportive in their own unique ways." Memories of Bryan's tenderness towards her surfaced, especially recalling his despair when she chose to remain in Romania. Darcia's light-hearted nature, reminiscent of a fun aunt taking her shopping and sharing in laughter, came to mind as well. Emotion welled up in Amy's eyes. Given that the alleged monster was merely a ploy to unite her with her family, perhaps she should ask her biological parents about reuniting with her extended kin.

Unbeknownst to her, Amy dozed off, awakening near midnight. She moved to the shower area, reflecting on the rapid changes her body was undergoing with triplets growing within. "I should discuss my diet with Gabriel," Amy pondered aloud, gazing at her reflection. Venturing into the living quarter, she found Caleb alone. "I was looking for my father," she mentioned. At her inquiry about his well-being, Caleb's laughter sounded.

"Not in the slightest, dear Amy," he confessed. "With your mother alive, she seems to detest my presence. Gabriel isn't the best company, you know." Amy acknowledged this with a nod. "Especially given his treatment of you and now, with you expecting triplets. Truly, a remarkable father." Amy chuckled at Caleb's sarcasm, eliciting a smile from him.

"My hunger's setting in. I need to speak with my father about what he fed my mother during her pregnancy. Dietary needs might differ for shapeshifters compared to humans. If you'll excuse me," Amy began, but soon realized Gabriel had all the basement keys. Returning to the main floor, she fetched a bottle of blood. Pouring a glass, Caleb soon joined, helping himself to some.

"Cheers to this grand life of secrets," Amy said. Caleb chuckled and raised his glass. "So, what are your plans for the evening?" Just then, Ginger came into the kitchen and grabbed herself an empty glass. Amy placed the bottle closer to her.

"I might take a solitary nighttime stroll, observing humans of all ages going about their business," Caleb mused, then turned to Ginger. "Must be exhilarating, preparing to become an aunt, right Ginger?" She shot Caleb a cold look, opting to sit without responding. "Too soon?" Caleb tried again. Ginger's silence persisted. "You truly are your mother's daughter," Caleb quipped.

Ginger glanced at Caleb, irritation evident on her face. "What's your problem? I'm not in the mood for small talk. And to answer your question, no, I'm not ready to become an aunt. Amy's too young to be pregnant with triplets. How this all happened is beyond me, but I try to stay out of drama," Ginger declared. Caleb, sensing the tension, raised his hands in surrender and exited the kitchen. Amy rinsed her empty glass to wash away the leftover blood, then placed it in the dishwasher.

Ginger studied Amy, concern evident in her gaze. "I can't believe Gabriel did this to you, Amy." Amy's smile was tight, strained. "I hope our mother can guide us better. Remarkably, she's still her same beautiful, intelligent self. Maybe I take after her." Amy chuckled wryly at Ginger's comment. "What?"

"I'm nothing like Gabriel, if that's what you're hinting at, Ginger," Amy retorted sharply. "If anyone's like our mother here, it's me – a mix of common sense with a side of frustration." Ginger laughed lightly.

"I don't want to argue. Let's drop this," Amy said, her tone brisk. Just then, the basement door swung open, revealing Gabriel and Arabella. "Father, I need to discuss something crucial," Amy approached them, urgency in her voice. Gabriel flashed a warm smile.

"Of course, my sweet child, but let me first get a little drink for your mother and myself," Gabriel said as he walked past Amy. Arabella, her face pallid and drawn, settled at the dining table.

"Mother, are you okay?" Ginger inquired, noting Arabella's frail appearance. Arabella, her eyes dark yet piercing, nodded. "Your father will help me recover," she murmured. Gabriel swiftly drained a glass and fetched another bottle from the cabinet. "This is my personal stock, fortified with more minerals and vitamins," he explained, pouring a generous serving for Arabella. She drank eagerly. Gabriel poured her another glass.

"Amy, you wanted to ask something?" Gabriel prompted. Amy, seeing her mother's state, felt a pang of worry and sadness. Gabriel's voice grew gentle, reassuring. "Your mother just needs to recuperate. She'll be fine soon." Amy took a deep breath, "What diet should I follow while pregnant with triplets?" Suddenly, Arabella choked, spattering blood on the table.

"Oh! I'd forgotten about your pregnancy, with everything I've been through," Arabella admitted. "Gabriel, what did Hildegard give me when I was expecting?"

"You were still human then. She provided regular food. But now I realize – had she given you some of my blood, perhaps you'd have survived the birthing complications. It's ironic; as the leader of the shapeshifters in our family, I overlooked that crucial detail." Arabella furrowed her brow, clearly deep in thought. "Would you like more, my love?"

Arabella pushed the glass away. "I think I've had enough for now. Your revelation surprised me, my dear husband. How could you not have considered that?" Gabriel's face fell in regret. "Having children never crossed my mind, Arabella. I didn't believe it was possible. I assumed that since Hildegard fed you human foods, everything would be fine. And then we lost you. I won't let the same fate befall Amy. She's strong, with both our blood coursing through her veins." Arabella retorted, "Indeed, she has. We're both strong. Amy will persevere and be one of the best mothers in our lineage."

Feeling overwhelmed, Amy quickly exited the dining area, with Ginger trailing behind. In the courtyard, Ginger called out gently, "Amy, would you like some company?" Halting, Amy's emotions surged. "Or maybe you'd rather be alone?"

"It's not you, Ginger," Amy said, her voice rising in distress. "I'm just overwhelmed. This situation is becoming unbearable. How can I cope?" Her breath quickened alarmingly.

Ginger swiftly enveloped Amy in a comforting embrace. "Just breathe, Amy. You'll be okay." Amy resisted momentarily, but Ginger's grip was firm. Guided by Ginger's soothing instructions, Amy's panicked breaths began to even out. Soon, she was calm. "I'm releasing you now, but try to stay tranquil." Gratefully, Amy nodded and headed towards the balcony, seeking solace under the waxing gibbous moon. Meanwhile, Ginger retreated to her bedroom, exhaustion evident in her posture.

Seeing her daughter deep in thought on an outdoor chair, Arabella approached gently. "Amy," she began, "how are you holding up?" Looking up, Amy forced a smile. Arabella's voice softened, "I deeply regret all of this," she said, touching Amy's shoulder gently. "If you ever need a mother, know that I'll be there. While I'm certain

Emma did her best, I wish to surpass that for you and my soon-to-be grandchildren."

Sitting beside her daughter, Arabella took Amy's hand. The two exchanged a comforting squeeze. "Thank you, Mom," Amy murmured. "All of this feels so surreal. It seems Gabriel's adapting to the shapeshifting lifestyle better than us." Arabella chuckled, "Or perhaps not?"

"Your father is something different, Amy. He might be the leader of all shape-shifters in our family, but even the strong falter sometimes." Amy smiled. "Both you and Ginger are doing way better than him, Amy. Goodness, how terrified Ginger must have been to find out what she actually is. Going from a regular college girl to being a potential princess and future aunt. No, my sweet Amy, your father is definitely something else. Whoever this Caleb is, I am not sure if I want him near you or Ginger. I am not sure what to do about that situation at the moment, but I can always come up with a plan."

"And what about Katrina, Mom?" Amy probed. "I have my reservations about her, too. When I met her and Gabriel, she seemed distant. For a moment, I thought she was my biological mother, but our looks differed." Arabella laughed softly. "In many ways, I feel I'm more like you, Mom," Amy continued, looking away. Arabella gently kissed the back of Amy's hand and released it.

"How old are you, Mom?" Amy asked. Arabella dismissively waved the question away, indicating age was immaterial to shapeshifters.

"I was thirty-six when I met your father and perhaps thirty-eight when I... departed. Age feels inconsequential now. Both you and Ginger are on the cusp of twenty. You'll remain youthful and radiant. As for Gabriel, I believe he was in his late thirties when he transformed. He never shared details of his past—never spoke of his shapeshifting nature or unique diet. I can only recall our initial romantic encounters. The long black hair, the pale complexion, the overwhelming passion. He showered me with gifts and treated me lavishly. Thinking back, our moments together were quite mesmerizing," Arabella reminisced.

Amy listened intently, momentarily setting aside her father's flaws and indulging in the romance her mother painted. She reflected on Bryan's gestures of love and wondered if he'd ever behave similarly with their offspring. Her thoughts drifted to Alistair and Darcia, and she quickly discarded the idea. "What was your impression of Alistair, Mom?" Amy inquired. Arabella chuckled again.

"He was delightful. Playful and humorous. Darcia was smitten from the start. They were truly a beautiful couple. In fact, after my passing, they would have been ideal guardians for you and Ginger. From what I observed during their trial, they exhibited immense love and care for both of you. Despite their human limitations, they could have eased your transitions. I hope to reunite with them soon," Arabella mused, standing up. "I'll check on your father now. Take care, Amy," she said, bending down to plant a kiss on her daughter's forehead.

# Family Reunion

Back at the motel, Alistair, Darcia, and their seven sons returned from their hunt. "I've often wondered if it's possible for us to consume blood sources other than humans," Darcia mused as she headed to the bathroom to wash her hands. "It reminds me of how Amy must have felt when we traveled with her." Alistair approached from behind and embraced her.

"She did just fine, my beloved Darcia," Alistair whispered. "Seeing some of those girls we've hunted in the past brought back those thoughts." Raymond settled on one of the beds, a smile playing on his lips. Across from him, Bryan mused from a chair, "Could Arabella really be alive? Sometimes, I question my powers and strengths." Raymond quirked an eyebrow. "Gabriel hasn't reached out, and neither have Amy or Ginger."

"I do wonder what Amy has been up to," Bryan continued, observing the dried blood on his hand. "First we travel with her and lie to her about everything, then Gabriel has a moment of almost killing his daughter, then she goes back to Oregon, and now she is officially acclimated with her new lifestyle. Perhaps it is best not to overthink these things," Bryan said.

Darcia and Alistair returned to the room, taking seats, while Joshua and Steven observed with worried expressions. "What's our next move, Father?" Joshua inquired. Alistair sighed, "This situation shouldn't have arisen in the first place."

Darcia nodded and shrugged. "I agree with our sons, my beloved," Darcia said. "I wish we could have just enjoyed our lives, let our sons meet their future spouses, and let the family expand in its own way. Now it seems like we are back to waiting on orders from Gabriel again."

Just then, the motel phone rang. Alistair and Darcia exchanged curious glances. Alistair picked up the receiver. "Motel residence," he greeted.

"Good evening, dear family," Gabriel's jovial voice came through. "Hope you and your beloved wife and sons are doing well?" Alistair looked over at Darcia with a smile. "We are all doing quite well, Gabriel," Alistair said. "What can we do for you?"

"I have delightful news. An old and beloved friend has awoken from the dead. She wishes to invite your family to the castle for a drink. Are you interested?"

Alistair smiled while holding the phone. "Of course, we would be honored, Gabriel. Arabella is back from the dead?" Then was a pause.

"Alistair, how did you know?" Gabriel's voice held a touch of worry. Alistair glanced at Raymond. "I never knew you had that kind of power."

"It appears that our Raymond has a special gift that we have not realized till recently, Gabriel. It came to him like a lightning bolt and we got the news through his sense."

Gabriel sighed. "I look forward to our evening together again, Alistair. We will be serving drinks around eleven in the evening. Just bring yourselves. Until then." With that, Gabriel disconnected.

"I guess we just got invited to have drinks with our leader," Alistair said, regaining his composure. "It seems he wasn't aware of our son's powers." Darcia, now apprehensive, approached Raymond, pulling him into an embrace. "I am sure it will be okay. At least we get to finally see Arabella again. It will be nice to see her true form in person."

As the clock struck eleven, Gabriel, situated in the living quarters and nursing a glass of blood, felt swell of anxiety. *Who possesses such a gift to foresee the future?* he pondered, gaze distant. The castle chime rang, announcing Hildegard at the entrance. Rising to his feet, Gabriel noticed Vladimir, Daniel, Amelia, Lucien, Adrian, and Katrina arrayed behind her. But where was Arabella? Proceeding to the sleeping quarters, he found no sign of her but eventually discovered Arabella, Amy, and Ginger in Amy's room, engrossed in his journals.

"Our guests have arrived, my beloved family," Gabriel said with a hint of fear in his voice. Arabella looked up at Gabriel in a confused manner. "I am sure Darcia and Alistair are fascinated to hear about your return, my love. Join us?" Arabella nodded and placed the journal on Amy's night table and the four of them walked down to see Alistair and his family waiting patiently by the staircase. Once Arabella showed up at the top, Alistair and Darcia both smiled.

"So you've returned, dear Arabella," Alistair exclaimed, arms outstretched for an embrace.

Darcia beamed, "Time hasn't touched you, dear sister. You look radiant, especially considering you've returned from beyond." Their warm reunion evoked tears from Arabella, which Darcia gently wiped away. "The sentiment is mutual, dear sister." Amy, spotting Bryan's impassive countenance, bypassed the gathering to take a seat beside Gabriel. Ginger chose a spot by Arabella, and the rest filled in the available seats.

"It is so wonderful to have our family back together," Gabriel said as Hildegard placed the glasses and two bottles on the table. I hope your lodgings are safe and comfortable?" Alistair couldn't help but laugh.

"Yes, motel rooms are quite comfortable." Just then Darcia couldn't help but join him in his laughter.

Arabella looked over at each member, analyzing them. "It is wonderful to have my beloved wife back home. Arabella, dear, how I was so torn and horrified to have lost you for all this time. I never wished for you to have gone through all of the horrific moments in your life. We have created two beautiful and strong women. Dear Amy and Ginger, how proud I am to have you both in my life as future leaders of our coven. You will be excellent in whatever you decide."

Amy smiled and raised her glass. "To family," she said. Everyone else chimed in and tapped their glasses.

Arabella took a small sip and placed her glass on the table. "I appreciate all the loving and caring words about me, but I have some concerns regarding my daughters. There are a few uncomfortable topics I'd like to bring up." She cleared her throat and closed her eyes momentarily before continuing. "I went through some passages in Gabriel's journal. While most of what he has shared with me aligns with his writings, there's no mention of how he became an immortal shape-shifter. There was also nothing about your parents, Gabriel, only about the hardships you faced."

Gabriel raised his hand to speak. "Forgive me for interrupting, Arabella, but perhaps now isn't the time for such inquiries."

Arabella sighed and shook her head. "That is such a typical move from you, Gabriel. Whenever something important gets mentioned, it's never the right time."

Gabriel sighed and leaned back in his chair. "It's just that Darcia and Alistair are here to reconnect with you, not to delve into how Amy and Ginger transitioned from the human world back to us."

"Yes, because I was dead for over almost two decades, my love. You lied to me, impregnated me, and kept me as a ghost in your home. Now, our Amy seems to be in a similar situation." Both Alistair and Darcia glanced at Amy, noting her altered appearance, then back at Gabriel. "You're all aware of this, aren't you?" Arabella asked.

Alistair and Darcia nodded. "My dear Amy, as much as it makes me happy that we will be getting new family members, it also saddens me regarding the circumstances. No woman should ever be subjected to decisions made on her behalf because of another's choices. Please excuse me; I'm not feeling particularly well. Perhaps it's the blood."

Darcia approached Arabella, embracing her. "We'll meet again under better conditions, dear sister," she whispered, planting a gentle kiss on Arabella's cheek. "I've missed you so much. We have a lot to catch up on." With a smile and a wave to the others, Arabella retreated to her quarters.

Gabriel let out a weary sigh. "So, Alistair, you mentioned your son possesses a unique gift. Which one of your boys has it?"

Alistair gestured towards Raymond, who nodded in acknowledgment. "That would be me," he confirmed. "It seems I might have the rare ability to foresee the future."

Gabriel furrowed his brow, his gaze fixed on Raymond. "Since when? I don't recall anyone from Croatia, Greece, Rome, or even Australia with such an ability. Darcia, Alistair, were either of you aware?"

Darcia shook her head with a smile. Gabriel turned back to Alistair, "Do any of your other sons possess unusual talents I should be aware of?"

Alistair lifted a hand. "Gabriel, if I may ask, why is this of such importance? Each of us has our own unique powers and gifts."

Gabriel fixed a piercing gaze on Alistair. *How was your son able to see Arabella awaken from her deep sleep, Alistair?* Alistair seemed entranced, his eyes shifting from blue to a deep black color.

*Gabriel, I had no idea about any of my son's powers. I never knew Raymond was able to see her awaken. Why does that matter?*

Gabriel looked away and Alistair's eyes returned back to its original color.

"There have been too many complications going on. Arabella means the world to me. I can't bear to lose her again. If word about her spreads, I might not have answers to the inevitable questions. I wish to keep my affairs under wraps. Larry Harrison is probably scheming my demise, and Gregory from Greece is facing execution for endangering my daughter. If other coven members possess similar foresight, Arabella's resurrection could jeopardize my position should issues arise in the future. For nearly two decades, she was lost to me, a mere specter. I wish time could stand still, allowing me to strategize properly."

Alistair rose from his seat, approaching Gabriel. He rested his left hand on Gabriel's right shoulder, offering reassurance. "Gabriel, you're not defenseless. Granted, you nearly executed my wife and me during our trial. But understand that such experiences can muddle emotions. Remember, you aren't alone in this. We have your back. Larry poses no threat to us, and soon, you'll be a doting grandfather. Give Arabella the grace period she needs to adjust. It's uncharted territory for her too." Gabriel placed his left hand over Alistair's.

"Thank you, Alistair. Your words bring solace. Maybe I've been overly harsh with Arabella, not considering her feelings and concerns. I'll strive to be better."

"Those are your words, okay?" Gabriel chuckled, picking up his glass.

"I reckon my wife, sons, and I should depart, unless you fancy inviting the other members to acquaint themselves with Arabella?" Alistair inquired, retaking his seat.

Gabriel shook his head, absentmindedly nibbling on his thumbnail. "Not now, it's all a bit too much. Sometimes I yearn for simpler days, where I was the lone immortal shape-shifter, perhaps meeting my end before ever crossing paths with Arabella."

Just then, Darcia spat out her blood and coughed. "Gabriel," Darcia said in a hoarse voice. "How can you say that in front of us all, especially your daughters? These moments happen and it does not mean you should give up and not care anymore. Sometimes there are stormy days in our lives and you must not ever give up. You are over thousands of years, so this is not the first time you ever felt this way, so try and use your past knowledge and experiences to keep moving. We are all together. None of us are dead. Arabella is back in our lives, so I want you to hush up about your sorrow and create a good plan to take on Larry Harrison and other bumps in the road. I do not want to hear such words again. We love you, Gabriel. You are smart, beautiful, gifted, strong, our father figure, so please do not forget that."

Gabriel smiled, nodding. "Thank you, Darcia. It will all work out," he whispered. Everyone nodded. Sensing the tension in the room, Bryan chimed in. "So, Amy, have you thought about what you will be naming your children?"

Amy choked on her sip and coughed. "Um…No. Why do you ask, Bryan?" Bryan smiled and shrugged.

"Do you have any suggestions for me?"

Bryan shook his head. "I was just curious, nothing more," Bryan said as he gulped down the final bits of blood from his glass.

Alistair cleared his throat. "Gabriel, I do think that the other members should hear about the news going on here, like Arabella being alive and our new family members showing up."

Gabriel stood, hands raised placatingly. "Alistair, let's pause. Everyone will be informed in due course. Right now, I need to check on Arabella. Please excuse me."

Exiting the dining area, Gabriel headed to Arabella's location. Bryan glanced at Amy. "Considering our hosts have left us, perhaps we should take our leave too, Alistair?" Alistair nodded in agreement. The group bid Amy and Ginger farewell.

"We shall keep in touch, my dear nieces," Darcia said before she released Ginger from her grasp. As the castle doors closed behind the departing guests, Amy and Ginger lingered at the table. The remaining members also left.

Amy was still processing Bryan's unexpected question about baby names.

"Ginger, what should I name my children? I have no real motherly feeling inside of me to want to keep these kids. Plus, if we are immortal shape-shifters, does that mean that the birthing comes earlier or later than human births? I wonder if there is a book in our gigantic library that could give me more answers than to rely on Gabriel for his 'wisdom'," Amy quipped. She got on her feet and left Ginger alone. Once Amy entered the library, it was quite dusty and wondered why Hildegard never thought of wiping off some of the dust. Skimming through sections on arts, math, science, and religion, Amy spotted a book on immortal beings. To her surprise, it seemed more like a children's tale than a scientific guide.

Amy flipped to the glossary of the book, skimming topics from creation to diets and births. When she landed on the section about immortal births, the graphic illustrations—depictions of ancient surgeries with blood spatters and chilling instruments—made her recoil in horror. She quickly slammed the book shut. Moments later, Ginger entered the library and approached Amy. "Find anything useful?" she inquired. Amy gestured to the closed book with a grimace.

"It reads more like a horror story," Amy remarked. "Quite gruesome." Ginger curiously flipped through the pages, commenting, "There are depictions of wolves, various animals, and landscapes. Who wrote this?" Upon checking the book, Ginger noticed the absence of an author's name. "Odd," she mused, "but just because it's in a book doesn't mean it's true."

Amy scoffed and shook her head. "Look at us. Remember our transition during my fabulous wedding?"

Ginger grimaced at the memory of Amy's staged wedding, a charade orchestrated for Gabriel's sake. "True," she conceded, "but just because this book lacks an author doesn't prove that these supernatural beings exist." Amy nodded, scanning the bookshelves for more information.

Ginger's voice grew soft. "I wonder if I'll ever have my own children. I'm thrilled for you, but it makes me reflect on my own possibilities."

Amy approached her sister, wrapping her in a comforting embrace. "You'll find love, Ginger. Maybe with one of Darcia and Alistair's sons or perhaps someone even more special."

Ginger smiled into the hug. "Thanks, Amy. I vow to support you throughout your pregnancy and to spoil your little ones with loads of treats and fun."

Laughing, Amy gave Ginger a playful slap on the back of her head. "They'll grow up on a healthy diet and live wholesome lives, thank you very much."

Ginger feigned indignation. "Either way, with you as their mother, they're destined to be wonderful, intelligent, and gifted."

Elsewhere, in a dimly lit basement, Gabriel approached Arabella, who lay curled up with her back to him. "My dear wife," he whispered, "are you okay?" Turning to face him, Arabella nodded, fatigue evident in her features. "Is the blood causing issues, or are you merely exhausted?" he asked. Stretching, Arabella yawned.

"Meeting Darcia and Alistair again was overwhelming. The reality of everything is hard to digest. I need time to adjust. Contrary to popular belief, death doesn't equate to rest, especially not for me."

Gabriel nodded. "I understand, my love. Would you care for some company and comfort?" Arabella gestured for Gabriel to join her, and he removed his blazer, loosened a few buttons on his shirt, and climbed into bed beside her, drawing her close. "I think we all deserve some rest before we get the other covens involved with our news of you and our future grandchildren."

Arabella gazed up at him. "The notion of being a grandmother hasn't settled in. All I wanted was to live out our days together, just as we used to. I never envisioned becoming an immortal shape-shifter. And now, with everything that's changed, I'm struggling to adjust to this new way of life and the altered diet. More than anything, I hope Amy will manage the birthing process. I couldn't bear seeing our children in pain."

Gabriel gently brushed her cheek. "Things will be different this time. When you were pregnant, you were human. Amy, however, isn't, and she's carrying Caleb's children." Arabella's expression darkened.

"Caleb? He's to be the father of our grandchildren? What transpired, Gabriel?"

Gabriel closed his eyes, trying to find the best way to help Arabella understand. "Gabe, what did you do?" Gabriel got out of the bed and stood in front of the bed.

"My love, I did not realize the potion I had given Amy was the pregnancy potion. I thought it would help her sleep, but I must have grabbed something different. Amelia was the one who helped me with the concoctions, just so you know." Arabella checked the time on the clock on her night table.

"It's one in the morning. Amelia might still be up. But for now, rest could aid your transition." The weight of it all threatened to crush Arabella. "Everything will be alright. Believe me," Gabriel implored, reaching out to comfort her.

Arabella shook her head. "I will try my best to regain my strength again, but I would like a word with Amelia tomorrow evening, my love." Arabella murmured before she lowered herself onto the mattress and her head on her second pillow. "I wish I could go back to the moment when I had no worries or concerns in my life." Arabella whispered.

Gabriel's voice was soothing. "Rest now, my love. Things will improve with each passing day." Arabella closed her eyes, seeking solace in the quiet. Gabriel lay beside her, encircling her with his arms, trying to shield her from the world's chaos.

While Arabella and Gabriel found solace in one another, Alistair and his family had returned to their motel. Darcia entered their room, trailed by the boys who took the adjacent one. "I sensed a strange aura from Arabella," Darcia mused, settling into a chair. "It seemed like she wasn't thrilled about reuniting with Gabriel. Or am I overthinking?" Alistair smiled and sat on the bed.

"She's probably grappling with the oddity of being back among the living after existing as a mere ghost in Gabriel's life," he suggested, kicking off his shoes and rubbing his feet.

Darcia's gaze shifted from Alistair to the door. "Amy appeared different, noticeably pregnant compared to our last encounter. The whole potion situation still confounds me. I thought couples approached things differently, not resorting to potions or serums," she remarked. Alistair just shrugged.

"I sincerely hope she thrives in her new role as a mother," he replied. "I trust Gabriel won't let harm befall his beloved daughter, although his judgment when it comes to family matters can be questionable. It's unfortunate that Gregory will soon face a dire fate, all because Gabriel didn't entrust the care of his newborns to Hildegard or another."

Darcia scoffed. "Such a fool he can be, my love," Darcia said as she got on walked over to her bed to lie down. "Ginger was also never part of the whole journey of meeting the other ones. I am surprised she did not have any mental breakdowns of any kind. Being in the human world with Emma and Aaron, and believing she was actually human. Goodness, how I can understand how Arabella feels. Very disturbed, unhappy, and perhaps even a bit disgusted."

Alistair chuckled as he took off his jacket and tossed it on the same chair Darcia sat in before, so he could lie down. "I could not have said it better myself, my love," Alistair said.

In the adjoining motel room, Bryan, Raymond, Joshua, and Steven, Silas, and Xander were gathered, flipping through television channels. "Could you please pick something, Bryan," Silas snapped, feeling anxious. Bryan blankly kept clicking without moving. "Bryan, are you even alive?"

Unperturbed, Bryan murmured, "Naming two daughters and one son is not something an outsider should even be asked."

Raymond quickly snatched the remote from Bryan's hand and turned the television off. "Thank you," Xander said as he was rubbing his eyes. "The flashing of the channels started to hurt." Raymond placed the remote control on top of the television and sat in front of Bryan who kept staring out in front of him. Raymond snapped his fingers to get Bryan's attention, but nothing seemed to work.

"Bryan!" Raymond yelled, but nothing worked. The other boys chuckled and got on their feet. "On the count of three, tickle him alive," Raymond said with a smile. One, two, and…three" the other boys started to tickle Bryan, which made Bryan push them all away and get on his feet.

"Great, at least you are not internally dead, dear brother," Raymond jested. "Why are you so bothered by this whole pregnancy thing, because Gabriel managed to get his daughter pregnant with some kind of serum? Is that what happened?"

Bryan rolled his eyes and shook his head. "I have no idea, brothers, but whatever happened, it is very disgusting and wrong. To get someone pregnant against their will and to force them to live a life that was never meant for them." The other boys nodded in agreement. "Especially if it is a serum from Caleb. I truly despise that man," Bryan snapped. His thoughts then shifted to another individual. "And don't get me started on that Larry Harrison. What ever became of him?"

The other boys shrugged and exchanged glances. "I think I might want to go on a search for him. He is still a potential threat to Amy and Ginger," Bryan said.

"I agree with Bryan," Raymond said. "He could perhaps harm her children, as well. Joshua, do you know of anything regarding

Larry's whereabouts?" Joshua looked up confused and shook his head.

"How did you know that Arabella was alive again but when it comes to news about Larry, your mind goes blank?" Bryan asked, keeping his gaze focused on Joshua.

"I do not know what to say, my dear brothers," Joshua said before he started to bite his fingernails on his right hand. "Regarding the news on Arabella, that came to me like a flash of lightning. News regarding Larry does not seem that important or dangerous. Perhaps Larry might need to be nearer to us for me to sense him. What about you, Xander? Or you, Silas?" Joshua snapped.

Both Xander and Silas exchanged puzzled glances. "I've sensed nothing," Xander said. Silas shook his head afterwards.

"What are your powers, anyway? If I can sense the future of rebirth, what can the rest of you do, aside from shape-shifting?" The boys exchanged glances.

"We can try them out as we spar with each other to see what our powers are all about? We can go to that same park where we saw Larry a while back? Perhaps he might be there again?" Bryan said with glee in his eyes.

The other boys chuckled. "Sounds like fun to me," Raymond said as he headed for the door of their room. The other boys followed toward the park. As they reached the entrance, it seemed very empty and quiet. The boys pricked up their senses and looked around with their sharp eyesight and ears.

"Perhaps this was a bad idea," Silas whispered. The other boys ignored him and continued walking. As they were walking, they heard the wind blowing through the trees and heart the fountains splashing on the water.

Suddenly, Bryan's attention was seized by a fleeting shadow. Shifting into his lupine form, fangs bared, he readied himself for a potential confrontation. The others followed suit, uniting in a resonating howl. The shadowy figure grew nearer until a familiar voice rang out, "Wait!" But Bryan, instincts taking over, lunged at the source of the voice. "Bryan, stop! It's me, Helen, from Croatia! I'm Kristjan's wife and Gregory's mother," she cried out.

Bryan returned back to his human form and held his hand out for her to take it. "Helen, what are you doing here in Romania?" Bryan asked sternly. "You do understand that what Gregory had done was not right."

Helen nodded and held up a hand to speak. "I understand that, Bryan," Helen said, trying to calm herself down. "Our son does not deserve to die. If blame is to be placed, it shouldn't fall on my family, but squarely on Gabriel's shoulders. This entire debacle stems from his actions, and my son shouldn't bear the brunt for simply following his instincts. He's a good lad. Had he known Amy would be involved, he might've been better prepared. We did our best, albeit with questionable acting. Recall Kristjan's stress-clutching of that couch pillow? He's terrified of anything related to Gabriel. We might be distant kin, but that doesn't mean Gabriel can just sentence our son to death."

Bryan sighed and shook his head. "Have you been feeding well, dear Helen?" he asked, shifting the topic.

Helen looked around and pointed at the bushes. "I stick to smaller prey, like birds and rabbits. Hunting for humans outside my territory is daunting."

Raymond scoffed and pushed Bryan aside gently.

"What brings you here, Helen? We're not the arbiters of Gregory's fate. True, we were roped into watching over Gabriel's daughter, which was unsettling in its own right. We've always been conscious of our own precarious stance in all this," Raymond stated. "Is Kristjan accompanying you?"

Helen shook her head.

"You came all this way from Croatia to Romania. How did you travel?" Helen remained quiet. "I am sorry for this great loss of yours, but if you want to beg someone, Gabriel is about twenty minutes away from where we are staying and I do not think he would like to receive any visitors right now."

"I just do not know what to do right now. I love my family and my children. If anything were to happen to either one of them, that would be like a stake in my heart." The boys nodded in agreement.

"I understand, dear Helen, but like my brother, Raymond said, we don't possess the clout to intervene in this matter. You can always try to go to Gabriel yourself. Take care of yourself." Bryan started to walk away. The other boys started to follow. Xander looked behind them with the feel of betrayal and pointed in the direction of where the castle was located. Helen smiled before she left the park.

Bryan stopped in front of his brothers and turned around. "That kind of ruined my evening. Seeing Helen in this state. I wish there was something we could do."

Raymond rolled his eyes and shook his head. "That sounds noble, dear Bryan, but there is absolutely nothing we can do to stop this." The boys continued their way, with Bryan momentarily lagging before catching up.

Meanwhile, at the castle, Lucien descended to the basement area, gently rousing Gabriel. "Brother, wake up. Helen from Croatia is here to see you."

Gabriel's features contorted in annoyance. "And why would she be here?"

Lucien shrugged and pointed at the door. "I will be upstairs, waiting for you to show up to greet our guest." Lucien left the sleeping quarter. As Lucien exited, Gabriel delicately disentangled himself from a deeply slumbering Arabella, murmuring a reassurance, and planting a tender kiss upon her cheek. He then donned his jacket and ascended to the main floor.

"Helen, what an unexpected pleasure to see you. Are you here in Romania on vacation with your family?"

Helen looked at Gabriel with tired eyes and shook her head.

"Is there something I can help you with?"

Helen nodded.

"Please join me in the dining quarter, then. Lucien, would you fetch us one of our special bottles?"

Lucien nodded and walked ahead of them.

Gabriel courteously pulled out a chair for Helen and once she was seated, he took the chair beside her. "Fancy a drink?"

"I don't want Raymond to die, Gabriel," Helen snapped, her voice sharpened with urgency. "My son is innocent and he does not deserve to get the death sentence."

As Lucien proceeded to pour drinks for both of them, Gabriel awaited his brother's departure before responding. Helen just stared at the glass and back at Gabriel. Gabriel took a quick gulp and placed the glass back on the table.

"What he did to my daughter was unacceptable and dangerous. You all knew about my plan and her journey. Neither you, Kristjan, nor any of your other children expressed reservations—except Gregory. How did that happen, sweet Helen?"

Helen scoffed at the way Gabriel called her and rolled her eyes. "Gregory may not have fed himself properly that day, but Amy was not harmed. Please have mercy on my son, Gabriel. If I can take the blame for being a bad mother to him, I would prefer to give up my life and let him live."

A curious glint appeared in Gabriel's eyes. "So you'd willingly you're your end rather than let your son accept his fate?"

Helen took a deliberate sip from her glass. "Parents assuming blame for their offspring isn't unheard of. Is that the bargain you're suggesting?" Helen's voice dripped with sarcasm.

"And what of Kristjan? How does he cope with the potential loss of his life mate? One can always have another child, but can Kristjan ever replace you? You both seemed destined for one another, as far as I recall."

Helen's patience seemed to fray at Gabriel's insinuations. "How dare you, Gabriel Ambrose? Your patriarchal position doesn't grant you the license to be callous over a mere misstep."

Gabriel couldn't help but smile at her response.

"How did you feel about losing Arabella?"

Suddenly, Gabriel's eyes went dark with fury.

"Ah, did I just touch a sore spot on you, Gabriel?" Helen asked.

Gabriel got to his feet and hovered over Helen. "Tread carefully, Helen," he warned, towering over her, "Her name is sacrosanct and off-limits."

Helen, sensing the tangible danger in the atmosphere, meekly nodded.

Regaining his composure, Gabriel refilled their glasses. "For the record, my decisions are beyond the purview of family scrutiny. I acted on my convictions and won't tolerate dissent. Anyone opposing me can face collective obliteration," he retorted, downing his glass once more.

Just then, Arabella glided into the dining quarter, donning a silk robe and matching slippers. "Gabriel, what is with all the commotion up here?"

Upon seeing Arabella, Helen's eyes widened in surprise.

"And who might you be?" Arabella inquired.

Quickly rising, Helen bowed. "This is Helen, Kristjan's wife from Croatia," Gabriel interjected. "She and her family graciously hosted our daughter Amy a while back. They were most hospitable, my dearest Arabella."

Approaching Arabella with an extended hand, Helen introduced herself. "I'm Helen. You're back from the dead? That's truly remarkable. I imagine many will be overjoyed upon hearing this."

Gabriel cleared his throat. Both Helen and Arabella looked at him. "This news is yet to be publicized. I wish to keep my wife's miraculous return discreet until we're prepared to divulge it. Isn't that right, love?" Arabella responded with an affectionate nod.

Suddenly, a glimmer of an idea flashed across Helen's face. She considered leveraging the secret of Arabella's return as a bargaining chip for her son's life. Catching her insinuation, Gabriel sternly glared at Helen.

"Perhaps it's time for me to return to Croatia and check on my family. We'll be in touch if that's agreeable with you, Gabriel?" Helen suggested, barely masking her smugness.

Exhaling deeply, Gabriel responded, "Sounds like a wise plan, Helen. I believe it's best for you to depart, allowing my wife and me to resume our rest."

As she confidently made her exit from the castle, Gabriel followed closely, eventually shutting the door behind them. "Your audacity to challenge me in such a manner knows no bounds. Would you like to accompany your son in his impending fate?" he threatened.

Helen scoffed and stuck her tongue out.

"For someone nearly my age, that's quite immature," Gabriel rebuked. After a moment's pause, he added, "Very well. Your son will be spared. However, under no circumstances are you to divulge any of this to your family."

In response, Helen formed a heart with her hands, pressing it to her chest and mouthing, "I love you."

Gabriel shook his head in disgust and walked back into the castle. Upon his entrance, Arabella was standing in the doorway, staring at Gabriel. "Is everything okay?" Gabriel smiled and nodded. "Good. I am starting to feel a bit hungry, my love," Arabella said. Gabriel gestured for Arabella to enter the dining quarter and placed Helen's used glass in the sink.

# Return of Darkness

In the early morning light, Arabella wandered into the library, drawing in the familiar scents that reminded her of her daughters. She observed the myriad of open books on immortals, shapeshifters, werewolves, vampires, mythological tales, and more. Moments later, Gabriel entered, a hint of amusement in his eyes as he watched Arabella. Unable to resist, Arabella met his gaze and grinned. "I see what you're up to," she teased.

Gabriel felt playful and approached her like he was stalking his victim. Arabella chuckled and ran behind the table. "Not this time, Gabe," she whispered playfully.

He countered by moving to the opposite side of the table, narrowing his eyes in mock challenge. "Why ever not?" Gabriel queried, feigning seriousness. "Can a man not have a little fun with his wife?"

Arabella rolled her eyes.

"I've never given up on us, beloved," Gabriel murmured, a more genuine tone replacing his playful banter. Arabella hesitated, stepping back, prompting concern to flash across Gabriel's face. "You can always speak to me, you know."

Turning to him, Arabella admitted, "Everything's still so fresh. I'm not entirely myself yet. It's like there's a barrier between us – a massive boulder blocking our path."

Growing increasingly frustrated, Gabriel pressed, "What do you mean by that? I feel no such obstacle."

Arabella exhaled and looked at the various books, trying to think of how to handle this potential conflict.

"I have never given up on you. Yes, I was lonely and needed an actual mate in my life, but I have never given my true self to her. We only made love a few times, but it was never to replace my love for you," Gabriel said.

Arabella remained calm. "When will you get rid of her? Katrina? Since I am back from the dead, I wish to keep my position as your queen in your life again. Be the mother of Amy and Ginger Ambrose, and as your true companion."

Resting his palms on the table, Gabriel sighed heavily, "There's a lot unfolding right now. We must ensure Larry Harrison poses no threat. Then there's Helen, pleading for her son Gregory's life. Life has been... overwhelming, to say the least. It's been a relentless tide of pain and challenges."

Meeting his gaze fiercely, Arabella countered, "What of my pain, Gabriel? The lies, losing my family, navigating this situation now?"

Amused by Arabella's fervor, a smirk played on Gabriel's lips.

"You think this is all funny? Being stuck as this creature, having two children that I am just learning about over the past week, and now there are more complications? Gabe, what will happen in the weeks to come?"

Gabriel walked around the table towards Arabella. She retreated until her back met a bookcase. With tenderness, Gabriel laid his hands on her shoulders and offered a reassuring smile. "Everything is going to be okay, my sweet wife," he soothed. "Nothing bad will happen." Before Arabella could react, Gabriel gently tilted her chin upwards and planted a soft kiss on her lips, engaging his trance powers. Arabella's eyes darkened, becoming compliant. "From tonight onwards, there will be no concerns in our lives. We'll live our fairytale. Be a loving mother to our daughters and grandchildren, and leave everything else to me. Once I awaken you from my spell, nod in understanding."

Gabriel snapped his fingers, bringing Arabella out of her trance. Her eyes returned to their normal hue. "Forgive my interruption,"

Gabriel murmured, taking Arabella's hands and pressing a kiss to each. "I have important matters to attend to. Feel free to explore the castle. Maybe check on the girls." With a blown kiss, he exited the library, leaving a somewhat dazed Arabella behind, who now looked around as if seeing the library for the first time.

As Gabriel retreated to his study, both Amy and Ginger moved to the dining area in search of another blood bottle. Arabella soon joined them in the kitchen. "Would you like a glass, Mother?" Ginger offered, uncapping a bottle and filling two glasses. Arabella responded with a smile and a nod. "Amy, could you fetch a glass for our mother?" After filling Arabella's glass, the trio sat together, each taking measured sips.

"So, Mother," Amy began, setting her glass down, "does any of this seem familiar from before our births?"

Arabella took a moment, her gaze distant. "From what I recall, much of this castle feels familiar. I remember when your father first brought me here. How he had Hildegard and maybe someone else prepare a meal while he sipped his burgundy drink from across the table. His shiny black hair, those deep, possibly reddish-brown eyes often fixed on me. I can't remember introducing him to my family. He was incredibly generous, showering me with dresses, shoes, flowers, and even exquisite European chocolates," Arabella reminisced, a soft smile gracing her lips.

Both Amy and Ginger smiled at her with fascination. "I never realized Father was so romantic," Amy remarked, looking to Ginger, who nodded in agreement. "His journals hardly captured these intimate moments with you." Arabella chuckled at Amy's observation.

"I probably was not born yet from the time he was alive and hunting. How are you girls managing your new lives?" Ginger smiled and shrugged, but Amy remained neutral.

"It was quite a challenge, Mother," Amy said in a somber tone. "I just have no idea why Father just abandoned us like that. I really wished someone in our own circle could have helped us a bit more." Arabella placed her right hand on Amy's left hand. "Thank you," Amy whispered. Arabella nodded.

"I understand how the transition must have been scary to you, my little doves," Arabella said, finishing her drink. "I just wished I could have been there for you both. I may have missed your first eighteen years for being a ghost, but from now on, I'll be here whenever you need me. I hope you can grow to trust and feel comfortable with me as your mother once more."

Amy smiled warmly. "I know we will. Right, Ginger?" she prompted. Ginger smiled and nodded. Amy refilled everyone's glasses, and they clinked them together. "To a brand new family," she declared. Ginger laughed softly, locking eyes with Arabella.

"Soon," Ginger whispered. Her words took Amy by surprise, making her choke on her drink. "Sorry about that," Ginger said, sipping her own glass. Amy cleared her throat, smiling weakly.

"No worries, sister dear," Amy said before she got to her feet and placed her glass in the sink. Arabella finished her glass and placed hers in the sink, as well.

"What are the plans for this evening?" Amy asked as she looked at both Ginger and Arabella.

"How about an evening walk outside? Perhaps some fresh air would do us good," Arabella said. "I will get my coat. Would you two like to get yours?" Both Amy and Ginger nodded. Once they were ready, Amelia, Lucien, Daniel, and Vladimir came over to them. "Would you join us for an evening walk?" Arabella asked. Amelia smiled and put her coat on. The men also nodded, but remained in their blazers.

"Any particular destination in mind?" Arabella asked. Amy eagerly chimed in, "One the eve of my transition, I remember how Alistair and Darcia took me and their boys out to this park. It is quite nice and relaxing." Arabella smiled.

"Sounds good to me," Arabella said as she led the way outside the castle. As they were walking, the men walked behind the women. Lucien was scanning the area and keeping his ears sharp.

Daniel and Vladimir exchanged glances, doing the same and keeping their ears sharp, as well. Amelia felt a strong presence and stopped in the midst of her walk. "I am not so sure this park is a good idea," she murmured, as she looked around. "Perhaps an area where there are more humans and where there are more street lights would be appropriate?"

Arabella, unable to discern the unease the others felt, looked around questioningly. "Is everything alright?" she asked. The others hesitated before glancing around once more. "We're not alone, are we?" Arabella surmised.

Just then, a rustling emanated from a nearby bush, accompanied by a menacing growl. Suddenly, a dark creature lunged at Amy, but Ginger managed to push Amy away. A taunting voice broke the tension, "Well, well, well, what a lovely family outing. Where's dear old Dad?"

Amy quickly regained her footing, glaring past Ginger. "Larry. How did you track us down?" she demanded. Arabella swiftly moved to stand beside Amy, holding her protectively.

"Who's this? A substitute for Gabriel's plaything?" Larry snapped, locking eyes with Arabella. "Oh... you must be the... the... oh, what's the word?" Larry said, snapping his fingers. "Ah, the wife." Amelia growled and bared her teeth. "And you," Larry said, focusing on Amelia, "you're quite the fiery one. And then we have the escorts of the group," Larry quipped, eyeing the three men behind them. "What? Daddy doesn't let his women out without supervision?" he added sarcastically.

"What do you want?" Amy asked, feeling herself vulnerable inside. "Please, leave us be."

Larry scoffed and took one step toward Amy. "I want Gabriel's head on a platter. I want my old life back. I wanted to become something different than this creature." Larry started to bare his teeth. Lucien stepped in between Larry and Amy. "And what is this? Will you become the next leader of your family? Or is it prince charming over there?" Larry said, pointing at Vladimir.

Lucien remained calm as he stared at Larry. "I need you to leave us alone," Lucien said in a calm manner. "Before you get hurt."

Larry scoffed and took a step back.

"Whatever your problem is with Gabriel, do not harm Amy or Ginger in any way." Larry growled and felt himself getting angry. "Go ahead, make your best move, but they are innocent and will remain alive." Larry started to back away slowly. Lucien kept his focus on Larry.

"Mark my words forever," Larry growled as he retreated. "A war's coming. And I'll be feasting on Gabriel's corpse when it's done." With that, he disappeared into the shrubbery.

Daniel laughed, clapping Lucien on the back. "Well done, brother," he remarked. "I would've just torn his head off, but you scared him off just fine." Vladimir rolled his eyes. "Oh, 'Prince Charming' here might've had a few moves too," Daniel teased. Vladimir gave Daniel a playful punch as the group began to exit the park.

"I think that's enough excitement for one evening. Should we check in on Gabriel?" Amelia suggested, linking arms with Arabella.

Back at the castle, Gabriel sensed danger. He bolted outside, suddenly aware of his own vulnerability. From a distance, he saw Arabella, Amelia, and the others approaching. He rushed over, embracing Arabella. "Is everyone alright?" he asked anxiously. Lucien nodded with a reassuring smile.

"I took care of the situation, but it seems Larry's hell-bent on starting a war soon, Gabe."

Gabriel shook his head in disbelief. "This situation needs to end real soon. Are you all okay, my loves?" he asked, scanning the group.

"No harm, dear brother," Lucien confirmed. "But perhaps it's wiser for us to stay within the castle walls and not venture out alone." Gabriel nodded, taking Arabella's arm, and they headed back to the castle.

"Forgive my absence, my love," Gabriel began. "I believe it's best for us to remain within the confines of this castle." Arabella nodded, though she wasn't fond of being led so forcefully by Gabriel. Once inside, Gabriel let go of Arabella, allowing the others to enter. Amy started feeling herself get hot and clammy.

"Father, am I supposed to be feeling this hot?" Amy asked, glancing at her flushed skin. Gabriel moved closer and touched her forehead. "You're burning up, my love," he noted, guiding Amy towards Hildegard. "Hildegard, could you run Amy a warm bath?" Hildegard nodded and gestured for Amy to follow.

Upon entering Amy's bathroom, Hildegard started the water, waiting for it to warm before plugging the drain. "How are you feeling, Miss Ambrose?" she asked, noticing Amy's glazed-over eyes. "You seem a bit off. Could it be the pregnancy?" Amy gazed at her reflection, the bump on her abdomen more pronounced.

"It might be, Hildegard," Amy responded. "People often say pregnancy looks radiant from the outside, but those experiencing it often suffer in silence." Hildegard offered a compassionate smile.

"I will fetch your robe and slippers," Hildegard promised, leaving Amy to her privacy. Once Amy was settled in the bath, Hildegard hung her robe neatly and set the slippers below.

"Call if you need anything," Hildegarde reminded her. Amy nodded appreciatively.

"Thank you, Hildegard. I am starting to feel much better." However, as Amy tried to relax, her mind kept wandering back to Larry's intense, reddened gaze. How had he transformed from that intriguing man in Oregon to the frenzied creature they'd encountered? Or had he always harbored vengeance towards her father?

A knock interrupted her thoughts. "Come in," Amy invited.

Arabella and Ginger entered. "How are you, dear?" Arabella inquired, settling on the edge of the tub. "I wonder if Amelia could whip up a tonic with the nutrients you might be lacking. I've already suggested it to her, and she's working on it." Amy managed a weak smile.

Ginger, peeking over Arabella's shoulder, marveled at Amy's burgeoning belly. "How did you even become pregnant? How does that work in our kind, mother?" she curiously asked.

Arabella smiled. "Our kind's pregnancies are quite unique compared to humans. I don't recall much traditional intimacy; I was given various elixirs which might've played a role in my transformation, or even my conception. Why Gabriel decided it was Amy's turn, I'll have to discuss with him later — once he's cooled down a bit." Amy nodded.

"The bath is soothing, but there's still this burning sensation, Mother," Amy admitted. "Did you experience anything similar during your pregnancy?" Arabella paused, casting her mind back.

"Yes, I remember a similar burning. It might be due to the unique nature of our shape-shifting offspring – they demand a lot from their mothers, especially when carrying multiples, like your triplets."

"How did you manage, Mother?" Amy asked, adjusting her position against the bathtub. "With both of us inside you, did we weaken you?" Arabella's face showed concern.

"Of course not, my loves. Never think such things. You two were meant to be here with me, and I am so blessed to have two beautiful girls in my life. I won't deny that the birthing was excruciating, but holding you both, even briefly, was the best moment of my life. I'm overjoyed to be your mother, always. I'll be there for every step of the way, supporting you both. Always remember this: no matter what happens, I love you unconditionally." Amy reached up to hug her mother. Arabella embraced her, resting her head on Amy.

While Amy and Ginger were with their mother, Alistair and Darcia stirred from their sleep. "I wonder what our sons have been up to," Darcia mused, stretching her limbs. Alistair rose, moving to freshen up. "I'll check on them," she decided, leaving Alistair behind as she knocked on Bryan and Raymond's door. Bryan greeted her with a smile.

"Mother, to what do we owe the pleasure?" Bryan inquired, opening the door wider.

From his bed, Raymond looked over his shoulder. "Mother, what's happening?"

Darcia stepped inside, wearing a gentle smile. "I was just checking in on my boys. How are you all doing?"

Bryan exchanged a glance with Raymond, who returned his smile.

"We might've done something... very stupid," Bryan began cautiously. "Do you remember Helen, Kristjan's wife? When we were out, she approached us, almost tackling me, pleading for our help concerning Gregory's death sentence." Darcia furrowed her brows, her expression growing serious. "We might've pointed her towards Gabriel's castle."

Darcia shook her head, making her way to the front door. "Please don't mention this to Alistair. We didn't plan on getting involved with them." Darcia opened the door, her mood lightening slightly.

"Just perfect," Bryan remarked with a hint of sarcasm. Another knock sounded, and Silas, Xander, and Joshua awaited entrance. Bryan sighed, "Our family drama seems to be deepening."

Alistair opened the front door to their room and glared. "What did you boys do?" Alistair snapped as he walked over to Bryan.

"Father, we didn't anticipate any of this. We were just bonding as brothers until Helen confronted us. How were we supposed to foresee this turn of events?" Bryan defended.

Alistair shot Joshua a perplexed glance. "How did you miss this, Joshua?" he chided sharply. "You can sense Arabella, but not Helen? What's become of your senses?"

Darcia gently laid a hand on Alistair's arm. "My love, go easy on them. Clearly, they didn't expect to encounter Helen. Whatever Helen discussed with Gabriel, I'm sure it's settled now. Let's return to our room," she suggested, attempting to defuse the situation.

Taking a deep breath to quell his rising anger, Alistair said, "Let's see how this plays out. I might be overreacting, but you need to be more vigilant in the future. Understand?" The five young men nodded in agreement, watching as Alistair and Darcia exited.

Meanwhile, back at the castle, as Amy concluded her bath, Gabriel approached, finding her in her nightgown. "My family," he began, entering the room and spotting Arabella and Ginger flanking Amy, "What transpired out there?"

Clearing her throat, Arabella began, "Larry Harrison wants you dead, my love," her eyes clouded with apprehension. "How did it come to this?"

Gabriel exhaled deeply, pulling up a chair to face them. "Centuries ago, let's say a hundred years back, I was unaware of my identity. All I knew was this insatiable craving beyond human food. Regular food seemed bland and unsatisfying. My health declined with each bite. Everything penned in my journals stands true. I recall waking up one day, with no memory of my origins, in a chilly room of a scorched building. I'm unsure if I caused the fire or if someone tried to harm me."

Arabella kept her eyes locked on Gabriel's. "What does this have to do with Larry Harrison, Gabriel?" she inquired.

Gabriel raised his hands in a placating gesture. "Bear with me. I'll get there. As I wandered aimlessly, penniless, in tattered clothes, and tormented by a relentless hunger, I resorted to stealing fruits from markets. But it did little to satiate me. Bread, too, had adverse effects. Desperation drove me to the brink of suicide. High falls, self-inflicted wounds – nothing seemed to harm me. The sun's burning rays provided some discomfort, but I knew I had to seek other solutions."

Both Amy and Ginger felt a wave of sadness upon hearing their father's tale. "Do not weep for me, my little ones," Gabriel implored, pausing his narrative momentarily. "The story takes a brighter turn as we approach the present." Both Amy and Ginger nodded, encouraging him to continue.

"Where was I? Oh right, so I decided to see if raw flesh could help, and it did. I would wait until all the markets were closed and see if there was some wildlife in the area where I was wandering around, somewhere in Europe. I heard various languages being spoken and was able to learn different tongues. Anyway, that is another fun story to talk about. Back to how I met Larry. Anyway, I saw various forms of creatures that I was able to take down. Then the first time I was able to taste blood, I got this shot-like jolt through my body, giving me a lot of energy and fulfillment. I kept going after raw meats and blood till I found my hearing getting sharper, my eyesight was sharp, and I saw my nails growing more. My canines were already sharp, but it felt good to sink my teeth into a warm mammal."

Arabella's expression grew horrified, especially noting the feral intensity in Gabriel's gaze.

"Please forgive my animated retelling," he apologized, his demeanor softening. "Throughout my travels, I crossed paths with diverse individuals — hairstylists, law enforcement officers, parents, chefs, and others. It felt as though I was settling into a rhythm until

I chanced upon a bustling tavern. Inside, there was a cacophony of sensations — music, dance, intimate moments, raucous fights. Such raw humanity. As I turned to depart, a tap on my shoulder halted me. It was Larry Harrison — a striking figure with porcelain skin, azure eyes, and caramel blonde hair. Yet, he had a delicate build. Uninterested, I aimed for the exit but his voice pulled me back. 'Mister, where are you off to?' he inquired. I responded simply, 'Home,' and continued on my way.

"Larry would not leave me alone. He kept going on and on and one about my appearance. At a certain point, I stopped and turned around to face him. "Why are you following me? Where are your parents? Larry had told me that he was an orphan, but how he was living with his uncle who worked for a coal-mining group and how abusive he was to Larry. I still had no interest in taking him in, so I sent him away and I saw how he slumped back to the tavern. Once I was back at my temporary miniature home, somewhere in some woodsy area, I felt the need to rest. I closed my curtains and got into bed. I had a nightmare, as if I was being hunted down and how my home got burned down. I saw a faint figure of a voluptuous woman in a light pink dress with her hair up.

"I'm not sure what else I could discern about her before she draped a blanket over me. Then I heard her scream. I awoke to brightness outside my curtains, a parched mouth, and a gnawing hunger. I knew I had to wait for nightfall before venturing out.

"As darkness descended, I sought animals for sustenance, but all seemed securely locked away in barns. Unwilling to draw attention, I ventured back to the familiar smoky tavern in hopes of finding a potential meal. The atmosphere was more subdued that evening. I approached the bartender, an elderly, rotund, bald man with a distinct accent. Though unfamiliar with his dialect, we managed to converse in English. When asked about Larry, he appeared puzzled, informing me that boys weren't permitted inside.

"Exiting the tavern, I heard Larry's voice around a corner. He was accompanied by another man. As I approached, Larry introduced me as a wealthy aristocrat intending to adopt him. Though I denied it, there was something unsettling about the man beside Larry. With a friendly gesture, I led Larry away.

"I asked about his parents and he told me how there was a fight over some land between him and another man and that the other man beat his father to death. His mother had suffered another form of tragedy and had looked around his hometown trying to find another family member till he heard about how his uncle worked in the coal mining business. I had no refreshments to offer to Larry, but I also felt like I should do something. I went out again to look for some wolves or other forms of creatures in the area and killed them, so I could perhaps offer him some meat that were to be cooked over a fire. Larry managed to prepare himself some rabbits that I managed to find and I watched him with disgust as he ate those lagomorphs. I could not help but hear Larry's fast heartbeat as his body was digesting his petty meal. Once he had finished his second rabbit, I told him how he could stay with me for a while, but Larry refused and said how his uncle would hunt him down. This kid confused me. Why was he hoping that someone like me would adopt him, but then he would go back to his uncle?

"Days morphed into weeks, and rumors arose of Larry assuming control of his uncle's enterprise by nineteen.

"I decided to leave my temporary home, anticipating that soon humans might notice a shortage of wolves, cattle, chickens, and other livestock. Before departing, I took one last look at the tavern. Larry was engrossed in conversation with a young woman, her laughter echoing each time he spoke. Our eyes met, and he approached with a furrowed brow. Informing him of my imminent departure, I saw sorrow cloud his eyes before he embraced me. I reciprocated and vowed to return soon.

"Moving to another town, the residents struck me as rather unsightly. Nonetheless, I had no desire to befriend them. Months passed as I maintained a low profile. Occasionally, I would seek solace in a church, gazing at the stained glass artistry. Although much of it seemed foreign, I refrained from overthinking. Each day added to my strength and wisdom," Gabriel narrated.

Gabriel paused, noticing the diminishing interest among his listeners. Arabella, her eyes weary, inquired, "You abandoned Larry. Is that the root of his animosity?"

Chuckling, Gabriel responded, "Let me continue. We're approaching the story's climax. Over the weeks, the villagers grew alarmed at the mysterious depleting livestock. Fingers pointed in all directions, but none suspected me. After what felt like three years, I returned to Larry's country. While I was in my early thirties, my appearance hadn't aged. Desperately needing sustenance, I headed for the familiar tavern. Inside, patrons were boisterously throwing bread, laughing, and shouting. Hunger gnawing at me, I spotted a young girl in a pink dress. Before I knew it, I'd whisked her outside, consumed her life force, and devoured her flesh. Rejuvenated, I suddenly recognized a familiar scream. It was Larry, now more mature and dressed in a suit. Tragically, the girl I'd consumed was his fiancée. Enraged, Larry lunged at me with his sword cane, piercing my heart. But death eluded me. Pulling the blade out, I implored his forgiveness. Yet his horror was evident. With the tavern's patrons oblivious, engrossed in revelry, I realized there was only one choice left: I had to consume Larry as well.

"I bit into him, but I felt too full to consume him entirely, so I carried him off to a secluded woodsy area and left him," Gabriel said.

# Balance between Good and Evil

Arabella exhaled in relief when Gabriel finished. "Have you concluded your story?" she inquired. Gabriel nodded, leaning back in his chair. "Did you ever discover who your parents were, Gabriel? Can you sense them?" He shook his head.

"I've lived for over a thousand years and still can't discern my origins. I'm not proud of who I was or the atrocities I committed. Yet, I had no answers either," Gabriel admitted.

"That poor girl," Amy murmured, eyes downcast. "Why a petite blonde? Why not a drunken man?" she questioned.

Gabriel met her gaze. "I wasn't in the right frame of mind, my dear family. The hunger was overwhelming."

Amy nodded, glancing at Ginger, who stifled a laugh. Gabriel, smiling, reached for his daughters' and wife's hands. "I assure you, we are all safe here," he said, leaning back. "If ever there's a battle, we're equipped to face any challenge. For now, we must keep Amy sheltered in our home. I won't risk losing any of my treasures. Sharing my story has drained me; I'd like to rest."

Arabella rose, offering her hand. "I'll accompany you, my love." Together, they exited Amy's room. Amy and Ginger exchanged glances, noting the time: four in the morning. "Maybe we should rest too," Amy suggested, sliding under the covers. Ginger agreed, heading for the door. "Sweet dreams," Amy called.

"You too, sister," Ginger replied, closing the door. In the room's darkness, Amy quickly drifted off.

She dreamt she was in a forest, donned in an 18th-century pink dress, her belly swollen. A deep hunger gnawed at her. Spotting a wolf, she approached, its back to her. Hidden behind a tree, she admired the creature's grace before lunging, teeth bared. The wolf's yelp echoed as she sank her teeth in, tearing flesh and drinking its blood.

When she regained her composure, she looked down and it was Larry Harrison in his human form with a big bite mark in his side. "Oh no, Larry!" Amy screamed. "What have I done?" Amy woke up screaming and crying. Ginger came running into her room and held her in her arms shushing her.

Regaining her senses, she saw Larry Harrison, human and wounded. "Larry!" she cried in horror. "What have I done?" Amy awoke in tears, Ginger rushing in to console her.

"It's okay, Amy. You're safe. What happened?" Looking around, Amy recognized the familiarity of her bedroom.

"I had a nightmare about Larry," Amy said. Ginger sat down on the edge of the bed, but kept her hands on Amy's arms. "I bit him and killed him, sweet sister," Amy whispered. Ginger gently kissed Amy's forehead. "You're safe, dear sister," she soothed. Amy, feeling more grounded, asked, "Would you stay with me for the rest of the morning?" Ginger nodded, joining Amy under the covers.

"Thank you," Amy murmured, turning her back to Ginger. Soon, the two sisters drifted off to sleep.

Upon awakening around six in the evening, Amy felt a familiar hunger pang. In the dining quarter, she opened a new bottle of blood and quickly downed two glasses. Katrina wandered in and poured herself a drink.

"So," Katrina began, "there was quite a commotion last night. Bad dreams?"

Amy chuckled, nodding. "Pregnancy seems to bring out the strangest dreams," she shared, refilling Katrina's glass.

Katrina, eyes on Amy's belly, smirked, "I can't say I envy you, Amy, dealing with all the hormonal changes and everything else pregnancy entails. Gabriel never gave me a choice about children. Otherwise, I might've considered it." She took a seat.

Amy, taking a chair opposite her, asked, "Did my father ever share his life story with you, especially his origins?"

Katrina looked thoughtful. "Only bits and pieces. His early life? That's always been a mystery. Sometimes, I felt he kept his distance, like he was holding back."

Amy sighed. "I'm still in the dark about his origins, too. I only recently learned about his history with Larry. I've read some of his journals, but they leave me with more questions than answers."

Katrina raised an eyebrow. "His journals? How far back do they go?"

"About five hundred years," Amy replied, refilling her glass. Seeing Katrina's empty glass, she asked, "Another?"

Katrina smiled and nodded. Amy poured Katrina another glass ad placed the bottle back on the table. "Are you worried about Larry, Katrina?" Amy asked. Halfway into Katrina's sip, she stopped to swallow.

"Not really, but it seems Larry has some serious unfinished business with your father," Katrina said. "In our world, there usually is a balance between good and evil. But who defines what's good and what's evil? Maybe Gabriel intentionally harmed Larry's fiancée, or perhaps it was an accident, and he did his best with the limited resources and help he had," Katrina reflected. "Do I think Gabriel is evil? Yes, in some aspects. But as his daughter, would you feel the same?" she asked.

Amy pondered. "I have no answer to that right now. When I believed he wanted to harm me, I would've said yes. But now that I know he's my father, probably not. Right now, I'm not sure about good or evil; I just seek peace and clarity," Amy responded. Katrina nodded, offering a comforting smile.

Suddenly, a jolt, like an electric shock, surged through Amy, making her gasp. "What happened?" Katrina asked, rising swiftly. Amy exhaled, "I don't know; perhaps we should find my father." But Katrina gently pressed Amy back into her seat.

"I'll get him. I don't want you or your unborn children to be in any danger," Katrina assured, leaving in haste.

Then, an uncanny vision unfolded before Amy: she could see her unborn children, the size of baseballs, tethered to her placenta. The vision faded, and she returned to reality just as Gabriel rushed in.

"My sweet, are you all right? Do we need to fetch you a healer?" Amy smiled and shook her head. "Huh," Gabriel said before he looked over at Katrina with irritation. "She seems fine to me, Katrina, why did you have to disturb me?"

Katrina could not answer and pointed to Amy and her belly. Gabriel waved her off and looked back at Amy.

"Are you okay, Amy?" Gabriel asked.

"Yes, Father," Amy said. "I am not sure what had happened, but I felt this weird electrical feeling inside of me and suddenly I was able to see my tiny sized babies in my womb. They look so beautiful already," Amy said. "I have no idea how I would be able to do that again." Gabriel smiled and placed his left hand on Amy's shoulder.

"I am happy to hear that you are okay, my sweet child," Gabriel whispered. "Katrina made it seem like you were close to dying, but as good as she meant it, it still frightened me. I will go back to my tasks. If you need anything else, Amy, Hildegard will be at your disposal," Gabriel said before he walked back to his study.

Katrina, back in her seat, chuckled, "Well, that was something." Leaning back and nibbling on her index finger's nail, she asked, "How are you feeling now?"

Amy smiled and shrugged.

"At least that is something positive," Katrina said. "Shall I put the bottle away or did you want more?"

"No thank you, Katrina, I think my children and myself are good for now."

Katrina nodded, placed the bottle back in the cooler, and set their glasses in the sink. "I'll go about my regular activities, sweet Amy, but if you need anything, don't hesitate to ask," Katrina said before leaving Amy.

Amy lingered, humming softly while caressing her belly. Elsewhere, Alistair and Darcia recalled the oversight of Larry's unexpected visit to Amy's family. Alistair entered Bryan and Raymond's room. "Boys," he began gravely, "Why didn't you mention that Larry is back? Joshua, what happened?" Darcia entered, her face a mask of disbelief. "Speak up!" Alistair demanded.

Silence filled the room until Silas, Xavier, and Joshua arrived. "I don't understand why I could hear Arabella but not Larry. Is something wrong with me, father?" Joshua inquired, a note of worry in his voice. Alistair, visibly irritated, closed the curtains. "You're ailing because you're not honing your gifts. I sensed a dark presence, but I thought you boys were just fooling around. Now I know it was something external. What happened?"

Bryan exhaled heavily in frustration, drawing a hiss from Alistair. "Alistair!" Darcia interjected, "Don't snap at him. I get it; this is concerning. But it's not fair to blame our sons."

Alistair's voice grew tense. "Remember our trial? How we nearly faced execution for failing to protect Amy? How Adrian's involvement almost ended us? Forgive my angst, but I won't let our sons' errors jeopardize us."

Darcia, understanding his concerns, cradled Alistair's face. "I get it. But my maternal instincts flare when I see our sons, no matter their age, in distress. Have you heard from Gabriel?" Alistair gently freed his face from her grasp.

"No, Darcia. I just crave peace, free from strife," he murmured. Darcia tenderly kissed him.

"As do I, my sweet husband," Darcia whispered. The boys rolled their eyes at their parents' affection. "That is what people do to each other when we love and care for each other," Darcia teasingly said. The boys all chuckled. Alistair could not help but chuckle at Darcia's comment. "For now, there appears to be no problem whatsoever. Helen is probably home in Croatia and Gabriel is probably safe and sound with his family. For now, shall we go out for another meal, my sweet family?" They all nodded and headed toward the front door of their motel room.

Back at the castle, Amy was still seated till she heard footsteps approach her. "Amy," Ginger said. "I heard a bit of a commotion while I was with our mother. Are you okay?" Amy smiled and tried to reach for Ginger's hand, so she could place it on her belly.

"Do you see anything, Ginger?" Amy asked.

Ginger looked at Amy very confused.

"Huh," Amy said. "Nothing?" Ginger shook her head and tried to release her grasp from Amy.

Amy snorted. "I was able to see my babies inside of me somehow, Ginger," Amy said.

Ginger smiled and placed both her hands on Amy's belly again. "Huh, still nothing for me," said Ginger. "I will probably see them soon in person." Amy smiled and nodded.

"Where is our mother?" Amy asked as she looked behind Ginger, but saw no one.

"She's probably still upstairs. I think our father's story about his connection with Larry frightened her somehow. She wanted to be left alone," Ginger said before she sat down next to Amy. "I can sadly understand why someone like Larry would hate our father. Dad's impulsiveness likely sparked the feud. Being turned against your will is undoubtedly traumatic. Then there's his history of leaving us with humans, deceiving us, attacking you, and his bizarre involvement in your pregnancy. The way he acts as if it's all water under the bridge... I can't fathom him sometimes," Ginger mused, staring into the distance.

Amy solemnly agreed, "I share your sentiments, sister. Still, regardless of the hurdles we've faced, I believe we can steer our destinies. How do you envision your future?"

Ginger exhaled a sigh, shaking her head. "It's a blur, Amy. I'm uncertain about leaving this castle or even how long our father might live." Amy chuckled at Ginger's phrasing.

"What? It's true! But what about your vision for the future?" Ginger inquired, her eyes seeking Amy's.

Amy's gaze softened, "I dream of a life with Bryan, raising our kids in a serene cottage, enlightening them about the wonders of our world. I hope you're always there, Ginger, playing the role of the doting aunt. My bond with my elder sister is irreplaceable."

Overwhelmed, Ginger stood and tenderly embraced Amy. "Thank you, Ginger," Amy murmured, "For everything. Our banter may be sharp at times, but with you by my side, I feel safe."

Ginger smiled, maintaining her embrace. "Always, sweet Amy. Always," she whispered. As they separated, Ginger picked up the same bottle that Amy and Katrina had enjoyed, quickly draining the last drops of blood from it. She placed the empty bottle in a crate for Hildegard to fill later, then retreated to her room for some rest.

Amy, gathering strength, rose to check on her mother. As she neared the bedroom, she found Arabella engrossed in a photo album given by Emma. Arabella's face lit up with fleeting smiles as she perused the images, then lifted her gaze to meet Amy's.

"Emma gifted that to me when I left Oregon for good," Amy reminisced.

Arabella, pointing to a picture of infant Amy and Ginger, commented, "You both were so radiant and precious in these snapshots.

"Yes, we were," Amy agreed, settling beside Arabella on the bed. "Emma and Aaron cared for us diligently till we graduated high school."

Arabella responded with warmth, "I never thought I'd say this, but I'm grateful to those humans for their care. While Hildegard was our supply runner and both Darcia and Alistair were pillars of support, they really did their best for my children." Pausing to close the photo album and set it aside, she asked, "What have you been up to, Amy?"

"I do not know how this happened, Mother, but I was just relaxing till I felt the presence of my own babies," Amy whispered. Arabella laughed and wrapped her arms around Amy.

"What? I have never experienced anything like that before," Amy said excitedly.

Arabella kissed Amy on top of her head and held her close.

"I have felt that way, too, my sweet child. When I was still a human. I saw both you and your sister inside of me. It appears that this is quite common for the women in our family. I wonder if Darcia or Helen, or any other female of our coven has ever experienced that before," Arabella said.

"Whatever it was, will it happen again, Mother?" Amy asked. Arabella leaned back, so she could look at Amy.

"Yes, my sweet child," Arabella said. "I will add this part. For humans, the average time of carrying is nine months. For our family, it is about six months," Arabella said. "Right before your body is ready to release the younglings into this world, you will get another one of these moments. Your father, however, was not very supportive of my birthing situation. I do understand why he acted the way he did, but I was quite scared and sad about my eyes seeing darkness. I really wished I did not have to die," Arabella said.

Amy hugged Arabella. "You are back now and are stronger than ever. Whatever Gabriel did, he brought you back and gave you some of his inner strength, sweet Mother," Amy said before she kissed Arabella on the cheek. "I need you to be strong for me and guide me in any way possible through these weird pregnancies. Soon, I would like to know how serums can impregnate our kind," Amy said.

Arabella chuckled and nodded.

"Shall I see if Amelia can guide you in harnessing your strengths? Would you like to accompany me, or would you rather remain in your room?" Arabella inquired. After a moment's reflection, Amy nodded.

"I'll accompany you to see what Amelia suggests. I'd like to gain insight into what I should consume to fortify myself," Amy replied. Together, they approached Amelia, who was engaged in conversation with Daniel, Vladimir, and Adrian in the living quarters. The group paused and greeted them with warm smiles upon their arrival.

"Good evening, ladies," Daniel greeted, rising from his seat and motioning for them to sit on an adjacent sofa.

"We were hoping to speak with Amelia, if that is okay?" Arabella asked as she looked at Daniel and then at Amelia. Amelia smiled and got to her feet.

"Of course, my dears. How may I assist you this wonderful evening?" Amelia asked.

Arabella smiled. "Amy is soon to be a mother, but I feel that her body may need some more support in her strength. Could you show her all the different types of potions?"

"Absolutely. Follow me to my chamber; that's where I keep my potion records," Amelia beckoned. Both Arabella and Amy followed her. The path to Amelia's chamber was reminiscent of the route to Gabriel's room, though situated on the opposite side of the castle. The trio descended a flight of mahogany stairs leading to a rosewood door adorned with a golden handle and lock. Upon entering and securing the door, they walked a short distance to another similarly designed door, this one fitted with a silver lock. Inside, they were greeted by an ornate wooden bead curtain leading to a room dominated by a grand cherrywood bed. A plush red carpet blanketed the floor, complemented by a redwood bookshelf housing an array of tomes. Amelia clicked her tongue thoughtfully, scanning the shelves for her potions book.

"Ah, here it is," Amelia, said as she got on her toes and reached up for this silver hardcover book titled 'Potions.' "Let's move to my sitting area," Amelia suggested, guiding them to a cozy nook furnished with a quaint fireplace, a beautifully patterned white and red rug, a snug sofa, and an accompanying chair. "Please, have a seat," Amelia invited, motioning to the sofa for Amy and Arabella.

Amelia sat in the chair adjacent from where Amy was sitting and paged over to the glossary section. "Baby, birthing," Amelia murmured. "No, pregnancies. I need to be in the 'P' section," Amelia said to herself. "Party, pregnancies," Amelia read aloud, then looked up at Amy and Arabella with a smile. "Okay, here, Amy," Amelia said as she handed Amy her book. "Here are the different types of vitamins and minerals you will be needing. We need to get you a lot of iron, but perhaps you may get sufficient from the blood. Next, we need to get you some anti-nausea herbs to help you with those special moments. Then we need to get you a few of these herbs," Amelia said, pointing to specific herbs unfamiliar to Amy.

Amy furrowed her brows and gently closed the book, sinking into the sofa. "This is overwhelming," she sighed, rubbing her temples. "I can't imagine navigating all of this. Children sound wonderful, but here I am, barely twenty in human years, no college degree, surrounded by almost strangers in a castle, and trapped due to some monster targeting either me or my father." She took a deep breath, her hands covering her face. "How can I cope with these feelings of panic and overwhelm, dear mother and Amelia?"

Amelia placed Amy's right hand in hers, offering comfort. "It will all soon pass, my love," Arabella said. "This too shall pass, my love," Arabella murmured. "It's a whirlwind of emotions right now. The toughest part, unfortunately, is still ahead, towards the end of your pregnancy. I remember a phase of insatiable hunger; eating endlessly but never feeling full. The restless nights — fluctuating between feeling too hot or too cold, bouts of nausea, and then sudden bursts of joy," Arabella shared with a light chuckle.

Amelia smiled, listening intently. "Your mother is a wonderful woman, dear Amy," she said. "Her inner beauty radiates outward. Speaking of which, have you heard from Bryan recently?"

Amy offered a slight smile and shrugged. "I last saw him about a week ago. But there was no spark or joy; he seemed withdrawn and distant when I descended the stairs to greet Alistair and Darcia."

Amelia pondered Amy's words before responding. "This pregnancy will be a lot for him to handle too. I just can't envision someone like Caleb supporting you through this," Amelia observed.

Arabella scoffed and shook her head. "That name. Who is he, anyway? Why did Gabriel even have him turned into one of us?" Amy remembered seeing Caleb at her high school prom and later in her human bedroom.

"I remember being alone with Gabriel during my first nights of being back in my biological home," Amy said. Both Arabella and Amelia looked at Amy. "He had told me that he had wished for a son and that he got two daughters instead. When he was not certain if we were to return back to him, he decided to create Caleb," Amy said. Arabella growled at that name again, which caused Amelia to laugh.

"How can we get rid of him?" Arabella asked as she looked at Amelia. Amelia reached for the potion book. Amy handed it back to Amelia and kept her focus on Amelia. Amelia went back to the glossary, searching for something related to "disappearance," but found no specific section. "And how do we get rid of Katrina? Now that the mother of Gabriel's children is back, Katrina serves no actual purpose anymore," Arabella said.

Amy looked at Amelia thoughtfully. "Is it possible to send them both away? However, I wouldn't want them to ally with Larry and turn against us," she mused. Arabella nodded in agreement. "Up to now, they haven't caused any major issues, except that I cannot stand that woman's voice," Arabella said, irritated. Amelia sighed, closing the book and returning it to its shelf.

"I think we should see what the other ones are up to. I am starting to feel myself getting a bit hungry," Amelia said as she headed toward the door to unlock the three doors and send Amy and Arabella upstairs. "Have you two eaten yet?" Amelia asked. Amy nodded, but Arabella shook her head.

"Perhaps we can have our own sisterly moment and have a little hunt, what do you say, Arabella?" Amelia asked.

# Back to the Beginning

It was a dark foggy evening in Romania. Back at the motel, Alistair nervously bit the nails of his right hand. From her bed, Darcia recognized the sound. "My beloved," she called out gently. "What troubles you?" Alistair turned around to face her. "You shouldn't bite your nails; it's a bad habit."

Alistair smiled, resting his hands on his lap. "I can't comprehend why all this drama is unfolding again," he sighed, rising from his seat to approach Darcia, who lay still. "How would you feel about a holiday away from the family? Perhaps Spain, Brazil, or Barcelona?" Darcia responded with a soft smile and a shake of her head. "Why? What if Gabriel is attacked, or if something happens to Amy or Ginger? Shouldn't we stay here for any important updates, my dear husband?"

Alistair settled on the edge of Darcia's bed, gazing at her. "But what if we're just stagnating here, growing more restless each day? Don't we also deserve a respite? I was reflecting on the fact that we never celebrated our narrow escape from execution last year. It still haunts me. Gabriel entrusts us with his children, and then when things go awry, we're the ones at risk," Alistair admitted with a shudder.

Darcia propped herself up on her elbows and offered a comforting smile. "We would never perish, my dear," she whispered. "We are stronger and wiser than many of our kind. Why do you think Gabriel entrusted his most cherished treasures to us? He knew we'd be capable guardians for his children," Darcia asserted. "How about we simply cuddle for a bit? I could use some rest." Alistair, with a smile, adjusted himself closer to Darcia, enveloping her in a warm embrace.

In the adjacent room, Bryan, Raymond, Xavier, Silas, and Joshua were gathered in Bryan and Raymond's quarters. Bryan turned to his sibling, inquiring, "Josh, is Gregory still among the living?" Joshua, casting a glance at Bryan, just shrugged. Bryan, a tad frustrated, pressed on, "How do your abilities even work, Joshua?" Joshua simply responded with another shrug. "You're quite the conversationalist, aren't you? Anyone can shrug," Bryan remarked, dripping with sarcasm.

Joshua sighed and looked over at Bryan. "Must you always be snarky to me?" Bryan scoffed. "And that, as well? I was only aware that Arabella had awakened, but had no insight into Larry or Amy's offspring." Bryan shook his head and looked back at the television. "Say, are you going to be the new father figure to those younglings?" Joshua asked. Bryan looked over and growled at Joshua. "What now?"

"What's gotten into you? Why harp on matters that clearly aren't my concern? I don't know what the future holds for Amy and me. But what's clear is that we're trapped here, waiting hand and foot, anticipating our next directive." Bryan's irritation was evident. Joshua, choosing to disengage, simply turned his attention back to the television.

Raymond, sensing the tense atmosphere, stood up. "How about we hunt down our own diversion? Perhaps a party or a club?" he suggested, hoping to rally his brothers. "We could all use a break from Gabriel and our elders. Just some quality brotherly time." Bryan agreed, rising to his feet, as did the other boys, except Joshua. "Coming, Josh?" Raymond inquired. Joshua simply shook his head. "Want us to bring something back for you?" Another shake of the head from Joshua. Raymond sighed, leading the others out of the room, leaving Joshua in solitude.

After a moment of contemplation, Joshua stood and opened the door, realizing his brothers had already departed. Deciding on some solitary exploration, he wandered to a familiar park where he'd previously spotted Larry and Helen. He paused to admire a magnificent fountain depicting a woman cradling a seashell, water gracefully cascading from it. Finding a bench overlooking a tranquil pond, Joshua settled down, lost in his thoughts.

Around him, there were some joggers and some dog walkers that we going in each direction. He started to feel himself getting hungry, but knew that there were too many witnesses. He started to walk away from the people and try to find someone who was alone. As he kept walking, the groups of people disappeared. He knew he had to find something quick. He started to feel shaky and clammy till he noticed a young man jogging near him, looking at him out of concern. "Scuzați-mă, domnule, dar sunteți bine?" the man asked.

Joshua looked up at him with hunger. "English?" Joshua asked. The man looked confused and thought about it.

"Need help?" the man asked.

Feeling weakened, Joshua shook his head, collapsing to his knees. The man hastily pulled out his smartphone to call for medical assistance. "No, please," Joshua murmured, reaching out to touch the man's arm. With the last of his strength, he dragged the man down and drained him, feeling revitalized afterward.

What Joshua did not realize is that there were sirens coming in their direction. Joshua quickly grabbed the man and threw him over his shoulder and ran toward the exit of the park. The ambulance showed up and saw Joshua holding the man and grabbed a gurney. "Cât de rău este?" asked one of the paramedics. Joshua was hesitant about giving the man over since he had bite marks on his jugular. "Domnule?" Joshua shook his head and took off with the dead man in his arms, so he could dispose of it somewhere else. The paramedics looked perplexed at the whole scene and called for backup. "Se pare că există un nebun care poartă un mort," said the driver over his walkie-talkie. The ambulance took off in the direction where Joshua ran to.

Upon reaching the motel, Joshua found he was the first to return. He discreetly placed the body inside, resolving to find a more suitable disposal spot. Ordinarily, Bryan managed such situations, but Joshua knew he had to address this himself. He approached the motel's main office where an older man stood behind the counter. "Bună seara," the man greeted.

Joshua smiled and nodded. "English?"

"How may I assist you?" the man responded in a heavy Romanian accent. Joshua pondered how best to request a shovel. "I need a shovel," he finally said. The man, visibly perturbed, seemed reluctant to question Joshua's intentions. "The janitor, the one who handles repairs, has a cabinet. Would you like the key to borrow a shovel?" he proposed.

Joshua smiled and nodded. "That sounds perfect. Thank you for helping me." The man opened up a drawer by the table and grabbed out the key for the janitor's cabinet and handed Joshua the key. "Over there," said the man pointing at this closet with a keyhole in it. Once Joshua got the closet open, he saw various tools and just a small shovel that was half his size. He picked it up and analyzed it. "Okay, this will do," Joshua said before he thanked the clerk and walked outside to dig a grave for his unfortunate victim.

While scouring a wooded area near the park, Joshua heard laughter and screams from men and women. Drawn to the commotion, he spotted his brothers with a few women. Hoping to remain unnoticed, he found a patch of moist soil and began digging a rectangular hole. Eventually, his heavy breathing caught Bryan's attention, who quickly approached, startling Joshua.

"What are you doing here, Josh?" Bryan inquired.

Joshua, focused on his digging, replied, "It's none of your business, Bryan. I need to cover my tracks. I landed myself in quite the predicament earlier."

Bryan clucked his tongue, shaking his head. "What did you do?"

Pausing momentarily, Joshua looked up, guilt evident in his eyes. "I let my hunger control me, and I killed an innocent man who thought I was injured or unwell."

Bryan chuckled and shrugged. "These things happen, brother," Bryan said in a hushed tone. "Where's the body?" Joshua pointed at the room. "If you could get me the body, I will help you."

Joshua nodded but could not smile at that moment. Retrieving the body, he had to wait for other guests to clear the area. Spotting a young blonde couple entering the adjacent room, Joshua seized an opportune moment, lifting the corpse and racing towards Bryan, who had finished the grave. Together, they buried the man.

Joshua looked at how dirty his clothes were and tried to wipe off as much of the dirt as possible. He then gave Bryan a quick smile and looked behind him. "How is your gathering, Bryan?" Joshua asked. Bryan quickly forgot about his supposed date and smiled. "Care to join us, Joshua?" Joshua smiled and shook his head.

"I think I will let you five enjoy yourselves. I have had enough excitement for the evening. Please do not mention this to the others," Joshua asked.

Bryan nodded. "Nothing happened. You were just sulking in our room," Bryan said teasingly.

Joshua smiled and turned around to walk back to their room and wait for the other brothers to join him. As Bryan and his brothers came back to their room, they were covered in blood and flesh.

"Does this place have a laundromat or a place where we can get our clothes washed?" Bryan asked. Bryan walked over to the main office of the motel resort but it was closed. "Just our luck. I guess we can wait for Darcia to help us with our clothes," Bryan said to himself before he walked back to his room.

Back at the castle, Arabella and Amelia came back from their hunt. They entered the living quarters to find Gabriel lounging on a sofa, entranced by the fire crackling in the hearth. "Good evening, ladies," Gabriel greeted, glancing their way. "Did you enjoy your meal?"

Amelia and Arabella both chuckled and shrugged. "Nothing new, but it was interesting to see how well Arabella was able to charm these guys. She really knows how to seduce people, Gabriel," Amelia said with a giggle.

With a warm smile, Gabriel beckoned them to join him. While Amelia excused herself, an invigorated Arabella took a seat beside her husband. "You're looking radiant, my beloved," Gabriel remarked, lifting Arabella's hand for a gentle kiss.

Arabella beamed at the compliment. "And how are you feeling?"

"I feel good right now, perhaps better than before. I am starting to understand the ways of our kind, but I still feel an occasional sadness inside of me when I know whether these humans have families or mates in their lives, my dearest Gabriel," Arabella said.

Gabriel nodded. "I understand that completely," Gabriel said. "It can sometimes be quite heavy and exhausting to realize how humans are very precious to others. That is why I have decided on hospital blood banks and have Hildegard run those errands for me to keep up our blood supply. An occasional human is also entertaining," Gabriel said as he moved his gaze to the fire. "I am happy to have you back in my life again, Arabella," Gabriel said. "I was not well in my mind of what I had done to our girls, but I promise that it will all get better each day. I know we will be wonderful grandparents to our little ones." Gabriel said with a hint of fatigue in his voice.

Caught in her thoughts, Arabella hesitated to voice her concerns about Amy's unexpected pregnancy. But as if reading her mind, Gabriel preempted her, "Our kind doesn't procreate like humans. I'd hoped for children once you transitioned. I recall our intimate moments, yet, in our state, they're devoid of sensation. Amelia developed a serum to grant you the potential for motherhood. Initially, I couldn't distinguish if the injection contained my blood or the serum, which might've endangered you due to potential complications. Later, I discerned it was indeed the pregnancy serum."

Arabella's anxiety was palpable. "Was it the same serum Amy received?"

Gabriel was quick to allay her fears. "No. Amy received Caleb's essence. It was his, not a serum."

Arabella breathed a sigh of relief. "You had me worried, Gabe." She paused, gathering her thoughts, "Why did you want Caleb for Amy?"

Gabriel exhaled deeply. "Caleb is a striking young man. I believed that once Amy embraced her true nature, they could produce powerful descendants, and the same goes for Ginger."

Arabella sighed in disbelief. "Why force them to be with those you've chosen? What if they wanted to be with someone they genuinely loved? Why decide their fates without asking them, my husband?" Arabella's voice quivered with anger. "I might not have lived my dream life, but I always wanted our daughters to have the freedom to choose their own paths," she said, her voice filled with emotion. "It saddens me that you made these choices for them without consulting me. They are my children too. Amy clearly has feelings for that Bryan boy, and Ginger will find her own way. I can't fathom why you'd do this," she said, rising abruptly to leave the room.

Gabriel stayed silent, watching Arabella exit. After a few moments, he reached for a bottle of sustenance, drinking deeply before placing it back on the table. Lucien and Adrian entered, their faces etched with concern. "Everything alright, Gabriel?" Lucien inquired. Gabriel merely gestured towards the bottle. Lucien smiled, fetching glasses from a cabinet.

"I saw Arabella back there. Is everything all right with her?" Adrian asked as he watched Lucien pour him a glass of blood.

Gabriel responded with a hint of sarcasm, "She's upset about the choices I made for our daughters." He continued, "Perhaps I let my protective instincts take over, wanting only the best for our family. In my mind, I believed creating Caleb to be the biological father of my future grandchildren was a good decision. Maybe my judgment was clouded by my grief over losing Arabella. What brings you two here?" he asked, shifting his attention to Lucien and Adrian.

Lucien drained his glass and set it down. "We should discuss Larry Harrison. Although I dealt with him recently, it doesn't mean he's gone for good. We might need a formal gathering, similar to Alistair and Darcia's trial, with the leaders of all the covens. Having backup seems prudent," he said, glancing at Adrian who sipped his drink leisurely. "We can't risk any harm coming to us, like when Alistair and Darcia tried to take Amy back to Oregon. Remember that ordeal, Gabriel?" Lucien queried.

Gabriel nodded and chuckled at the absurdity of the memory. "Family dynamics at its finest, is that not true?" Gabriel asked with a smile. Both Adrian and Lucien chuckled. "Very well, we shall have our family meeting with everyone around the world. I just wonder if they have already sensed Amy's situation, or if they might hold a grudge against me for what I did to her," Gabriel said.

Lucien rolled his eyes, smiling. "Save that thought for another time, Gabriel. If they notice anything or sense the abnormality of Amy's situation, so be it. You are our patriarch, Gabriel Ambrose. You need to stand your ground and not let anyone push you around or even think of you as less of a leader than you were meant to be. Amy is doing just fine, and so is Ginger. They might ask about Arabella, but then again, Amelia is kind of our sorceress who makes potions; so just tell them about her spell book and how you were the one who actually saved her and brought her back from the dead. All of them will admire a story like that," Lucien said.

Gabriel nodded. "I like that story, Lucien," he replied with a smile. "For now, I would like to rest up as it is getting close to dawn. Tomorrow evening, we can get everyone involved in this potential war or battle. Have a good slumber, brothers," Gabriel said to his brothers. They all wished each other a good slumber and went over to their own beds.

As everyone was getting ready to go to sleep, Amy walked over to Ginger and saw her looking at the picture book that Emma had given to Amy. Amy smiled as she climbed into Ginger's bed, resting herself on her right elbow. Ginger smirked at some of the pictures and looked over at Amy. "How has your evening been, sweet sister?" Ginger asked.

"Quite well, sweet Ginger," Amy said. "For some reason, my room feels a bit cold. Could I spend the night with you?" Ginger rolled her eyes. "Please, I feel like if I am cold that my babies might get upset with me." Amy said with pleading eyes. Ginger smirked and nodded. After Ginger turned off the light, light started to shine through the curtains. Amy fell into a deep sleep and dreamt how she was walking in a beautiful, hill-like area where daisies bloomed and the sun shone brightly. Then, in her dream, she wondered how it was possible to walk out into daylight. She looked at her floral white dress and matching heels, then down at the stroller to see a tiny puppy inside. Amy scrunched her brows as she leaned closer. The puppy was a little wolf pup with blue eyes.

When Amy was about an inch away from the pup's snout, it yelped. "Amy?" asked a familiar voice. Amy quickly turned around to see Larry, but he was in the same outfit he wore when she had first met him. "How is our daughter doing?" Amy looked back inside the crib and saw a small baby swaddled in a blanket with the same blue eyes. "Amy, we are meant to be together. You must never leave me."

Amy started to back away and saw the sky turn from sunshine to dark clouds. Larry slowly started to shape shift into a wolf and approach her slowly. "Stop it! Please leave me alone!" Amy screamed, waking up with a gasp. Ginger was still asleep next to her. Amy felt her forehead; it was hot and clammy. She leaned over to Ginger's night table as gently as possible to check the time—it was eleven in the morning. Amy leaned back slowly against the mattress and pillow, deciding to go over to her own bed to avoid waking up Ginger.

Once the evening came, Amy walked down to the dining quarter, though she had no hunger for blood. She remembered the spell book that Amelia had, trying to remember the different types of herbs she could consume to help her babies grow strong inside of her. Amy opened some cupboards in the dining quarter, revealing silver cans labeled with different types of herbs, such as galangal, cloves, echinacea, cinnamon, saffron, and others. Not wanting to haphazardly grab ingredients, Amy walked back to Amelia's chamber and knocked on her door until Amelia appeared in her white robe, her long black hair messy, and her black eyes sleepy.

"Amy, what are you doing up so early?" Amelia asked groggily. Amelia then realized how Amy needed something for her body. "Wait here while I get my potion's book. Try to follow the instructions or have your mother help you if needed," Amelia said as she walked back to her room and came back with the book. "Try to be careful, my sweet girl," Amelia said before she closed the door. Amy returned to the dining quarter and found she needed pepper, cinnamon, cacao, and curcumin. She mixed the herbs together in a pan, boiled some hot water, poured it into the pan, and let it bubble for a few minutes. Then, she transferred the mixture to a glass and waited.

The smell wasn't too bad, but the colors were unappealing. After waiting a few minutes at the dining table, Amy took a tiny sip, wincing. "That tastes bad," she said hoarsely. "How is this supposed to help me?" Leaning back in her chair, she closed her eyes, feeling her body warm up gently. The feeling wasn't unpleasant, so she took another sip, trying to acclimate to the sensation. After finishing her drink, she felt a bit nauseous and waited a bit longer. She placed her glass in the sink to soak. As she walked to the living quarters, she felt her body strengthen, as if she'd slept for a solid week. When she checked the main clock, it was about one in the afternoon.

Amy reminisced about her times hanging out with her old friend Jenna during the afternoons on weekends and the final moments of her human life with Martha. She then recalled her encounter with some of her shapeshifting uncles in the mall's parking lot, realizing how unethical they had been in their attempts to bring her back to her father. From what Amy also remembered from her father's library, spectacles of that sort were often considered illegal. Gabriel, or his henchmen, would execute those who exposed themselves or caused any sort of drama. Amy sat down on one of the sofas, gazing at the unlit fireplace, feeling no need for additional warmth. She pondered whether she should consider meeting Larry again to explain why his actions were wrong.

Before Amy thought about anything else, she felt her body get heavy with extreme fatigue wash over her. She curled up on the sofa and fell asleep. She was then hours later abruptly awoken by a loud. Amy got to her feet quickly and groggily looked around. There was nobody to be seen. She looked outside the kitchen window and saw Larry standing outside staring at her. Amy felt this sharp pain inside her body and stood inside frozen with fear. "Amy," Larry mouthed as he pointed to the doorknob. Amy could not move and kept staring at him. "Please let me in, Amy," Larry said. Again, Amy was frozen with fear. "We need to talk," Larry said.

Amy managed to take another step back and felt dizzy. "Please, Amy, remember our wonderful evening together in Oregon? How you had met my family?" Amy's eyes welled with tears as she continued to back away, heading towards the dining quarter. Suddenly she felt two arms around her. It was Gabriel, holding her close in his arms, shushing her. He was wearing his black satin pajamas, a matching robe, and black suede slippers. Amy broke down, crying into his chest as he led her away.

"It is okay, sweet Amy," Gabriel whispered as he held her close. "He cannot enter this place. We are safe from him." Amy tried to control her breathing and leaned against Gabriel's chest.

"Here, let me take you back to your room, so you can rest," Gabriel said as he walked Amy back to her room and tucked her into her bed. He closed the curtains and sat on the edge of the bed. "You are safe, Amy," Gabriel said. "Try to keep as calm as possible, for the sake of your kids." Amy closed her eyes and remembered the tactic Alistair had used on her at the airport when her cravings had become overwhelming.

Taking deep breaths, Amy inhaled and exhaled, repeating the process about five times until she felt centered again. Gabriel, concerned, asked, "What actually happened, Amy? Why were you down in the living quarter?" Regaining control of her breathing, Amy opened her mouth to respond, "I…I had a bad dream about Larry and pushing his puppy in a stroller, out in daylight." Gabriel tenderly placed his right hand on Amy's left cheek, gently stroking it. "I woke up, thought about making one of Amelia's potions, and then I fell asleep," Amy explained.

Gabriel nodded, patiently waiting for Amy to finish speaking. "Perhaps I should ask Hildegard to bring your drinks and meals to your room, so you can rest as much as possible," Gabriel suggested before standing up. "I still need another four hours of sleep, Amy, but please try to rest as much as you can. Okay?" Amy nodded, snuggled under her covers, and closed her eyes. After leaving Amy's room, Gabriel quietly closed the door behind him and returned to his quarters. Arabella was still in a deep sleep, breathing softly. Gabriel carefully removed his black robe and slippers, gently slipping back under the covers to avoid waking her. "Gabe?" Arabella whispered softly. Gabriel wrapped his arms around Arabella's shoulders, reassuring her. "Is Amy okay?"

"Yes, she is. She just had a bit of a nightmare, but she's back in her room now," Gabriel whispered. Arabella hummed softly and drifted back to sleep. The next evening, around six o'clock, Gabriel got up and made his way to the main floor. He grabbed a half-bottle of blood, swilled it down, and then placed the empty bottle in the crate for Hildegard to return to the blood bank. Lucien and Daniel arrived moments later.

"Gabriel, what happened this morning?" Lucien asked, concerned. Gabriel turned to face them and smiled.

"Nothing much, except that Larry fellow is bothering Amy. I wonder what he is planning," Gabriel said.

Daniel sighed. "Gabe, I think we need to have a family meeting this evening to discuss this serious situation," he suggested. Gabriel nodded in agreement. "I agree. Could you, Adrian, or Amelia organize the meeting for all of us?" Gabriel asked. Lucien frowned, confused. "I feel the need to be closer to my children and Arabella for a while, to keep them centered and safe," Gabriel explained.

Lucien rolled his eyes. "You are the patriarch, Gabriel. You should at least inform them that you will be hosting this meeting. Asking your brothers to do it might make the family feel skeptical and uneasy about the sudden gathering," Lucien advised. Gabriel smiled and nodded in acknowledgment. "Okay, I appreciate you initiating the meeting. I believe you still have all of their contacts on your electronic device," Lucien said before leaving the dining quarter. Daniel grabbed a fresh bottle of blood from the cooling case and an empty glass from the cupboard, catching Gabriel's attention.

"Daniel," Gabriel said. "I want to thank you for all of your support towards me and the other ones. I may not always show it all that much, but I appreciate you as a brother in many ways." Daniel smiled and nodded.

"You are welcome, dear brother," Daniel said as he poured himself a full glass. "Care for some, Gabriel?" Gabriel nodded and grabbed an empty glass and placed it on the table. Daniel poured him a glass and raised it in a toast. "To a future full of complications and problems that we can handle together," Daniel said, which caused Gabriel to chuckle.

Gabriel gulped down his glass and sat down. "I do hope it will all be okay, dear brother," Gabriel said. "Especially since they will all have questions for me or Arabella about her return." Daniel smiled and sat down.

"Why are you afraid of dealing with such questions, Gabriel?" Daniel asked.

Gabriel thought about his answer. "Well, I just do not want any of them to think of me of being weak, I think," Gabriel said.

"Why would they think you are weak, Gabriel? You brought Arabella back from the dead, you have two children who love you, and you still have us in your life. What is with this unusual thought?" Daniel asked. "The fact that you will be battling this Larry kid, so you could protect your daughter. That is not being weak, in anyway," Daniel said.

Gabriel exhaled, shifting his focus from the chair across from him to Daniel. "You think so?" Gabriel asked. Daniel rolled his eyes and shook his head.

"Yes, of course, brother," Daniel said. "If you need any help organizing this meeting, I am willing to help you, but only after you have had enough sustenance to better focus."

Gabriel smiled. "I am fine for now, as I had already finished a bottle before you and Lucien came into the dining quarter."

"Let me finish my meal and then you and I will get everything organized," Daniel said.

Just then, Amelia came into the dining quarter and grabbed a glass. "Could I have some or are you both sharing that bottle?" Amelia asked. Daniel beckoned for Amelia to join them.

"Amelia," Gabriel said. "Amy had a nightmare last morning and said that she was creating something from your potion's book. Why?" Gabriel asked.

Amelia took a sip before responding. "She and Arabella both came to me and requested some sustenance for Amy's pregnant body. I gave Amy my spellbook because she was awake at eleven in the morning and she looked a bit pale," Amelia said as she sat down across from Daniel. "Is she okay?"

Gabriel nodded. "Yes, she is, but I wished you would have also discussed your plans with me, as her father. These grandchildren are the future of my foundation and they must remain healthy, whether I am alive, passed away, or have abdicated in any form," Gabriel said.

Amelia nodded. "I understand, Gabriel. Perhaps Arabella is not the only one who actually has been down the pregnancy road," Amelia said sarcastically. "Perhaps her father might be a better source?" Gabriel looked at Amelia with a serious expression. Daniel put his hand on Gabriel's hand and held it tightly.

"I am okay, Daniel, I just want to be more included in these affairs, especially since I have not been able to for nineteen years, and I want to know all the details of everything that I will be facing and dealing with," Gabriel said.

Amelia rolled her eyes and took another sip from her glass. "Well, okay, Gabriel. I shall consult with you as well whenever Amy or Arabella approach me," Amelia said.

Gabriel nodded and got to his feet. "Brother, are you about done with your drink?"

Daniel nodded and grabbed both his and Gabriel's empty glasses and soaked them with warm water before he and Gabriel walked over to Gabriel's study.

Upon entering the study, Gabriel pressed his hand against an electronic scanning device located outside. The doors clicked open, and he walked inside first, followed by Daniel. "Okay," Gabriel said with a sigh. "There is what the humans call a laptop. Are you familiar with that term?" Daniel nodded. "Good. I will be here for support, but I need you to be the one to organize it," Gabriel said as he sat in a chair across from his own, behind the table.

Daniel took Gabriel's usual chair behind the laptop, clicked on some icons, and typed a few words.

*To all our family members,*

*Gabriel has proposed a family meeting regarding an urgent matter: a dangerous creature named Larry Harrison. He is plotting to have him and Amy killed or at least severely harmed. Please respond to this message and attend our meeting at midnight, so we can all discuss a plan to deal with this situation.*

*With regards,*
*Daniel Ambrose, proxy for Gabriel*

After Daniel had sent off the message, he signed out of some accounts, but left Gabriel's laptop on. "Done," he announced, looking across to Gabriel. "Now we shall see which members will attend our meeting. Between you and me, Gabe, what would you consider to be an important strategy to handle this Larry Harrison?"

Gabriel thought about his answer and nodded. "I have no actual intentions of having him killed, but like the humans would say in this world, it's kill or be killed. If he wants to harm any of my family members, I think death would be appropriate."

Daniel nodded in agreement. "Okay, that sounds like a plan. And what are you hoping to get from the other members from around the world? Would you like them to come over and protect Amy and Ginger or would you just have a few members sent out?" Daniel asked. Gabriel looked at Daniel with a confused expression.

"Why would I just have half of the members sent out here, Daniel?" Gabriel snapped. "Of course I would have all of them here." Daniel rolled his eyes and shook his head.

"I am just trying to help you, Gabe, but you are making it very hard on me when you act like that," Daniel snapped back, his voice rising. Gabriel bared his teeth and growled at Daniel, who growled back.

Just then, Lucien, Vladimir, and Adrian entered the study, having used Lucien's fingerprint for access. "Stop it!" Lucien yelled. "This is not helping the situation." Gabriel relaxed himself and leaned against the chair. Daniel did the same, but got to his feet to leave Gabriel's study. "Did you two make an announcement of our meeting?" Gabriel nodded and got to his feet.

"Actually, it was Daniel who did most of the work. What would be a good strategy to use in this situation, dear Lucien?" Gabriel asked. Lucien just looked at Gabriel with tired eyes.

"We shall take this meeting as it comes. I think the other ones will have some good ideas to bring to the table. Right now, it is eight o'clock in the evening, which means we have four more hours to prepare. Should we get Alistair and Darcia involved in our meeting, as well, Gabe?"

Gabriel smiled, reminiscing about the chaos that ensued during Alistair and Darcia's trial regarding Amy's perilous incident. "I think I shall invite them," Gabriel decided, sitting down in his chair. He swiftly opened an electronic messaging service and sent Alistair a message about the meeting. Afterward, he got to his feet and walked down to the basement's sleeping quarters, where he found Arabella putting on her clothes and brushing her hair.

"My beloved wife, how pretty you look right now," Gabriel said, placing his hands on Arabella's shoulders, kissing the top of her head. "How did you sleep?"

Arabella glanced at Gabriel through the mirror and smiled. "Quite well, dear husband," she said. "I did wake up briefly when I felt your return to our bed about Amy's wellbeing. How is she?"

"She is wonderful, sweet Arabella," Gabriel said. "She is resting a bit. From now on, I shall have Hildegard prepare her meals and drinks. I was wondering, dear Arabella," Gabriel said. "We will be having a meeting with the other coven members. Would you like to attend or not?"

Arabella looked up at Gabriel with a serious expression. "Why would I not attend? I am the queen, am I not?" Arabella asked. Gabriel smiled and nodded.

"Perfect," Gabriel said. "I shall let the other ones know how my beautiful and smart queen will be attending. Please excuse me for a moment," Gabriel said before he walked back to the main floor. He was looking around for Lucien or Daniel and could not find them immediately.

He saw Ginger descend the stairs from her room, dressed in her usual attire, her silk-like hair flowing behind her. "Good evening, my sweet child," Gabriel said, acknowledging Ginger's presence. "How did you sleep?"

Ginger smiled, waiting until she reached the main floor before responding. "Quite well, Father," she said. "I had Amy with me for a while, but then I noticed this evening she was back in her own room. She doesn't sleepwalk, does she?"

Gabriel chuckled, shaking his head. "No, I don't think so. I believe she may have had a nightmare, but I managed to lead her back to her room and tuck her in," Gabriel said. Ginger nodded.

"I'm going to get myself something to drink. I'm feeling quite hungry and thirsty right now. Excuse me," Ginger said, excusing herself. She walked over to the dining area, grabbed an opened bottle, and took several gulps. Deciding to check up on Amy, she made her way back up to their sleeping quarters and opened Amy's bedroom door, finding her sleeping peacefully. As she was about to close the door, Amy called out to Ginger.

"Yes, Amy?" Ginger said. "What can I do for you?"

"Could you get our father for me? I need to ask him about my feeding schedule," Amy said. Ginger closed the door and went downstairs to find Gabriel, who was in the living quarter, conversing with Lucien. Noticing Ginger, Lucien greeted her.

"Good evening, Ginger," Lucien said. Gabriel looked up and smiled.

"My child, what can I do for you?" Gabriel asked as he focused his gaze on Ginger.

"Amy needs you, Father," Ginger said.

Gabriel nodded, excusing himself from Lucien's company, and made his way to Amy's room. Upon knocking, she called him in. "My child, what can I do for you?" he asked warmly.

"I was wondering if you could help me decide what nutrition I need to maintain my strength and that of my children," Amy said, snuggled under her covers.

"I shall consult Amelia to see what she can suggest. How are you feeling otherwise, Amy?"

Amy shrugged. "Average, I guess. Occasionally, I feel tired, then hungry, and then tired again," she said. Gabriel smiled and nodded.

"Anything else you need? Otherwise, perhaps Hildegard could assist you for a while, since she probably has more experience with these sorts of matters. I can give you all the information you want about our existence, but regarding womanly problems and needs, I leave that up to other professionals in that area," Gabriel said. Amy scoffed and smiled after that.

"Anything else, my sweet child?"

Amy shook her head and rested her eyes a bit longer. Gabriel left her room, making his way back to the dining area where Adrian, Vladimir, Arabella, and Amelia were enjoying a drink together.

"Amelia," Gabriel said. Amelia looked up, intrigued. "Could you come with me for a moment?" Amelia smiled and gulped down the last few inches of blood in her cup and placed it on the table.

"I am not done yet, fellow family members," Amelia announced, before joining Gabriel.

Gabriel led her out towards her sleeping quarters, and they both waited outside of Amelia's first locked door. "Before we both enter, what did Amy make herself last morning, Amelia? It seems that it may have helped her." Gabriel said.

"That is good to hear, Gabriel," Amelia said. "I've been looking into some of the ancient literary works from the past about what the Romans, Greeks, and other cultures used for their herbs and spices. I managed to have Hildegard purchase some of the important spices from various markets," Amelia said. "As long as it helps our sweet Amy, I'm relieved."

Amelia turned the lock and opened up the door, allowing them both to enter. Once they reached her slumbering area, Amelia grabbed her potion book and handed it to Gabriel. "Perhaps it would be best to keep this in Amy's room for a while, until she no longer requires any of these potions." Amelia said.

Gabriel took the book in his hands and leafed through it, discovering various topics on potions, such as blood cleansing, increased speed, and enhanced sleep—some of which he had never heard of. He closed the book. "Thank you, sweet Amelia," Gabriel said. "I shall give this to Hildegard and have her gather some more herbs and spices to ensure Amy gets through this pregnancy safely. Between you and me, Amelia, I never intended for any of this to happen. There was just some form of miscommunication that resulted in this situation."

Amelia smiled warmly. "I would never doubt your intentions, Gabriel. You've taken good care of us, and I believe whatever happened was outside of your power."

Gabriel smiled back and tenderly stroked Amelia's face with his right hand.

"I shall take my leave. Thank you for the book." He then left her in her room.

Reaching the main floor, Gabriel walked over to the dining quarter, only to find that his family members were nowhere in sight. He placed the potion book on the table and proceeded to his study. Upon entering, he noticed his electronic device, a laptop, was open—something he didn't recall doing. Perhaps Lucien, whom he trusted the most, or even Daniel, needed to look up something.

Just then, there was a knock on his door. Opening it, Gabriel found Arabella standing there. "My sweet husband," she greeted him. Gabriel gestured for Arabella to enter his study and closed the door behind her

"Quite well, my sweet wife," Gabriel said. "How are you, yourself?" Arabella sighed and looked around.

"Nothing in this room has changed, I believe," she observed before taking a seat in one of the guest chairs. "I myself am doing well. However, as I walked through the kitchen area of our home, I noticed Amelia's spell book lying there. Is that what you used on me to keep me confined in your room, Gabriel?" Arabella asked, her tone laced with curiosity.

Gabriel began to feel uneasy at Arabella's question. "Why do you ask, Arabella?" he said, quickly taking a seat in his chair. "I remember how I couldn't bear to lose you, and Amelia came up with that idea herself, you know," Gabriel explained. Arabella fixed a stern gaze on Gabriel and remained silent. "Why are you bringing this up now, Arabella?"

Arabella sighed and shook her head. "If anything were to happen to Amy, I hope she wouldn't end up in the same situation I was in, Gabriel. This whole pregnancy, with Caleb's blood and carrying three kids, is still bothering me."

Gabriel's expression shifted from relaxed to stern as well. "I've already told you that I never intended for any of this to happen, Arabella. I promise that our daughter will be safe. Please, stop bringing this up," Gabriel implored, striving to maintain a calm tone. Arabella remained still. "Amy is strong and powerful. She has my blood in her to keep her strong. You were just a human when you died, Arabella. Amy will not die."

Arabella's eyes started to water. "I just cannot bear the thought of losing one of my kids, Gabriel. I have only seen them for about three weeks and our pregnancies are about six months, so I barely had any moment of being with our daughter."

Gabriel got to his feet and walked over to Arabella to hold her in his arms. "Amy is strong, my sweet wife," Gabriel reassured her in a soothing tone. "She has managed everything from navigating high school among humans, to traveling the world, and finally accepting her true self in this life. Instead of dwelling on the worst-case scenarios, my wife, think about the three beautiful children we will hold and nurture with our love and resources. Amelia is a skilled sorceress. If her books could bring you back from the dead, they will protect our family from any harm," Gabriel said.

Arabella nodded, seeming somewhat reassured. Gabriel released his hold on her and took a step back "Is there anything else I can help you with, my life mate?" Gabriel asked. Arabella shook her head.

"Not for now, Gabriel," Arabella said, standing up. She looked around the room, noticing various paintings of Gabriel, and one of her in a golden frame from when she was human. "I never knew you had that made, Gabriel. When did you have a painting of me made?"

Gabriel smiled. "I have a vivid memory of who you were and what you looked like. If you had remained dead, at least I would have this beautiful picture of you to help me through my duties as the patriarch of our group," Gabriel said. Arabella studied her portrait. Even though she knew it was her, she still felt that it looked slightly off, with discrepancies in her nose size and the spacing of her eyes.

"If you would excuse me, we have a meeting in one hour. I must put on my work suit," Gabriel said as he waved goodbye to Arabella.

Arabella made her way to the sleeping area, her eyes scanning the closet filled with pink and yellow dresses. "I will see if Amy still has her trial suit that she wore the day she met Gabriel," Arabella murmured to herself as she approached Amy, who was sitting up in bed, cradling her enlarged belly. "Amy, my darling," Arabella began, "do you still have the black suit that Darcia bought for you a while back?"

Amy looked up, gesturing towards the walk-in closet adjacent to her personal bookshelf. "In there, I believe. That suit looked too expensive to get rid of, so I had Darcia keep it for me," Amy said. "Why will you be needing it, Mother?"

Arabella walked into the closet with her back to Amy, pushing the clothes back and forth. "Your father is arranging a meeting regarding that Larry kid," Arabella said before she found the pants and white blouse. Then she looked further and found the matching blazer. She laid the clothes on Amy's bed and began to change. "By the way, how are you feeling, my child?" she asked, slipping into the suit, which was a bit large for her—a preferable alternative to it being too tight.

"I'm okay. Just a bit tired and nauseous, but my mind is still clear," Amy responded.

"Amy, I swear on my blood that I will never lose you. Okay? You are strong and can handle anything that comes your way," Arabella declared, as she focused her gaze on Amy. "Amelia is our family's greatest sorceress, and her books will help you through these turbulent times. I promise to spend more time with you, to help you regain your strength and energy. Most importantly, I promise to give up my life for both you and Ginger, should that time ever come," Arabella vowed, kissing Amy gently on the head. "For now, I must prepare myself for the evening," she added, planting another kiss on Amy's forehead before heading towards the bedroom door.

"Mother," Amy called out. Arabella stopped before the threshold to turn around. "I am so happy to have you in my life and would hate to lose you," Amy said. Arabella smiled and blew Amy a kiss.

"You will never have to worry of such things, my sweet child," Arabella said before she walked down to the main floor and over toward the area where Gabriel had held Alistair and Darcia's trial. Lucien, Adrian, Amelia, Vladimir, and Daniel were all suited up in the area, placing all the needed equipment for their electronic communication.

"By the way, before I forget," Gabriel started off. "Has anyone notified Alistair and his family?"

Amelia nodded. "I believe it was yesterday. I got an electronic message on this cellular device that they are on their way," Amelia said as she held out her rectangular phone. "They should be here in a few minutes. That reminds me, I need to grab seven more chairs for our other members," Amelia added, heading back towards the kitchen area.

Moments later, the door chimes went off. Hildegard walked over to the front door and gestured for Alistair and Darcia to enter with their sons. "Welcome, my dear family," Gabriel said as he opened his arms up for Alistair to hug him, and then Darcia. "I believe it will just be fourteen of us attending this meeting. My daughters are resting up for the evening; Amy has gotten a bit bigger, so I felt it was best for her to get as much rest as possible," Gabriel said as he moved his gaze from Alistair over to Bryan, who appeared somewhat annoyed. "Daniel, my brother, is everything ready for our meeting?"

Daniel clicked on some keys on the laptop's keyboard, resulting in a black screen appearing on a larger display.

"The meeting is set to start in fifteen minutes," Daniel said before he left the laptop to join the others on the two sofas. "I guess we should wait for them to show up." Gabriel smiled and nodded. "Thank you, Daniel, for your hard work and dedication," Gabriel said before he sat down across from the big screen in his own throne-like chair, watching the numbers change on the screen.

Soon after, the screen came to life with Logan from Australia, followed by Dante and Francesca from Italy, Alarick and Vanessa from Greece, and finally, Kristjan with Helen. "Welcome, my dear family members from around the world. I trust we are all acquainted with one another?" Gabriel inquired, scanning the faces in the room and on the screen. Everyone nodded in confirmation.

Arabella chose that moment to enter the room, prompting audible gasps from those on the screen. Helen couldn't suppress a chuckle, while Gabriel shot a glare at the reactions. "It seems I have a pre-announcement before we start our meeting. My beloved wife, my queen, my life's blood, has returned from the dead," Gabriel announced. Kristjan turned to Helen with a questioning look. "Were you aware of this, Helen?" he asked.

Helen simply smiled and shrugged. The room's attention shifted back to Gabriel as Kristjan pressed, "How is this possible, Gabriel? And what does this mean for Gregory's fate? Is he sentenced to death?"

Gabriel firmly shook his head. "No, Kristjan," he stated, his gaze now focused on Helen. "I have reconsidered the situation and realized that death is too severe a punishment for your son. Perhaps remaining in Croatia would be a more fitting consequence," Gabriel suggested. Kristjan exhaled deeply, his shoulders relaxing in relief. "Hvala vam puno," he expressed his gratitude before stepping away to wipe the tears forming in his eyes.

"Okay, but questions regarding Arabella's existence will have to wait. I have called you all with regard to a great dire situation that needs to be attended to. Larry Harrison from my past has come back to try and kill me," Gabriel said.

Logan, Dante, and Alarick all growled in response, prompting a nod of acknowledgment from Gabriel. "I appreciate your support," he said. "For now, I need you all, especially you, Kristjan, to consider coming here. Leave Gregory at home, but bring the other family members. We are stronger together, and if Larry is plotting something, we need to be prepared," Gabriel urged.

The other members agreed. "How is Amy doing anyway?" Vanessa asked, remembering how they came across Adrian in his wolf form. "I just remember taking extra good care of her in Greece," Vanessa said.

Gabriel smiled. "She is wonderful, sweet Vanessa," Gabriel said. She is just resting up, but I shall give all your regards to her once she is alive and energetic," Gabriel said with a chuckle. Vanessa smiled.

"I hope to have you all at my castle, somewhere at the end of this week and we can plan and strategize how we can take care of this problem," Gabriel said. All the members nodded simultaneously. "Good. Now, with regard to Arabella's rise from the dead, I shall let Amelia take over the answers to that question," Gabriel said.

# The Planning

After the meeting concluded, Alistair, Darcia, and their boys finished their drinks and left the castle. Alistair, somewhat taken aback, remarked, "I wasn't expecting that. A regular meeting turned into preparations for an upcoming battle." Darcia kept her gaze forward, deep in thought.

"I cannot believe this, my love," Darcia said. "Having to deal with conflicts and battles." Alistair wrapped his left arm around Darcia's shoulders, holding her close to him. "Nothing bad will happen to our family, my sweet Darcia," Alistair said as they walked back to their rooms.

Unbeknownst to them at first, they stumbled upon a chilling scene in the motel parking lot: around ten bodies lying on the ground. Darcia peered into the clerk's office, her eyes widening at the sight of blood spatters everywhere and the clerk slumped face-down on the table.

"Alistair, do you hear that?" Darcia whispered, stopping in her tracks. Suddenly, Joshua's eyes turned pitch black as he stared up at the sky.

"Joshua?" Alistair called out, but Joshua was unresponsive.

"Larry is creating an army of humans and turning them into shapeshifters," Joshua said in a monotone voice. "He already has fifteen members around him."

Darcia and Alistair exchanged worried glances, now noticing the smashed windows of their rooms. "Perhaps it's best if we find another place to hide out, maybe go back to the castle," Darcia suggested, taking Raymond and Silas by the hand. "Come, family," she urged.

As they headed back, Larry appeared from behind a tree, his newly created creatures surrounding him.

"Well, well, well," Larry taunted, clapping his hands together. "Are you all lost?" he asked sarcastically.

Bryan bared his teeth, his body starting to change. "Bryan," Alistair warned, grabbing his shoulders. "Not now. Do not let him provoke and intimidate you," he whispered urgently. Bryan returned back to his human form, but kept a fierce gaze on Larry.

"Good boy," Larry sneered. "Perhaps Daddy will let you out of the crate sometime?"

Ignoring the taunt, Alistair nudged Bryan behind him, his right hand resting protectively on his back.

"What do you want?" Alistair demanded, his voice stern. Larry slowly approached, his entourage following. "Keep your distance, Larry, or this might end badly," Alistair warned, his tone sharp. Larry smirked, stopping about ten feet away from Alistair, the tension palpable.

"A little birdy told me that you and your family are plotting to have me killed; is that right?" Larry asked.

Darcia scoffed and hissed at Larry.

"You tell me to keep my distance, but you let your wife hiss at me. Alistair, you all have no manners whatsoever," Larry snapped. Darcia relaxed her body and jaw. "Now, you had asked me what I wanted, and I responded with how I heard that you are planning a war against me. Remember this. I did not choose this life. Whatever Gabriel has told you all is a gigantic lie," Larry asserted. "I had no intentions of being with him, whatsoever or to become this weird creature. I have my reasons for my hatred towards him. He took my life away from me, so I feel that it is justified for me to take his life away from him," Larry said.

Alistair chuckled at that comment. "We were born this way, you know, Larry. We are no humans either, so your belief in freedom and free will is misplaced. Gabriel was quite foolish when he was young, long before he met his wife," Alistair said, not realizing how dangerous it was to mention that. Larry's interest was piqued. Alistair quickly stopped talking and took a step back.

"Ah, Gabriel has himself a girlfriend, does he?" Larry asked provocatively. "Where can I find her? Was she made out of love or out of lust?" Alistair looked away and started to walk away. "You think that walking away from your problems will help? You don't think we will escalate this further, Alistair?" Larry challenged.

"Family, ignore him. How about we go on a little walk for the evening," Alistair said, grabbing Darcia by her arm and urging her along with him. Larry just stood behind them, shaking his head, smirking at the thought of going after Alistair next. Once Alistair and his family were out of sight, Larry walked back to his group.

"I think we need a couple more dozen of us to take down that family," Larry said as he looked at a new girl he had transformed, and then at a younger guy. "Perhaps you all can help me grow our little family?" Larry proposed. His new members nodded their heads. "Good. Whatever looks appetizing, go ahead and claim your victims," Larry said before taking the lead and guiding them toward unlit areas of different streets.

Once Alistair felt that it was safe, he turned around and exhaled out of exhaustion. "I had no idea we would even survive that moment, dear family," Alistair said, panting. "He looked like he was ready to take us on."

Darcia looked over at him and then at her sons. "We are stronger than those tots, my sweet husband," Darcia said in a reassuring tone. "We would probably take on Larry quite nicely, but I am glad we did not have to fight them right now. Plus, I would hate to have anything bad happen to my boys. As strong as you all are, you are still my little pearls that I will always want to take care of," Darcia said as she smiled at each of her boys. They all smiled back and chuckled.

Alistair exhaled. "Now, we need to find a different route to Gabriel's castle. I think if we walk a few blocks over there, make a right, and then go straight through, it should take us about forty minutes to get to his castle," Alistair said, looking ahead and analyzing the entire journey. Once he felt confident about his plan, the seven of them walked in the direction Alistair had indicated.

Back at Gabriel's castle, Hildegard was preparing accommodations for Gabriel's extended family members. She busily closed all curtains and turned on soft lights in each room. There were over thirty members needing a place to sleep and somewhere to hang their fine clothes. Meanwhile, Arabella walked over to her sleeping quarters and sat on the edge of her bed. She had no interest in dealing with such conflicts, especially when they were a result of Gabriel's actions. It made her ponder whether Gabriel's courtship, the massacre of her family, and her subsequent confinement were really all out of desperation. She wondered if now was the right time to bring up such heavy topics, or if it would be better to wait until after dealing with Larry.

Gabriel, in his study, was overwhelmed with feelings of loss and despair. He questioned his own survival in the upcoming battle and wondered how his daughters would feel about him going on a slaughtering spree against innocent victims. Thoughts of giving up and ending his own life had been looming heavily on Gabriel's mind ever since Arabella's return. He remembered all the horrific things he had done out of pure lust and egotism. He realized he had had no regard for humanity, no genuine desire for women beyond their physical appearance, and certainly no wish for children. He had aspired to be powerful, influential, and adored by all members of his coven. Now, Gabriel was beginning to realize how all those desires and hopes were dead.

Back in Amy's room, Amy was grappling with the energies and discomforts of carrying three creatures inside her, draining her resources, and leaving her weakened. How was she going to survive the pregnancy? What if she were to become so weak that she would die or even end up paralyzed somehow. These fears raced through Amy's head as she lay still in her bed. She sometimes wished she was never a shape-shifter, or even that she had never been born. It seemed like giving up would be an easy escape from her situation.

Yet, after those dark thoughts, a spark of positivity would remind her that if she remained strong, despite her dwindling energy, she could be a wonderful mother and a protector of her coven, her family, and her future family members. With this shift in perspective, Amy would momentarily forget her worries and despair, focusing instead on all the positive contributions she could make.

As Amy was going back and forth with her thoughts, Ginger was in her room, looking at the picture book that Emma had given to Amy some time ago. She smiled, relcting on the development and growth of both herself and Amy. How happy they had been, how fun all of those memories were, and how loved she felt by Emma and Aaron when she was supposedly still human. Even though she felt unhappy about her current situation, knowing that she was loved somehow turned her sadness into optimism. She got to go to college and meet different types of humans from various backgrounds. She got to attend some interesting classes from different professors. She had a very good youth when they were placed in swaddled blankets at the hands of two humans.

As grim as some situations might become, Ginger harbored a feeling that everything would turn out okay. She might even have a bright future ahead. Perhaps she would find true love and start a family of her own. While Alistair and Darcia's sons were entertaining, she wasn't particularly interested in them. However, she pondered the possibility of finding love in a different western country, outside of the covens' influence. Maybe she could find someone who would love her despite her being a shape-shifter, or perhaps she could turn someone into a shape-shifter. First, she realized an imminent battle was looming. She wondered if it was worth participating, as Amy might need her in the future, and if Ginger were to die in battle, she would never forgive herself for not being there. It might be wise to consult her father, Gabriel, about her and Amy's participation in the battle, especially her own involvement.

After placing the closed picture book on her bed, Ginger descended the stairs and noticed Hildegard diligently cleaning the area. She contemplated offering assistance but decided it was more crucial to talk to Gabriel about the battle. Approaching Gabriel's study, she knocked on the door. Gabriel opened it, his expression transitioning from surprise to happiness. "My child, what can I do for you?" he asked, gesturing for Ginger to enter.

Ginger sat down in one of the chairs across from him and waited for Gabriel to be seated as well. "What can I do for you, sweet Ginger?" Gabriel asked, smiling. Ginger gathered her thoughts before responding.

"Okay," Ginger said. "Regarding this upcoming battle between us and them, are Amy and I required to take part in it or are we to hide or relocate to another country?"

Gabriel's expression turned serious. "You two are not required, and I would never want you to take part in this battle. You two, and perhaps your mother, will be relocating with Hildegard once the battle starts near this castle," he explained. Despite the relief, Ginger couldn't help but feel a sense of loss hearing those words.

"What about you, father? I'm worried about your life as well. What will happen to us if you were to die?"

Gabriel smiled and kept his focus on Ginger. "If—and I emphasize strongly—if something were to happen to me, you or your sister, whichever of you feels fit to be the future queen, will assume that role as queen or matriarch of all the covens. That is bound to happen in the long run, of course, but if it comes to it, you, or both of you if you choose, will take over from me," Gabriel explained. Ginger couldn't derive any sense of optimism or comfort from his words. She felt compelled to take part in the battle, to protect as many members as she could.

"Ginger," Gabriel said, reaching across the table. Ginger placed her hands in his. "You have nothing to fear about me or your future, my sweet child. You and Amy are going to be wonderful at whatever you choose to do with your life. Enjoy as much as you can and learn as much as you can about various subjects. This world, despite the many years I've lived, has experienced its share of wars and conflicts, but it has also seen many good moments. No matter what happens to me, your mom, or the other members, you need to remain strong for yourself. You need to be your own person, boss, woman, caretaker, and teacher in various aspects of life. I couldn't be there for you during your childhood, but I hope to help you discover your inner strengths now. You have that strength within you," Gabriel said before releasing Ginger's hands. "The other members will arrive in a few days, and I will ensure that you, Amy, your mother, and Hildegard are taken to a safe location, the whereabouts of which only I will know. For now, I need to focus on some important preparations. If you don't mind, I need some time alone," Gabriel said. Ginger nodded, rose to her feet, and left the room.

After closing the door behind her, Ginger felt tears streaming down her cheeks. She felt scared and weak as she leaned against the door to her father's study, wishing for someone to console her, to hold her in their arms, and reassure her that everything was going to be okay. She wondered if she should seek out her mother. Descending the stairs, she unlocked a few doors with her skeleton key and eventually knocked on the door to Arabella and Gabriel's room.

"Enter," Arabella called from the other side of the door. Ginger walked in, wiping her eyes with her right hand. Arabella looked up, surprised. "Oh, my sweet child," Arabella said, walking over to embrace Ginger. "What happened?" Unable to hold back, Ginger cried into Arabella's shoulder. "Here, how about we both sit down on the bed?" Arabella suggested, guiding Ginger to the edge of the bed and holding her tighter. "What happened, my sweet Ginger?"

Ginger tried to control her breathing, aiming to relax as much as possible. "I don't want to deal with any conflicts or wars. I don't want any of us to die so soon," Ginger whimpered. Arabella held Ginger close, stroking her hair and her back, offering comfort. "I can't lose you, Amy, or even Father, despite his foolishness." Arabella smiled at that last comment, appreciating Ginger's candor and concern.

"Nothing bad is going to happen to us, my sweet girl," Arabella assured, pulling back slightly to meet Ginger's gaze. "Your father is very strong and fully capable of handling these situations. I doubt this is his first battle," she said. "I believe he can take good care of himself in many ways."

Ginger took a moment to steady her breathing and wiped away her tears with the back of her hand. She felt dizzy and tired, yet she did not want to leave her mother's side. "I think Amy and I will probably not be involved in this whole situation. I'm unsure of what I should do. Should I participate to increase our chances of winning this battle, or should I stay behind with my daughters and relocate?" She waited until she felt composed enough to speak.

"Father already told me his plans for you, Amy, Hildegard, and me to go somewhere only he knows of. He intends to stay behind with the other coven members and confront Larry's group," Ginger explained. Arabella remained silent, absorbing the information.

"Perhaps that is for the best. The four of us could use a break from everything, a chance to see the world from a different perspective," Arabella said, releasing her hold on Ginger.

"Would we ever return, Mother? If Larry is defeated, would you want to come back to this castle?" Ginger asked. Arabella smiled warmly.

"That, I'm not sure of. Perhaps I'd prefer a smaller, cozier home for just the four of us. I might not even want to be around Gabriel anymore, not after some of the things he did when I was younger," Arabella confessed. Concern flashed across Ginger's face.

"Like what, Mother? What has Gabriel done?" Ginger pressed, her gaze intently focused on Arabella.

Arabella smirked, shaking her head dismissively. "It doesn't matter anymore, my sweet child. The past is the past, and I should start looking ahead, thinking about what I hope for our future," she said, gently steering the conversation away from Gabriel's past actions. Yet, Ginger couldn't easily let go of her curiosity about what her father had done to her mother.

"Should I be worried about our father, Mother?" Ginger inquired, a hint of concern in her voice. Arabella redirected her attention back to Ginger, offering a reassuring smile.

"Focus on your own life, Ginger. Concentrate on achieving the goals and ambitions that matter most to you," Arabella advised. "For now, let's just enjoy having the castle to ourselves. Soon it will be bustling with other family members. The night is clear; would you and Amy be interested in taking a walk outside, or at least enjoying the soft breeze?" Arabella suggested. Ginger's face lit up, and she nodded in agreement.

"I would like that," Ginger said. "I'll go check on Amy and ask if she'd like to join us." After receiving a loving kiss on the forehead from Arabella, Ginger left to find her sister. Arabella, deciding to seek clarity on Gabriel's plans for her and the girls, ascended the stairs to the main floor and made her way to Gabriel's study. She knocked on the door, overhearing him murmur, "Can't I get a break in this place?" When he opened the door, his expression shifted to a welcoming smile. "Arabella, what brings you here?" Gabriel inquired. Arabella offered a smile and a nonchalant shrug in response.

"I heard that Amy, Ginger, Hildegard, and I would be relocating somewhere else. Were you ever going to mention that important news to me, husband?" Arabella snapped. Gabriel gestured for Arabella to enter, but she held her ground, staying in the doorway. "Look, we are supposed to be life partners, yet I feel that you have made all the decisions without consulting me, your wife, about any of them. About our daughters' futures, about me being a ghost, about your conflicts with creatures outside of our family. Now you want me, Amy, Ginger, and the servant to leave. Why don't you and your family members move to where Larry may be, like the nearby park, while I stay here with my girls and Hildegard? Have you even considered that important aspect? Amy is in no condition for long-distance travel, especially since she may be carrying shape-shifting babies. What if she were to die, Gabriel? What am I supposed to do, grab Amelia's spell book and bring her back? Honestly, Gabriel, what goes on in your mind when you plan these things?"

Gabriel sighed, his expression weary. "I'd prefer to discuss this in a more private setting, with the door closed, rather than having my brothers and Amelia overhear. I also wish you'd lower your voice. I did what I felt was appropriate at the time. Sending the three of you away seemed like the best option, as this castle would be the first place Larry, or anyone else, might target," Gabriel said, his voice laced with a growl.

Arabella sighed and relaxed her body before entering his study. "I just want you to respect me as your life partner and not just treat me as an accessory or relic that fits your life the way you want it to," she said. Gabriel waited for Arabella to take a seat in the right chair across from his desk so that he could sit in the left one.

"My sweet, beloved wife. My heart's blood. My muse. My world. You are my equal and amazing partner. The reason I haven't mentioned the travel arrangements to you immediately is that I wanted to wait until right before the battle, perhaps in about two days, to tell you where to take our children and Hildegard. I'm unsure of Larry's abilities—whether he has strength, sharp hearing or vision, or something else I'm not aware of," Gabriel explained, his voice softening. "I promise you, I'm not keeping secrets from you because I want to. I just don't want others to know, in case they tell him out of fear or panic. I love you enough to want to keep you safe from any harm. Please, believe me when I tell you this," Gabriel said before he took Arabella's hands in his, lifting them to his lips.

"I understand the love part, sweet husband, but what I am having trouble with is that I want you to include me in all decisions. Amy is my daughter too, and I would have never allowed you, Lucien, or the others to impregnate here. She is a woman with her own desires in life, and now she is a fearful mess with extra burdens," Arabella said as she tugged her hands away, needing space to express her feelings.

"I could not even get over how you found me and massacred my family, Gabriel," Arabella said. "I was an innocent girlsoon to be wed to another man from an upper-class family, until I was, presumably, kidnapped or at least taken by you, ending up in the bedroom that we now share. How my memory shifted from blank shock to a cold, sad reality was a hard transition, my sweet Gabriel," Arabella said.

Gabriel could not help but feel a sense of sadness inside him as Arabella spoke about the past. How he wished he had never been an immortal shape-shifter, craving blood and lust. How he wished he could have had a regular life with family and friends to share beautiful moments, and a wife who loved him despite his faults—not a bitter wife who hated him. Arabella looked over at Gabriel, placing her right hand on his cheek. "However, the past is to be left behind us. I will take good care of our children, and I know we will soon be reunited somehow, Gabriel," Arabella said before she stood up.

Gabriel smiled and got to his feet. He wrapped his arms around Arabella, holding her close to him. "I love you, my sweet wife," Gabriel whispered.

Arabella smiled and closed her eyes. "I love you too, Gabriel," Arabella whispered, placing her hands on Gabriel's back. They stood there for a few minutes before Arabella released her hold.

"I shall see what Amy is doing. I promised Ginger that the three of us would have a nice evening walk together," Arabella said before leaving Gabriel's study.

Ginger was already in Amy's room, sitting on the edge of the bed. "You do look a bit pale, sweet sister," Ginger noted. Arabella entered, her worry evident at Amy's appearance. "Amy, how are you feeling? You look somewhat unwell," Arabella said. Ginger stood, allowing Arabella to sit in her spot. Arabella placed her hand on Amy's forehead, feeling it somewhat cold. "Shall I get Hildegard to send you up some iron or something that will make you warmer, my sweet child?"

Amy looked up at Arabella with glassy eyes and nodded. "I just feel very weak inside. Nothing seems to really make me feel more energetic, especially with three younglings inside of me," Amy said, remaining under the covers. Arabella nodded, standing to find Hildegard. "Ginger, would you mind staying with your sister?"

"Yes, Mother," Ginger said, sitting back down on the edge of the bed. "I will wait for you." Arabella left the room to find Hildegard, who was collecting empty bottles in a crate.

"Hildegard," Arabella said. "Could you get me some of these herbs to help Amy regain her strength somewhat? She is looking quite unwell in her room."

"Of course, madam," Hildegard said. "I shall first get a new batch of blood and perhaps a few more crates for our guests. Then I will see what I can find from your list," Hildegard said, taking the crate to the garage and placing the crates in the trunk of her car.

Arabella walked back to where Amy and Ginger were and sat at the foot end of the bed. "Hildegard is finding some more herbs and spices for you, my child. Are you hungry or thirsty?" Arabella asked.

Amy looked over at her. "Perhaps something to drink? Something warm? I know that the iron that we drink is cold, but I feel like I need to warm up my body since these younglings are draining me of my internal source," Amy said.

"Okay. Anything else?" Arabella asked. Amy shook her head, closing her eyes some more. Arabella walked down to the main floor, trying to find something warm for Amy.

Katrina entered the dining quarter, leaning against the wall furthest from Arabella. "So, the little mother-to-be is not feeling so well?" Katrina asked. Arabella turned around to face Katrina, glaring at her.

"Why are you still here?" Arabella snapped. "I thought Gabriel would release you back into the wild after my return?"

Katrina slowly walked over to Arabella, smirking. "What about you being released back into the woods? There may only be one queen in this castle, and since you died, I've taken your position," Katrina snapped back. "I can help you, if you need it."

Arabella inhaled and exhaled, trying to control her anger. "What is wrong with you? Just because Gabriel wanted me back, does not mean you should treat me this way. I am the official queen and mother of Amy and Ginger, so why you are still here is still a mystery to me," Arabella snapped.

Katrina held Arabella's gaze until Daniel, Lucien, and Amelia approached. Katrina quickly turned and left the dining quarter.

Arabella relaxed her mind and body, waiting for the three family members to enter the dining quarter. Amelia looked at Arabella with concern. "Are you all right, Arabella?" she asked, walking towards her. Arabella nodded and rolled her eyes.

"Katrina needs to go, Amelia. I think we need to get rid of her, and quickly," Arabella whispered. Amelia smirked.

"Is there anything for us to drink here?" Lucien asked as he walked to the cooler to find one last bottle. "Has Hildegard gone out to fetch us some more?" Arabella nodded. "Good. I hope she has more for our guests coming here soon," Lucien said. Arabella turned to Amelia.

"Say, Amelia, would you perhaps have something to warm up Amy? She is feeling quite cold in her room," Arabella said. Amelia thought about it for a moment.

"Yes. I think there is cocoa drink I could make for her, which is usually quite tasty and also beneficial to her body. I shall return in a few minutes," Amelia said before heading to her own sleeping quarters.

Arabella remained in the dinning quarter, and moments later, Vladimir and Adrian entered.

# Night Terror

After Amelia had returned with a glass cup and lid on it, she handed it to Arabella. "Be careful, Arabella" Amelia said. "It may still be quite hot. This has various warming herbs in it with the flavor of chocolate. Perhaps Amy can try a sip and see how it makes her feel?"

Arabella took the cup in her hands, feeling its warmth but ensuring it wasn't too hot to carry. "Okay, I shall see how Amy responds to this beverage," Arabella said before she walked over to Amy's room. Once there, with the cup in hand, she found Amy sitting up in bed, leaning against the frame, while Ginger maintained her concerned gaze on Amy's poor complexion. "Amelia made this for you, my Amy," Arabella said before handing Amy the cup, complete with a lid. "You might want to take the lid off before you drink it. Plus, it's quite warm, so check if it's not too hot for your body," Arabella added.

Amy took the lid off and handed it to Ginger who then placed it on her night table. Amy took a sip and swallowed.

"Hot chocolate?" Amy asked. Ginger couldn't help but chuckle at Amy's expression. "How will this help?" Amy asked. Arabella thought about what Amelia had told her, but could not help but also think about Katrina, as well. "What else do I taste? This spice? Is it pumpkin or turmeric?" Amy asked. Arabella was still deep within her thoughts. Amy looked over at her mother who focused her gaze out in nowhere. "Mother, hey?" Amy asked. Arabella quickly moved her gaze back to Amy.

"Huh, what?" Arabella responded, her focus now back on Amy.

"I was asking about the spices in the drink," Amy said, a hint of frustration in her voice.

"There are some good herbs in that beverage. I shall ask Amelia what she put in there. I don't think it was pumpkin or the other herb you mentioned," Arabella assured her.

"Are you all right, Mother?" Amy asked as she focused her gaze on Arabella's faint expression. "Mother?"

Arabella sighed. "I cannot get my exchange with Katrina out of my mind. She probably sees me as a threat and wants to get rid of me, but now that I am back and stronger than ever, she has to go," Arabella said to herself.

Amy and Ginger both exchanged glances. "What is the plan?" Ginger asked as she got to her feet. "Would you need some help from me?"

Arabella smiled and gently cupped Ginger's face. "Not at all. Amelia said she would help if that time were to come. I want both of you to be safe from any family drama. It might be good for the three of us to leave Romania for a while. I'm not sure where your father will have us relocate, but I think it would do us good to be away from all this drama and trouble. Plus, this whole mess with Larry is practically Gabriel's fault anyway. It doesn't seem right for us to be a part of it," Arabella explained.

Ginger felt a sense of betrayal, realizing how right Arabella was. Gabriel's clumsy handling of Arabella's death was his fault, and it was something Ginger found hard to forgive her father for. "Perhaps it is for the best," Ginger agreed. "That the three of us, along with Hildegard, leave."

Just then, Amy started to feel a warm sensation flow through her, prompting Ginger to exclaim, "Amy!" Noticing the return of color to Amy's complexion and the sharpness in her eyes, Ginger asked, "How are you feeling?"

Amy chuckled and shrugged. "Much better than before. I feel warmer and more awake." Satisfied, Arabella checked Amy's forehead and smiled, relieved to see her daughter's condition improving.

"Much better. You are warmer, and your complexion has returned. I shall ask Amelia to create more of that chocolate drink for you since it seems to be helping," Arabella said. "Right now, I have no reason to leave you two."

Meanwhile, Alistair, Darcia, and their five sons were nearing the castle again. "Alistair, do you think Gabriel will find it odd that we're back so soon?" Darcia asked. Alistair, focused on the path ahead, responded, "I don't care what Gabriel thinks, my dear wife. All I care about is that we are safe from Larry and his creatures. How he managed to have them all changed since we last saw him, which was what, about a week ago?"

Darcia glanced behind her and noticed Joshua looking in her direction. "Joshua, what do you think? Have you felt or noticed anything out of the ordinary?" she asked. Joshua sighed, "I've been feeling various sensations ever since we arrived in Romania. I had no idea Larry would be here, except when Raymond brought him over so Bryan could try to kill him. Remember that, boys?"

Joshua's question sparked Bryan's memory of the incident in the park where he had attacked Larry, only to have Darcia and Alistair show up after Larry had disappeared. "Yes, I remember. It was Raymond who brought him over so I could try to kill him," Bryan confirmed, looking back at Joshua.

"That is what I just said, Bryan. So I don't understand why you're repeating it back to me," Joshua snapped.

Alistair stopped in his tracks, addressing his sons, "Boys, can we all just get along for a few more days? Once this battle with Larry is over, I think we should all relocate somewhere cooler and more remote. The problems started when we were called to take Amy and Ginger to Oregon. Then we had to pick them up, lie to them, and protect them—even from our own family members, like Gregory and Kristjan," he explained.

Darcia wrapped her arms around Alistair, offering words of comfort, "This will all be okay. We are strong, and we can handle any conflict and battle. Remember fighting Gabriel when we had to take Ginger back to Oregon?" she chuckled. "We've been through many problematic situations, but we've always managed quite well."

Alistair smiled, kissing Darcia on the top of her head, "You boys should be grateful to have a mother like Darcia. She is a very beautiful and strong woman, and she has been an incredible partner—even in our fights against those other guys," he praised, to which the boys all smiled and nodded in agreement.

"I think we can handle a slimy creature like that Larry fellow," Bryan declared confidently, starting to walk again. "I have no fear whatsoever."

Alistair resumed walking, with the others following suit. When they were about a block away from the castle, Gabriel sensed Alistair's presence. He looked out of the window and saw Alistair and his family approaching. "How is this possible? I don't recall inviting all coven members so soon," Gabriel muttered to himself. Leaving his study, he headed to the entrance. Before Alistair could ring the bell, Gabriel had opened the door, revealing himself to Alistair and Darcia, with their sons standing behind them.

"Alistair, Darcia, what brings you and your boys back here?" Gabriel asked sternly. Darcia looked up at Gabriel with concern, while Alistair remained silent for a few moments.

"Larry Harrison is amassing quite a force for his war against you, Gabriel. We are here to support you and your family," Alistair said. Gabriel sighed and gestured for them to enter. After Joshua entered last, Gabriel closed the door behind them. "I believe Hildegard has finished preparing some of the accommodations for you and the other members, but she is still busy running errands for our food source," Gabriel said.

"That is okay," Alistair said. "We have managed living in motel rooms, so a bed and the darkness will work out for us." Gabriel nodded and started to walk towards the living quarters. "So, when are the others ones supposed to arrive, Gabriel? I do realize that we are quite early. Larry's friends broke into our motel room, I believe. We wanted go to a safer place and realized we were not far from your home. We came across him, by the way. He is very much obsessed with having you killed and serving your head on a platter. Forgive my ignorance, of course, but why does someone actually want you dead, Gabriel?"

Gabriel sighed and stared deep into Alistair's eyes. "What has he told you, Alistair?" Gabriel asked, trying to control his emotions. "I may have accidentally killed his fiancé without realizing it, but I had no control over my own life at the time. I had no one to run to for guidance or support. The fact is that, about five hundred years ago, when you and I first got acquainted, I was at this tavern. I had to find a quick way to remove Larry, but could not finish my supposed second meal with him. I had to get rid of the body without realizing that what I had done could have drawn attention to me, possibly resulting in my death," Gabriel explained.

Alistair kept his focus on Gabriel's story. "It sounds quite complicated, Gabriel, but we shall try our best to deal with this conflict. Did you try to talk it out with him or at least explain the situation?" Alistair asked. Gabriel scoffed and shook his head.

"Yeah, right, Alistair. I should have gone back to him after he got turned and apologized for killing his fiancé and then for abandoning him. No. I did what I thought was best: I left the situation and returned to my place. Many decades later, my foundation of immortal shapeshifters expanded to current times. Now, I plan to kill anyone who wants to harm my family or me. Please, Alistair, do us both a favor and stop asking questions from now on," Gabriel said before leaving Alistair, Darcia, and their sons alone.

"Oh, by the way," Gabriel added, "Your rooms will be on the first floor, next to Amy and Ginger's rooms. I am sure they will be happy to see you all again."

Alistair furrowed his brow and shook his head. Darcia took Alistair's hand in hers and held it tightly. "I sometimes wonder whether it is worth our life and time to be helping someone with their own conflict," Darcia said. "I mean, do you think Gabriel would have done the same for us if we were in a situation like this?"

Alistair sighed and, with Darcia by his side, walked over to the staircase. "I'm not sure about anything right now. I'm starting to doubt this whole battle we might be facing. If Gabriel did something wrong to that Larry guy, he should deal with it himself and not risk our lives," Alistair said in a hushed tone. Bryan, with his sharp ears, overheard Amy, Arabella, and Ginger talking together in Amy's room. Darcia glanced at Bryan and shook her head.

"I think we should give them some space," Darcia said. "Soon, once we have our family reunion, I think you can see how Amy is doing. For now, I think it is best that we just stay together in one room."

Bryan sighed and continued up the stairs. Once they reached the second floor, he followed Alistair and Darcia into their room. Inside, he saw three double beds in a room with burgundy walls, illuminated by a faint orange light from the overhead fixture. Large windows with red curtains pulled to the side let in the night, and a door led to the washroom. A tall, empty chestnut closet stood against one wall.

"Huh," Bryan said. "There are seven of us, but only beds for six. How are we going to work this out?" Alistair walked over to the window and looked out into the courtyard, where bats were flying and the wind was rustling through the trees and bushes.

"One of us can sleep on the floor, and we can rotate each night, taking turns with a sleeping bag," Alistair suggested, returning his gaze to Bryan and the beds. "Or we can flip a coin?" Bryan smirked at that comment and looked over at his brothers. "Would Amy prefer to have some company in her bed?" he asked cheekily. Alistair shot Bryan a glare.

"We are to be on our best behavior in this home. That means, no drama or complications with Gabriel's daughters. Is that understood?" Alistair snapped. Bryan nodded with disappointment.

"That was partly a joke, Father. I don't really have any reason to get involved with Amy right now."

Just then, there was a knock on the door, and Caleb appeared at the entrance. "The rumors are true. Alistair and Darcia are back." Darcia looked over at Caleb and then at Alistair, who wore a confused expression.

"And who might you be?" Alistair asked. Caleb entered the room and extended his hand.

"Caleb. I'm supposedly the father of Amy's children," he introduced himself. Bryan growled and bared his teeth. "Oh dear," Caleb remarked, noticing Bryan's reaction. "Is this a bad time? I can come back later."

Bryan slowly advanced towards Caleb. "You got Amy pregnant?" Bryan snapped. Caleb started to back away, fear in his eyes.

"It was not my intention whatsoever," Caleb said. "This whole situation is Gabriel's doing."

Alistair cleared his throat. "Bryan, enough," Alistair said. "Leave Caleb be for now."

"No, Father," Bryan snapped. "This guy just happens to be the biological father. How am I supposed to deal with that? Was Amy even serious about me helping to name her children, or was she just teasing me?" Bryan questioned, his frustration apparent. Darcia sighed and turned her attention to Bryan.

"I do not think she was teasing you at all, Bryan. I really do believe that she wants you to be involved in their future, if that's something you want as well," Darcia said, trying to calm the situation.

"While you all figure this whole situation out, please excuse me," Caleb said before leaving the room. Bryan waited until Caleb had closed the door behind him before throwing a pillow at it in frustration.

"Bryan," Alistair said. "Please try to be more rational and think about how our goal is to get rid of this Larry guy and then we can leave Gabriel alone for a longer time. Perhaps even forever?"

Bryan glared at Alistair and took a seat in the nearest chair by a table. "I think this situation is going to take longer to resolve than you think, Father," he said.

Alistair had a sneaking suspicion that Bryan might be right about the timeframe. What was Larry even planning, and who would be forced to give up their life? Darcia, sensing Alistair's thoughts, took his hand in hers.

"Let's not get too caught up thinking about the future. Right now, we're all together in this room. Sure, our belongings at the motel are probably ruined or stolen, but we still have each other. We have our future together, and everything will be okay," Darcia assured him in a calm voice.

Alistair smiled, wrapped his arms around Darcia, and held her close to him. "Thank you, my sweet wife," he whispered before releasing her.

"I think I am going to ask Hildegard about an extra bed or mattress or even a sleeping bag," Bryan said before he left the room.

"Bryan, please remember," Alistair said. "No drama in this house. We need to be on our best behavior."

Bryan ignored Alistair and closed the door behind him. He stood by the closed door for a few minutes till he heard a familiar voice behind him. "Bryan?" Amy asked.

Bryan turned around to face Amy and smiled. "Well, look at you, future mother," Bryan said teasingly. "How are you feeling?"

Amy smiled and shrugged. "I have had better days in my life, but I am glad to have you all back in my life again. Here, feel," she said, taking Bryan's hand and placing it on her belly. "Can you see them inside of me, or is that just a gift for the mothers in our family?"

Bryan placed his hand gently on her belly, but he couldn't see anything beyond her light pink blouse and white dress. "No, I can't see anything, Amy," Bryan admitted. "By the way, I was wondering if this castle might have an extra bed or mattress for me to sleep on since it seems my brothers have already claimed all the beds in our room."

Amy smiled. "What about we sharing my bed, Bryan?" Amy asked. "I am quite a deep sleeper." Bryan smiled at that comment and shook his head.

"I am sorry, Amy, but I think I should remain with my brothers and parents till this whole situation blows over," Bryan said. Amy felt a bit disappointed by hearing those words from Bryan, but nodded.

"I understand," Amy said. "I think Hildegard knows more about the accommodations for you all. She should be back by now or on her way since it's about two o'clock in the morning."

Bryan smiled before he started to walk away from Amy. "See you around, Amy. I know everything is going to be okay regarding this whole Larry problem. Nothing bad will happen to any of us." Amy smiled and gave a small wave to him before she walked back to her room.

Once Bryan reached the main floor of the castle, he heard different voices from various family members around the area. He walked over to the dining quarter to see Lucien and Daniel in conversation. When Bryan was in the vicinity, they both stopped and looked at him.

"Oh sorry, I did not mean to disrupt your conversation. I am just looking for Hildegard, hoping she might be able to offer me a more comfortable bed," Bryan explained. Lucien smirked, and Daniel kept his focus on Bryan. "You must be one of Alistair's sons," Daniel noted, adjusting himself in his chair. "I am Daniel Ambrose, the second eldest brother to Gabriel. And you are?"

Bryan extended his hand in Daniel's direction with a smile. "Bryan. Just plain old Bryan," he replied, waiting for Daniel to accept his handshake.

Lucien extended his hand to Bryan and shook it. "Pleasure to meet you, Bryan. I am Lucien." Bryan shook hands with him, smiling at both of them.

"So, where is this Hildegard?" Bryan asked. Lucien and Daniel exchanged glances.

"Hildegard should be back any moment, Bryan, but you are welcome to wait here with us till she gets back?"

Bryan felt a bit uncomfortable and started to back away. "I think I shall look around the castle a bit more and get acquainted with the hallways and different rooms," Bryan said.

"Wait," Daniel said. "May I ask you a question? It might come across a bit harsh, but I assure you I don't intend to be rude or mean," Daniel clarified. Bryan steadied himself and exhaled. "Are you and Amy a couple, or are you like her boyfriend?" Daniel asked.

Bryan rolled his eyes, feeling his anger start to simmer. "Daniel," Lucien intervened, "Why must you ask such personal questions to people you hardly know?" Daniel scoffed and shot Lucien a hard stare.

"Why do you even care about Alistair's kid anyway, Lucien? How can you even see them as equals in this place?" Daniel questioned, emotion evident in his voice. Lucien realized that Daniel hadn't had his feeding and recognized that shape-shifters could become very aggressive when not fully fed. "Bryan, you should probably go back to your family and remain there until Hildegard arrives. I'm sure you'll know when she's back. If you have good hearing and smell, you can easily track someone like her down," Lucien advised, keeping his focus on Daniel, who relaxed his back and shoulders.

Bryan walked away from the situation and up the stairs toward his room. Upon entering, he found Alistair and Darcia sitting together on one bed, while the other boys were engaged in conversation. "Hey, family," Bryan greeted. Alistair looked over at Bryan with concern. "Hildegard isn't back yet, so I'll wait and see about getting a nice, comfy sleeping bag or mattress," Bryan updated them.

Alistair nodded. "Their maid is not back yet, I believe," Alistair said. Bryan shook his head and sat down on Silas and Xavier's bed. "I think it is best if we kept to ourselves till this is all over," Alistair said. "This new setting is different from when we each had our own rooms, but we can make do," he added, his optimism evident. Darcia smiled at Alistair's positive outlook. "I mean, I understand that you're all bored, but this will soon be over," Alistair said, chuckling.

Darcia laughed at Alistair's comment, prompting the boys to join in. "Boredom is a fitting word to describe our situation. Maybe we can do something different tomorrow evening," Darcia suggested. Alistair smiled and wrapped his right arm around her.

Meanwhile, in his study, Gabriel was trying to devise a strategy to get rid of Larry. He started to feel flustered and overwhelmed. "What if Arabella and the girls aren't safe outside of the castle?" Gabriel wondered aloud. "What if Larry goes after Amy and her children just to harm me? Perhaps I should talk to Larry by myself." Resolved, Gabriel stood up, grabbed his overcoat, and headed for the front door, just as Hildegard was inserting her key into the lock.

"Good evening, Hildegard," Gabriel said, opening the door for her and allowing her to remove her keys. "I hope you've brought enough bottles for my guests?" he inquired. Hildegard nodded.

"Of course, Sir Gabriel," she responded, walking past him.

Gabriel then left the castle and headed towards the park, recalling Arabella's mention of it earlier that evening. As he reached the entrance, he appreciated the quietness, the stars, and the crescent-shaped moon. He looked up, identifying different planets and imagining shapes they could form.

Suddenly, Larry emerged, clapping loudly enough to be heard. "Well, well, well, if it isn't our dear and beloved Gabriel Ambrose, the king and master of his flock," he taunted. Slowly, about twenty other members appeared behind him, their eyes and stances hungry and aggressive. Gabriel held up his hands.

"Lawrence Harrison, might I have a private talk with you? Man to man?" Gabriel requested.

Larry scoffed and shook his head. "Why, Gabriel? So you could kill me and call it done between us? What could possibly make me agree to that? I never agreed to you killing my sweet, beautiful bride-to-be. I never agreed to you almost killing and abandoning me. So, why should I agree to talk with you?" Larry retorted, his anger evident.

Gabriel sighed, lowering his hands and steepling his fingers. "I was hoping to end this problem between you and me. My family has nothing to do with it." Gabriel said.

Larry smiled and shook his head till his smiled faded to anger.

"My daughters are very precious to me and Amy is pregnant, so I cannot have them harmed," Gabriel said.

Larry's expression changed to curiosity. "Pregnant? How did she manage that with that watered-down puppy, Bryan?" Larry snapped.

Despite the tense situation, Gabriel couldn't help but laugh at Larry's description of Bryan. "I did… well, technically, it was with Caleb's blood," Gabriel said.

Larry scrunched his brow and looked at his group with disgust. "That sounds disgusting, Gabriel. Not only are you a monster and a child abandoner, but also you are also very sick inside. I regret having ever met you many years ago," Larry said, his face contorted in disgust. "What should we do about this? Fair is fair. You took my life, so I should have the right to have you massacred, as well. Don't worry, Gabriel; I'll make it quick, unlike how you left me in the woods to die," Larry said as he slowly approached Gabriel.

Gabriel started to back away, noticing his group slowly closing in on him from various angles. "Larry, this is your first and final warning. We need to end this, or it could escalate to a disastrous scenario. I have no intention of going after you or your fiancée, Larry. I was still adapting to my diet and way of living back then. Remember how I took you into my home and fed you those rabbits?" Gabriel asked.

Larry's eyes darkened, and he bared his teeth. "That means nothing to me, Gabriel. Just because you did one nice thing, you still ruined my chances of a beautiful future," Larry said before lunging at Gabriel. Gabriel dodged the attack, bared his teeth, and growled. Soon, the others also attacked Gabriel, but his speed and strength allowed him to fend off most of the attackers.

Gabriel began to feel overwhelmed as over twenty of Larry's associates grabbed him. Larry opened his mouth and took a substantial bite from Gabriel, causing him to scream. Lucien, Daniel, Vladimir, and Adrian, along with Amelia and Arabella, ran toward the park, their eyes wide with horror. Gabriel managed to throw Larry against a nearby tree and pushed the others off.

Larry looked at Gabriel's family members with horror and anger and took off running. "Gabriel!" Arabella screamed as she ran toward him. "Here, have some of mine," she said, offering her wrist to his lips. Gabriel gently pushed Arabella's hand away. "Please, your wound needs to heal," Arabella insisted, her voice filled with fear.

Lucien came over to Gabriel and kneeled beside him and grabbed a little pocketknife from his jacket pocket, letting some of his blood drip into Gabriel's mouth. "What were you thinking, Gabriel? Why would you come here by yourself? We needed to face him together, as a unified alliance. Did you really think you could handle him and his friends alone? I have so much respect for you, Gabriel, but this was a fool's errand, and you let yourself get hurt," Lucien said, his tone soothing yet concerned.

Daniel knelt beside Gabriel on the opposite side, extending his hand for Lucien to pass him his pocketknife, so he could offer some of his blood. "You were quite brave, though. I mean, there was so much doubt within you, yet you still possess that dark and sharp edge within, dear Gabriel. Always remember that," Daniel said.

As dawn began to break, the entire group hastily retreated inside the castle, ensuring all the curtains were drawn shut. Lucien and Daniel gently accompanied Gabriel to his sleeping quarters, where they found Arabella in her nightgown, brushing her hair, her expression turning to horror upon noticing the scar on Gabriel's shoulder. "My poor love," Arabella uttered as she approached the bed, assisting Gabriel under the covers.

Arabella joined him, wrapping her arms around him tightly. "Thank you, my sweet wife," Gabriel whispered. Arabella smiled, remaining awake until Gabriel drifted off to sleep, after which she too closed her eyes and fell asleep.

In his dream, Gabriel found himself back in the tavern, but this time Larry was not a boy but the same man he had seen in the park. As Gabriel entered, he noticed Larry's friends, including the bartender, all present, with bassinets turned away from him. The sound of cooing infants filled the air. "Larry, what's happening? Are my children in there?" Gabriel asked, pointing at a bassinet.

Larry chuckled, shrugged, and gestured for Gabriel to see for himself. Gabriel approached, only to find a recording device emitting baby sounds. "You lied to me," he whispered. Larry simply stared back. "You evil child, where are my children?" Gabriel demanded, panic rising as he spun around in circles. Suddenly, he faced Larry again, who now held a baby in his arms, looking remarkably like Amy as an infant. "Give her back to me, Larry," Gabriel pleaded.

Larry just laughed, and a young man with dirty blonde hair and green eyes handed him a knife, smirking as he said, "We're all quite hungry, Larry." Frozen, Gabriel kept his eyes on Larry's hand, holding the knife. "Take me instead. Leave Amy out of this," Gabriel demanded. Larry paused, the knife tip perilously close to the baby's chin. "Take me. I am the one you want, Larry Harrison. I shall die for my children," Gabriel begged.

Larry chuckled, set the knife on the table, handed the baby to the young man, and declared, "With pleasure, Gabriel." He then grabbed the knife and lunged at Gabriel, who woke up screaming.

Startled, Arabella woke up screaming as well. "My love, what's happening? What's wrong?" she asked urgently.

# Arabella's Story

After sunset, Gabriel found solace in the living quarters, seated on a sofa and gazing intently at the flames dancing in the fireplace, an effort kindled by Hildegard's assistance. In his right hand, he held a full glass of fresh blood. Amy, her belly noticeably larger, waddled into the living quarters. "Amy, what are you doing out of bed?" Gabriel inquired, his attention partially diverted as he caught sight of her.

"Father, what happened out there?" Amy's voice quivered with fear. "I overheard that you were attacked and had to consume Uncle Daniel's and Lucien's blood. Why?" Gabriel, not wishing to engage in a heated discussion about the incident, simply smiled and shrugged.

"Just a heated debate, nothing more. I want you to take good care of yourself, dear Amy," he gently urged. "Don't let anything stress you out. You need to stay strong for your children, and let the grown-ups handle this situation. Tomorrow evening, some of our family members are coming over to resolve the issue with Larry Harrison. Please stay out of it," Gabriel said.

Amy stood frozen, her emotions a turbulent mix of fear and anger. "I don't know if I can handle it, Father," she confessed. "It's all too much for all of us." Gabriel offered her a reassuring smile.

"Ease your troubled mind, sweet child. This will all be over soon enough," Gabriel said. "Please, go on and rest up as much as possible. Has Hildegard been feeding you?" Gabriel asked. Amy nodded before exiting the room.

Approaching the staircase, she encountered Caleb descending the stairs. "Good evening, sweet Amy. How are you feeling?" he greeted her warmly.

Amy, choosing not to engage, waited silently for him to reach the bottom step before she laboriously began her ascent. "Okay, well, have a nice evening," Caleb said, undeterred, before he walked away. Reaching the first floor, Amy felt an overwhelming heaviness in her legs. Unaware that she was about to faint, she fell backward with a soft moan of "Ouch."

Just then, Bryan came over to her and picked Amy up by her shoulders and lifted her back onto her feet. "Do you need help getting back to your room," Bryan said as he placed his hands on Amy's upper body. Amy nodded and allowed Bryan to partially carry her over to her room.

"There you go," Bryan said , gently placing her on her feet and pulling back the covers to help her into bed. "I heard you from the second floor. Do you need anything else, Amy?"

Amy reached out, taking Bryan's hand in hers. "I could use some company, especially from someone I feel a deeper connection with. The many trips we've taken together have created a bond, don't you think?" she inquired. Bryan smiled, sitting down at the edge of the bed.

"My father thinks it might be better if we kept our distance from each other. The reason we are here is because of that Larry Harrison kid. He really knows how to get under my skin," Bryan said. Amy could not help but to giggle at Bryan's facial expression and comment.

"I have no interest in him whatsoever. The fact is, he was there for me while I was babysitting, taking me out to lunch, inviting me over to his family, and even having that strange sleepover," Amy said. At the mention of the word "sleepover," Bryan's eyes hardened. "Oh, am I bothering you with my story?" Amy asked.

Bryan shook his head quickly, smiling. "No, I was just deeply engrossed in your story. I might have looked stern, but I was actually quite fascinated," Bryan assured her. "Okay. Well anyway, enough about that guy. What have you and your family been up to?" Amy asked. Bryan shrugged.

"Not much. We are pretty much just relics and servants of the Ambrose family, I believe. We don't really have any actual freedom in this family," Bryan said. "We haven't been doing much. Hildegard gave us a spare sleeping bag to use on the floor. It's not as comfortable as a bed, but then again, our accommodations weren't really prepared for our stay either," Bryan said.

Amy nodded in agreement. "You know, you can always stay in this bed. As long as Gabriel and your father understand that it's only for sleeping purposes and perhaps also for protecting me as a fragile new mother, I don't think they would oppose the idea. I'm just throwing it out there so you don't have to suffer with sleeping problems," Amy offered. Bryan smiled, taking Amy's hand in his and kissing the top of it.

"You are quite a remarkable person, Amy," Bryan said. "Your children are going to have a wonderful future with you as their mother. Whoever the father figure is, that shall remain a mystery for a long time, but I have no interest in ever finding out."

Amy focused on Bryan, listening to his words and feeling a sense of comfort and relaxation in his voice. She didn't realize how quickly her relaxed state turned into sleep. Bryan watched as her eyes closed and decided to stay in the room with her for a while. Suddenly, there was a knock at the door. Bryan rushed to answer it, placing his finger to his lips to signal Darcia to be quiet.

"Amy is asleep? That is good to see and hear," Darcia whispered. "If you want, you could stay in this room with her?" she suggested. Bryan smiled and shook his head.

"What would Alistair think of us being together again, in the castle of his lord or master?" Bryan said sarcastically. Darcia smiled and gave him a gentle punch on the shoulder.

"He is your father and he will always feel a sense of fear, especially when it is focused on his offspring, you know?" Darcia said.

Bryan smiled. "Would Alistair not mind us being together in this room?" Bryan asked. Darcia looked around before she placed her lips close to Bryan's ear.

"Just go ahead and stay with her. I will talk to Alistair myself and knowing how protective you were of her during her traveling, I am sure he would be okay with it. The girl does need someone with her aside from Ginger or Arabella, even though I respect their strength in many ways," Darcia whispered.

Bryan nodded in agreement. "Okay. That sleeping bag is not as comfortable as it looks, you know?" Bryan said. Darcia could not help but to chuckle at that comment.

"See you around, Mother," Bryan whispered to Darcia, and she kissed his cheek softly before she left. Bryan walked back to Amy and sat in the same chair, observing how comfortable and at peace she looked. He leaned against the chair, reminiscing about all the different countries he had visited with Amy. He remembered feeling occasionally uncomfortable around her since she was Gabriel's daughter, yet he also felt a sense of comfort and a desire to protect her.

Meanwhile, in her own room, Ginger was pondering the need to do something more fruitful with her time. She wondered what would happen to her and Amy if Arabella decided to take them away from all the drama. Would they be happier and more alive, or would that complicate the situation even more? Lost in thought, she stared at a blank part of her wall, her thoughts going in circles. She knew it was important to talk to someone about any planning.

Deciding to act, Ginger left her room and headed toward the main quarter, where she found Gabriel, Vladimir, Adrian, Lucien, Daniel, and Amelia in conversation. Noticing her arrival, Gabriel looked up. "My child, is everything okay?" he asked.

Ginger, fidgeting with her nails, pondered how to respond. "When are Amy, mother, and I supposed to leave this place, father?" she asked. "I mean, if our guests are arriving tomorrow, shouldn't Amy and I at least be packing our luggage or something along those lines?"

Amelia looked over at Gabriel with a confused expression. "What is this, Gabriel? Are you sending them away? Why?" she asked, with frustration in her tone. "What about me or your brothers?" Gabriel shifted his focus from Ginger to Amelia.

"Nobody is going anywhere. I have changed my mind. What happened out there with Larry was just a taste of what he can do, but as far as I am concerned, we are stronger and we have a bigger group than he does, so I am not too concerned with him," Gabriel said.

Ginger rolled her eyes and crossed her arms. "Why are we not being placed in a safer location, Father? What about Amy? She's due in a few weeks, so why does she have to remain here in the castle while everyone is out fighting and not protecting her?" she asked, desperation in her voice.

Gabriel raised his right hand to hush Ginger. "My child, everything is going to be okay. Nothing bad is going to happen to Amy, and nothing bad is going to happen to you or your mother, okay?" he assured her.

Ginger felt a sense of anxiety washing over her and decided to turn around to walk away.

"Have a nice evening, sweetie," Gabriel snapped sarcastically.

Ginger turned around in anger.

"Normally, when a conversation is over, we greet each other pleasantly. I have no quarrel with you, sweet child, but my patience wears thin when I feel that my wishes and ideas are not respected," he said firmly.

Tears welled up in Ginger's eyes. "You're so cold, you know that?" she said sadly before leaving the room, covering her eyes. Amelia stood up, shaking her head in disgust at Gabriel.

"We are all stressed out, you know. Ginger is just looking out for her sister and her mother. You could show a bit more support toward your children," Amelia snapped. Gabriel's brothers remained silent, the tension in the room growing.

Lucien cleared his throat, attempting to steer the conversation in a more productive direction. "So, Gabriel, what's actually the plan? What are you thinking right now?" he inquired, his tone serious.

Gabriel, deep in thought, focused his attention on the table in front of him, analyzing the carvings on the wooden surface. Realizing he was not responding, Lucien tried again to grab his attention.

"Gabe?" Lucien called out, whistling and snapping his fingers until Gabriel finally shifted his focus back to him. "Whatever it is, we will support you, no matter what," Lucien reassured.

The other brothers nodded in agreement. "I think your daughters should know that they are safe here, so perhaps adding some fatherly advice would perhaps warm up the situation a bit more, rather than resorting to sarcasm?" Lucien suggested, his words thoughtful.

Gabriel smiled, a gesture that was mirrored by his brothers. "I know what I did wasn't smart, but then again, facing Larry last evening wasn't smart either. I just wish this whole immortal shapeshifter thing hadn't been bestowed upon me. It may look fun and exciting in movies and TV shows, but once you're stuck in that situation, it loses its excitement after a few seconds. Especially when you realize people consider you more of a monster and feel the need to go after us, rather than leave us alone," Gabriel expressed, his frustration evident.

Daniel nodded, understanding Gabriel's sentiment as he looked around at all his brothers. "We completely understand, Gabriel. But what's done is done, and now all we need to focus on is getting rid of the bad people. If we want others to see us as the good guys in this story, we must eliminate the evil creatures that pretend to be us but are not," Daniel stated firmly.

Gabriel cleared his throat, adjusting himself in his chair as he collected his thoughts. "I have no interest in fighting, but if it's a necessary evil, then it needs to be taken care of," he declared. "Are any of you in need of a drink? Because I need to warm up my throat a bit," he added.

The five of them rose from their seats and walked toward the dining quarter, where they helped themselves to one of the fresh bottles that Hildegard had brought back for them. They clinked their glasses together before taking their first sip, and then Gabriel poured everyone another glass.

Just then, Arabella entered the room, dressed in one of her old floral dresses, complemented by matching slippers. The guys all looked over in admiration. "Oh, stop it," Arabella teased, a playful glint in her eyes. "You all know better than to hit on another man's wife, hm?" she chided, eliciting chuckles from the group.

"Say, Gabe, may I have a word with you in private?" Arabella asked. Gabriel nodded, quickly finishing his second glass before following Arabella into the living quarter. Once Gabriel was seated on one of the sofas, Arabella took a seat on the opposite one, facing him. "Ginger was quite upset just now, saying that you treated her disrespectfully. Is that true?" Arabella asked, her tone serious.

Gabriel's expression changed from happiness to anger. "She went to her mother to complain about me, is that it?" he retorted, his tone sharp.

Arabella raised her hands, signaling Gabriel to stop. "I'm not here to shield or defend her. But what's this about us not going anywhere? Why not, Gabriel? Here we go again. You're updating plans without sharing them with me? Are all the plans made solely by you? I think it would be best if I took the girls and Hildegard elsewhere, while you deal with your own problems. Amy needs extra support and protection, and being here in the castle is not going to help her at all," Arabella asserted, her voice filled with frustration.

Gabriel waited for Arabella to finish speaking before he exhaled deeply. "When I briefly fought Larry out there by myself, I thought I might be able to talk to him about our conflict. But he is adamant about having me killed. I even had this horrible nightmare about him, Arabella," Gabriel confessed. "He'll probably try to kill Amy off first, before getting a chance to go after me. While Amy is here with us, protected by about twenty people in this castle, her chances of survival are higher than if she were just with you, our firstborn, and a human servant."

"So what you're saying is, you don't trust your new shapeshifting wife or firstborn daughter to protect Amy? You think we're frail women with no skills whatsoever and that you need to be there for us?" Arabella challenged, her voice rising. Gabriel's eyes darkened with anger. "Does it anger you when I ask such questions, Gabe?"

Gabriel struggled to control his breathing, his eyes remaining pitch black. "Why do you see me as such a control freak, Arabella?

I've done everything I thought was appropriate to keep you, even when you were a ghost, and to protect our daughters from harm. What if I had gone after Alistair or Darcia when they took them? Not all plans work out, but I did what I thought was best. And look—they are both alive and educated," Gabriel retorted, his eyes returning to their normal blue color.

Arabella sighed, leaning back against the sofa. "Against my own wishes as well, Gabriel. And what was your plan? To have my family killed off so you could have me as your life mate?" she questioned, her tone bitter. Gabriel stood up abruptly, waving off her comment. Arabella snapped back, "Is that your answer to everything? Dismiss important questions because you can't deal with the truth?"

Gabriel started to walk away, his emotions boiling over. "I have no love for you anymore, Gabriel Ambrose. Not after everything you've done to me, and now, to your daughters. Amy was supposed to have a happier and healthier life. Now she's practically surviving on herbal drinks because you thought that was appropriate. Goodness, Gabriel. I have no love for you anymore," Arabella declared, her voice breaking as she quickly walked past Gabriel toward the basement sleeping quarters.

Gabriel was left stunned and nauseated by Arabella's harsh words. Her comment had hit him hard. He steadied himself, feeling a sharp pain flow through him. Dizzy, he staggered and slammed against the wall, heading toward the dining quarter. Gabriel let out a shrill moan, and Lucien and Daniel rushed to him in alarm. "Gabriel, what happened? Are you unwell?" Lucien asked urgently. Gabriel shook his head as he tried to regain his strength.

"Arabella," Gabriel began, his voice shaky as he leaned into Lucien for a hug. "She says she doesn't love me anymore," he moaned, his breathing labored and strained. Lucien rubbed Gabriel's back in an attempt to help him relax. "She wants to leave me."

Lucien let out a deep exhale. "I'm sure this is just a phase, Gabriel. Everyone's on edge with the upcoming fight, but I believe Arabella will come around, and things will be okay again," he reassured, slowly releasing Gabriel from his embrace. "Brothers, could we get Gabriel a drink? It might help calm him for now." At Lucien's request, Adrian went to the table, filled an empty glass, and brought it over to Gabriel.

Gabriel took a small sip, wincing slightly. "That hurt a bit, but I think I'll be okay," he whispered, gently pushing Lucien away as he felt steadier on his feet. He made his way to an empty chair in the dining quarter and sat down, the other brothers taking seats around him, all eyes on Gabriel.

"I will be okay," Gabriel murmured, closing his eyes and leaning back in his chair. "This too shall pass. I think the whole situation is getting to everyone, but I hope Arabella still loves me. I can't help but want to support her, even though she seems to want distance. Was I wrong in my actions, brothers? I may not have handled things in the best way, but I did what I believed was right. I lost my wife in childbirth, was left with two daughters I had no idea how to care for. What are your thoughts on this issue between Arabella and me?"

The brothers all smiled and exchanged glances. Daniel looked at Lucien, who then looked at Adrian. "Well," Lucien began, "perhaps it would have been better to try and revive Arabella after she died, rather than keeping her as a ghost. Doesn't Amelia have something in her spellbook about bringing the dead back to life? Plus, sending your daughters out into the human world was a risky move. What if their powers had developed earlier than expected, without them knowing anything about it? They could have been killed or locked away, Gabriel."

Gabriel surveyed his brothers. "Do you all feel the same way about what Lucien just said?" he asked. The room fell silent. "What's wrong? Are you afraid to agree with him, thinking I might retaliate? I've even contemplated sacrificing my own life to ensure your safety," he said, his tone laced with desperation.

Lucien swiftly turned to Gabriel, his expression one of alarm. "Brother," he exclaimed, "how could you even entertain such thoughts? We can't afford to lose you or any of our family members. You need to banish that idea from your mind immediately."

Gabriel held up his hands, signaling for a pause. "Enough for now. That was just a fleeting thought, nothing more. Would you all excuse me? It's nearly four o'clock in the morning. We should all get some rest in preparation for the arrival of our extended family tomorrow evening," Gabriel said. He then made his way to the sleeping quarters, where he found Arabella sitting in her chair by the boudoir, brushing her hair, a look of sadness in her eyes.

Gabriel opted for silence as he took off his shoes and changed into his satin pajamas and robe. He then climbed into bed, lying on his back. Through the mirror, Arabella watched him, remaining silent.

Arabella got into her side of the bed, lying on her other side, facing away from Gabriel. Gabriel turned his back to Arabella as well, but sleep eluded him. The same was true for Arabella. They lay together in silence until Arabella sat up in bed and looked over at Gabriel, who still had his back to her. "I know you're awake, Gabriel," she said. Gabriel remained silent. "Okay, just listen then," she continued. "Why am I upset with you? You've been nothing but manipulative and lustful since we got together. I'll admit, I did fall in love with you for many reasons. But sometimes I wonder if you used spells or magic to make me fall for you. It was mean-spirited of you to keep me as a ghost and not find a way to bring me back to life sooner. Why not earlier, Gabriel? I can't help but think you never loved me. How can I love someone who doesn't show that love in return?"

Gabriel sat up against the headboard and sighed. "The fact that I didn't let you die, that I brought you back to life, shows that I still love you, Arabella. Isn't that proof enough that I still care?" Gabriel asked. "I could've just let you die and burned your body. I don't understand why you keep making me repeat myself. I love you, and I've given you so much. Our daughters are safe. What more can I do for you, my beloved wife? Please, tell me."

Arabella turned her gaze away, remaining silent. "I'm very frustrated being here. I don't feel like I belong to this family anymore, Gabriel. You have Katrina in this castle; she can participate in the battle between you and Larry. I have no interest in being involved with this family any longer. The only person I respect here is Amelia, who has been more comforting to me than you have. After tonight, I'm taking the girls and leaving. I think it's better that way, so Amy can be safer than being stuck in her room."

Gabriel looked at Arabella as if she had lost her mind. "Absolutely not, Arabella," Gabriel snapped. "She needs to stay here where my brothers and I can protect her. If she's somewhere I can't reach her, she'll be even more vulnerable than if she's with you. You've become stronger, but I have hundreds of years more strength than you do. Right now, I don't fully trust you with my children," Gabriel snapped before he turned around to lie down.

Arabella got out of the bed and walked out of the room, heading to the main area of their sleeping quarters and walked up to the main floor. She walked over to the dining quarter and grabbed herself a fresh bottle of blood and started drinking from the bottle.

Hildegard entered the room, her expression one of surprise. "Milady, shouldn't you be asleep right now?" she inquired. Arabella continued drinking until the bottle was nearly empty, then removed it from her mouth to gulp down the remaining sip.

Setting the bottle on the table, she turned her attention back to Hildegard. "Gabriel and I are experiencing some issues at the moment. Besides, all the curtains are drawn, so I'm not concerned right now," Arabella explained, finishing off the last of the bottle. "Where did Gabriel say we should go when the battle starts, dear Hildegard?"

Standing about ten feet away, Hildegard approached Arabella. "He mentioned relocating to an apartment complex he prepared for situations like these—somewhere warm and less attractive to other shape-shifters. Then, he talked about staying here. Honestly, I'm not sure what to think anymore, except that we are expecting guests in about twelve hours. It might be best for us to get some rest to be ready for their arrival," Hildegard advised.

Arabella rolled her eyes. "Perhaps I'll sleep with one of my daughters tonight. Ginger, maybe, since Amy needs her rest, and

I might be more disruptive to her than to Ginger," she decided, heading to the staircase that led to Ginger's room. Gently opening the door, she sneaked in and eased the covers back to slip in without disturbing Ginger, who remained fast asleep. Arabella snuggled under the covers and fell asleep.

The next evening, around five o'clock, Ginger awoke to feel someone next to her and gasped in surprise upon seeing her mother. "Mother?" she whispered. "Mother?" Arabella slowly opened her eyes, rubbing them with her fingers. "Yes, Ginger?" she responded, squinting in the dark room. "What are you doing here? Where's Father? Is he sick?"

Arabella chuckled softly. "No, he is fine. I just needed some space from him—needed a break from all the family drama and fighting," she explained, sitting up against Ginger's headboard. Ginger looked puzzled. "What kind of family drama and fighting? Are you and father fighting right now?" Ginger asked. Arabella shook her head.

Arabella shook her head. "No, my sweet Ginger," she reassured her. "I'm talking about the fight between your father and Larry." Ginger got out of bed, put on her slippers and a cotton robe, and turned to face Arabella, who was still in her bed. "But why do you need distance from Father, dear mother?" Ginger asked.

Arabella took a moment to choose her words carefully, then sighed. "Your father did something terrible to me when we first met, Ginger. Should I even tell you this story, or would that ruin your relationship with him?" she questioned, lifting her gaze to meet Ginger's. Rolling her eyes, Ginger stared down at Arabella. "What did he do? How bad is this story?" she asked, feeling a surge of anger inside her.

Arabella sighed once again, rose from Ginger's bed, grabbed her own satin robe, and sat back down. "Many years ago, when my father owned a farm, I met your father. I was in town one evening to purchase some items from our local market, but I had to hurry back home because a rainstorm was approaching. That's when I saw this dark, mysterious-looking man – your father. Ginger, if you only knew how much you resemble him, you would understand his allure,"

Arabella recounted, smiling at Ginger. "Of course, I was captivated by his looks, but something inside me urged me to leave. So, I left the market and headed home. That night, we heard a horrific roar or growl – I'm not quite sure how to describe it – and I looked outside to see this monstrous creature attacking our livestock. I tried to make out what it was but couldn't. My father went out with a gun in an attempt to kill it, but the creature killed him instead. My mother, horrified, rushed to lock the doors and then ran to the room where I was sleeping with my two sisters and one brother. She told us to hide. To cut a long story short, she was killed as well. My brother tried to fend off the creature but was brutally attacked. That's when the creature turned to me and just stared. As it approached, I was frozen in fear. Then, it transformed into the same man I had seen in the market earlier that night. After that, everything is a blur. When I regained consciousness, I found myself here in this castle, lying on a sofa in my nightgown, with him sitting on the opposite sofa, staring at me. I was so weak and disoriented that any sudden movement made me dizzy. Days later, I woke up in a large bed with a bronze frame and purple satin sheets. There was an unmarked bottle and a glass on the nightstand. My throat was incredibly dry, so I reached for the bottle. With the little strength I had, I managed to unscrew the top and took a sip. Although the drink made me wince, it helped soothe my dry throat, so I took bigger sips and soon felt my energy returning. I put the bottle back on the table, walked over to the door, and opened it. He was right there, as if he had been waiting for me," Arabella shared.

"Good evening, Arabella," Gabriel said. "How are you feeling?" Arabella looked around, panic-stricken, and started to back away from him. "You," she pointed at him accusatorially, her voice filled with sorrow, "you killed my family. It was all you." Gabriel closed the door behind him and raised his hands in a placating gesture.

"I have been searching for the perfect partner to help me with my legacy sweet Arabella. I traveled to various countries to find someone who I knew would be my one true love," Gabriel explained. Arabella scanned the room, looking for a way to escape, and made a run for the door. However, Gabriel quickly grabbed her from behind, causing Arabella to scream.

"Please, my sweet Arabella. We are destined to be together forever. Can't you see that?" Gabriel pleaded, struggling to keep a resisting Arabella in his arms. "I need you," he whispered. Arabella stopped squirming, waiting for Gabriel to loosen his grip. Once he let her go, she turned around and began to dry her eyes.

"What does all of that mean? I do not even know what to call you," Arabella said. Gabriel nodded. "Gabriel Ambrose, but my friends and family just call me Gabriel."

Arabella looked at him with fear in her eyes and shook her head. "I have never met you before, so how can we even we destined for each other, Gabriel?" she asked.

Gabriel gestured for Arabella to sit on the bed as he made his way to sit on the edge. "I have been following you, or what humans might call stalking. I've seen how you interact with others and noticed that you often seem lonely and sad. I have been searching for the perfect wife, someone to be mine for all eternity," Gabriel explained. Confused, Arabella furrowed her brows. "What do you mean 'for eternity,' Gabriel?" she asked.

Gabriel smiled and nodded. "Perhaps I should explain that part to you as well. I am not human, as you might have noticed back at the farm. I can shape-shift into various creatures, from animals to monstrous beings. I don't eat human food; I feed on the warm flesh and blood of living creatures. I felt such a deep connection to you that I knew I had to claim you as mine," Gabriel revealed.

Arabella shook her head in disbelief. "I cannot believe this, Gabriel. This all seems insane," Arabella said. "I want to leave. Please, do not follow me out of this place," Arabella said. Gabriel sighed, focusing his gaze on Arabella.

"I need you more than you would ever know, Arabella. Please, stay with me for the night. It's dangerous outside. If you really want to leave me after that, I will respect your wishes," Gabriel said.

Arabella fell silent and cleared her throat, prompting Ginger, who had been intently listening, to speak up. "Then what happened?" Ginger asked, curiosity lacing her voice. Arabella smiled and shrugged.

"He seduced me quite nicely, my sweet Ginger," Arabella said. "He had Hildegard, who was just a young girl at the time, prepare meals for us, and he would have her bring me lavish gifts—dresses, jewelry, and other niceties. I felt like a princess. Then came the lovemaking. That was quite wonderful. He treated me like a precious diamond. I was his, and he was mine," Arabella said, her eyes filled with a lustful nostalgia. Ginger couldn't help but chuckle at Arabella's expression.

"Then we came into the world, is that what happened next?" Ginger asked with a smile on her face.

Arabella smiled. "Not for many years after that. I got to meet his brothers and then I got to meet Amelia. We were just one big happy family in this castle and all of my past memories of my family were just repressed by such wonderful care and passion," Arabella said. "Now that we are in the midst of these crisis moments, I feel it's important that we start taking steps backwards and distance ourselves from these things. Hildegard mentioned an apartment complex somewhere in a warm country. Perhaps I should ask Hildegard more about where we might find it and let Gabriel deal with his problems alone," Arabella said.

Ginger looked over at her closed door with concern. "What about Amy? I would rather that Amy did not relocate anywhere. She is in a vulnerable state and we must protect her at all cost," Ginger said. "Plus, with our other family members around, Larry and his followers would not be able to stand a chance against our family," Ginger said. "I have faith that we are quite capable of handling this upcoming battle."

# Family Reunion

Amy was in her room putting on a maternity gown that Hildegard had purchased from a maternity store. She put the gown over her head and saw how big she had gotten the last time, which was about a month ago when she saw herself in the mirror. "The beauty of pregnancy," Amy murmured to herself. She heard a knock on her bedroom door. "Come in," she called out.

Bryan opened the door and closed it behind them. "How do I look?" Amy asked with a nervous smile.

"Beautiful," Bryan said. "Some of our guests have arrived. I believe Dante and his family are here and Alarick and his family, as well. Then we just have to wait for a few more families and then we can probably strategize how we can take down this Larry Harrison," Bryan said.

Amy smiled and reached out for Bryan's hand. Bryan took her hand in his and moved over so he could hug Amy gently. "How are your kids doing inside of you?" Bryan asked, placing his hands gently on Amy's belly.

"I think they are doing good. I do occasionally feel a nice jolt of pain, which I believe is a good sign. Other than that, my appetite has increased a lot," Amy said. Bryan smiled and nodded. "That is good to hear," Bryan said. "So, are you ready to meet your extended family again?" Bryan asked as he escorted Amy down to the main floor. Bryan slowly helped Amy down the stairs and they both were able to hear different voices talking. Amy could hear Alistair and Darcia talking and a few other voices she vaguely remembered.

When Amy entered the room with Bryan supporting her, all conversation ceased as everyone turned their attention to Amy, their expressions a mix of surprise and curiosity. "So, the rumors are true. Amy is with child," Francesca, whom Amy remembered from Italy, remarked.

Helen looked over with a smirk and chuckled. "How far along are you, dear Amy?" she asked.

Amy looked around, recognizing all the faces staring at her. "About six months," she responded. "I think I'm due in a week or two, but with Larry Harrison on the loose, I think my babies will be born after he's dealt with," she added confidently.

Just then, Gabriel came in from behind Amy and cleared his throat. "We are still expecting a few more people for this family reunion. Please, help yourselves to some more of our fresh bottles of warm blood and enjoy the time together. I am sure you all want to catch up, as this is probably only the second time we have had a family reunion in person instead of through those electronic devices," Gabriel said.

Alistair scanned the room, waiting for someone to break the silence. Then Arabella made her entrance, donning a black pants suit—the same one Amy had worn the first time she met Gabriel. The room filled with gasps as everyone turned their attention to Arabella. With a smile and a wave to each person, she greeted, "It is good to see you all again in person. I am sure Gabriel has shared stories of me with you all, right, husband?" she asked, turning to Gabriel.

An awkward tension filled the air as everyone shifted their focus to Gabriel, concern etched on their faces. "I do not recall any story that we were told by Gabriel," Dante admitted.

Just then, the bell chimes rang. Logan and his family showed up. Hildegard walked over to the front door and let the final guests in. Logan, leading his family, entered the living quarters, nodding in acknowledgment to the room before focusing on Gabriel. "Good evening, Gabriel," Logan greeted. "It's good to be here in person. It's been a while since we last saw each other. Please, allow me to reintroduce you to my family," he said, gesturing toward his wife and children.

Audrey and Mackenzie immediately turned their attention to Amy and then to Arabella. "I don't remember Amy being that large, Logan," Audrey commented, glancing over at him. Logan's gaze followed, moving from Amy to Arabella and then back again. He smiled at Caleb, who stood quietly in a corner. "Did you have anything to do with Amy's pregnancy, Caleb?" Logan queried. "And how did you get so close to Gabriel? What made you decide to leave Australia?" he pressed.

Gabriel cleared his throat, raising his right hand to quiet Logan's barrage of questions. "I did not invite you all here to scrutinize Caleb, Arabella, Amy, or myself. We have a serious problem that needs addressing," Gabriel stated firmly. "Has anyone here ever encountered a Lawrence Harrison?" he asked, looking around at the coven members who exchanged glances and shrugged in response. "Well, it seems that due to my new life, I've found myself in a bit of a bind with our current problem. I may have accidentally turned this kid into one of us without intending to," Gabriel admitted. "Now he wants revenge. He almost attacked my sweet Amy in Oregon with intimidation, aggression, and—what was it, Bryan? A potion his father had given her that made her ill?" he asked, searching the room until his eyes landed on Bryan, seated next to Alistair.

Bryan nodded. "That is true. I was the one who saved her from her illness that night, if you by any chance remember that, Amy? The night of your sleepover with Larry?" Bryan asked. Everyone looked over at Amy who felt quite exposed for having all eyes on her. Amy nodded.

"Yes. I remember that dreadful night. I was extremely feverish and very ill. It was just horrible," Amy recalled, tears starting to well up in her eyes. "Forgive me; these pregnancy hormones are really getting to me lately," she added, her voice quivering. Everyone in the room nodded understandingly, and their attention shifted back to Gabriel.

Dante stood up. "So, you gathered us all here to confront this Larry and potentially kill him? Why can't you handle this kid on your own, Gabriel?" he questioned. "It seems like this is your problem, and I don't see why we should all risk our lives for it." After Dante had spoken, Logan stood up as well.

"I agree with Dante on this matter," Logan said. "I have no interest in participating in a futile battle, especially when it seems that this issue is entirely yours, Gabriel. And Caleb, I'm very disappointed in you as well. I can't fathom why you left our group to live in this castle, or how your children ended up in that poor girl's body," Logan remarked, his tone laced with disapproval.

Gabriel cleared his throat, a stern expression on his face. "Hold on a second, all of you," he interjected sharply. "Before you proceed with your judgments and disappointments, understand that this problem concerns us all. He is building his own army and could expose himself as non-human to the world. If blood banks, hospitals, and clinics start noticing Hildegard's blood pickups, humans could start tracking us down as well. Please understand that while this is primarily my fault, if you feel any sense of loyalty to me—as your leader, patriarch, protector, and comforter—then please, help me keep my daughters and wife safe from any harm we might face. Yes, I chose Caleb's blood for Amy because he seemed like the best option. I had no reason to choose anyone else to father healthier grandchildren for my wife and me. But please, when we stand together as a united front, no one will get hurt or die. And once this is all over, I will never ask anything of you again," Gabriel pled.

Logan and Dante exchanged glances and looked back at Gabriel. "I really do not understand how you cannot handle a kid like this Larry," Dante said. "You are stronger and wiser than most of us, and especially someone like Larry, I am sure you, Lucien, Daniel, and Vladimir could all take him down together, so I do not know why you would have us all come over here. Perhaps I just need to see this Larry kid before I make the final decision and if it is true that you say, Gabriel about not asking for anything after this, I will accept that. I love you as a father, Gabriel, but I have no reason to risk my life or my family's lives in a conflict that has nothing to do with a global crisis."

Gabriel nodded. "Thank you for that, Dante. I promise that this will be the final request I have," Gabriel said with a smile. "Now for a nice meal together, Hildegard has prepared us a nice feast of various blood types from various blood donors at the table. All you have to do is ask for which type and she will pour it for you in your own glass. Please, join me," Gabriel said.

Everyone took their seats around a long rectangular table adorned with crystal wine glasses. Their eyes roved over the various unmarked bottles in front of them as they awaited Hildegard's finishing touch—opening the first bottle.

Gabriel patiently waited for his guests to help themselves before gesturing for Hildegard to fill his glass. "So, how were your travels and journey coming over here? Was it challenging or smooth?" Gabriel inquired, his gaze shifting to his right, where Logan sat with his wife and daughter, followed by Alarick and Vanessa, and then Kristjan and Helen.

Alarick smiled and nodded. "It was quite straightforward. We ran through various woods and hopped on different modes of transportation to get here. We did consider flying, but we also wanted to explore other means of travel," he explained.

Dante, with a smile, added, "We opted for public transportation, although being amidst humans in such confined spaces was quite the challenge." Francesca chuckled at Dante's description, adding, "Flying didn't seem appealing at the time, but we might consider it for our return journey, right Francesca?" She smiled warmly, squeezing Dante's hand in hers.

Kristjan and Helen looked around the table before speaking up. "We left our son Gregory back at home, just to let you know, Gabriel," Kristjan said, as Helen turned her attention to Amy, her expression apologetic.

"Again Amy, we are so sorry about that incident that we had back in Croatia. We had no idea our son would behave that way around you, and I didn't realize you were still in your human form when you visited. I wasn't strict enough with my children regarding your arrival," Helen admitted.

Amy smiled and nodded. "I understand and thank you again for such kind words, Helen. That was quite a moment that I will remember."

Kristjan looked over at Gabriel, who met his gaze with a stern expression. "Gabriel," Kristjan began again, "I really appreciate your decision to let us keep our son. He knows he was wrong to attack that night."

Gabriel maintained a neutral demeanor as he turned his attention to Arabella, who seemed engrossed in her drink. "Let's leave it in the past, shall we?" he suggested. "I don't want any more expressions of gratitude regarding Gregory. I went against my nature in making that decision, but I have no interest in bloodshed over an accident," he stated firmly.

"Now," he continued, addressing the entire table, "I've got an outline and a rough draft of our plan ready. But for the moment, let's enjoy our drinks and each other's company before we delve into the serious matters."

Gabriel then turned to Amy and Ginger, his expression softening. "My dear girls, I think it would be best for you both to rest after finishing your drinks," he suggested gently. Ginger, concern etching her features, looked between Gabriel and Arabella.

"I can understand that Amy needs her rest, but I am not pregnant, Father. Why must I leave?" Ginger asked. Gabriel exhaled and closed his eyes before he answered Ginger's question.

"You two are my precious jewels. I cannot and will not lose either of you. Your mother has decided to take part in our battle, and I know she is capable of taking care of herself and the other family members. Hildegard will be there for you two if you need anything, and that is final," Gabriel said sternly. "Go ahead and finish your final glass before you go up to your rooms."

Ginger quickly downed her final glass and stood up, walking away from everyone. "I cannot believe this," she whimpered to herself.

"I am fully capable of handling myself. I even took Gabriel down during a fight between him, Amy, and me some time ago." Ginger slammed her door shut and walked over to her bed, continuing her soliloquy. "I am not a child to be sent to her room while the adults talk. I am not a vulnerable human. I am a strong shape-shifter and the princess of our family."

A knock at the door interrupted her thoughts. Ginger initially ignored it, but when the knocking persisted, she sighed and responded. "Yes? Please enter."

Arabella opened the door, stepped into Ginger's room, and closed the door behind her. "My dear child," she began, "your father, in his own loving way, is looking after you and Amy." Ginger rolled her eyes and looked away, but Arabella continued. "You are not weak, nor are you a child, Ginger. You are your father's daughter, which means he is very protective of both of you. He and I had an argument a while back about his decisions, but now I realize that he gave you both up because he wanted to protect you from his anger and destructive nature. If it's true that his lust is what started this conflict with Larry Harrison, then he did the right thing in giving you two to the mortal world, bringing you back around the time of your transition."

Ginger felt a surge of anger. "How can you actually believe that, Mother?" she snapped. "How can you even side with him? What he did was selfish and dangerous. He never wanted daughters; he said so himself. That's why Caleb came into the picture. He disgusts me, too," she added before retreating to her bed.

Arabella held up her hands in a gesture of surrender. "I didn't come here to argue with you, Ginger. I'm just trying to help. I understand how frustrating this all is. Trust me, I've been in vulnerable positions in my life, and now I'm the queen of a shape-shifting family. How many people can say that?" she asked, glancing around Ginger's room. Ginger managed a small smile and a nod in response.

"I know you mean well, Mother, but I just hate being categorized with Amy, who is very vulnerable, while I'm a strong female shape-shifter of the family. I even took Gabriel down the first time we fought," Ginger said. "I couldn't believe my strength that evening. It was very strange, but also invigorating in other ways. What would have happened to Amy and me if we had transitioned amongst humans? We could have been hunted down like wild animals or locked away in an asylum. What then, mother?" Arabella nodded in understanding and approached Ginger, gently stroking her hair.

"I understand the questions and concerns that you and your sister could have faced, but I need you and your sister to remain as safe as possible," Arabella said before she kissed Ginger on top of her head. "I will go back down and see how everyone else is doing," she added, leaving the room and gently closing the door behind her.

Gabriel, having shifted back to his original self, adjusted himself back to his true form. He descended the stairs towards the group and noticed Arabella conversing with the other members. As Gabriel entered the room, everyone fell silent. "How are our girls?" Arabella asked as Gabriel sat back down next to her.

"They are calmer now. I had to offer them some fatherly advice before the final battle takes place. I love those two girls so much and really want them to be safe from any harm," Gabriel replied. The others in the room exchanged smiles and glances. "So, has everyone had their fill of blood, or does anyone need more?" Gabriel inquired. Everyone shook their heads and placed their empty glasses on the table.

"Okay. Hildegard, would you be a dear and take care of the used glasses and napkins. I will go to my study and bring out my plans and strategy. Please excuse me," Gabriel said before leaving the table to retrieve his laptop and papers from the study. As he opened the door, he noticed a dark figure moving away from the window outside. Quickly, Gabriel ran to the front door, but there was nothing to see.

Alistair arrived behind Gabriel seconds later. "Are you okay, Gabriel? Did you see something?" Gabriel, still focused on the perimeter outside his castle, eventually turned to face Alistair.

"I thought I saw someone, but now I am not so sure anymore," Gabriel said , closing the castle door and walking back to his study. Finding nothing more to see, he grabbed his equipment, allowing Alistair to grab the other equipment, and together they both walked back to the living quarter where everyone was lounging around.

"Okay, family," Gabriel said as he placed the paperwork and laptop on the living quarter table and sat behind it. Just then, the sound of a broken window echoed from the study. Gabriel bared his teeth and ran back to the study to find a rock with a message attached. "How petty of you all to vandalize my house like this," Gabriel yelled at the broken window. "And how petty to be sending such weak messages." Alistair, Darcia, Dante, Alarick, Vanessa, and Logan all showed up at the study.

"Gabriel, what happened?" Logan asked as he walked through the door of Gabriel's study, eyeing the rock. "What is that?"

Gabriel picked up the rock and scoffed at it. "'Dear Ambrose family, I am losing my patience. I wish to meet with you all for a nice evening chat about our conflict. Please meet us at the park fountain, and I promise that there will be no fight. With regards, Lawrence Harrison,'" Gabriel read aloud. "Are you all up for finally meeting with the horrible creature that we will be facing?" Gabriel asked.

Dante smirked, and Alarick rolled his eyes. "I believe we've had our fill for the night, but what say we have a bit of dessert?" Alarick suggested. Everyone chuckled and walked back to the living quarter, where Gabriel walked over to Arabella and hugged her tightly.

"If you want to stay out of this conflict, my dear wife, you can," Gabriel whispered. Arabella smiled and nodded. "Good. I want you and our daughters to be safe from any kinds of problems," Gabriel said before he kissed Arabella softly on her lips and turned around. "Okay, shall we take care of this problem that Larry is so eager to deal with as well?"

All the coven members nodded and smiled. "We are ready," Dante said before they all left the castle, leaving Arabella and Hildegard in the living quarter. Moments later, Arabella heard Amy scream from her room and ran up to her bedroom quickly, seeing Ginger at the edge of Amy's bed, holding her hand.

"Mother!" Ginger screamed. "Amy is probably due tonight." Arabella walked back to the hallway.

"Hildegard, I need your assistance right now," Arabella screamed. Hildegard came running up to Amy's bedroom and called a human medic she was close with, and then hurried away. Amy was breathing heavily and moaning through the pain.

"Amy, please focus," Arabella said in a soothing tone. "You are going to survive this, okay?" Arabella said. "You are not going to die here. You are going to have three beautiful babies. Try to focus on the breathing. Hildegard is getting a medic to come over here right now to help you," Arabella said.

Amy nodded and continued with her breathing. Ginger felt horrified and upset about everything, but remained as calm as she could. "Keep breathing, Amy. Perhaps you might want to lean against the bedpost, or even walking could sometimes help," Arabella suggested as she allowed Amy to support herself on Arabella's shoulders and get off her bed. Both Arabella and Ginger supported Amy with the walking where Amy felt her body slowly snapping.

"Ouch! This hurts, Mother. What is happening to me?" Amy cried. Arabella gently placed Amy back on the bed and noticed that her body was somehow changing to release her children. "I think your body is preparing you for your children, Amy. Perhaps it would be best to lean against the headboard.

As Amy, Arabella, and Ginger were helping Amy with her birthing, Gabriel and his group were around the fountain in the park. It was around one o'clock in the morning, but Larry was nowhere to be seen. Dante scoffed and shook his head. "Are you even sure you did not just hallucinate any of this, guys? Where is this child?"

Just then there was growling around them. Gabriel got into a defensive position, as did his other members. Larry came out in his wolf form with an aggressive expression in his eyes. "Whatever you guys find appropriate to change into, do whatever feels strong to take these thirty-odd creatures down," Gabriel yelled. Larry lowered himself into a pouncing position and growled at Gabriel before he lunged at him. Gabriel dodged his attack, but another wolf attacked him, causing him to stumble.

Daniel and Lucien shifted into their wolf forms, and the rest of the group did the same, launching into attack mode. Gabriel tackled Larry and threw him against a lamp pole. Then another member of Larry's group attacked Gabriel, but he managed to dodge this time. Suddenly, Gabriel heard a loud scream from the castle and realized that Amy was having her children. The other members of Larry's group went after Gabriel but were stopped by the other members. Gabriel started to feel disoriented by the screaming and the fighting.

Larry managed to tackle Gabriel, knocking him to the ground. With Larry on top, he drooled over Gabriel's face like a rabid animal, pulled back his head, and leaned down to sink his teeth into Gabriel's flesh. At that moment, another wolf from Larry's team joined the fray, piling on top of Larry. Meanwhile, Amelia transformed into her wolf form, followed by Arabella.

Arabella pushed Larry off of Gabriel, revealing deep cuts and wounds all over Gabriel's face. Arabella then turned her attention to a few other members of the opposing team, attacking ferociously until four of them retreated into the darkness. Eventually, everyone reverted to their human forms, taking in the aftermath of the battle. Lucien was severely wounded, Daniel moderately so, Dante had sustained a few cuts, and Logan had deep flesh wounds. Then, Logan's eyes fell on Audrey, lying unresponsive on the ground. He fell to his knees, cradling her in his arms. Nearby, Mackenzie was on the brink of death but managed to show signs of life with slight movement. Vanessa, despite being badly wounded, managed to stand, and Helen was in a dire state, coughing up blood.

Gabriel, in shock, touched his face, his hands coming away bloody. The rest of the night passed in heavy silence.

# New Beginnings

Amy lay on her back as Hildegard and the medic, Josiah, entered her room about half an hour later. Arabella and Ginger were at Amy's sides, providing support. Josiah, assessing the situation, encouraged Amy to spread her legs a bit wider.

"You are quite close, Amy," Josiah noted. "When you're ready, push as hard as you can."

Amy, gritting her teeth, pushed with all her might, quickly delivering her first baby.

"That was fast," Josiah remarked, somewhat taken aback.

Arabella, glaring at him, was quick to remind him, "She has two more children inside her. How is she looking?"

Josiah, refocusing on Amy, noticed another baby. "This... is unusual. Regular human births don't typically work like this," he commented.

Hildegard, placing a hand on Josiah's shoulder, shook her head, signaling him to be more considerate.

"Apologies," Josiah muttered. Turning back to Amy, he said, "When you're ready, Amy, go ahead."

With another push, Amy delivered her son.

"Oh, wonderful, a boy," Josiah exclaimed as he placed the baby beside its sibling. Both babies were now crying.

"One more," Arabella prompted.

Josiah nodded , and with one final push, Amy delivered her second daughter, leaning heavily into Arabella's supportive grasp afterward. Hildegard picked up the first baby, noting its resemblance to Amy, with the same eyes and nose. The second baby, to Amy's dismay, bore a striking resemblance to Caleb, while the third was a mix of both parents.

"I shall leave you ladies to swaddle and care for the children, but if you need any further assistance, don't hesitate to call," Josiah said, placing his business card on Amy's nightstand. Just then, Amy moaned and threw up a bit of blood.

"Oh dear, is she okay?" Josiah said with fear in his eyes. "I think I should call an ambulance."

Arabella waved him off, gesturing for Hildegard to escort him out.

"Have a nice evening, and congratulations on your new children," Josiah said as he was led out, leaving Arabella shaking her head in disgust.

"Hildegard, how can someone like him be a good medic? Our births are quite easy, if you want to know the truth. I was human when I had these two," Arabella gestured to her children, "but Amy, I am so proud of you. You are not dead, and you have three beautiful children right here with you."

Ginger leaned down and hugged Amy gently, whispering, "Congratulations, sis. You are going to be a wonderful mother. I just know it." Amy, feeling quite weak, and closed her eyes.

Arabella left the room with Hildegard to grab some blankets for swaddling the three babies. When they returned, they found Amy deeply asleep, with Ginger watching over her.

"They are so beautiful, are they not, Mother?" Ginger whispered.

Arabella nodded, picking up the second daughter to swaddle her. Hildegard swaddled the boy and handed a third blanket to Ginger, who swaddled the last baby. The three women held each baby in their arms while Amy continued to breathe softly, remaining asleep for the rest of the evening.

Back in the living quarters, Gabriel and the others were slowly regaining their strength again.

"Logan, my condolences to your family," Gabriel said, drinking from a bottle of blood that Hildegard had provided for healing their wounds. "I am so sorry for all of this, family," he added, wincing from his own pain.

Arabella, Ginger, and Hildegard then appeared, each holding a baby. "Good evening, family," Arabella greeted. "May we introduce you all to the new family members?"

Everyone, except for Logan, approached to fawn over the infants. Gabriel approached Arabella, taking Amy's first daughter from her arms.

"Welcome to the new world, my little one," Gabriel whispered to the baby. "You are going to do wonderfully in this world. I promise you."

Logan stood up. "I will take my leave now. Dante , could you help Mackenzie outside? She is very weak, and I will carry my deceased daughter while Gabriel enjoys his new family." Dante, feeling a sense of anger towards Gabriel as well, carried Mackenzie out of the castle in a bridal style.

Francesca, along with Dante and Logan's children, joined them outside. "Are you all leaving us?" Gabriel called out, holding a sleeping baby in his arms. "I really hope you will return back to me."

Logan scoffed and walked out the door. Dante turned around, sadness in his eyes. "I think we shall call it quits for now, Gabriel. This whole problem is your problem, and it cost Logan his life in many ways. Alarick and Kristjan, decide what you want to do. But if you feel that it is not worth putting your lives on the line, feel free to leave whenever you want. Gabriel may be our patriarch, but he does not own us," Dante declared.

Gabriel looked over at Alarick and Kristjan with concern. "I may not be perfect," he snapped, "but I am not the bad guy in this story either. Remember how well I have taken care of your family, spared your son from a death penalty, and provided for you all. Feel free to listen to those two, but I have never harbored any ill feelings towards any of you, even Logan or his family."

Alarick sighed and got up. "Look at us, Gabriel. We are all torn in different ways, and I have a feeling that this Larry guy will continue till you are dead. Perhaps it might be something to consider." Gabriel gently handed the baby back to Arabella and approached Alarick, his teeth bared.

"Are you suggesting I should have myself killed so this feud can end? I had no intention of going after Larry many years ago, boys. So, to think I should consider a thought like that is quite troubling. I want you to leave, Alarick, and join Logan in your hatred towards me. However, I have no reason to consider you part of this family any longer," Gabriel said sternly. "Now, leave."

Alarick slowly walked out of the castle with his family, looking back to see Kristjan still in the living quarter. "If you feel the need to leave me as well, Kristjan, go ahead. Follow the others out of the castle. I could have had your son killed off, but I also know how much it hurts to see your children die. I had no intention of having Logan's children killed off like that. It was purely accidental, and I feel bad that this all happened. However, I cannot say that I am entirely to blame either."

Kristjan and Helen got to their feet and walked out of the castle, leaving Gabriel in a state of betrayal. "Fine. Go and leave me," Gabriel snarled. "After everything I have done for you all."

Gabriel marched out of the living quarter, leaving Arabella, Ginger, and Hildegard in the room alone. He was too caught up in his own rage to realize he had forgotten to check on Amy.

Meanwhile, Amy remained in bed, feeling weak and tired, with mild pain in her body. She realized that she was still alive, not dead. She looked around, saw she was in her room, and managed to raise herself up against the headboard. She noted her body had transitioned from a pregnant state to a slender figure with a marble complexion and an even healthier physique.

Amy pushed the covers aside. Though not strong enough to stand on her feet, she managed to sit on the edge of the bed, supporting herself. She looked at her blood-stained Victorian gown and tried to speak, her voice breaking, "Where are my babies?"

Just then, there was a knock on the door. "Enter," Amy said hoarsely.

Bryan entered the room, his expression somewhat uncomfortable. "Congratulations, Amy. You are now a new mother to three beautiful children. How are you feeling?"

Amy smiled and massaged her throat. "Could you get Hildegard to bring me something to drink?" Bryan nodded and left the room, leaving the door open. He approached Hildegard in the hallway and asked for a bottle of blood.

"Oh, forgive me," Hildegard said, looking for a place to put the baby boy down. Bryan opened his arms, allowing Hildegard to place the swaddled boy in them. "I shall return quickly," Hildegard said before fetching an unopened bottle of blood and quickly walking back to Amy's room.

Bryan looked down at the peaceful, sleeping face of Amy's son, his smile involuntary at the sight. "You will be a wonderful father figure to them, Bryan," Arabella remarked. Bryan's head snapped up, his expression one of horror.

"Excuse me?" Bryan asked, baffled. "Why would you think I would be the father figure to him? Where is Caleb, anyway?" Bryan's gaze darted around the room. "And where is Katrina?"

Arabella smiled, cradling the second daughter close. "I told them both to leave this place and never to return. A castle can only have one queen, Bryan. Similarly, Amy's family can only have one father figure. Please, at least consider taking care of Amy's fledglings. I am sure Alistair and Darcia raised you well enough to be a good spouse and father to Amy."

Ginger, holding Amy's firstborn daughter, smiled at Bryan. "And don't you forget, Bryan, I will be here to help as their aunt. You're not entirely alone. In this family, we might have our moments of clashing—like Amy and I have experienced before—but we always protect and care for each other, no matter what." Arabella smiled and nodded in agreement.

"Just try and relax as much as you can, Bryan. Everything is going to be okay. Amy is quite strong and capable of handling anything thrown her way. She has endured so much in this world including the birthing of her three children, and she will be a wonderful mother and protector, and a wonderful partner to you as well, Bryan. If she takes after me and not so much her father, you two will be together forever," Arabella assured him.

Bryan felt overwhelmed but took solace in the fact that Amy was still alive, even though fear started to creep in. He needed to see how Amy was doing. As he approached her open door, he heard the sounds of her drinking from the bottle. Slowly, he entered the room and was struck by how beautiful and strong Amy looked. "Wow," Bryan whispered.

Amy looked over at Bryan with confusion and then smiled when she saw what he was holding. "Meet your son, Amy."

Amy extended her arms for Bryan to place the swaddled baby in them. The baby opened his eyes, looked up at Amy, and Amy was flooded with mixed feelings of joy, sadness, excitement, and fear. "Good evening, my son," Amy whispered before planting a kiss on top of his head. "Welcome to the family." The baby cooed in response. Amy then looked up at Bryan.

"Where are my other two?" Amy asked with concern and fear in her voice.

Bryan smiled reassuringly. "Downstairs with your mother and sister," he informed her. "They look so beautiful."

Amy smiled and handed the baby back to Bryan, so she could try to stand. She moved slowly, her body feeling heavy, but she managed to make her way toward the hallway and stood at the top of the staircase. "How about I carry you down while you hold your son?" Bryan offered.

Amy nodded and took her son back into her arms, allowing Bryan to pick her up. He carried her down to the living quarter where Arabella and Ginger were waiting. Upon their entrance, both women looked up and smiled warmly at them.

"You look amazing, Amy," Ginger complimented, her eyes shining. Arabella smiled warmly.

"Meet your two daughters. They've inherited so much from you, Amy. They have your eyes, nose, and hands. Such precious angels," she gushed. Bryan gently placed Amy on the ground and took her son from her arms, allowing her to walk over and meet her daughters. Tears welled in her eyes as she exclaimed, "They are so precious. I've created such beautiful children in this family."

Ginger, smiling broadly, handed the second daughter to Amy. She watched with love and happiness as Amy looked down at her daughter.

Amy's eyes scanned the room, searching. "Where is father?" she asked. Arabella's expression changed as frustration bubbled within her.

"A father who cannot be here for his daughter's fledglings? Excuse me, everyone," Arabella said tersely, handing the firstborn daughter to Ginger. She stormed over to Gabriel's study, knocked on his door, and waited for him to answer.

"Arabella, what can I do for you? Before you say anything, I want to thank you for saving me from Larry. Without you and Amelia there, I would have been in a bad state, my love," Gabriel expressed, his voice sincere. Arabella sighed and nodded.

"You are quite welcome, Gabriel. Now, are you ready to meet your grandkids again and see how well Amy is doing?" Gabriel's eyes widened with glee.

"Amy survived? Where is she?" he asked, rushing past Arabella before she could respond. Entering the living quarter, he saw Amy, Ginger, and Bryan, each holding a baby.

Amy looked up at Gabriel, surprise and shock in her eyes. "Father, what happened to you? Why are you scarred like that?" she asked. Gabriel smiled, shaking his head.

"Let's not focus on me right now, my sweet child. Let me take a good look at you," he said. Amy stood up, and Gabriel's chest swelled with pride as he noticed how much healthier and stronger she looked. He approached her gently and hugged her, careful not to disturb the baby in her arms. "Congratulations, my child, on everything. For being strong. For becoming a mother. For being my daughter. You truly are an amazing woman, dear Amy," Gabriel praised.

Ginger looked up at Gabriel , her expression confused. Gabriel's gaze shifted to her. "And you, Ginger, are an amazing woman yourself. You've been a wonderful protector to your sister. You will be an incredible aunt and, hopefully, without any interference from me, a wonderful mother yourself one day." Gabriel then turned to Bryan, standing before him with open arms. "And you, Bryan, are a true gentleman. Whenever you're ready, I hope you'll consider being my son as well. I don't know where Caleb has gone, but I hope you choose to stay and become a part of the Ambrose family. You've already shown in many ways that you belong," Gabriel said warmly.

Bryan stood, extending his left arm to hug Gabriel while cradling Amy's son in the other. "Now that we've all met the little ones, I'll leave you to it. I need to get through some paperwork. Please excuse me," Gabriel said, leaving the living quarter. Arabella followed him to his study, stopping at the threshold.

"What are you doing now, Gabriel? Planning your next attack seems pointless, especially since we are at peace now, aren't we?" she questioned, her tone laced with concern.

Gabriel rose to his feet, pulled Arabella into his study, and closed the door behind them. "Not at all, Arabella," Gabriel snapped, his tone sharp. "We are far from being at peace. Did you not hear how Alarick thought it appropriate for me to give up my life to satisfy Larry? I couldn't believe my ears hearing that from my own family, Arabella. I'm uncertain if Logan, Alarick, or even Dante are siding with Larry right now, but I feel compelled to resolve this issue before it escalates like it did a few hours ago. Arabella, I'm done blaming myself for everything. Right now, I just need a bit of sympathy. I'm strategizing to keep all of you safe, including the three new grandfledglings, my sweet wife," Gabriel said, his eyes filled with sadness.

Arabella shook her head and crossed her arms , her expression stern. "Perhaps I should stay here to help protect us all, as well," Arabella murmured. "I find this entire situation repulsive. If you'd like, I could attempt to meet with this Larry creature and see if we might reach some common ground, aside from having you killed."

Gabriel scoffed and rose quickly to his feet. "Absolutely not, Arabella. What makes you think that plan of yours would work? Huh?" Gabriel demanded, frustration evident in his voice. Arabella stared at Gabriel, trying to control her own rising anger, and exhaled deeply. "I'm still working on a plan, Arabella. Either stay here and help me or go assist your daughters with their newborns and be a wonderful grandmother to those fledglings," Gabriel instructed sternly. Arabella shook her head and turned, walking back towards the living quarter.

Meanwhile, Bryan was contemplating the whereabouts of his own family. Closing his eyes, he tried to communicate telepathically with Alistair. *Alistair, where are all of you? Please let me know where you are.* There was only silence in response. Bryan then attempted to reach out to Darcia telepathically. *Darcia, where are you? Alistair isn't responding. Please tell me where you are.* Yet again, he was met with silence from her end. Bryan's worry intensified, and he rose to his feet. "Has anyone seen my family?" Bryan asked, looking at Ginger and Amy, who both shrugged and scanned the room.

Suddenly, a voice resonated in Bryan's mind. *Bryan?* It was Darcia. *Bryan, where are you? We decided to stay at the park to track Larry when he ran off.* Bryan considered his response, placing Amy's son gently on the sofa next to him. "My family is still at the park. Please excuse me," Bryan said before taking off, running into the dark.

Upon reaching the entrance of the park, he saw no one. Closing his eyes, Bryan allowed his heightened senses to guide him until he heard rustling from a large hedge. Darcia and Alistair emerged, followed by Raymond and Joshua from another shrub, and then Silas and Xavier from another direction. Bryan ran towards them, relieved, and hugged Darcia and Alistair tightly.

"Were you able to find Larry?" Bryan asked. Alistair and Darica both shook their heads. "No, son," Alistair said. "We did our best, splitting up to search for him, but he managed to vanish without a trace. His scent disappeared as well." Bryan glanced at his brothers, noticing the leaves and dirt on their clothes, and then looked down at his own pristine attire. Darcia sniffed Bryan's jacket and smiled.

"Amy had her kids, did she not, Bryan?" Darcia asked. Bryan smiled and nodded. "The are absolutely beautiful creatures, family. Such a wonderful batch of fledglings that she was able to produce."

Alistair gently patted Bryan on his shoulder. "Not sure if this is an appropriate time, but congratulations, Bryan. I am sure you will be a great father figure to her kids." Bryan growled at Alistair and took a step back.

"Why does everyone, including Gabriel, think I would be a good father to Caleb's children? Where is he, anyway? Shouldn't he be paying alimony to Amy?" Bryan snapped. Darcia smiled and shrugged.

"He might be teaming up with Larry. Who knows," Darcia said. Bryan scoffed and crossed his arms.

"How is Gabriel, anyway?" Alistair asked. "He looked quite torn up before he ran after Larry." Bryan looked back in the direction of the castle with anger.

"He is fine. He's healed up mostly, but Logan's daughter is dead, his wife is severely injured, and all of Gabriel's family just up and left. I'm not sure what they're planning," Bryan said.

"Oh dear," Darcia said, her voice filled with sadness at the news about Logan. "So, I assume Gabriel is on his own now, except for us, perhaps?" Bryan simply shrugged.

"I'm just overwhelmed and angry about this whole situation. Remember how happy we were, making plans for ourselves before we got called over to help Gabriel when Arabella died?" Bryan questioned.

Everyone nodded, smiling at the memory. "I just remember how happy we all were. You were going to marry that Giselle girl, right Bryan?" Darcia asked. Bryan rolled his eyes.

"That was just one moment of pure lust. After her mother confronted me at that parlor with Amy, I realized I may have dodged a metaphorical bullet with that family. There's just something about Amy, the complete opposite of Giselle—her strength, determination, and ambitions in life. I remember wanting her so much, but now, with everything that's happened with Gabriel and Caleb, I just don't feel the same urge to help her. I know it's important, but technically, they're not my kids; they're the kids of a deadbeat," Bryan admitted.

Alistair smiled understandingly. "Okay, I get where you're coming from, Bryan, but maybe we should check on Gabriel to get a better understanding of what needs to be done. Larry might come back, alone or with a new group of allies, and we need to be more prepared than ever." With that, Alistair led the way to the castle's entrance, and they all walked back together.

Gabriel sensed Alistair from a distance and peered out of the window from his study, observing them as they slowly made their way back together, Bryan included. Where had Bryan been? Gabriel wondered. He hurried over to the living quarters at a brisk pace, only to find Amy, Ginger, and Arabella once again cradling the three babies. "Where is Bryan?" Gabriel asked.

Amy looked up at Gabriel. "He went to find his family, Father," she replied. "Hasn't he returned yet?" Gabriel shook his head, visibly angered. "Huh," Amy murmured. "I'm sure he will find them. In the meantime, I have my mother and sister with me. The babies have just been sleeping in our arms." Just then, the castle's chimes rang out. "Perhaps that's them," Amy suggested before returning her attention to her daughter. Intrigued, Gabriel made his way to the castle's front door, his expression one of surprise.

"Alistair, Darcia, Bryan, and the others," Gabriel greeted. "Where have you all been? I was beginning to wonder if Logan had turned you against me as well."

Alistair offered Gabriel a reassuring smile. "We tried to track Larry down while you were recovering from the fight, but we lost him," Alistair explained.

Gabriel nodded and gestured for Alistair and his family to enter the castle.

"Bryan mentioned that Amy's children are here. Would now be a good time to meet them?" Darcia inquired. Gabriel responded with a nod, leading the way to the living quarters.

Upon entering, Darcia was filled with a sense of love at the sight of the three infants in Amy, Ginger, and Arabella's arms. She gently approached and quietly sat next to Amy, who cradled a sleeping girl. "Would you like to hold her, Darcia?" Amy asked. Darcia opened her arms, allowing Amy to place the child in her embrace.

"She is so tiny and light," Darcia whispered. Amy smiled. "Have you named them, yet?" Darcia asked. Amy shook her head.

"If you ever want some suggestions, I have a few names you might consider for your children." Amy chuckled, observing how gentle Darcia was with her child. She remembered Darcia's fierceness during a hunt and found it fascinating to see this tender side of her. Alistair entered the room, smiling at the sight of the three children.

"Congratulations, Amy. You've done an amazing job so far with these kids." Amy smiled.

"Thank you," she said softly. "The pregnancies and births weren't easy or fun, but in this moment, nothing else matters. The pain I felt before has practically disappeared."

Arabella looked over at Amy, smiling at her. "She was incredibly strong and brave through it all," Arabella remarked. "I am so proud of her and Ginger." She then acknowledged Ginger with a glance, and Ginger couldn't help but chuckle at the comment. "Being a new mother is hard, especially with all the uncertainties and scares we've had. But Amy, you did an amazing job getting through it all."

Amy turned to Arabella with a smile and expressed her gratitude, "Thanks, Mother," she said. "I really have overcome a lot. From being misled in the past, traveling around the world, and enduring pregnancy, to encountering our family's archenemy, along with other terrifying experiences. And now, the biggest but also the most rewarding challenge awaits—raising these little ones."

At that moment, Gabriel entered the room, acknowledging everyone present. "You won't have to face this alone, my dear child. Your family is here to support you in many ways, so you have nothing to worry about. Leave Larry Harrison to us. Focus on being a wonderful, caring, and supportive mother to your children, Amy, and we will take good care of you," Gabriel assured her.

Amy smiled and nodded. "Thank you, Father. Despite our rocky moments in the past, I feel reassured being a part of this family," she said. Bryan took a seat on the other side of Amy, observing the babies as they slept and stretched their little bodies.

As dawn broke, Amy, with the help of Arabella, Amelia, Hildegard, and Ginger, arranged little beds for the infants to sleep in. "This afternoon, I'll visit some maternity stores and gather the basic supplies that you and the children will need," Hildegard stated. "You're going to need a sizable crib, or perhaps three, along with clothes, diapers, hygiene products…" She continued listing the necessary items before leaving the room and the castle.

Amy, grateful but exhausted, shook her head with a smile. "Goodness, I'm really tired right now. I think I'll call it an early morning," she declared. Everyone exchanged goodnights and soon fell asleep. In her dream, Amy found herself walking in a wooded area outside the castle, pushing her infants in a triple stroller. The wind blew gently through the trees, and birds fluttered around, creating a peaceful atmosphere. She felt content and at ease.

Suddenly, a familiar voice called out from behind her. It was Caleb. "Caleb, where have you been?" Amy inquired.

Caleb remained silent for a moment, his gaze intense as he looked at Amy. "You can't hurt me or my children," Amy declared firmly. Caleb raised his hands in a gesture of surrender. "What do you want?" Amy demanded.

"I am sorry for everything, Amy," Caleb spoke in a flat tone. "Your father is the one to blame. He's a monster, Amy," he accused. "And he will get what's coming to him." As Amy began to push the stroller away from him, he raised his voice, "Don't forget what happened, Amy!" Amy hastened her pace, putting as much distance between them as possible.

Suddenly, she heard rustling in the bushes. Acting quickly, she moved the stroller behind a tree to shield her children and adopted a defensive stance.

Larry emerged, walking alone. "I'm not here to fight, Amy," he said calmly. "I just want to talk. I have no quarrel with you, so please, hear me out," he implored. Amy maintained her defensive position but stayed still. "What your father did to me, to Caleb, and even to you, was wrong. We didn't choose this life, so I can't understand why you're still with him, living in that castle. It worries me, Amy," Larry explained.

"Please keep your distance from me and my children, Larry. Whatever you want, this is not the right time," Amy said sternly, asserting her boundaries. "I don't want to be bothered by you, whether in my dreams or in person."

Larry sighed and crossed his arms. "You keep avoiding me, Amy. That evening, when I was outside the glass door until your father came to protect you, I just wanted to see how you were doing. I had no intention of harming you or letting my parents back in Oregon harm you during your sleepover at our place. We just wanted to see if you had already transformed into your shape-shifting body. Maybe that was wrong of us, but you managed to survive it, remember?" Larry challenged.

Amy scoffed, taking a few steps back to put distance between them. "I want you to leave me alone. Stop bothering me, whether it's in person or in my dreams," Amy snapped, her tone firm. "Please leave." As Larry started to walk towards her, Amy got back into a defensive pose. "Stop," Amy commanded. Larry halted but cast a glance over at the stroller.

"Your children need to know how corrupt your family is, Amy. Perhaps I can help with that," Larry suggested, making a move towards the stroller. Amy reacted instantly, jumping onto Larry. She woke up in a state of shock, her heart racing, and heard her babies crying. She quickly got out of bed and placed each of her children on the bed, trying to soothe them. At that moment, Ginger walked into Amy's room.

"Are you okay, Amy?" Ginger asked, seeing Amy in a state of panic. "Here, let me help you."

Ginger picked up one of the children, rocking them gently. "Maybe they're hungry. What do we shape-shifters do to feed the little ones?" she questioned, looking to Amy for answers. Amy just shrugged, unsure herself.

"Where is Hildegard? She might have some of the answers," Ginger suggested, proceeding to sneak around the castle, making sure to walk in unlit rooms in search of Hildegard. When she couldn't find her, she sighed and returned to Amy's room.

"I could not find her, Amy. But do you have any bottles to give to them?" Ginger asked. Amy looked around, finding nothing except for her own personal bottle.

"That might not be such a good idea, Ginger. Not sure if their little tummies can handle such a heavy beverage," Amy said.

Ginger sighed. "What about from you, Amy? Like any new mother." The suggestion made Amy tense up, a mix of anger and fear crossing her face. "Okay, never mind. I'm just trying to help you with these kids," Ginger quickly backtracked, noticing Amy's reaction. Amy took a moment to calm her mind and body.

"I'll wait in the dining quarter to see if Hildegard will return. I'll be back, Amy," Ginger said, leaving Amy with her children. The crying started to dim down somewhat, but Ginger's suggestion lingered in Amy's mind, making her ponder the right course of action.

As Ginger sat in her pajamas, robe, and slippers in the dining quarter, she tapped the table with her long well-manicured nails, waiting for Hildegard to show up. After what felt like over an hour, Hildegard finally came into the castle from the garage side and entered the dining quarter, carrying two big bags of items and groceries. Ginger tracked her movements, waiting for Hildegard to notice her. "Oh, Ginger," Hildegard gasped, finally acknowledging her presence. "What are you doing here in the middle of the afternoon?" Ginger let out a sigh of relief and frustration.

"Amy needs to feed her kids. Do you have any experience on what she should do? Since our mother died in childbirth, she might not have the answers to some of these questions," Ginger stated.

Hildegard furrowed her brows, confused. "What mothers normally do when they feed their kids, Ginger. Has Amy tried that?" Hildegard asked. Ginger just shrugged. "Is Amy awake now?"

Ginger nodded. "Perhaps you should come up to her room and see if she needs any help from you," Ginger said, waiting for Hildegard to remove her jacket and purse before accompanying her to Amy's room. Upon reaching the door, which was closed, Ginger knocked. "I am indisposed," Amy responded from inside.

Hildegard nodded, understanding. "It seems like she has figured out what she needs to do," Hildegard observed. "Please excuse me, Ginger. I need to put away all these items that require cooling."

After Hildegard walked away, Ginger knocked on Amy's door. "Not now," Amy said. "I am busy."

"Okay," Ginger said , deciding to leave. "I shall return to my room." She walked back to her room, quickly falling asleep. After Amy finished feeding her kids, she felt too weak to do anything else and soon fell asleep as well, leaving the children on the other side of her bed.

Once dusk fell and midnight arrived, Amy woke up, not realizing that her children were on her bed until she turned on the night lamp. "Oh, dears," Amy said softly. "I am so sorry for leaving you three in that position. I must have been extremely tired." Then there came a knock on the door. "Yes?" Amy asked. Ginger entered the room.

"How are you feeling, Amy?" Ginger asked, approaching the bed slowly. "Were you able to feed your children and take care of them?" Amy nodded. "Good to hear. That must have been stressful, but I am glad you managed to take care of your kids."

Amy nodded and smiled. "Being a new parent is not easy from what I have seen. I wonder how Aaron and Emma must have felt, seeing two infant daughters brought to them by a non-human father," Amy mused, chuckling. "That must have been really stressful for them." Ginger couldn't help but giggle at that remark.

"I wonder how they are doing right now? It must have also been hard to say your goodbyes to them when you were there, wasn't it?" Ginger asked. Amy nodded, trying to control her emotions. "It was," Amy murmured softly. Ginger nodded.

"I am sure they are both doing well," Ginger said. "They did have a good handle on raising us, even though we should have been around our own kind." Amy nodded in agreement. "Your children are going to be okay, Amy. At least you don't have to deal with humans and adoptions, or any other stressful things like that." Amy nodded once again.

"Plus , I have a family and a sister who can help me through these moments as well," Amy added, smiling. "Say, I might have chosen names for my two daughters, Ginger." Amy's statement caught Ginger's attention, her eyes lighting up with excitement. "Remember the story about our ancestor, Maggie? I shall name my firstborn Gabrielle Amelia Ambrose. For the second daughter, I would name her Maggie Rose Ambrose," Amy declared. Ginger chuckled in joy, delighted by the names Amy had chosen.

"Beautiful names, Amy," Ginger exclaimed. "I would have never considered those names at all, but they do have a nice flow to them. What about the boy, Amy?" Amy pondered for a moment, realizing there were angelic names in her family's male lineage, like Gabriel and Daniel. "How about Nathaniel for the boy?" Amy suggested.

Ginger thought about it for a moment and nodded. "That's a strong name for a son," she said. "What about his middle name?" Amy reflected on a second name, wanting to honor a man she had respected for many years. "Nathaniel Alistair Ambrose," she decided. Ginger smiled and nodded in approval. "He would be quite honored to hear that, Amy," she said. "He truly was an amazing father figure to you during your travels, and he loved you as if you were his own."

# Changes

Weeks passed, and the children grew steadily. Each baby was able to crawl quickly from one wall to the other, and Amy found foods they could gum down. Hildegard frequently visited the grocery store, stocking up on various meats and a bounty of fruits and vegetables to keep the children healthy.

On a quiet, dark evening, Amy brought Gabrielle into the dining quarter, where Gabriel, Daniel, Vladimir, and Adrian were gathered. They all welcomed her with cheers, and Amy smiled, proud to show off her quickly growing children. "Say, Father," Amy addressed Gabriel, who looked up attentively. "At what age should I start giving her some of our blood supply?" she inquired.

Gabriel thought about it for a moment and shrugged. "I'm not too certain about the exact age, but judging by the looks of your children, it might be quite soon. Has Hildegard mentioned anything to you, Amy?"

"Well," Amy began, uncertainly, "she's told me some basic things, but we haven't really discussed the whole blood-drinking part." Gabriel nodded in understanding.

"You might try a teaspoon sometime soon, but it seems like the basic foods you are giving them are doing well. And Amy," Gabriel added with a smile, "I am honored that you named your firstborn daughter after me."

Amy smiled warmly and nodded. "She deserves to have a beautiful strong name in this world, Father," she responded before excusing herself to step outside. Holding Gabrielle, fully clothed in baby attire, Amy pointed out various objects—the sky, trees, stars, and the moon—while walking around the courtyard, staying as close to the castle as possible. Suddenly, she felt a chilling sensation down her spine and froze, fear gripping her as Gabrielle began to squirm. Amy rushed back inside the castle, closing the door swiftly behind her.

Gabriel quickly rose to his feet, placing his hands on Amy's shoulders. "Is he back, Amy?" he asked urgently. Amy shrugged, glancing behind her to find no one there. "Perhaps I overreacted out there, but it seemed a bit cooler than normal, Father," she admitted. Gabriel nodded, urging Amy away from the door before locking it securely. "Perhaps we should wait until they are young adults before you take them outside again, Amy." Amy nodded and walked back toward the staircase.

Larry and Caleb observed from a distance, their eyes filled with hunger. "What's the plan, Larry?" Caleb inquired, glancing over at Larry who maintained his focus on the castle from the trees. Swiftly, Larry jumped off the branch, landing deftly on his feet in the grass, and waited for Caleb to follow suit.

"We shall wait for the opportune moment, Caleb," Larry said. "Right now, they are all quite guarded. I tried communicating with Amy in her dream, but she is resistant to me at the moment. What's that term called when the victim falls for the perpetrator?" Larry asked.

Caleb pondered for a moment before snapping his fingers. "Stockholm Syndrome," he answered.

"Yes, Caleb, that's right," Larry confirmed. "These girls are completely oblivious to what a monster their father is. How can they still respect him after all the horrible things he's done to them when they were infants? It baffles me," Larry expressed, shaking his head in disbelief.

Caleb shrugged. "I feel the same way, and Katrina does too, especially when it comes to Gabriel." Back at the house owned by Larry, Katrina sat in the living room, still clad in the same robe she wore at Gabriel's castle, but now filled with anger. When Larry and Caleb returned, she looked up expectantly.

"Find out anything new, boys?" Katrina asked, her blonde wavy hair, dark eyes, and marble complexion standing out against her pink fuzzy robe. Both of them shook their heads.

"They know something is up," Larry said. "We will wait for the opportune moment to strike. Amy's children are a vulnerable factor."

Katrina hissed in disdain. "I've really come to hate them," she confessed. "Especially Arabella. I thought she would remain a deceased ghost while Gabriel and I reigned as king and queen of the family. But deep down, I believe he only used me." Larry and Caleb nodded in agreement. "So, where are the others that you created, Larry? Are they scouting for new members, or did you get rid of them?" Katrina asked.

Larry thought about it for a moment and realized how two of his members were not told to make spectacles around humans. "Hmm," Larry murmured, "I'm not quite sure at the moment. But if anything happens, we can just report Gabriel and his family to the humans, right?" Katrina laughed at Larry's suggestion, and Caleb joined in, albeit hesitantly.

"That sounds like a fun idea, Larry," Katrina said , her laughter continuing. Caleb, however, stopped laughing, deep in thought. He had no issues with Amy or Ginger and hated the thought of anything happening to them.

Noticing Caleb's serious expression, Larry asked, "You alright, Caleb?" Caleb nodded, forcing himself to relax. "Okay, good," Larry responded, exchanging a glance with Katrina before heading to his bedroom. Katrina remained seated on the couch, and Caleb sat down beside her.

"How do you feel about all this, Katrina?" Caleb inquired, genuinely interested. Katrina simply shrugged, lost in her thoughts.

"The pain I once felt from Gabriel's betrayal doesn't hurt as much now, but my anger and frustration are still lingering. I do agree with Larry; they all should realize what Gabriel has done.

Hypothetically, even if what he did was justified—his lust, killing Larry's fiancé, leaving him in the woods, finding me, turning me into this, and promising me the world—it all turned out to be a big lie and deception," Katrina said.

Caleb nodded, aligning himself with Katrina's perspective on the conflict. "I was also turned in hopes of becoming the male heir to Gabriel's fortune and legacy," Caleb shared. Katrina glanced over, curious.

"How old are you, anyway, Caleb?" Katrina asked, analyzing Caleb's appearance.

"About twenty-two years old," Caleb said. "Back in my time, I could have started a family. Now, I am somewhat younger than Larry by a few hundred years, but not by much. What about you, Katrina?"

Katrina chuckled. "My, my, asking a lady about her age, are we?" she teased. Caleb shrugged, looking down at his shoes. "I was thirty-seven, or at least I was," Katrina revealed. "I was promised a wonderful life with Gabriel, but it turned into a nightmare." Caleb nodded, and they both sat together in the house that Larry had somehow acquired.

Back at the castle, Amy returned to her other children, finding Arabella, Amelia, and Ginger gathered around the kids. "I have to tell you all something strange that happened while I was outside with Gabrielle," Amy started, her tone serious. The three women looked up at her with concern. "I felt a cold sensation like never before in the courtyard," Amy explained. Arabella glanced at Amy's windows, noting the darkness outside.

"Maybe it would be best if you and the children stay indoors for a while. And if you do want to go outside, perhaps take some of us with you so you're not alone," Arabella said.

Amy nodded and walked over to Nathaniel, then to Maggie, admiring how beautiful they looked in their fuzzy onesies. She couldn't help but think of the baby pictures that Emma had saved for her and Ginger, remembering how cozy and warm they looked in their blankets and clothes. Arabella watched Amy, concern in her eyes, until Amy looked up at her. "What?" Amy asked. Arabella kept her focus on Amy, smiling softly. "Yes? Are you reading my thoughts, Mother?" Amy asked. Arabella shook her head.

"These children take so much after you, Amy. There's a lot of you in them. It just made me wish I could have been there for you and your sister," Arabella shared, her voice soft.

Amy felt a wave of sadness hearing those words. "I wish that too, mother. I really wish you were the one to bathe us, feed us, change us, cuddle with us, read to us, and walk around with us," Amy admitted. "Just because I didn't get the proper welcome or a standard life doesn't mean my children should suffer the same. They deserve a steady and relaxed home." Arabella smiled, touched by Amy's words.

"And they shall," Arabella said. Ginger looked between Amy and Arabella.

"Plus, these kids will have many of us to guide, teach, and support them." Amy smiled and thought of all the wonderful plans she has for her kids. How much fun it was going to be with three younglings.

Hildegard came into the room with some extra towels and blankets. "When you're ready, I can help you bathe the little ones," she offered. Amy gratefully handed Maggie to Hildegard, who then left the room. Smiling again, Amy turned to her mother, aunt, and sister.

"Thank you all for helping me with everything. My life may have started off quite chaotic, but I feel that it's heading toward a happy ending." Arabella, Amelia, and Ginger all smiled and nodded.

"We're happy to have such a wonderful young woman as yourself in this family," Amelia said. "So strong and confident in many ways."

"She takes after me with those traits," Arabella teased. "I mean, the apple does not fall far from the tree, does it?" Ginger smirked at that comment. "Of course, you do too, Ginger. You are quite strong yourself." Amy's mind drifted to a memory of her and Ginger at the airport in Oregon because of Caleb, remembering how Ginger had been her greatest support and comfort when they had to return to Romania.

"She is a wonderful sister," Amy said. "One of my best friends and greatest support in this world."

While the women enjoyed their time together in Amy's room, Gabriel walked from his study to the living quarters and found his brothers there. "Congratulations, grandfather," Lucien teased. "How are they all doing? It sounds like they are quite happy." Gabriel smiled.

"I was not expecting this to go so smoothly," Gabriel admitted quietly. "I really didn't think Amy was going to survive, and then I would have given Arabella another reason to hate me, not to mention Ginger." He rubbed his hands together nervously.

Daniel chuckled at Gabriel's nervousness. "Yet survived it all, Gabriel." Gabriel looked over at Daniel and shook his head.

"I know that, brother, but I couldn't be there for Amy. Births aren't timed, and we could have lost more of our group members. It all made me feel quite uncertain. Perhaps Alarick was right. Maybe I should surrender to Larry and admit my wrongdoings, even though it was purely accidental. I can't help but think about what else could have gone wrong yesterday. I may be the patriarch and creator of all, but I also feel quite vulnerable in many ways. You see those movies where the bad guys lose and the good guys recover from their losses or battle scars. Logan lost his daughter, and it made me realize that Amy could have died while I was being attacked by Logan and his group. It was quite scary," Gabriel said.

Lucien, Daniel, Vladimir, and Adrian exchanged glances. "What are the plans regarding this Larry kid anyway," Adrian asked. "We could easily track him down and end him right now. We are five strong men with hundreds of years of learning and experiences from the past. We could probably go over to him now and, then instead of him killing you, it would be the opposite?"

Gabriel thought about it. "Before we delve into that matter, brothers, has any of you seen Katrina lately? I don't recall seeing her at our fight yesterday and haven't seen her since," he inquired. The others exchanged looks. "Katrina would never leave the castle or get lost out there," Gabriel added. Lucien stood up, followed by the others.

"I wonder if Larry might have had her killed, or if she has run away to escape this conflict. Should I ask Amelia or Arabella?" Lucien pondered.

Gabriel considered Arabella's possible involvement. "I shall speak to the women myself, brothers. Please excuse me." Gabriel walked over to Amy's room, where he found two clean babies and Hildegard bathing Nathaniel. "Arabella, may I have a word with you?" Gabriel asked. Arabella got to her feet and walked out of Amy's room, letting Gabriel follow her.

"Yes, Gabriel? Is everything okay?" Arabella asked before she closed the door behind them.

"Where is Katrina?" Gabriel asked directly. Arabella glared at him before rolling her eyes. "Well? What have you done with her, Arabella?" Gabriel pressed, his tone sharp. Arabella took a step back and crossed her arms.

"I send her away, Gabriel. I did not want her here any longer. I am your queen, your first wife, the mother of Ginger and Amy, and the grandmother of Amy's children."

Gabriel's anger flared. "Where, Arabella? Why didn't you come to talk to me before sending her away? I might have considered a safer place for her," he retorted angrily. Arabella's anger mirrored his.

"I told her to leave, along with Caleb. They do not belong in this family, Gabriel. Just because you kept me as a ghost and supposedly remarried or found another woman as your temporary queen does not mean they have any right to stay here."

Gabriel stepped back, taking a moment to sigh. "What you did was incredibly dangerous, do you realize that?" he snapped. "Where are they going to live, Arabella? How will they survive without making spectacles of our kind, risking humans tracking us down?"

Arabella sighed. "Why do you think I take matters into my own hands right now, Gabriel? For many years, I have felt our communication has been lacking. I share my grievances, and it feels like you disregard my feelings, ideas, and plans. You've done so much behind my back, never once asking for my perspective. So, how dare you interrogate me about this? We'll deal with the Katrina and Caleb situation if and when it arises. But as long as they're hidden somewhere, it's more their problem than ours," Arabella retorted sharply.

Gabriel bared his teeth but quickly walked past Arabella down the staircase. "This is not over, Arabella!" he yelled. "I will find those two and bring them back here. Brothers, I need your help. Do whatever it takes, but we are going to find Katrina and Caleb," Gabriel declared. The men all rose to their feet and exited the castle through the front door.

"Gabriel, what is going on?" Lucien asked. Gabriel picked up the pace to a jog, and the rest followed suit. "We need to find them. Use all your senses—smell, hearing, any sensation you can," Gabriel instructed sternly. Eventually, they all stopped and closed their eyes, tuning into the surrounding environment. They could hear distant laughter, birds chirping, airplanes overhead, and then… Gabriel's eyes snapped open. "They're closer than we realized, brothers. Follow me."

Gabriel led his brothers through the park for about half an hour until they reached the other side, where a small house stood, its curtains drawn closed. Peering through, Gabriel used his sharp vision and noticed silhouettes inside. Katrina was sitting on a sofa, and Caleb might be there too. But then he saw something alarming— Larry was standing in front of her.

"Brothers," Gabriel whispered. "They might have joined forces with Larry, or he could be holding them hostage."

Lucien, Vladimir, Daniel, and Adrian crouched down, poised as if ready to pounce, yet they remained still. "What's our move, brothers?" Gabriel asked, his voice low. "I have no desire for another battle, but we need to understand what's happening in there."

Just then, there was a rustling sound from behind them. Gabriel growled, Lucien growled, and the others bared their teeth. Alistair emerged from behind a shrub, his hands raised in a gesture of surrender.

"Forgive me, Gabriel. I should have announced my presence more gracefully. But there's something you need to know," Alistair said softly.

Gabriel's expression softened slightly. "What is it, Alistair?" he inquired.

Alistair crouched down to their level. "Katrina and Caleb have sided with Larry in his fight against you and your family. My son Joshua—you met him a few weeks ago—has visions," Alistair explained. Gabriel nodded in acknowledgment. "I must stress, you cannot surrender and let yourself be killed. What happened was an accident, as you've said. I know you would never intentionally harm Larry's fiancée or compromise him in any way. The same goes for Arabella's death," Alistair asserted.

Gabriel's mind eased further. "Is there anything else, Alistair?" he asked.

Alistair shook his head. "No, that's all."

"Alright. We might need to speak with Joshua again, if that's alright with you," Gabriel said. Alistair nodded in agreement. "Good. You and your family are welcome back at the castle, and this time you'll have better accommodations since the others have returned home, I believe."

Alistair shrugged. "You've always been generous to us, Gabriel. We've cared about you and your family from the beginning."

Gabriel nodded, a smile gracing his lips. "And I appreciate your loyalty, Alistair. My home is always open to you and your family, especially now that Bryan has become the primary caregiver for my grandchildren."

Alistair smirked at that.

"He is a wonderful young man, Alistair. I see where you have really put effort into turning your boys into such caring and protective men toward my daughters," Gabriel said.

Gabriel took one last glance behind him and got to his feet to walk back to the castle. Once they all arrived at the front door, Hildegard opened the door for them to let them all in. Gabriel walked over to the living quarters and saw that it was two o'clock in the morning. "Where are your boys and Darcia right now, Alistair?" Gabriel asked.

"They're back at the motel room. Larry won't bother us there anymore. His intimidation tactics won't keep us from returning. In fact, we managed to get our deposit and the money back for the supposed vandalism, straight from the manager who owns the place," Alistair responded, chuckling at the memory.

Gabriel smiled. you'll all consider moving into the castle. You deserve a better and safer place to live," he stated. "When they're ready, feel free to call or send a message using those electronic devices humans use," Gabriel said.

Alistair laughed, appreciating Gabriel's attempt to stay current. Gabriel, shaking his head at Alistair's teasing, walked over to the cooler to grab a fresh, unopened bottle of blood and six glasses for himself, his brothers, and Alistair.

"After our moment together, I must have another word with Arabella, my sweet and faithful wife," Gabriel said, his voice dripping with sarcasm. He downed three full glasses of blood before placing his glass in the sink. Making his way toward the basement area of his living quarters, he found Arabella brushing her hair in front of her vanity. "Arabella, we need to talk. Outside of my frustration with you for excluding me from your decisions, it appears Larry has recruited both Caleb and Katrina to his side. What are your thoughts on that, wife?" Gabriel inquired, his voice stern. "I'm not pleased, Arabella. I had hoped to decide their fate on my own terms, or rather, our terms, which meant... dealing with them personally," he added, his voice tense as he clasped his hands together.

Arabella remained silent for a moment before furrowing her brows. "What's gotten into you, Gabriel? Why this sudden change in tone? You created this mess, and now you're playing the victim? Were you planning to dispose of them to avoid further problems, drama, or conflict? Is that it? That's always been your way, Gabriel— running from your problems, ignoring the warning signs," she accused, her voice rising as she aggressively brushed her hair. "You know what? I'm done with the drama. I want you to leave me alone about Katrina and Caleb. I may not harbor anger or cruelty inside me, Gabriel, but that doesn't mean my patience is limitless," she declared, stopping her brushing abruptly, placing the brush on her vanity, and rising to her feet.

Gabriel crossed his arms. "Should I just give up and let you all go?" Gabriel asked. "Should I just let myself get killed off for all of my accidental actions?" Arabella shook her head.

"I am not that cruel, Gabriel. I also care about Amy and Ginger's well-being. If they love you, I think you should be there for them, accept your mistakes, and come to terms with the fact that not many hold you in high regard anymore. Our dynamics have definitely changed. I protected you from Larry and his friends because I do respect the remorse you feel for our children, but after what you did to me, Gabriel, I can no longer say I love you. I'm relieved that the worst is behind us, but once this conflict with Larry is resolved, I have no intention of staying here with you. You can call Katrina back or find another woman to stand by your side, but I'm done. The girls can decide what they want for themselves, but I need you to understand how deeply you've hurt me. If roles were reversed, I would never have done what you did. If you had died, I would have tried to bring you back as soon as possible. I would never have given up our daughters to some humans, possibly compromising their lives as well. There's never a good time for anything, so I'll help you resolve this issue with Larry, but our relationship as it was can never be restored. I'm sorry for that, but at the same time, I'm not," Arabella expressed.

Tears welled up in Gabriel's eyes. "I am truly sorry, Arabella. I had no idea who or what I was in this life. I never meant to harm your family. I never intended for any of this to happen. I'm done apologizing for my accidental actions, but I can't bear to lose you. My love for you was real and true. I never meant to cause any harm. I love you, Arabella. I still want to fight for us, for our relationship. Please, Arabella, just please," Gabriel pleaded, wiping away his tears. "Don't give up on me. I want to be a better father to Amy and Ginger. I want to be there for them. I have given them so much love and support. I truly believed that giving them up would provide them with a chance to be with a supportive family, away from a chaotic and frustrated environment. I am not a monster or a criminal, Arabella. I never intentionally caused problems for our family. I care deeply about everyone— you, Amelia, my brothers, Dante, Alarick, Kristjan, everyone in this family," Gabriel asserted, his voice raised, his anger boiling to the surface. "Please, I can't lose you. I need you in my life, for our children's sake as well."

Arabella sighed and shook her head. "I want to love you, Gabriel. I wished for everything to be sunshine and rainbows for all of us. I wished for a loving and fun family. But why should I stay with you after everything you've done? We are immortal, which means we don't die of old age and get to watch our children live their lives. Instead, we're stuck in this endless cycle of problems, Gabriel," Arabella stated, her voice laden with sorrow. "We've been fighting non-stop ever since I returned from the dead. Being stuck in limbo as a ghost was no fun, watching you make all the decisions about our children, getting Amy pregnant, and barely giving them any freedom until now," Arabella expressed, sounding exhausted. "I'm just worn out from having to witness all of this."

Gabriel sighed and sat down on his side of the bed. "Is there any chance, any spark within you, that might consider giving me a second chance once this whole drama with Larry is over?" he asked. Arabella closed her eyes and exhaled deeply. "If I didn't care about you, Arabella, I wouldn't be here trying to fix the situation. I'd be upstairs, drinking the night away with my brothers, waiting for Larry to attack us. I love you, Arabella. My wedding vows were sincere. My smiles, every time I saw you, were genuine. Everything I have done and felt for you is real."

Arabella looked over at him, beginning to feel a sense of relief from hearing Gabriel's words. "I'd like to keep that option open, Gabriel. For now, I'll help with this situation with Larry, but I want to see how I feel afterwards before I give you a definitive answer," she said. Gabriel nodded, understandingly.

"I appreciate your honesty, Arabella, and that you're keeping options open," he responded. Arabella remained silent, noticing that it was four o'clock in the morning on Gabriel's watch.

"I think I shall call it an early night," she said, getting under her covers. Gabriel went back up to the main floor and noticed that everyone had left, and all the glasses were neatly placed in the dishwasher. He heard Hildegard closing all the curtains, so he decided to check on Amy in her room.

# A New Plan

Amy heard a knock on her door. "Come in," she said. Gabriel entered her room and saw her getting under the covers. "Father, what a surprise," she remarked. "Shouldn't you be heading to bed as well?" Gabriel nodded.

"I just wanted to see how you're doing, Amy," he said sincerely. "I realized I wasn't there to see you bring your young ones into the world because of the fight with Larry. I am sorry for that."

Amy smiled and shrugged it off. "Thanks, Father, but honestly, it wasn't a big deal," she reassured him. "The pain was actually quite bearable. I don't know why so many women in movies scream hysterically," she added with a chuckle. "I should get some rest though. Feeding the little ones takes a lot out of me."

Gabriel nodded, understandingly, before leaning down to give her a gentle kiss on the forehead. "I want to be there for you, Amy, and for your children," he said softly, before leaving her room, closing the door gently behind him. He made his way back to his sleeping quarters, finding Arabella fast asleep. He walked quietly over to the room where Katrina was sleeping, noticing she had left all her possessions there. He considered talking to her about why she had left, but he was wary, remembering the last time he tried talking to Larry alone. Deciding to put that thought away for now, he got into bed, wrapping his arm around Arabella, seeking some solace in her presence.

The next evening, Gabriel awoke to find Arabella missing from their bed. He glanced around, noticing only her nightgown draped over a chair as a trace of her presence. Rising from the bed, he donned his regular suit, the same one he wore every day, and ascended to the main floor of the castle. There, he encountered Lucien and Daniel, also stirring from their quarters, but there was no sign of Arabella.

"Have you seen my wife?" Gabriel inquired, his tone laced with concern. Lucien and Daniel, however, could only offer shakes of their heads in response. "Normally, she's a rather deep sleeper."

Undeterred, Gabriel continued his search, heading first to the living quarters, only to find them deserted. Next, he made his way to the dining area, where he found Vladimir and Adrian in the process of opening a bottle of something, presumably alcoholic.

"You guys have not seen Arabella down here, have you?" Gabriel asked, his voice tinged with desperation. The two men shook their heads, prompting Gabriel to think aloud, "Perhaps she's up with her daughters. That might be a good place to look."

With that, he made his way to the staircase, only to find both Amy and Ginger's doors firmly shut. His concern for Arabella deepening, Gabriel was left to ponder her whereabouts. Had she decided to leave without a word? And if so, why?

His train of thought was abruptly interrupted as he descended back to the main floor and caught sight of Amelia and Arabella together, walking toward the dining quarter. A wave of relief washed over him, momentarily eclipsing his concern.

"Arabella, where have you been? I thought you'd left me," he exclaimed, rushing to her side. Arabella, however, merely offered him a look of frustration, which Gabriel chose to ignore as he followed her into the dining quarter.

His brothers were gathered there, drinks in hand, seemingly unphased by the situation. "Oh, right. Arabella is with Amelia," Daniel noted, prompting Gabriel to nod in agreement. "Good, you've found them."

Allowing himself a moment to collect his thoughts, Gabriel then reached for an empty glass, his mind already shifting to the tasks at hand. "What are the plans for today?" he asked the room at large. "Are Darcia and Alistair still enjoying their own rooms in this castle? Has anyone heard from them?"

Almost as if on cue, Alistair and Darcia descended the staircase, joining the gathering. "Our beds are quite comfortable," Alistair remarked, his tone appreciative. "The boys are thrilled to have their own rooms here. We can't thank you enough, Gabriel."

Feeling a semblance of normalcy returning, Gabriel seized the moment to address the group. "Family," he began, his tone serious, "I feel the need to have another talk with Larry. And this time, I think it would be best if we all went together, as a united front. Last time it did not end so well between him and I."

Alistair, however, was quick to express his reservations. "That sounds like a bad idea, Gabriel," he said, shaking his head. "If we all show up together, it'll look like we're gearing up for another round with him. Maybe it would be better if Darcia and I approached him. Though, considering we chased after him not too long ago, he might not be all that receptive to a visit from us, either."

Before any further plans could be discussed, the sound of the front door chime interrupted, drawing everyone's attention. The chime sounded again, prompting Hildegard to check who it was. The room fell silent, all eyes on her as she returned.

"Master Gabriel," Hildegard announced, her tone formal, "There is a young man by the name of Caleb here to see you."

Gabriel furrowed his brow, taken aback by the unexpected visitor. He turned to the others, allowing them to follow if they wished, as he made his way to the front door.

"Should I send him away?" Hildegard asked, her hand poised to open the door.

Gabriel shook his head, signaling for her to stand aside. "Leave him to me, Hildegard. I can handle this," he assured her, his tone resolute as he prepared to confront the young man named Caleb.

"Caleb, where have you been? Why are you outside the castle and not in your own quarters?" Gabriel demanded, his tone sharp. Caleb's face bore expressions of guilt and shame. "Surely, you'd want to come in, right?" Gabriel pressed, but Caleb shook his head.

"Not really," Caleb said. "I have found other quarters outside of this castle, Gabriel. Your wife had me sent away because of the whole pregnancy thing with Amy. I never felt like I was part of this family to begin with."

Gabriel sighed, his arms folding across his chest as his demeanor softened slightly. "Then why are you here, Caleb?" he asked, his tone now soothing. "This doesn't have anything to do with Larry, does it?" Gabriel prodded further, but Caleb avoided eye contact, remaining silent. "Or does it?" Gabriel pressed, but still, Caleb remained silent.

"Your silence is provocative, Caleb. You can either speak up or leave. But whatever your reason for being here, I'm not buying it, and I'm not convinced by anything you have to offer. This is your final warning. Are you here on Larry's behalf?" Gabriel's tone sharpened once again.

Caleb nodded, yet he maintained his silence. Gabriel cleared his throat, attempting a different approach. "For what purpose, son?" he asked, subtly using a term of endearment to manipulate the situation. "What can Larry offer you that I have failed to provide? Whatever Larry has told you — that I'm a monster, that my actions were deliberately malicious out of lust — you should know, back then, I was probably around a hundred and thirty years old. To us, that's quite young. I had no idea who my parents were, no knowledge of who raised me or shaped me into who I am today. I simply woke up one morning, never to physically change again, growing stronger with each taste of raw flesh and blood."

Gabriel paused, his voice softening. "Caleb, if Larry is hoping to meet with me again, I insist on having at least two family members present. The last time we tried talking, he was resistant to my words and nearly had me killed. Plus, many in my own family dislike, if not hate me, for the fight we had with Larry and his friends. I'm not sure where you were at the time, but whatever plans I had for you, they were genuine. I wanted a son, someone beautiful, sensitive, and strong, with so much potential to offer this family."

He continued, earnestly, "I don't kill people for fun or sport like some of our kind might. My source comes from blood banks and hospitals, and it's only on very rare occasions that I might find someone. But those people, they are usually the louts and savages of this world."

Gabriel paused, giving Caleb space to absorb his words. "Whatever Larry has done to you, I would never manipulate or harm you in any way, dear Caleb. If you want to return home to us, all I need to hear is why you decided to leave and what you think associating with a creature like Larry could possibly mean for you," Gabriel concluded, taking a step back. "I want you to speak your mind, so I don't have to guess what you're thinking."

Caleb cleared his throat, seemingly preparing to respond, his expression contemplative as he sighed.

"I loved the idea of being someone's son, Gabriel. I relished the thought of being strong and powerful, and living in such a luxurious castle. However, I didn't appreciate being coerced into giving up some of my bodily fluids for your pregnancy plan with your daughter. I bear no ill will towards Amy or Ginger, but I felt pressured and pushed into that situation. I could never be a father since I never had a father to love and take care of me. Where would I gain the experience, Gabriel?" Caleb questioned.

Gabriel shook his head, his expression solemn. "I would have been more than willing to assist you as my own son, Caleb. I genuinely believed that I could turn you into a wonderful supporter for our family. I've spent many years observing humans, watching them on overcast days, noting how loving the fathers were to their children, regardless of gender. I never had a father figure either, Caleb, but I relied on my intuition to learn how to be a father," Gabriel said.

Caleb scoffed, his tone filled with sarcasm. "Right. Like giving up your daughters to some mortal family, then wanting them back, having me turned in the process, and then almost attacking Amy when you first saw her. And still keeping Ginger human. Yes, those were some stellar fatherly moments, Gabriel. I'll be sure to remember that for when I have children of my own, which will be,"

Caleb paused, counting on his fingers mockingly, "hm, never," he snapped. "I came here only to see how things were going. I have no intention of harming you or your children, Gabriel. But I also didn't appreciate being turned against my will and being fed false hopes and lies all my life. I'm leaving now, Gabriel, and I have no interest in ever being part of this family again."

After Caleb turned around and left, Gabriel closed the door and locked it. "Well, that was that, I guess," Gabriel murmured to himself before returning to the dining hall, sitting down at the head of the table with his glass and half-full bottle of blood. The rest of the family joined him, and they sat in silence. Alistair and Darcia held each other's hands. Shortly after, Amy and Ginger descended the stairs to join them in the dining quarter.

"Good evening, family members," Amy greeted, walking in first, followed by Ginger. The family exchanged greetings. "In case you're all wondering, my children are still asleep, so I'll wait until they wake up to feed them. Hildegard helped me prepare the milk bottles, which makes it easier for us all," Amy shared.

"Good to hear," Gabriel said. "And in case you're all wondering as well, especially after the situation with Caleb, I've lost interest in meeting with Larry. If he wants to see us, he can come to us. I've tried talking to both Larry and Caleb and have apologized in different ways for my past actions. But if they choose to remain angry, there's not much more I can do," Gabriel declared. "For now, I wish to spend time with my daughters," he added, a hint of warmth in his voice.

Ginger smiled, brought over a chair from another room, and sat next to Gabriel, taking his left hand in hers. "I would love that, Father. I'd enjoy listening to more of your stories and spending the evening and nights with you," she said. Gabriel smiled in return, kissed the top of Ginger's hand, and looked down the table to see Amy pouring herself a glass.

"What about you, Amy? Would you like to spend some time with your old man? I'm eager to hear more about your children and how they're developing and growing," Gabriel said. Amy smiled warmly and chuckled.

"I would like that, Father," Amy said, taking a seat next to Daniel. She then asked with a hint of curiosity, "Would this technically be the first time you spend time with a baby? Since Ginger and I were probably just lying on a table near our deceased mother when we were infants," Amy added. Arabella, sensing the need to intervene, placed her right hand on Amy's shoulder, capturing her attention, and shook her head slightly.

"Your father is interested in your children, Amy. Some extra bonding time with him, especially for you three, would be beneficial. He should know what it's like to hold a baby," Arabella suggested gently.

Amelia cleared her throat and raised her left hand. "He has held a baby before," she murmured. "He held Ginger, and I held Amy when they were just born." Gabriel smiled at the memory, the mixed emotions of that moment flooding back—the horror of the situation, yet the profound beauty of his newborn daughters. Amy relaxed her body, realizing her mistake. "Sorry about that," she said, her tone softening. "Perhaps my hormones are affecting my mood."

Arabella smiled, giving Amy's shoulder a reassuring pat before she reached for her own glass of blood. "The past is the past. We need to focus on the future of our bloodline. Since I was human, and we grew like any other humans, I'm curious about what it was like being a baby shapeshifter. Do you grow quickly, or is the process slow?" she asked, directing the question to the room.

Daniel raised his left hand, interjecting with a question of his own. "Um, if I'm not mistaken, weren't we all humans once, except for Gabriel? How else would this whole shapeshifting thing work? And Gabriel, you were probably once human too. So how did you become a shapeshifter at birth, and where are your parents?" Daniel asked, his voice rising with curiosity.

Caught off guard, Gabriel quickly stood up and left the castle, heading into the courtyard. The moon hung heavily in the sky, almost full. He walked deeper into the woods, finding himself at the same park where previous drama had unfolded. "Nothing makes sense," Gabriel whispered to himself, his voice laden with confusion. He walked further into the park and sat down on a park bench. Alistair, following him, found Gabriel sitting there.

"Good evening, Gabriel," Alistair said. "Things can get quite heated in this family, can't they?"

Gabriel smiled and gestured to the space next to him on the bench. "Please join me, Alistair," he said. "May I ask what brings you out here?" Alistair took a seat beside Gabriel.

"Joshua has seen something troubling, Gabriel. We're not certain it will come to pass, but it seems Caleb might be in danger." Gabriel furrowed his brow, focusing intently on Alistair. "He might try to deceive Larry in some way, but Joshua can give you the full details."

Gabriel cleared his throat. "Where is your son, Alistair? I would like to hear more about his vision," he said. "Is he nearby, or back at the castle?" In response, Alistair put his fingers to his mouth and whistled loudly. Moments later, Darcia and her sons appeared behind them. "Joshua, please share your vision with Gabriel," Alistair requested.

Meanwhile, back at the castle, Amy sensed her babies crying through their special connection. She hurried upstairs with several bottles of her milk, followed by Hildegard and Ginger. Each woman took a bottle and began to feed the infants, who appeared to be growing unusually quickly. "Huh," Amy observed, "They've grown quite a bit. Is this how it was for us, Ginger?"

Ginger smiled and shrugged. "Perhaps. But remember, we stopped growing once we reached our teenage years, so it's hard to say for sure," she replied. Hildegard, looking at Gabrielle, remarked on how adorable she looked feeding from the bottle. "Such precious angels," she cooed.

Arabella entered the room, her eyes lighting up as she saw the three women feeding her grandchildren. "May I?" she asked Hildegard. Without hesitation, Hildegard handed Gabrielle to Arabella, allowing her to take her place on the bed.

Arabella finished feeding Gabrielle, who let out a loud burp followed by a hiccup. "Would you like me to change her, milady?" Hildegard offered. Arabella, however, smiled warmly.

"Or I could do it. I never had the chance to care for my own babies, and I wouldn't mind at all taking care of these little ones," Arabella said. "Where do you normally do it?"

Hildegard pointed towards the bathroom area, where there was a tall changing table, a trashcan, and drawers filled with all the necessary baby care supplies. She then left Arabella to care for her granddaughter.

Back downstairs, Gabriel re-entered the castle with Alistair and his family. "So Larry wants to meet with us again, is that correct? I think this time we should go to his place, leaving the more vulnerable members of our group behind. Perhaps Bryan and Raymond could stay behind to take care of the women?" Gabriel suggested, looking to Alistair's other sons, who remained silent. "Nothing bad will happen. I just hope to talk things through with Larry and sort everything out. I'd rather Arabella not know our plans. Perhaps it's best to keep this a secret," he added.

Darcia's eyes filled with tears as she shook her head. "There has to be another way, Gabriel. You're too important to this family," she whimpered. Alistair wrapped an arm around Darcia, holding her close. "If anything were to happen to you, it would spell the end for all of us," he agreed.

Gabriel felt a surge of sadness but quickly suppressed his emotions.

"If we're going to deal with this, we should let the chips fall where they may and see if Joshua's vision holds true," Gabriel said decisively. "Sons, I trust you to take care of my daughters. Xavier, Silas, Joshua, you three will come with us."

Darcia, teary-eyed, wiped her face with her fingertips and took a deep breath. "I really don't like this," she murmured under her breath. Gabriel placed his right hand on her shoulder, waiting for her to meet his gaze.

"It will be okay, no matter what happens," Gabriel reassured her, channeling his powers to help calm her nerves. "Repeat after me, Darcia. It will all be okay."

Darcia's eyes turned black as she echoed, "It will all be okay." Gabriel prompted her to repeat the phrase twice more before he removed his hand, her eyes returning to their original color.

"Okay. Let us meet this creature and get this over with," Gabriel declared, taking the lead toward the house where Larry was staying with Katrina. Meanwhile, Bryan and Raymond entered the castle, joining Hildegard, Arabella, Amy, and Ginger in the room with the babies. Bryan, overcome with emotion, quickly wiped away his tears.

"Bryan, are you okay?" Amy asked, setting Nathaniel on the floor next to Ginger before walking over to embrace him.

"What happened?" she pressed, sensing his distress.

Suddenly, a loud scream, unmistakably Gabriel's, filled the air, sounding like another battle had erupted. Arabella and Ginger rushed out of the castle, leaving Amy, Bryan, and Raymond behind.

"What's happening?" Amy cried out. "Bryan, what happened?"

Bryan, speechless and overcome with tears, couldn't respond.

"Bryan!" Amy screamed. "Was that my father?"

Raymond, choked up with sadness, could only shake his head.

"Raymond, please, say something."

Raymond covered his eyes with his hands, shaking his head in disbelief. "Your father... he decided to give himself up, Amy," he choked out, breaking down. "Joshua had a vision. Gabriel was overwhelmed with remorse for his past actions. He mentioned Alarick, Dante, and Logan had convinced him to let Larry take him down."

The babies' cries intensified as Amy's world came crashing down. She covered her mouth, sobbing uncontrollably. "No," she whispered between sobs. "No! My father can't be dead. He's an immortal shape-shifter. It's not possible!"

Rushing out of the castle, she made her way toward the chaos and found her father lying motionless on his stomach, a blade through his body. Amy stood there, frozen in shock.

Alistair rushed to her side, enveloping her in his arms as she struggled to reach her father. "Amy," Alistair whispered, his voice filled with sorrow. "I am so sorry. It was inevitable."

Amy, tear-stricken and with red, bloodshot eyes, pushed herself out of Alistair's grasp. "Where is he?" she sobbed. "Where is Larry?"

Alistair, his expression filled with remorse, could only watch as Amy broke down. Ginger, equally shocked, stood frozen, unable to respond.

"My father can't be dead," Amy repeated, her voice a mix of disbelief and despair. "He is the most powerful shape-shifter in our entire family. How could a dagger end him like that? It doesn't make any sense!"

"Darcia, please take the girls and Arabella back to the castle. Joshua, Xavier, Silas, and I will attend to the body." Darcia nudged Amy and Ginger toward the castle, and Arabella slowly followed them. Alistair carefully picked up Gabriel's body, with the dagger still inside, and they all walked over to a place suitable for burial. The three boys began to dig a rectangular grave. Once done, Alistair removed the blade from Gabriel's body and gently laid him inside.

By the time the four women arrived at the house, Lucien, Daniel, Adrian, and Vladimir were there to greet them, enveloping Amy and Ginger in warm hugs. "Please, come in," Lucien invited. "Daniel, would you mind getting the girls some blood? You all must be famished by now." Amy felt dead inside, her body heavy as she almost collapsed to the floor. Arabella quickly caught her, holding her close. "It will all be okay, Amy," she whispered soothingly. Amy, unresponsive, allowed Daniel to hand her a glass of blood. "Please, drink some, my child," Arabella urged gently. Amy took the glass mindlessly but found herself unable to drink.

"How does someone like him even die from that, Mother? He survived so many years of hunters, so how does a dagger end him like that?" Amy's voice was filled with disbelief as she questioned her mother, tears welling up once again. Arabella simply held her tighter in response. At the table, Ginger sat with a shocked and unresponsive expression on her face.

"I can't believe it," she whispered, more to herself than anyone else. "He was too strong for everyone. Even when Amy and I took him down that one time, he probably let us win." Amelia approached from behind, wrapping her arms around Ginger in a comforting embrace.

"Take all the time you need, my sweet princesses," she whispered gently. "Take all the time you need." Ginger allowed herself to be held, closing her eyes as she soaked in the comfort. "Where are Alistair and the boys anyway?" she finally asked, her voice barely audible.

Amelia exchanged a glance with Arabella before responding, "They're probably still outside, giving your father a proper burial, I guess."

# The Transition

Back at Larry's house, the mood was entirely different. Larry had opened up a bottle of blood, handing glasses to both Katrina and Caleb. "To finishing a wonderful project! We did it, you two; the king is finally dead," he exclaimed, raising his glass for a toast. Caleb, however, looked numb and sickly, avoiding eye contact with Larry.

"What seems to be the problem, Caleb? Your creator is finally gone forever," Larry prodded, clearly not understanding Caleb's distress.

"I need the bathroom; where is it again in this place?" Caleb asked, standing up abruptly.

Larry, looking confused, pointed down the hallway. "Please excuse me," Caleb said, quickly making his way to the bathroom.

Once inside, he transformed himself back into Gabriel, quickly grabbing Caleb's cellular device. Deciding to call Alistair, he needed confirmation. "Did it work, Alistair? Is Caleb the one being buried right now?"

"Yes," Alistair said.

Just then, a knock came at the bathroom door. "Caleb, are you all right in there?" Larry asked, concern lacing his voice.

Using his ability to mimic voices, Gabriel responded in Caleb's tone, "Just fine, Larry. Just washing off the dirt and filth from that Gabriel creature," he said, trying to sound casual.

Larry laughed from the other side of the door. "Gabriel creature, that's hilarious. Whenever you're ready, we have more celebrating to do."

Waiting until Larry was out of earshot, Gabriel, still pretending to be Caleb, whispered urgently into the phone, "Alistair, how am I going to get out of this situation?"

Alistair paused for a moment before responding, giving Gabriel his undivided attention and consideration. "We just have to remain low-key for a while. I shall see what my family can do in this situation."

"Please hurry, Alistair. I am not so certain I can handle being in this disgusting place any longer." After they both hung up their devices, Gabriel shape-shifted back to Caleb and adjusted his jacket. "This is disgusting," Gabriel murmured before he walked out of the bathroom and back to the living quarters. When Gabriel returned as Caleb, Larry handed him a full glass of blood. "I may have taken some of that Gabriel's blood source personally, which should taste much sweeter like drinking wine with royalty," Larry said.

Gabriel raised his glass with Larry and Katrina and they all gulped down the glass. Gabriel whimpered and coughed. "You're right to do so, Caleb," Larry said.

"His blood is actually not that good. Like sewage water." Gabriel nodded and sat down on the sofa.

"So, Larry," Gabriel said shakily, trying to control his emotions. "What are your plans for the family? Are you considering Gabriel's daughters and wife, or are we done?"

Larry scoffed and sat down in a chair adjacent to the sofa. "We are done for now, but then again, I do have this hunger for wanting to go after his brothers, Lucien and Daniel was it? Then there were the other two," Larry said. Katrina then cleared his throat.

"Adrian and Vladimir," Katrina said. Larry smiled and nodded.

"That's it," Larry said. "I think I may have called one of them prince charming. Perhaps that was a weak statement to make of me, because of how none of them could ever be a prince. They are just bottom feeders of this world."

Katrina chuckled and looked over at Gabriel as Caleb. "What would you like to do, Caleb?" Katrina asked. Gabriel looked over at Katrina with sadness and guilt.

"I think we have had enough for now, friends," Gabriel said. "I think we should call it a day and perhaps even a life. Those other members are not worth our time. We managed to get the big guy out of the picture. Perhaps I might do some traveling or something along the lines of that."

Larry scrunched his brow in confusion. "My dear friend, we have only just begun. Would you not like to take over that castle someday or even help me become king or leader of all shape-shifters?" Larry asked. Gabriel smiled, realizing he had to control his anger and sarcasm from Larry.

"Perhaps someday, Larry," Gabriel said. "For now, I am quite satisfied with how we were able to kill Gabriel Ambrose, forever," Gabriel said before he started laughing manically, which caused Katrina and Larry to join him.

Gabriel faced down and dried off some of his tears. "Do not worry, friends, these are tears of joy from finally taking down the worst monster in our life," Gabriel said. Larry smiled, patted Gabriel on his shoulder, and raised his glass again.

"To Gabriel, never existing anymore," Larry said. Katrina tapped her glass against his, and they both gulped down the blood.

Back at the castle, Amy was in her room, controlling her fear, anger, sadness, and nausea from seeing the body of her father on the ground. Arabella came into her room and sat down next to her, placing her arm around Amy, holding her close.

"How are you doing, Amy?" Arabella asked in a soothing tone. "I just saw Ginger who is still in shock."

Amy remained silent, her gaze fixed in front of her while her children slept peacefully in a large crib, each swaddled in their own blanket. Arabella, noticing Amy's withdrawn state, tried to offer her support. "I will be here for you whenever you need me, Amy. If you want me to stay with you while you sleep, I can," she said gently.

Amy offered no response, her mind lost in thought. After a moment, Arabella rose to her feet. "I shall go to sleep now, my sweet jewel. Please feel free to wake me when you need to."

Left alone, Amy sat on her bed, her thoughts overwhelming her. "I just cannot believe it," she whispered to herself. "How could a shapeshifter who has lived for a thousand years suddenly die? He was attacked by Larry a while back but managed to recover. Something is not right here, and I need to find out what's going on." With that, she stood up and made her way to Ginger's room.

Gently knocking on the door, Amy heard groaning from inside. She opened the door to find the room in darkness, and Ginger, who was almost asleep, sat up at her arrival.

"Amy, what are you doing? Are you okay?" Ginger asked.

Amy walked over to Ginger's bed, closing the door behind her, and used her night vision to navigate in the dark. "Don't you find it weird that our father just suddenly died like this, Ginger? It makes no sense to me. He had already had a big fight with Larry before. So how did Larry overpower our father this time? He was with Alistair, Darcia, and Joshua, I believe," Amy said, her gaze now fixed on Ginger's night table.

"And Silas and Xavier," Ginger said. "Yes, I remember. You don't think Alistair and Darcia had anything to do with this, do you, Amy?" she asked cautiously.

Amy looked at Ginger, confusion in her eyes. "Them? Why would they send our father to his death like that, Gin?" she asked, her voice rising slightly. "You don't really think that, do you?" Before Ginger could respond, Amy's thoughts shifted. "Huh. Where are Bryan and Raymond anyway?" she asked.

"Probably in their own rooms, on the next floor?" Ginger suggested, her voice tired.

Amy quickly got to her feet. "Please try to sleep tonight Amy. I feel quite worn out from it all. Tomorrow I will have more energy," Ginger said.

Amy left the room, closing the door behind her, and walked up to the second floor. The hallway was quiet, all the doors closed. She approached Bryan's room and gently tapped on the door. It opened almost immediately, revealing Bryan standing fully clothed, his arms open in a gesture of comfort.

"I am so sorry about your loss, Amy. Gabriel was a wonderful leader and patriarch of our family. I actually started to care for him when he finally named me son," Bryan said.

Amy remained still and glared at him. "Want to come inside?" Bryan said as he gestured for Amy to enter.

Amy walked in, but her gaze never wavered. "Did you and your family have anything to do with my father's death, Bryan?" she snapped, anger flashing in her eyes.

Bryan looked taken aback, confusion and fear evident in his expression. "What? Amy, what is going on? I wasn't part of the outing yesterday. What would make you think that our family would side with Larry and have your father killed off?" Bryan asked, his voice filled with disbelief. Amy shook her head, her mind racing with questions and suspicions.

"My father does not die off that easily, Bryan. He's already had two fights with Larry, and he's the strongest shapeshifter in our family. He wouldn't just die off so quickly, especially with a dagger in his body like that. What is really going on, Bryan?"

Bryan remembered Alistair's instruction not to disclose Gabriel's plan to anyone, and he shook his head, feigning ignorance. "I have no idea what you're talking about, Amy. Larry must have somehow overpowered Gabriel. We did… or I mean, my brothers and parents went with Gabriel to confront Katrina, and that's where it all went wrong."

"I do not believe you, Bryan. I really can't trust you any longer based on your actions. My father is the most powerful shapeshifter, and he just can't die like that. Please, Bryan, for the sake of me and your children…" Amy began, but Bryan quickly interrupted her.

"What children, Amy?" Bryan snapped. "They are not mine; they belong to Caleb." Amy felt a surge of pain, similar to the agony she experienced when she saw Gabriel on the ground.

"Bryan," Amy whimpered. "It does not make sense to me to have to accept that my father is dead."

Bryan sighed and hugged Amy closely. "I understand that, Amy. If you want, I could stay with you while you sleep?" Bryan said. Amy felt her stance weakening by Bryan's caring words and shook her head. "Here, let me at least take you back to your room," Bryan said before he escorted Amy to her room and watched her get into her bed. He saw the light shining through her curtains and remembered how he had met Amy for the first time during an overcast day.

Amy kept her gaze on Bryan as he stood at the end of her bed. He looked back at her and approached the edge. "Would you like me to stay here with you, or would you like to be left alone for the morning?" Amy shook her head.

"I will be okay, Bryan. Perhaps I should get my rest and find out tomorrow evening what the plans are," Amy whispered. Bryan leaned down, kissed the top of her head, and left her room. Amy couldn't shake the feeling that he was being insincere and lying to her. There was no way her father could have died like that. Perhaps there was a conspiracy involving Alistair and Darcia. Maybe they were not as trustworthy as they seemed. Maybe Adrian showing up in his wolf form was a protective measure when everyone else was hunting, and she twisted her ankle.

Unable to calm her mind, Amy tossed and turned in bed, her thoughts going in circles. She recalled a time when Alistair had helped her relax at the airport one evening when she was craving blood. How did he manage to do that? Amy's confusion and frustration grew as time slowly passed.

Meanwhile, Alistair was at a motel room with Caleb, who he had tied up to a chair. "I'm sorry your life turned out this way, Caleb, but there was no other way for us to get closer to Larry, especially with Gabriel being a shapeshifter. I have no grievances toward you, but this was the only option we had at the moment."

Caleb glared at Alistair. "Just wait till Larry finds out that Gabriel is not me. He will surely have Gabriel's head on a silver platter before you know it," Caleb snapped. "And now that you have me as your hostage, I might want yours next to his, as well."

Alistair sighed and shook his head. "Soon this whole problem will be over and you will become a free man again, Caleb. Gabriel does feel remorse for what he had done to you and to Larry, but since the conflict cannot be resolved with plain talking, we all feel the need to have to defend ourselves from any form of harm."

Caleb scoffed and looked away from Alistair. "How are you even going to be feeding us, Alistair? Are you not getting hungry?" Caleb asked with a smirk on his face. "If you leave me alone in this situation, I might escape, so how will you be able to track me down?"

Alistair sighed. "I have some blood packs in our washroom in case you are hungry, Caleb. I have no need to leave this place for a while. I am also keeping you here, so you do not have to get brainwashed by Larry anymore," Alistair said. "It will all be over very soon."

Caleb growled and hissed at Alistair. "What if I get cold? Are you going to get me a blanket from your room?"

Alistair chuckled at Caleb's sarcasm and smiled. "Whatever you want, Caleb," Alistair said. Despite himself, Caleb chuckled as well. Alistair left the room and came back, draping a blanket around Caleb's shoulders while his hands remained tied behind his back. "Nice and cozy," Caleb commented.

"I do have a question for you, Alistair," Caleb said. "How do you feel about being turned from human to shape-shifter? Were you born like this, or were you turned by Gabriel?"

Alistair regarded Caleb thoughtfully. "I was turned, and then I met my wife, Darcia. I was so in love with her, and I was thrilled to spend eternity with her," he said. Caleb kept his focus on Alistair. "It was a bit of an adjustment, but in the end, I felt that it was the right choice."

"Why, Alistair?" Caleb asked. "Why would that have been the right choice? How were you and Darcia able to have kids, anyway?"

Alistair smiled. "Just like how Amy got pregnant. Our kind uses special serums and formulas to make it possible for the women to conceive. Lovemaking doesn't work with our bodies, but with a special potion that was created for us, we were able to have children."

"Huh," Caleb said. "I never would've thought I'd become what I am, especially after being lied to by Gabriel. He never mentioned anything about Amy or Ginger to me. I was promised a princely life once I was turned by him. Then, later on, Amy and Ginger show up, not to mention Arabella," he said, his voice rising. Alistair quickly put a finger to his lips, signaling Caleb to be quiet.

"Remember, these walls are quite thin, Caleb. It's best to keep your voice down," Alistair whispered. "I know all that, but murder and death won't solve your problems. Even if Gabriel had died hours ago, you'd still be the shapeshifter you are now. This isn't like those movies where you kill the head vampire or the main creature, and the spell is broken. We are who we are, and you have to live with it, or you can choose to end your own life," Alistair said, his voice growing louder, causing Caleb to giggle.

"Hypocrite," Caleb murmured. Anger bubbled at the edge of Alistair's tongue and fingers, but he quickly calmed himself. "Do you feel better now?" Caleb asked, a teasing tone in his voice. Alistair swiftly walked to another bedroom, locked the door, and sat on the edge of the bed. Meanwhile, Caleb remained seated in his chair, staring at the wall.

Back at Larry's house, Gabriel lay in Caleb's sleeping quarters, akin to a closet room with a small bed. He lay on his side, pondering how to take down Larry without alarming Katrina. Bringing Alistair back here would only complicate matters, not to mention the chaos if Caleb were to show up. Overwhelmed and weakened by the low-quality blood he had consumed, Gabriel couldn't sleep and tried to relax as best he could. He considered reaching out to Amy, but decided against it, knowing Amy and Ginger couldn't be let in on the plan to take down Larry, Katrina, and Caleb.

As dusk approached, Larry sat in his chair, biting his thumbnail, deep in thought about his next move. Katrina slowly woke up, while Gabriel remained awake, lost in thought about Arabella and her potential worry. "Caleb, are you okay?" Larry called through the closed door. Gabriel morphed back into Caleb's form and opened the door. "You've been acting strange lately. Everything alright?"

Gabriel nodded and smiled, maintaining his Caleb disguise. "Of course. I just needed some extra sleep after how exhausting last night was," he explained. Larry seemed satisfied with the answer.

"Okay. We have some fresh blood here if you need breakfast," Larry offered. Gabriel nodded and followed him into the living room where Katrina, clad in Larry's robe, sat on the sofa sipping from her own glass. Larry handed Gabriel a glass filled with blood.

"What kind of blood is this, Larry?" Gabriel asked. Larry smiled and looked over at Katrina who giggled. "It tastes very sweet."

"I might have followed some girls while you two were asleep and gotten some fresh source from them," Larry confessed. Gabriel's eyes narrowed in suspicion. "What?" Larry asked, noticing the change in Gabriel's demeanor.

"It just tastes different than the blood we had yesterday, that is all," Gabriel said, quickly recovering and downing the glass, though it made him wince. Larry chuckled and retreated back to his chair.

"So, here's what I'm thinking, dear family," Larry began. "Maybe we should pay our dear Amy a visit and see how her children are doing." Anger flared within Gabriel. "What now?" Larry snapped, growing impatient. "Caleb, you're showing a lot of aggression right now. I can tell something's bothering you. If you want to leave and find your own place, I won't stop you, but otherwise, you need to calm down."

Gabriel composed himself, trying to shift the conversation. "Let's forget about Amy and the others, Larry. We should be focusing on creating our own legacy and finding our own family," he suggested.

Larry thought about it for a moment. "What about the other members who attacked Gabriel the first time you met him?"

Larry's face darkened as he recalled that moment, and his subsequent anger towards Gabriel. "Were you there? I don't remember you being there. Maybe you can fill me in later," Larry said. "Those members are long gone. When Alistair and Darcia chased my friends and me away, they abandoned me. I felt completely betrayed," he admitted, his voice laced with bitterness.

Gabriel offered Larry a sympathetic nod. "Maybe there are other ways to find new coven members. Where did you say you saw those kids?" he asked, steering the conversation away from sensitive territory.

Larry seemed to recall plucking them off the streets, from alleyways and parks. "But, Larry, Amy has no value to you. Think about it. She's just a little girl who wants to live her life. She's never harmed you or us," Gabriel urged.

Larry scoffed, his tone skeptical. "Why do you sound so protective of Amy, Caleb? Do you like her? It sounds like you have a crush on that little girl," he taunted.

Gabriel couldn't suppress a low growl, but Larry quickly backpedaled. "I'm just kidding, Caleb. Goodness, you're not an evening person, are you? If you have feelings for Amy, I won't stand in your way. Though, you might have some competition with that Bryan guy," he said, a hint of provocation still in his voice.

Gabriel took a moment to think. He knew he couldn't contact Alistair or Amy directly, but Bryan could be a good ally since he had already told him not to mention the plan to Amy. He forced a smile onto his face.

"Bryan," Gabriel chuckled, playing along. "He's not important to me, but maybe I will want to see him sometime."

Larry laughed, though his expression quickly turned serious. "Huh, that might not be such a bad idea," he mused. "You did go to that castle a while back, didn't you, Caleb?"

Gabriel, recalling Caleb's visit to the castle, nodded. "Yes. I was there. I saw Gabriel, his brothers, and Arabella," he said.

Larry nodded approvingly. "Whenever you're ready, Caleb, don't let me stop you from pursuing your plans. Sometimes I think your plans are better and wiser than mine," he admitted.

Gabriel couldn't help but laugh hysterically at this, which caused Larry to hiss in annoyance. "Stop that," he snapped. "I was giving you a compliment, not an invitation to laugh at me."

Gabriel smiled and nodded. "I understand," Gabriel said. "Okay, I think I shall visit that castle, right now," Gabriel said as Caleb.

"Perhaps you can take Katrina with you for backup," Larry suggested.

Katrina looked excited at the prospect, but Gabriel shook his head. "I'd like to try going alone again, if you both don't mind. Sometimes approaching them one at a time seems less aggressive."

Larry nodded. "Okay. Perhaps one hour would be long enough for you to talk to Bryan," Larry said.

Gabriel nodded and left the house. He walked two blocks before transforming back into his original self and approaching the castle. He knocked on the door and waited. When Hildegard opened it, her face showed pure shock. Gabriel quickly placed his hand over her mouth and pulled her outside.

Gabriel discreetly explained the entire situation to Hildegard in a hushed whisper, and she responded with a nod, her eyes wide with fear. "I am supposed to be dead. I am entangled in this dreadful game with Larry, but I need to speak with Bryan," Gabriel murmured urgently. Hildegard, still nodding, made her way to the second floor.

As Gabriel waited outside, he saw Amy's silhouette through the walls, where she just remained in her bed motionless. "Soon, my child, we will all be together, again," Gabriel whispered to himself.

Bryan soon emerged from the castle, closing the door carefully behind him. "How are you holding up, Gabriel? Alistair and Joshua briefed me on the plan. It's really tough, having to keep another secret from the girls again," he whispered.

"I know, Bryan," Gabriel responded quietly, his tone laced with seriousness. "It's a burden for me as well. We need to be extremely cautious, luring Larry out when he's at his most vulnerable before launching a full-scale attack."

Bryan nodded in agreement. "But why are you back right now? Amy thinks we were all conspiring against you, Gabriel," he whispered, his voice filled with concern. "She's furious with us and is wondering about Alistair's whereabouts. Darcia hasn't seen Amy yet, but Amy is under the impression that we sent you to your death. How did you manage to pull off that illusion?"

Gabriel gave a slight nod. "Once this is all over, I will explain everything to everyone. We will sit together, enjoy a family meal, and put all of this behind us. That's a promise," he whispered. "I just wanted to check in, see how everyone was holding up. Larry thinks I'm here to threaten you, in the guise of Caleb. I'm glad we're all in this together, even though I never wanted us to face such a nightmare again," Gabriel whispered.

# Betrayal

Back at Larry's house, in his Caleb form, Gabriel found Katrina on the sofa, polishing her nails. "Larry stepped out, just so you know," she informed him nonchalantly.

Gabriel looked at her, his expression filled with confusion. "May I ask where he has gone?" he asked.

Katrina shrugged.

"I hope he didn't go to the castle. He said he wanted to give them a break from all this drama. With Gabriel gone, why would he need to pursue things further?"

Katrina's gaze shifted to Gabriel, now filled with confusion. "Why do you even care, Caleb?" she asked.

Just then, the front door opened and Larry came inside. Gabriel walked over to him.

"What is going on? I just had to run a little errand, nothing else," Larry said as he walked past Gabriel in the form of Caleb. "By the way, Caleb, were you able to see Bryan? What information were you able to get from him?"

Gabriel thought about his answer. "He's devastated by Gabriel's death. He'd rather leave Romania forever, never to return with his family. Amy is also deeply distressed and upset about losing her father," Gabriel said, keeping his tone steady.

Larry scoffed, shaking his head in disbelief. "How pathetic. The little girl gets abandoned by her father, and now she mourns his passing," he said sarcastically. "Maybe her knight in shining armor should pay her a visit, offer his condolences? What do you think, Caleb? Or maybe we should both go?"

Gabriel struggled to conceal his anger and emotions. Larry, noticing the change in his demeanor, voiced his confusion. "I don't always understand you, Caleb. You're quite pathetic with your reaction to Gabriel's death. You should be happy that the monster is out of your life, giving you the chance to live a happy future with us or with a new woman. Why do you even care about Gabriel or Amy?" Larry asked.

Gabriel, feeling his anger boiling just below the surface, managed to remain calm. "I just don't like conflicts, Larry. Now that Gabriel is gone, I think I'll find myself another woman and start a new family," Gabriel said. Larry, unexpectedly, felt a twinge of guilt inside.

"Forgive me, Caleb. I have no intention of sending you away," Larry murmured. Gabriel sighed, preparing to leave, but turned around to address Larry one last time. "Okay. For now, I think we should rest and relax. I have no intention of causing any more problems for Amy. I have no feelings for her or my children, but I think we should just take it easy for now. I've known humans who feel a mix of fatigue and relief once their goal has been achieved. Have you ever felt that, Larry?" Gabriel asked.

Larry sighed and nodded. "I get what you mean, Caleb. There is a part of me, though, my carnivorous side, that wants to pursue this further. Perhaps Amy and her children are not worth my time," Larry said. Gabriel nodded and smiled. "Would you care for another drink, Caleb?" Larry asked. Gabriel nodded.

"Why not," Gabriel said with a chuckle. Larry joined in the laughter, and they both walked over to Katrina, who was carefully blowing on her freshly polished nails. Gabriel handed Katrina a full glass of blood, and the three of them clinked glasses before gulping down their drinks.

Back at the castle, Amy was in her room with her three children when she heard a knock on her bedroom door. "Yes?" Amy responded. The door opened, and Darcia entered, closing the door behind her before approaching Amy. "Darcia, what brings you here?" Amy asked. Darcia glanced outside of Amy's room, noting the darkness.

"How are your little ones?" Darcia asked. Amy smiled and shrugged.

"Little night creatures. Sometimes they like to wake me up for no reason. Probably just to cuddle with me," Amy said with a chuckle. Darcia smiled.

"I heard that Bryan was with you. How are you feeling about your father's passing, Amy?" Darcia asked gently. A wave of sadness washed over Amy.

"It still hurts, Darcia. I just can't understand why my father would just... leave us like that," Amy whispered.

Darcia pulled Amy into a comforting embrace. "I know, my sweet Amy. If you need anything, I'm here for you," Darcia said before releasing Amy from her grasp.

"Thank you," Amy whispered. She then cleared her throat and sighed. "By the way, where is Alistair? I haven't seen him since my father's death, and he said he would give my father a proper burial. Shouldn't we inform the other coven members of my father's passing?"

Darcia remained still. "What?" Amy asked. "Why are you suddenly so quiet? What is going on, Darcia? Why does it feel like you all are lying to me, again?" Darcia swallowed hard and quickly left Amy's room. Amy decided to follow, but Darcia had already disappeared. "I know something isn't right," Amy snapped, feeling tears welling up inside her. "My father is still alive. I just know it."

Arabella heard Amy and walked up the stairs to Amy's room, wrapping her arms around her. "I understand how heartbreaking this all must be, Amy, but this will all soon pass," Arabella whispered. Amy pushed Arabella away and growled, "Why are you all lying to me? Where is my father?" Amy screamed. "Father! Gabriel, where are you?" Amy screamed again. Ginger came running out of her room, her eyes wide with fear.

"Amy, what is going on? Are you having a nightmare?" Ginger asked. Amy glared at Ginger and hissed. Ginger crouched defensively and said, "What are you doing? I came because I heard you screaming for our father," Ginger said. "He is dead. I am trying to cope with his loss, as well," Ginger snapped. Amy's body relaxed as she took a step back, looking at both Arabella and Ginger. "I know he is still alive. An immortal creature does not just die," Amy whimpered. She then walked back into her room and gently closed the door, mindful of her children who were awake and crying.

"Forgive me, my little ones," Amy whispered. "Mommy is here, and I need to remain calm," Amy said soothingly before picking up Gabrielle, then Maggie, and finally Nathaniel, feeding each of them a bottle of her milk. She then lay down in her own bed, her thoughts filled with her father and her desperate need for him to be with her right now.

*Father,* Amy thought, *I need you to know how much I wish for you to be here with me. You can't be dead.* Back at Larry's house, Gabriel heard Amy's voice and whispered her name. Larry suddenly glanced at Gabriel in his Caleb form, confused. *Please don't be dead, Father. You are so strong and important to me. Please come back home.* Gabriel felt tears building in his eyes. Joshua's plan no longer felt right. He needed to find a way back to his castle and permanently eliminate Larry.

*Gabriel* Alistair thought. *You cannot come back right now. I am here with Caleb at our motel room and we must wait for Larry to be at his most vulnerable moment before we go in for a full attack. Apparently, Caleb has been talking about how Larry has been running errands to create another army again. Try to hang in there for a bit longer.* Alistair said. Gabriel felt like his stomach was turning with guilt, shame, and fatigue. How was this plan even going to work out in the end? Nothing made sense to Gabriel anymore.

Gabriel as Caleb relaxed his body. Larry kept his focus on Caleb for some time. "Perhaps I should be more honest about what I was planning," Larry said to Gabriel and Katrina. Gabriel looked over at Larry. "I am building ourselves a bigger and stronger army, so we can take down the rest of those monsters. I realized this, Caleb and Katrina," Larry said. "I cannot let those other ones survive. It is important that they all realize and understand how every action does not go unnoticed. Gabriel is dead, but then again, I am still this monstrous creature."

Gabriel sighed and shook his head. "Since when did you have this planned, Larry? I thought I had persuaded you to not go any further," Gabriel said. "Where is your army anyway?"

Larry smiled enigmatically. "Here and there. I've been collecting blood from various victims out there," he chuckled. "Look, Caleb, I understand your desire to take a break, and you should do what you need to do. However, I feel compelled to seek justice for myself. You haven't turned mortal either, Caleb. Doesn't that bother you? The fact that Gabriel transferred some of his essence into Amy seems quite disrespectful to you, doesn't it?" Larry probed.

Gabriel remained silent, deep in thought.

"Unless you enjoy having that Bryan creature raise your children, Caleb, you do whatever you feel is right for now, but I feel the need to let them know how disgusted and hurt I am by their whole existence. The fact that Gabriel still has no idea how he came to be. Obviously, that is a lie. He must have been human before he even met me. Back at the tavern, there was something dark about him. I just remember how he took me in and let me cook those rabbits, but there was always something dark and uncertain about being around him that made me feel weird," Larry said.

Gabriel looked up at Larry, intrigued. "In what way exactly? What did Gabriel do that made you feel uncomfortable?" Gabriel asked. Larry glanced back at Gabriel, his tone laced with sarcasm. "Have you met Gabriel? A large, dark-haired creature who has hunted numerous humans, including my beloved fiancée, Viviana. Her blonde hair flowed like the waves of the ocean," Larry reminisced, lost in the memory of her beauty.

Gabriel remembered how she had tasted. Like strawberries and fresh air. He couldn't help but smile at Larry's description of Viviana, until he noticed Larry glaring at him with anger. "You find this amusing, Caleb?" Larry snapped. Gabriel quickly adopted a solemn expression and lowered his head. "No, Larry. I was just relieved to know that Gabriel is gone, that's why I smiled," Gabriel explained.

Larry shook his head in anger and left the house abruptly. Gabriel turned to Katrina, noticing her discomfort. "How do you feel about Gabriel's death, Katrina?" he asked. Katrina scoffed and shook her head.

"I'm certainly not a warmonger, but Gabriel deceived me, Caleb. He promised me a life of luxury and a bright future, but in reality, I felt like nothing more than his pawn. I usually kept out of his affairs, which always struck me as odd. His close relationship with Arabella made me jealous, and he was well aware of that," Katrina confessed.

Gabriel nodded, attentively listening to Katrina's grievances. "I mean, I feel sorry for him now that he's gone, considering his daughters must be quite uneasy about their position and future," Katrina expressed. Gabriel cleared his throat, raising his hand to speak.

"I have no personal regard for Gabriel myself, Katrina, and I understand your feelings towards him. I'm not trying to take his side at all, but when I was in the castle, promised to be his son, I was told that he did care about us in his own way," Gabriel shared. "Gabriel may not have been the exemplary patriarch of the family, but he did make an effort with his family—giving up his daughters and keeping his wife close…" he added.

Katrina's eyes focused intently on Caleb as he spoke. "How do you know all of this information, Caleb?" she asked sharply. "Did Gabriel personally tell you all of this, or did you find it out from someone else?"

Gabriel chuckled, looking away. "Come on, Katrina. Of course, he told me those stories. How else would he have earned my trust?" he responded nervously.

Katrina chuckled, turning her gaze outside the window. "Are you done with your story, Caleb? It's kind of boring me," she remarked.

Gabriel nodded. "I am done." Just then, Larry reentered the house. "Okay," he announced. "I was able to recruit ten more members. Including the recruits from the past two nights, that gives us fifteen new members of various ages, all willing to fight for me." Gabriel smiled and nodded.

"Good," Gabriel said. "Just ensure you know what you're getting yourself into, Larry. Lucien, Daniel, Adrian, and Vladimir are not as weak as they may seem," he teased. Larry glared at Gabriel, appearing as Caleb, and was about to strike him.

"Larry," Katrina snapped. "No violence in this house. I will not allow any more violence between the three of us."

Larry sighed, taking two steps back. "I am getting tired of being ridiculed by Caleb. Nothing more. I'm doing everything I can to make this situation work out for the best for us. I know the other members are strong, but so am I. I may have a couple of hundred years less experience than Gabriel, but I am still strong enough to handle any battle."

Katrina rolled her eyes. "Understood, Larry, but we also need to work together. I don't want any more of us leaving or getting abandoned because of family drama. We need to stick together," she insisted. Larry nodded and grabbed two packs of blood from the refrigerator, pouring three full glasses for Gabriel, Katrina, and himself.

"Forgive me, Caleb," Larry murmured. "I can sometimes have a short fuse and it is not one of my best traits."

Gabriel nodded. "I forgive you, Larry," he replied, his voice laced with a hint of sarcasm. Larry chose to ignore the comment, quickly gulping down his glass and leaning back in his chair. "Perhaps I am feeling a bit of that depression you were talking about, Caleb. About how people can feel somewhat down after completing their biggest task?" Gabriel looked down at his glass, then up at Larry, contemplating his next move.

"Right," Gabriel said. "I would not blame you for having mixed feelings, Larry. I can understand where you're coming from. Perhaps we could have a boys' night out sometime? Just the two of us?" Gabriel suggested.

Larry thought about it for a moment and smiled. "I would like to deepen our bond, Caleb. Sometimes I feel I don't fully know you, and I believe we could truly get to know each other on a deeper level," Larry responded. Gabriel smiled and nodded. "How about tomorrow evening?" he proposed.

"I accept, Gabriel," Larry said. "Tomorrow, you can also meet the new members. Perhaps there might be a girl for you to live your life with forever?"

Gabriel started to feel frustrated. "Perhaps another time for that. I just want it to be the two of us," he insisted. "I'm looking forward to some brotherly bonding. I hope you can share more about why you despise Gabriel. I've got a vague idea, but I'm eager to hear more of your stories. How about we enjoy a nice evening together, maybe with a few victims?"

Katrina chuckled. "Oh, come on, Larry. Enjoy some quality male bonding with Caleb. I am sure you two will have a nice evening together." Larry smiled and nodded.

"Okay. A fun evening for just the two of us," Larry said. Gabriel looked down at his watch. "Are you going to sleep, Caleb?" Larry asked. Gabriel nodded.

"Yes, dawn is only a few hours away, and my body needs rest," Gabriel replied before finishing his glass.

Gabriel rose to his feet. "I shall wish you both a good night's sleep," he said before retreating to his room and drawing the curtains closed. He lay down on Caleb's bed, staring at the ceiling. *Alistair, I may have a plan. Larry and I are going to have some male bonding time tomorrow. That's when I'll make him vulnerable and strike. What do you think?* Gabriel sent his thoughts out, but there was only silence. *Alistair?*

*Gabriel,* Alistair finally responded. *Do your best to lure him into the wilderness. I will be waiting there with Bryan, Raymond, Joshua, Xavier, and Silas. Darcia is at the motel, keeping Caleb company.*

*Okay. I shall lure the victim into the woods and have you all wait there. Katrina has been acting weird around me, Alistair. I'm doing my best to act like Caleb, even though it's quite difficult.*

*We shall keep in contact, Gabriel. Just bring him out and go back into your original form.* Alistair thought. *Sleep well, dear friend.*

Comforted by Alistair's words, Gabriel closed his eyes and found himself sleeping more peacefully than before, dreaming of being back at the castle, watching Amy's children grow up. Their eyes, their bodies—everything about them was perfect.

Dusk arrived quickly, and Gabriel got to his feet, transforming back into Caleb's form before leaving the room. Larry was in the living quarters, seemingly not having moved for a while. "Caleb," he greeted. "How did you sleep?"

"Quite well, Larry. And you?" Gabriel asked in the form of Caleb. "Are you okay?"

Larry looked up at Gabriel with a grin. "Very well. I've been thinking about going somewhere open for the evening. Maybe a park we've never visited before?"

Gabriel sighed. "Perhaps we can just see where the night takes us, Larry. However, I think it would be nice to be in a more secluded area." Larry maintained his gaze on Gabriel as he spoke, "There is this beautiful hike I was interested in back when I was a new fledgling in this world. It's filled with pine trees and offers a stunning view of a lake," Gabriel explained. Larry smiled in response, "What do you think?"

Just then, Katrina entered, donning a different outfit: a pair of black jeans and a white t-shirt. "How does this look for the evening?" she asked, adding, "I won't be joining you two, but I have my own semi-date that I'm looking forward to meeting." With that, she grabbed her jean jacket and purse and headed out the front door.

Gabriel, unfamiliar with such modern women's attire from his own time, commented, "I never knew women actually dressed like that." Realizing he might have revealed too much of himself, he quickly added, "I mean, I never knew women like Katrina would dress like that. She usually wears her feathery gowns and other dresses."

Larry smiled and got to his feet. "Let's see what this hike is all about, dear Caleb. I'm interested to know why you think it's important for us to go there."

Gabriel opened the door, and they both stepped out, leaving the house unlocked. Gabriel led the way, and after about a half-hour, they reached a wooded area. "It gets better the deeper we go," Gabriel assured. Larry looked around, sensing something amiss.

"Caleb," Larry said. "What made you choose a place like this? We could have also gone to a tavern or pub?" Gabriel turned around and noticed Larry's eyes darkening. "What is going on here?" Larry snapped. "Who are you, anyway?"

Suddenly, a growl echoed from the distance. Larry bared his teeth in that direction, demanding, "Show yourself." Gabriel shook his head.

"Larry," Gabriel said, revealing his true form. "You can't be foolish enough to believe I've been Caleb this whole time, right?"

Larry lunged at Gabriel, but Gabriel grabbed him and threw him against a tree. Immediately, Alistair and Bryan arrived in their wolf forms, followed by the other three brothers. "Not so fun being outnumbered, is it, Larry?" Gabriel taunted.

Larry tried to attack again, but Bryan knocked him down and pinned him. Gabriel smiled at the scene, "Larry, you're not foolish enough to think I was Caleb the entire time. You sensed something was off, didn't you?" As Alistair and Bryan forced Larry to his knees, Gabriel continued, "Look at you. Is this what you hoped to achieve in life, Lawrence Harrison?"

Larry growled and hissed at Gabriel. "I see," Gabriel said. "Well, I think I have no reason to keep you alive. If I release you back into the wild, my boy, you would probably have me killed...for real. So, any last words before your end?"

Larry, however, just smiled and began to laugh. "Not much for final words, but I guess that will do," Gabriel commented. Turning to his comrades, he instructed, "Alistair, Bryan, would you do the honors?" Within seconds, both had ripped Larry's arms and head off.

"Good," Gabriel said decisively. "Now, let's burn the body. Alistair, where's Darcia?" Alistair checked his cellphone, noticing some missed messages and a voicemail from Darcia. He turned on the speakerphone, letting everyone listen to the message.

"Alistair, Caleb overpowered me and escaped. I didn't think he would take me down so easily, but he's gone," Darcia's voice trembled through the speaker. Alistair and Gabriel exchanged quick glances before rushing toward the motel resort.

Upon arrival, they found the windows smashed, the door hanging off its hinges, and Darcia slumped against a wall inside. "My love," Alistair said gently as he approached her. Darcia opened her arms, allowing him to help her to her feet. "What happened?"

Darcia wiped her eyes and looked past Alistair to see Gabriel entering the room. "Caleb... he was just too strong for me, my love," she admitted. "I have no idea how he managed it, but he's gone now. Where is Larry?"

"He's dead. Bryan and I tore him to pieces, then burned his body," Alistair explained. Darcia smiled faintly before turning her attention to Gabriel. "I'm sorry, Gabriel, for letting it happen like this. I never knew Caleb was actually that strong."

Gabriel nodded. "He had some of my life source inside him, Darcia. He was quite capable of taking care of himself," he said. "I'm just glad you're okay. We've had enough drama and death for a long time. Would you and your sons join us back at the castle for a nice meal?"

Both Darcia and Alistair nodded, following Gabriel back to the castle. As they arrived, they were greeted at the front door by Amelia, Adrian, Daniel, Vladimir, and Lucien. "A little bird told me Larry is dead. How did you all manage that now and not before?" Amelia inquired. "And by the way, how have you come back from the dead, dear brother?"

Gabriel nodded and shrugged. "It's what we shape-shifters do. I managed to shift into Caleb's form, leaving him to be mistaken for my dead body. He took advantage of the confusion to escape," he explained.

Lucien scoffed, clearly upset. "I'm so disappointed and angry right now, Gabriel. Why didn't you tell us this before you left five nights ago? I mourned your death! We were planning a family gathering. I was even going to inform the entire coven, and now here you are, alive and well. How do I know you're not still Caleb?" he demanded, glaring at Gabriel.

"You'll just have to trust me, brothers, and Amelia," Gabriel replied. "I'm not Caleb. I tricked Larry into thinking he was spending a pleasant evening with us, and now we're all reunited as a family."

Daniel scoffed, gesturing for them to enter the castle. "Just wait until you see your children again, Gabriel. How well do you think Amy and Ginger are going to take your reincarnation from the dead?"

Gabriel sighed, his patience wearing thin. "It's over for now. We're done with the fighting and conflicts. Whatever Caleb has planned, it won't work. Katrina's gone with him, so she's an easy target, but trust me, we'll all be a big happy family again soon," he said, his voice strained. "Now please, give me some space and let me serve our guests our finest drink," he snapped, eager to move past the recent events.

Arabella approached them, her expression filled with surprise. "My goodness," she whispered, her eyes wide. "Gabriel, is that really you?" Following closely behind was Ginger, her face reflecting her shock. "Father? What happened to you? Where's Larry, and how are you still alive?"

Gabriel opened up his arms, enveloping Ginger in a tight embrace. "I managed to outsmart our tormentor once and for all. He's gone, out of our lives for good. Please, my sweet child, I need to attend to our guests and make sure everyone is fed. Excuse me," Gabriel said gently, pulling away.

Downstairs, Amy recognized a familiar voice and decided to investigate. Donning her cotton robe and slippers, she descended the stairs. Her lack of sleep left her unsure if she was dreaming or awake. As she reached the dining area, she spotted Arabella, Darcia, and Alistair from behind. Then she saw him. "Father?" Amy whispered, disbelief in her voice. Gabriel, looking up from his drink, opened his arms to her. "Come here, my sweet princess," he said warmly. "I have so much to tell you."

Amy, overwhelmed by emotion, walked up to him and, without thinking, slapped him across the face. Gabriel groaned, hissing at her in response. "What's gotten into you, Amy? What's happened?" he demanded.

"How could you do this to us, Father? How can you be so deceitful to your own family? What is wrong with you?" she snapped, anger evident in her voice.

Lucien and Daniel reached out to steady her, grabbing her by the shoulders, but Arabella intervened, placing her hand on Daniel's arm. "Let her go," she ordered sharply. "She has every right to be angry with Gabriel."

Amy shrugged off their hold, her gaze returning to her father. "What is wrong with you, Father?" she asked again, her voice trembling.

Gabriel nodded, understanding her anger. "There was no easy way to deal with Larry without shape-shifting into Caleb and pretending to be dead, Amy. It was the only way. If Larry had known I was still alive, he would have killed me for real. I had to catch him off guard and then attack. I'm sorry for the grief and pain you've suffered these past few days, but it was the only way," Gabriel explained, finishing off his drink.

Amy's eyes filled with tears once again. "I mourned for you, Father. I had a whole ceremony and speech prepared. God, I feel so stupid and disgusted right now. So, Larry is really gone? Out of our lives for good?" she asked, her voice softening.

Gabriel nodded.

"But how do we know he won't come back? If we're all immortal shape-shifters, he could be too, right?" Amy pressed, seeking assurance.

Gabriel furrowed his brows, confused by her line of questioning. "Father? Is that true or not?"

He shook his head, dispelling her concerns. "We burned his body. As far as I know, he won't be coming back," Gabriel reassured her.

Amy rolled her eyes, still struggling to come to terms with everything. "I understand the frustration and confusion from all of you, but he was going to go after you, Amy, and your children. I had to stop him before he could do any more damage," Gabriel explained, hoping to make her understand his actions.

Amy, overwhelmed with intense anger, retreated to her room. She studied her reflection in the mirror, taking in her beautiful complexion, hair, body, and eyes. Yet, despite her outward appearance, she felt a deep sense of repulsion within herself. She wasn't a human woman; she was a monster, just like the rest of her family. Her gaze dropped to her children, realizing that they too would grow up to be just like her. Amy began to reconsider her options, contemplating whether she should stay in the castle or brave the dangerous world outside.

Sinking into her bed, she was soon interrupted by a knock at her door. "Yes?" she called out. Gabriel entered, closing the door behind him. "Oh, Father," Amy said, her voice laced with surprise. "What brings you here?"

"My sweet, beautiful Amy," Gabriel began, his tone soothing. "It hurts me to see you like this, angry and upset."

Amy shook her head and rolled her eyes. "I am not angry or upset at you, Father, but at the entire situation. I wish I had been born into a loving family, not one filled with lies and deception," she expressed.

Gabriel nodded, understanding her pain, and sat at the edge of her bed. "The last thing I want is to drive you away. Know that I will respect your decision if you choose to leave. I do love you, Amy," he said, taking her hand in his. "I love you and Ginger so much. I would give up my life for yours in a heartbeat. Please believe that."

Feeling a surge of emotion, Amy released her hand from Gabriel's grasp and wrapped her arms around him. "I love you too, father," she whispered. "I just despise this whole situation. And I have a feeling that Katrina and Caleb are planning something against us."

Gabriel offered her a reassuring smile. "Leave those problems to me. I want you to live the life you desire. Raise your children with Bryan, if that's what you wish, and know that I will always protect you. Okay?"

Amy nodded, her voice soft. "I can't lose you, Father. I can't afford to lose any more family members."

Smiling, Gabriel kissed the top of her head. "You are free to do as you please for the rest of the evening," he said, standing up and leaving Amy's room.

Meanwhile, at a forestry park, Katrina and Caleb stood over Larry's burnt and mutilated body. Katrina wept for Larry's death, and Caleb held her close. "We will avenge his death," he vowed.

Just then, twenty new members arrived, surrounding them from various points in the forest. "You all are Larry's newcomers, correct?" Caleb asked.

The group nodded, forming a circle around Larry's body. "Gabriel Ambrose has a weakness: his children and grandchildren. If we take them down, Gabriel will fall next. I've scouted the castle, particularly around Amy's room. I believe there's a way to kidnap her children, luring Amy, Ginger, and Gabriel into a trap," Caleb explained.

Katrina, beaming with delight, clapped her hands together. "I've always dreamed of having a baby," she exclaimed. "Besides, they are technically Caleb's children, so it's only right that the kids have their father around."

Caleb, however, was less enthusiastic. He rolled his eyes and shook his head in disgust. "A father against my will. That monstrous creature practically forced me into fatherhood with Amy. It's repulsive," he spat out, his face twisted in distaste. Some members of his group couldn't help but chuckle at his candid reaction. "I'm serious," he added.

Unperturbed, Katrina's smile widened. "I think I might have a plan to snatch Amy's children. All I have to do is pretend to reunite with Gabriel, then seduce my way to the kids. We just need to wait for the right moment, when you all are ready near the castle, and then we can grab them and make a run for it," she plotted.

Caleb's mood lightened at this, and he clapped his hands in approval. "Go for it, my queen," he encouraged.

"My king," Katrina whispered sweetly, caressing his face with her right hand.

Meanwhile, back at the castle, Gabriel was in his study, sorting through his strategic papers and tidying up his desk. Suddenly, there was a chime at the front door. Hildegard, the housekeeper, answered it, only to find Katrina standing there. "Master Gabriel!" Hildegard called out, her voice filled with alarm. "Katrina is back."

Gabriel got to his feet and walked over to the front door. "Katrina? What happened? Where have you been?" Gabriel asked.

Katrina put on a show, her face contorting into a sad expression as she began to whimper. "I got lost in the woods, Gabriel. When I heard about Larry and the danger he posed, I couldn't bear the thought of being near him," she lied, fake tears streaming down her cheeks.

Arabella, Gabriel's wife, appeared from behind him, her eyes narrowed in suspicion. "What are your true intentions for returning, Katrina? There can only be one queen in this castle, and I am the rightful Ambrose queen, married to my husband," she declared firmly.

Gabriel raised his hand, signaling for Arabella to be silent, before turning his attention back to Katrina. "Continue," he said calmly. "You do realize that Lawrence Harrison is dead, don't you?"

Katrina feigned shock. "What? Dead? How did he die, Gabriel?" she exclaimed.

Gabriel, unimpressed and growing impatient, rolled his eyes. "Don't play dumb with me, Katrina. As far as I'm concerned, there's no place for you here. I'm going to have to ask you to leave."

Defeated, Katrina broke down into tears. "It's not fair," she sobbed. "I was meant to be queen of this castle. Why did you ever cast me aside, Gabriel?"

Without another word, Gabriel closed the door, locking it securely before turning back to Arabella. "My love," he said, his voice soft.

Arabella smiled at him, a glint in her eyes. "Yes? What can I do for you?"

"I'm considering asking you to be my queen again, Arabella," Gabriel confessed, his eyes filled with hope.

Arabella, amused, shook her head. "You're coming on strong, Gabriel. I might be willing to be your queen again, but I need time to readjust to this lifestyle."

Gabriel chuckled, then wrapped his arms tightly around Arabella, pulling her close. "Now, now, my queen. If you're going to be queen of the castle again, I do expect some form of payment," he teased.

Arabella, playing along, pushed Gabriel away gently and headed toward the dining quarter, leaving Gabriel to return to his study, chuckling to himself.

Back in the wooded area, Katrina returned to find Caleb and the others waiting in the same spot. "Well?" Caleb asked impatiently. "Why are you back here and not inside the castle?"

Katrina wiped her eyes, visibly shaken. "I didn't expect Arabella to be there. She was the main reason I was thrown out, Caleb," she explained. Caleb, however, was unimpressed and rolled his eyes.

"That's disappointing, Katrina. What are your strengths and weaknesses as a shape-shifter?" he asked, pressing her for information.

Katrina shrugged. "I'm not certain, Caleb. But what about you? Couldn't you shape-shift into one of Gabriel's family members, just like he has done before?" she suggested.

Caleb pondered the idea and closed his eyes, focusing. He visualized Larry and, to his surprise, managed to transform into him. Opening his eyes, he noticed Katrina's shocked expression. "So, you have the same abilities as Gabriel?" she queried.

Caleb nodded and closed his eyes once again, this time picturing Katrina. He transformed, causing her to gasp. "Now stop that, Caleb," she snapped, visibly annoyed.

Caleb, still in Katrina's form, twirled around playfully in her dress. "What's the matter? You don't like having a twin?" he teased.

Katrina scoffed and walked away, unamused. "Perhaps I can impersonate you and sneak around as Katrina, the ex-queen," Caleb mused, considering the possibility.

Katrina shrugged, indifferent. "I'd like to see how Gabriel reacts to being seduced by his ex-wife," Caleb declared, smirking as he walked back to the castle.

Upon arrival, Hildegard opened the door once again, but quickly shook her head. "Master Gabriel doesn't want you back, Katrina," she stated firmly. Without missing a beat, Caleb lunged at Hildegard, pushing her aside. "He will now," he proclaimed, mimicking Katrina's voice perfectly.

Hildegard, gasping for breath, managed to call out for Gabriel. Caleb, seizing the opportunity, cried out, "Gabriel, please, talk to me. Give me another chance. I didn't abandon the family; Arabella threw me out. I just want to be a nanny to Amy's children," he pleaded.

Gabriel approached, his expression filled with confusion. "I'm not sure I want you back here, Katrina. Why are you so adamant about returning?" he asked, his tone skeptical.

Caleb fell to his knees, clasping his hands together in a desperate gesture. "I still have feelings for you, Gabriel. I understand if you hate me, but I truly want to return, even if just as a nanny or housemaid. Please, don't cast me out into the darkness like your wife did," he implored.

Gabriel, feeling a twinge of guilt and compassion, sighed. "Okay, Katrina. I have a different living quarter for you downstairs. Please follow me," he said, leading the way.

As they descended, the air grew damp and musty. "By the way, how have you been, Ka...trina?" Gabriel asked, his tone suggesting he was onto Caleb's disguise.

"Oh, you know. It's been quite hectic for me lately," Caleb replied, attempting to maintain the facade.

Gabriel smiled knowingly. "Okay, now please follow me," he said, opening a door and swiftly pushing Caleb inside before locking it.

"Caleb, Caleb, Caleb," Gabriel said, shaking his head. "I knew it was you. Want to know how I realized you weren't Katrina? Katrina is more concerned with her appearance; she would never get down on her knees and beg like that. She'd try to kiss me or seduce me, but you, you completely broke character. You'll stay here until my family and I decide what to do with you."

# Surprise Visit

Gabriel walked back to the main floor, trying to shake off the intense encounter with Caleb. He decided to keep the ordeal to himself and have a bit of twisted fun at Caleb's expense. However, as he allowed the situation to consume his thoughts, he found himself losing control, becoming increasingly aggressive.

Lucien and the other brothers made their way to the dining quarter, only to find Gabriel guzzling down an entire bottle of liquor – a quantity that would normally last the entire family for a week – in mere moments.

"Gabriel, what's gotten into you?" Lucien demanded, concern etched across his face. "Why are you acting this way?" Gabriel simply smiled, drained the bottle, and slammed it onto the table.

"Why does everyone care so much about me, or this family, for that matter? Why didn't anyone try to stop me from taking my daughters when they were born? And why bring up that human couple in the first place, brother?" Gabriel spat out, his tone laced with provocation.

Anger simmered inside Lucien, but he fought to remain calm. "What's going on with you? Why are you being so hostile towards me, brother?" he implored, cautiously approaching Gabriel, who now had pitch-black eyes and unnaturally sharp teeth. "I've never done anything to deserve this from you, Gabriel," Lucien added, his voice filled with sorrow. "Is this about Larry's death, or did Caleb do something to you? Where's the kid, anyway?"

Gabriel smirked. "He's in a special room I reserve for traitors; I find their torment particularly enjoyable. Think of it as our personal dungeon," he chuckled darkly.

Daniel , unable to contain his anger, demanded, "Are you Larry or Caleb?" his voice filled with fury. Gabriel laughed loudly, shaking his head in amusement.

"Of course not, brother. It's me, Gabriel Ambrose, the patriarch of our entire coven," he proclaimed confidently.

Despite Gabriel's assurance, Daniel maintained a hard stare. "Then why are you acting so strangely? You're usually more strategic and composed," he pointed out.

Gabriel's expression darkened. "I've kept Caleb as a pet. Katrina is probably wondering where he's disappeared to, unaware that Caleb tried to shape-shift into her to get closer to Amy and her children. Why shouldn't I be furious right now? Yes, Larry is dead, as far as I believe. But reflecting on my entire existence, I realize I have no answers anymore. Perhaps he might find a way to return, but for now, I finally have some leverage for the upcoming final battle. Unless, of course, there are some younglings out there harboring ill will towards me," Gabriel mused.

Lucien frowned, visibly disturbed. "So, you're planning on torturing Caleb?" he clarified, seeking confirmation. Gabriel simply shrugged.

"Isn't that a bit extreme, Gabriel? Caleb was the son you always wanted, and now you feel nothing for him? Your behavior is causing the other coven members to turn against us. We're isolating ourselves, leaving no one to back us up." Lucien cautioned, his worry for both Gabriel and their coven evident in his tone.

Gabriel sighed heavily. "I'm tired of constantly defending myself against my mistakes, always with the excuse that I had the best of intentions. I am not evil or corrupt, brothers. I didn't kill Larry's fiancé out of lust or anger, and I never meant to harm Larry out of malice. It's somehow in my nature to act the way I have, but you can't blame a lion for chasing down a smaller animal. You can't blame a shark for all those shark attack stories.

Sometimes it's just the wrong place at the wrong time, and I am done having to explain myself. I am not evil; perhaps I am also a victim in my own way," Gabriel said, his gaze falling to the empty bottle in his hand.

With another sigh, he walked off, placing the empty bottle in the crate that Hildegard brings in, and returned to the group. "Perhaps I have no intention of torturing Caleb. However, I also have no desire to face any more threats and fears. Katrina was sadly a victim in her own way, but in the end, she also succumbed to her lust for power. She loved being queen and having me as her guard, doing whatever she pleased without consequences. She had no dignity either," Gabriel said.

The other brothers exchanged bored glances. "Perhaps we can talk again soon, Gabriel," Daniel said, getting up to grab a bottle. "I'll get us something to sip on." He went to the cooler, selected an unopened bottle, and poured four glasses for the men. Meanwhile, Gabriel retreated to his study and sank into his chair, deep in thought about his next move.

Up in Amy's room, Amy and Ginger were watching over the three children, who were now crawling around. Amy felt a swell of pride watching her children develop and grow. "Gabrielle, Maggie, and Nathaniel are such little angels," she said. Ginger smiled, watching them interact with each other through a series of mumbled sounds. "I must say, if it's true that Larry is out of our lives forever, I do feel a sense of calmness," Amy admitted.

Ginger nodded in agreement. "I feel it too, sister. I'm glad that part of the drama is over. But I do wonder about what Caleb and Katrina might be planning, and if they are causing trouble or going on a killing spree." Amy looked at Ginger, concerned.

"I never really considered that," Amy said. "I also wonder if something else could have happened to Larry, if he might be a ghost or something. Our mother was a ghost, you know?" she asked, looking to Ginger for answers.

Ginger considered this and decided to seek advice. "I think I might ask Amelia for some guidance. I'll be back shortly, Amy," she said, before leaving Amy's room and heading to Amelia's quarters. She found Amelia and Arabella in the room together.

When Ginger knocked, Amelia looked up in surprise but welcomed her warmly. "Welcome, Ginger," she said, gesturing for her to come in. "Your mother and I were just reminiscing about old times. What brings you here?"

Ginger exhaled, her expression serious. "I have a question about ghosts, Amelia. Is it possible that Larry could be a spirit somewhere?" she asked. Amelia furrowed her brows in thought, shaking her head slightly.

"Not to my knowledge, Ginger. Why do you ask such questions? I know that there are spells to turn someone into a ghost and to bring them back from the dead, but did someone even use such a spell for Larry?" Amelia asked. Ginger shrugged.

"I was not there during any of those fights," Ginger said. "I have no idea if someone has done that to Larry."

Amelia crossed her arms, her expression turning contemplative. "I think we should look into that, just to be sure and rule out some of these possibilities," she suggested. "We should talk to your father since he was there when Larry died."

Arabella, Amelia, and Ginger made their way to Gabriel's study. Arabella knocked on the door and they waited for him to respond. "Ladies," Gabriel greeted them as he opened the door. "What can I do for you?" he asked, curiosity in his tone. Amelia took a deep breath before speaking.

"When Larry had died, you had his body burned, right Gabriel?" she inquired. Gabriel pondered the question for a moment before nodding in confirmation.

"Yes. I left that task to Alistair and Bryan," he replied. Amelia furrowed her brows, pressing further. "You were there when they did that, right, Gabriel?"

Gabriel recalled delegating the burial to Bryan and Alistair, confident they would not let him down. "I'll double-check with Alistair. Please excuse me for a moment," he said, before heading to Alistair's room. Upon knocking, he heard Darcia's laughter mingling with Alistair's. Alistair opened the door, his expression one of surprise. "Gabriel," he exclaimed. "What brings you here? Is everything okay?"

"You and Bryan did burn up Larry's body after you dismembered it, right?" Gabriel asked urgently. Alistair pondered the question for a few seconds, then realization dawned on him. They had left the body behind due to Alistair being distracted by Darcia's messages on his cellular device.

"I am not so sure anymore, Gabriel," Alistair admitted, his voice laden with concern. "This could end up being a very big problem. He's a shape-shifter, right? He probably changed his appearance after we left him."

"Alistair," Gabriel snapped. "I am very disappointed in you. How did you let this happen?"

Just then, a scream emanated from Amy's room. "Larry!" Amy screamed. "How did you—" Her voice suddenly cut off. Alistair and Gabriel both raced to Amy's room, only to find her and the babies gone.

"You are going to help me get them back, Alistair. You and your family. In fact, I want you to call back the other coven members and explain how their princess got abducted," Gabriel commanded, his voice steely.

Alistair nodded, shame in his demeanor. "Perhaps I should take the death sentence for you, Gabriel. Maybe you should stay behind and let me fix this problem and clean up this mess." Gabriel hissed at Alistair in response. "I am not letting my baby girl suffer without the protection of her father," Gabriel stated firmly. "We will prepare a bonfire for him, complete with music and dancing."

Alistair nodded, understanding the gravity of the situation. "I am sorry, Gabriel, for this situation. I never thought it would come to this. I wonder where Bryan was after we left. Would you like me to ask him?"

Gabriel shook his head, determination in his eyes. "It's too late for that, Alistair. I need you all to find my daughter and her children and bring Larry to justice for his crimes against the family.

If anything happens to Amy or any of those children," Gabriel warned, his tone ominous, "I'll make sure you follow them."

Alistair nodded again, his demeanor filled with remorse. "I understand, Gabriel. Again, I am truly sorry for this situation."

Larry gripped the squirming Amy in his arms, motioning for Katrina to bring the restless children to the secluded woodsy area where Larry's group was stationed. "Okay," Larry declared, a sinister tone in his voice. "We finally have leverage against Gabriel Ambrose. The little princess can be our prisoner in exchange for Caleb."

Amy, struggling fiercely, managed to bite Larry hard, causing him to retaliate with a harsh smack across her face, leaving a deep flesh wound. "Now, now, Amy. I am sure Daddy would not be impressed with that type of behavior," Larry taunted.

Amy, her spirit unbroken, hissed at him, even as four of Larry's cronies moved to subdue her further. "Let my children go, Larry. You can keep me, but they are innocent in this matter," she pleaded.

"Why, Amy?" Larry asked. "As far as I am concerned, they are Caleb's children. He is the actual father, is he not?"

Amy tried to remain composed, though the sharp nails digging into her skin made it challenging. "I let my guard down while your father played me for the final time, Amy. This time, I know better than to let you all trick me. You are the real monsters of this world. I should have you tried by the human world and executed for taking part in those hunts for innocent humans," Larry spat out.

Amy scoffed, defiance in her voice. "Yeah right, Larry. What about your friends here?" she snapped, gesturing to the creatures restraining her. "These creatures holding me down? You probably enjoyed the hunt, didn't you, Larry?"

Larry smirked, reminiscing. "I remember when I first met you, back in Oregon. You were such a fragile little girl. I could have easily had you killed and let the human authorities declare you a suicidal fragile kid," he taunted.

Anger welled up inside Amy as she reflected on how charming Larry had seemed, all for the wrong reasons. "If there is anyone who is a monster, it's you, Larry. You manipulated me, just to get to my father. Why didn't you go to Romania yourself, Larry? Why take the cowardly route?" she challenged.

Larry hissed at Amy and raised his hand, as if to strike her again. "Go on, Larry. Hit me again. It's not like it really did that much damage. I heal from different wounds," Amy taunted back, her spirit unbroken.

Larry sighed, his attention shifting to Gabrielle, who shared Amy's hair color and eyes. "Perhaps I might see how well your children heal. Would you all like to see that?" he asked his friends, a sinister gleam in his eyes. Katrina, however, looked visibly worried about the whole situation.

"Larry, one strike is enough for now," she interjected cautiously. Larry nodded in agreement.

"I do think we should relocate to a different place. Let Gabriel enjoy the hunt for once in his life."

Amy, seizing the moment, tried to free herself from the grasp of the creatures holding her. "You will suffer, Lawrence Harrison. Mark my words. You will not survive this," she vowed, her voice filled with determination.

Larry scoffed, mockingly blowing a kiss to Amy. "We shall see, dear Amy Rose Ambrose. We shall see," he said, smirking as he led the group away from the castle, the children distributed among his followers.

Meanwhile, Gabriel burst out of the castle, flanked by Alistair, Amelia, Adrian, Vladimir, and Lucien. "Darcia," he snapped, urgency in his voice. "Call for the other coven members to help us find them."

"Yes, Gabriel," Darcia responded immediately, ready to act. Gabriel glanced back, noticing Arabella standing in the doorway, a look of concern on her face.

"What would you like, Arabella? Would you like to stay at the castle and wait for any word on Amy or would you like to come with us?"

Arabella, remaining in the doorway, glanced over at Ginger before responding. "Perhaps it would be wise for the two of us to stay here, Gabriel. Just in case Amy manages to return." Gabriel nodded in agreement and proceeded to lead his group away. Once Gabriel and his team were out of sight, Arabella secured the castle, with Ginger staying close by her side.

"I am so worried, Mother. I can't bear the thought of something happening to her or her children," Ginger admitted, her voice quivering as she fought back tears.

Arabella wrapped her arms around Ginger, offering comfort. "Nothing is going to happen to Amy. She's incredibly strong and more than capable of handling immense stress and anxiety, my dear child. Amy will return home to us."

After a moment, Ginger stepped back, allowing Arabella to release her. She then made her way to the dining area, where she found Hildegard stressfully wiping down the counters.

"Hildegard," Arabella spoke gently. "Please try to relax. We will get through this. We are strong women, born to withstand challenges."

Hildegard paused her cleaning and took a deep breath. "I understand that, Milady, but sometimes it's overwhelming, being the only human in this family. I'm surprised Larry never targeted me, especially considering he was able to move about during the day when he was seducing Amy."

Arabella pondered this for a moment. "Well, you are safe now, and everything else is going to be okay." Hildegard managed a small smile in response.

Meanwhile, as Gabriel tirelessly searched for Larry, Larry and his group had managed to traverse into a different Romanian city. "Perhaps we should consider relocating to Oregon. What do you think, Amy? Would you like that?" Larry taunted.

Amy remained silent, choosing not to engage.

"Ah. Playing the silent game with me. Okay. There are other ways to get you to talk," Larry snapped.

Amy continued to ignore him, casting occasional worried glances towards the creatures holding her children. "You are a coward, Lawrence Harrison," she finally spat out. "I will never forgive you for the attempt on my life at your family's apartment complex."

Larry abruptly stopped and turned to face Amy. "We never intended to kill you, Amy. That potion was meant to weaken you, not end your life."

Amy scoffed and shook her head dismissively. "You are pathetic. Where is your family, anyway? Shouldn't they be here as backup?"

Larry smirked and glanced at his watch. "Speak of the devil, Amy," he said, just as a van pulled up. Amy's heart sank as she recognized the faces of Buffy, Athan, their son William, and their daughter Bianca. They all exited the van, each on their own terms, to get a closer look at Amy.

"My, my," Buffy said. "You have become such a gorgeous creature."

Athan stepped forward, surveying the three infants. "And a new mother? I must say, I'm impressed, Amy."

William joined in, "Who's the lucky guy? Larry, you must be over the moon to have such beautiful children."

Amy scoffed once more. "The father is actually Caleb," she corrected them. "I hate to break it to you, but you're not the grandparents of these babies."

Buffy looked over at Larry with confusion.

"It is true, parents," Larry said. "Caleb is the actual father of these younglings, but Gabriel has captured him and is holding him hostage at the castle.

"What castle, Larry?" Athan asked. "Are you talking about that grungy looking building with all the foliage around it?"

Larry nodded. "The very same," Larry said. "I am keeping Gabriel's princess as a prisoner swap, so Caleb can be reunited with his children, again." Buffy clapped her hands with glee before she walked over to Gabrielle and placed her hand on her gently. Gabrielle started to cry.

"Leave her alone," Amy snapped. "She is not anyone's child, except mine. I am her mother and protector."

Athan erupted into laughter, quickly joined by William and Bianca. Larry, however, remained neutral and raised his hands, signaling them to quiet down. "Oh, I see you've brought friends with you," Buffy observed, looking past Amy to the more than twenty assorted creatures standing behind her, all appearing hungry and bored.

"My coven," Larry said. "I needed some backup, so I could take down that horrible monstrous creature."

Amy turned to Athan and Buffy with a questioning look. "I've been wanting to ask this for so long, but how are you all related to Larry, exactly?" she inquired. Athan and Buffy exchanged confused glances.

"We are his parents, of course," Buffy said. "How would he even have existed in the first place?"

Amy shook her head and sighed. "No, but what I mean is, were you humans before Larry became your son or did you turn him into a shape-shifter, or did he turn you two?"

Buffy burst into laughter at Amy's question, with Athan joining in. "Oh, my poor, ignorant child," Buffy said, shaking her head. "We created Larry. Athan is probably around the same age as your father, or maybe a bit younger."

Amy felt a wave of confusion. "What?" she asked, bewildered. "That makes no sense. Larry, what is this? Why have you been lying to me about wanting to kill my father? That whole story about the tavern was a lie, wasn't it?"

Larry waved her off dismissively. "So, how should we handle this, parents?" he asked, turning his attention back to Athan and Buffy. "I can't abandon my group, but I also can't leave Amy with her children. How about this? You take Amy and the kids back to your place. That way, if Gabriel tries to track my scent, he might think Amy is still with me, but she'll actually be far away. Then we can figure out our next steps from there."

Athan and Buffy both nodded. Katrina handed Buffy Gabrielle, and the two others, Maggie and Nathaniel. Larry pushed Amy into the van and made sure she was between William and Bianca. "Nice and safe from any harm," Larry said as he fastened Amy's seatbelt.

Amy hissed at Larry, which caused him to chuckle. "We shall see each other real soon, Amy. I promise." Larry said before he blew her a kiss and closed the van door. After Athan got into the driver's seat, Amy had to try and remain as calm as she could during such moments.

Back at the castle, Arabella and Ginger were sharing a quiet moment, sipping blood together, when the sound of the doorbell chimes echoed through the halls. Hildegard opened the door, and Bryan stormed in, making a beeline for Arabella and Ginger. "Where's Amy?" he demanded.

Arabella and Ginger exchanged confused glances. "She's been kidnapped by Larry. Where have you been, Bryan? You were there when Larry died. Why didn't you ensure his body was burned? Where are your brothers?" Arabella asked sternly. "My baby is gone because you and your family failed in this crucial task."

Bryan bared his teeth, irritated. "It wasn't my responsibility to ensure he was burned. Alistair was in charge of that, and, sadly, Darcia allowed Caleb to escape. He's probably out there somewhere now."

Ginger reflected on the situation and then realized something important. "No, Bryan," she corrected him, "Caleb is here, in the dungeon—or what my father refers to as the dungeon." Bryan furrowed his brow in confusion. "Where is this dungeon? I need to see Caleb," he demanded, his voice laced with urgency.

Ginger sighed and pointed toward the door that led to the staircase. Bryan quickly ran over to the basement dungeon area where he saw Caleb in a metal cage.

"Well, well, well," Caleb said sarcastically as he clapped his hands together. "Look who's here—the faithful watchdog."

Bryan growled at Caleb, which caused him to laugh. "Oh, Bryan, you do make me laugh."

"Where are Amy and Larry?" Bryan demanded, his patience wearing thin.

Caleb shrugged nonchalantly. "Oh, is Larry back from the dead? I would have thought that you would have had him burned to a crisp by now, Bryan. Was that too challenging for you?" he teased.

Bryan composed himself, straightening up and relaxing his shoulders. "Where are they, Caleb? If anything happens to Amy or her children, I promise you, you will suffer—slowly. Understand?" he threatened in a low whisper.

Caleb hissed in response, showing his disdain. "How would I know where they are? For all I know, he enjoys hanging out in that park outside the castle. Maybe he's there right now with your precious girl?" he said, smirking. "Or maybe not."

Bryan growled again, his anger palpable. "I might take you with me, Caleb, but probably in chains to ensure you don't escape. If you behave, we might consider a prisoner swap. But as of now, I think both of you deserve to die."

Caleb scoffed and turned away. "I am not going anywhere. You can go outside and look for them yourself. I am quite comfortable in this cell."

Bryan slammed the cell bars loudly in frustration, but Caleb just laughed even more. "Do you really think your intimidation tactics will work on me, Bryan? You might be strong in some ways, but you're also quite foolish. I have no interest in looking for that girl. I was meant to be Gabriel's son, so I'll wait for him to return and see what he has planned for me," he said defiantly. "Now leave."

Bryan hissed at Caleb once more before turning to leave. "This isn't over, Caleb. Mark my words," he said, his voice filled with anger.

Once back on the main floor, Arabella and Ginger were finishing up washing their glasses, waiting for Bryan's return. "Well? What did Caleb have to say?" Arabella asked, curious.

Bryan shrugged and shook his head. "He is useless and rude," Bryan said. "I'll try to find Amy myself. Maybe I'll find Alistair as well and ask him what happened after Larry was killed."

After Bryan left the castle, Arabella and Ginger moved to the living quarters and started a fire in the fireplace, settling down on one of the sofas. "I really hope Amy is okay, Mother," Ginger said softly, her concern evident. "I can't stand the thought of all this happening just because of our complicated family dynamics."

Arabella responded by holding Ginger close, offering her comfort in the unsettling situation.

"Amy is strong, Ginger. Remember that. You both are your father's daughters; you have his blood and shape-shifting strength within you," Arabella said in a soothing tone. As Arabella and Ginger sat together, Alistair, Gabriel, and his brothers were on Larry's trail, following his scent.

"Alistair, has Joshua mentioned anything of this to you? About the whole kidnapping of my daughter?" Gabriel asked. Alistair stopped to turn around.

"Not to my knowledge, Gabriel," Alistair said. "Wait a moment. Where are my sons, anyway? I should have let Bryan and his brothers burn Larry's body. Why did I not think of that?" Alistair wondered aloud.

Gabriel placed a comforting hand on Alistair's shoulder. "You were concerned about Darcia. I don't blame you for wanting to protect your life mate, Alistair. You won't die because of this inconvenient situation, but we must also ensure that Amy and her children remain unharmed," Gabriel reassured him.

Alistair nodded, visibly troubled. "Again, Gabriel, I apologize for this entire situation. I should have instructed Bryan to burn the body; I just... spaced out," Alistair admitted, feeling a mix of anger and fear coursing through his body. Gabriel cupped Alistair's face tenderly with his hands, forcing him to make eye contact.

"You are okay, Alistair. Repeat after me: I am okay. I am safe," Gabriel instructed. Alistair repeated the words. "Again," Gabriel urged, and Alistair complied. "One last time," Gabriel prompted. After Alistair finished, Gabriel released him and took a step back.

"Okay," Gabriel said, his senses heightened. "I can sense him somewhere close. Please follow me, brothers and Alistair." The six of them walked toward the scent they believed belonged to Larry, but they couldn't find him. Gabriel paused and activated his mind-reading abilities.

*Amy, where are you my sweet girl,* Gabriel thought, hoping for a response from Amy. Suddenly, Amy, amidst her uncomfortable situation, heard her father in her mind. "Father?" she asked aloud. Athan and Buffy both turned to look at her. Amy glared at them, then looked around, realizing she was in a van on a highway.

*Amy, you can hear me. Please tell me where you are. I will find you and your children. We will end this war with Larry,* Gabriel thought. Amy felt a sense of relief, knowing that she was being searched for. It gave her hope that she was going to survive this whole chaotic mess.

*Father, I am with Larry's parents and siblings in their van. I am not sure where I am specifically, but we are on a highway,* Amy thought. Gabriel sighed and turned around to face his brothers and Alistair.

"Amy has been taken by Larry's parents, and they're currently on a highway. Which highway is closest to where we are?" Gabriel asked. Lucien started to explain which highway was nearest, and they quickly headed in that direction. Meanwhile, Athan and Buffy exited the highway and drove into a small city, eventually arriving at an apartment complex.

"So, this is where Larry will meet us after he is done with your father, Amy," Athan said before he got out of the car from the driver's side. Bianca and William had each baby in their arms and Buffy had the third baby in her arm. "If you do anything drastic, Amy, like harm any of us or try to escape, your children will die," Buffy warned sharply before Athan opened both the passenger-side door for her and the sliding door on the other side of the van.

Amy was the first to get out, and Athan dragged her through the front door before pushing her onto one of the living room chairs, where they waited for the other members to arrive. "You all are insane and disgusting," Amy snapped, her voice filled with anger. "How did you all become so evil? I never did anything to you, and neither did my father, from what you told me earlier," Amy exclaimed. "Why do you even want him dead, and why did Larry create such a ridiculous story about that girl?"

Buffy scoffed. "That story is true, Amy, but there's more to it regarding your father's involvement. You see, your father is considered the patriarch of the family. We wanted so badly to be part of his coven. We felt that we were so similar and that we could benefit from each other's abilities and strengths, but your father cast us aside. Athan and I felt a deep sense of betrayal from being treated like that. This all took place in Romania, just so you know.

We had to find a place for ourselves, but then we overheard Gabriel sending both you and your sister off to Oregon. So, we tried to track you both down and kidnap you for leverage. However, Alistair and Darcia showed up, thwarting our plans. We did have you stay with us, if you remember? We tried to get you to release your powers to us, but then Bryan came for you, as well?" Buffy asked, her tone a mix of bitterness and reminiscence.

Amy kept her focus on Buffy. "So, we started resenting you all for our rejection of your family. Larry did start to have feelings for you, but I managed to talk him out of it," Buffy said. Amy rolled her eyes before she focused her attention on Gabrielle in Buffy's arms.

"May I at least have my children close to me? I do need to feed them occasionally, just so you know," Amy said in a relaxed voice. Buffy looked over at Amy and handed Gabrielle back to her.

"Whatever anger or resentment you have toward my father, my children should not suffer for it. I would have preferred if Larry and Katrina had just kidnapped me and left my children in my room. But involving them like this goes way too far," Amy stated firmly.

Buffy did not respond, but kept her focus on Gabrielle. "She does look like you, Amy," Buffy said. Amy did not respond and held Gabrielle close to her.

"Would you mind if I used your bathroom, so I can feed my babies?" Amy asked. Buffy directed Amy to the bathroom. After Buffy left Amy in the bathroom, she remained outside to make sure Amy was not going to escape through the bathroom window.

Bianca and William both sat on a sofa in the living room, each cradling a baby in their arms. "They smell weird," Bianca commented. Meanwhile, Buffy smiled and remained outside the closed bathroom door. When Amy emerged, Gabrielle was making cooing sounds. "I would like Maggie and Nathaniel now," Amy requested. Buffy took Gabrielle from Amy, allowing Bianca and William to hand her both babies, and then she closed the door behind Amy.

Athan approached Buffy and waited for Amy to finish feeding her children. After Amy reappeared, Athan took Nathaniel, while Buffy held Maggie. "Okay, Amy, no more requests now. Your children are safe, but that doesn't mean this conflict is resolved. Please, take a seat again," Athan instructed sternly. Amy returned to the same chair she had been pushed into earlier. "I will check what Larry is planning," Athan said before he handed William the baby and stepped out of the room with his cellular device in hand.

"Father?" Larry answered the phone, his tone filled with concern. "Is everything okay?"

"Everything is fine, my son," Athan said. "We have the girl and her children with us. How far away is Gabriel from you right now?"

"I'm not entirely sure at the moment, Father," Larry admitted. "We led Gabriel to this wooded park, but he seems to have headed practically in your direction, towards the highway. If you notice anything, please let me know," Larry requested.

"Will do, son," Athan said. "Everything is going to work out better this time."

"Okay, but I should hang up now. Perhaps we might end up going in that direction as well," Larry said before he hung up.

Back at the castle, Ginger decided to go down to the basement to see what Caleb was doing. Standing in front of him, she caught his attention, and he smirked. "You look so much like your father, Ginger," Caleb observed, his tone laced with a mix of admiration and something darker. "But more beautiful."

Ginger remained silent, her expression steady. "I am worried about my sister, Caleb, and knowing that you played a part in this disgusts me," Ginger expressed, her voice tinged with sadness.

Caleb , sensing an opportunity, decided to play on Ginger's emotions. "I understand, Ginger. Sometimes, I can't stand myself, especially when I get involved in these kinds of activities. I never intended to harm your sister, or you, for that matter," Caleb said, adopting a soothing tone.

"I want to believe you, Caleb, but I'm not naive enough to think you genuinely care about Amy," Ginger retorted sharply. "Whatever issues you have with Gabriel, that's your problem. Amy and I are just as much victims of his lies and deception. So, for Larry to go after my sister, kidnap her and her children... I truly hope he gets what he deserves in the end. And that goes for you, too," Ginger declared firmly.

Caleb smirked. "Do you see me with Larry right now, Ginger? I'm not the ruthless one here. I've always been more of the quiet type. So, to threaten me like that? I don't appreciate your tone, Ginger," Caleb responded calmly.

Ginger hissed before she turned around to leave. Caleb remained calm and unresponsive.

Meanwhile, Bryan had reached the wooded area, spotting Larry's group from a distance. Suddenly, Joshua, Xavier, Silas, and Raymond appeared behind him.

"Where have you all been?" Bryan whispered urgently.

"We got lost somehow, Bryan," Raymond whispered back. "Where have you been? How is Larry even alive? I thought we had ripped him apart," Silas said. Bryan shook his head.

"We had to burn him, as well, brothers. Alistair never mentioned that part to us at the moment and took off to find out where Darcia was. By the way, where is she?"

Darcia then approached them from the trees. "Here I am," Darcia said before she walked over to Bryan.

"I am guessing Alistair is with Gabriel?" Bryan asked. Darcia nodded. Arabella and Ginger are back at the castle. I saw Caleb in their dungeon in a cage." The other brothers looked over at Bryan with confusion.

"Gabriel has a dungeon? The man has many secrets, does he not?" Raymond asked. Bryan chuckled. "So, what is the plan this time? It seems like we are always close to our goal and then we get pushed back to the beginning," Raymond said.

"I think he is trying to bait one of us, or even Gabriel, to attack him," Bryan whispered. "Perhaps we should see where they would lead us." Slowly, Darcia and her sons followed Larry and his coven from a distance. Larry was in front of his group with Katrina next to him.

"Katrina, how do you feel about this whole situation with Gabriel?" Larry asked as they walked next to each other. Katrina smiled and shrugged.

"Mixed feelings," Katrina said. "I do not care about drama and fighting, but then again, I do not like being lied to either, Larry."

Larry nodded. "I was quite surprised how my body was able to regenerate itself. I would have never known that was possible. To have a new body within a few minutes," Larry said.

Katrina quickly looked over. "Oh goodness, I forgot to ask how you felt," Katrina said. Larry smiled. "Well?"

"Like a baby deer that learned how to walk after being pushed out into this world," Larry said. "I feel okay."

Katrina nodded. "I just totally forgot about that, because of the whole kidnapping and meeting your parents," Katrina said. "I am glad you are going okay." Larry looked behind to see sullen and hungry faces from his coven. "How are you all doing back there? We will soon be eating some good gourmet food, my fellow comrades," he said.

The coven members all nodded and kept walking behind Larry and Katrina. Katrina chuckled at their response and looked over at Larry. "I think they might be hungry right now, Larry. Do we have anything to offer to them for their services?" Larry rolled his eyes and shook his head. "We are not stopping or going down a different path right now."

While Larry and his coven were walking towards his parents' home, Amy remained as quiet and relaxed as she could, as a hostage would in such a circumstance. Amy closed her eyes and let her body relax as much as possible. "Oh look, Nathan, it appears that our guest is getting tired," Buffy said sarcastically. Amy quickly opened up her eyes and sighed. "Do not stop us from your need of rest, Amy," Buffy said. "Feel free to let your mind wander freely."

Amy glared at Buffy and adjusted her seating position to face her. "Fine," Buffy said. "We cannot let you out of our sight, just so you know." Amy did not respond. "Then again we cannot let you starve either, since you are leverage for us, Amy," Buffy said. "Nathan sweetie? Could you get Amy a little drink?"

Nathan entered the room and asked, "Like what, honey?" Buffy glanced at Amy before asking, "What blood type do you prefer,

Amy?" with a grin on her face. Amy remained silent. "Perhaps some rat blood?" Buffy suggested. Amy chuckled at the comment, prompting Nathan to shrug and step outside to see if he or his kids could find any live rats.

"No thanks," Amy said hoarsely. "I am not hungry or thirsty. Especially for a rodent beverage," Amy said.

Buffy leaned back against the sofa, while keeping her focus on Amy. "This shall pass, Amy," Buffy said in a soothing tone. "Your father will be out of our lives, Caleb will have his children back, and you can decide if you wish to remain here with us or go back to your monster castle."

"Do you enjoying taunting me, Buffy?" Amy asked. "As far as I am concerned, I never did anything to you, so why you need me as leverage is understandable, but also wrong. Especially how my children will remember this moment forever."

Buffy scoffed, "You sound like your father—such a petty creature he was. Why he felt Nathan and I were not good enough is beyond me. We are quite strong in our own ways, Amy. But he was, and will always be, very rigid." Just then, Nathan returned with two dead rats in his arms, poured their blood into a glass, and offered it to Amy. Amy declined the drink. Nathan slammed the glass onto the dining room table and threw the rat carcasses outside.

"I believe our guest is not that hungry, Buffy," Nathan said. "If you'd like, you can rest upstairs and leave William and me with our captive." Buffy nodded and stood up.

"We will talk again soon, Amy. For now, I shall get my beauty rest." Buffy walked over to the staircase. Amy watched Nathan and William sit down on the same sofa that Buffy was sitting on.

"So, Amy," William said. "It has been quite a long time since we last saw each other. I remember seeing you in our family's library after you had some sort of nightmare, was it?" William asked. Amy did not respond. "How is Bryan anyway? Are you two like a couple right now? Is he the one who will help you raising your little pups?"

Amy glared at William but stayed silent. "What? Has the cat got your tongue, Amy?"

# A New Emergence

Gabriel sensed that he was getting closer to Amy's whereabouts. He, along with Lucien, Daniel, Vladimir, and Alistair, were just a few blocks away from the location. "Why would Larry have Amy placed in this upscale part of Romania?" Alistair pondered aloud.

Gabriel maintained his focus and responded, "All I care about is bringing her and her children safely home. I don't care about his reasons." Alistair nodded, and the group continued their focused approach toward the location. Suddenly, Alistair sensed a chilling presence behind him. He turned around, tapped Gabriel on the arm, and said in a calm yet frightened voice, "Gabe, look what's behind us."

Gabriel turned around to see some of Larry's associates appearing behind them. Larry's coven remained still and stopped walking. "Gabe, I'm not sure about this place. I think we should go back before it gets any worse," Alistair suggested, his unease evident in his voice.

Gabriel stopped in his tracks. "Alistair, why are you acting so scared right now? You're stronger and quicker than those younglings. Just because it's five of us against over ten of them doesn't mean we should worry about our fate. Larry only managed to pin me down in our first battle because I underestimated him. I've learned from my mistake, and this time, I will show no mercy whatsoever," Gabriel said assertively. "We're almost at the house where Amy is being held captive. We just need to see what she's doing and lure her out as quickly as possible."

About forty yards away, Bryan remained still, his attention fixed on Larry's movements, while he and his brothers discreetly followed Larry's coven. "Bryan, I'm worried that things might not work out so well this time," Raymond expressed, concern evident in his voice. "Even Joshua looks quite scared."

Bryan glanced at Joshua, who was fidgeting with his nails and glancing around nervously, resembling a scared animal. He walked over to Joshua and placed his right arm around his shoulders, asking, "What's wrong, brother? Why are you suddenly so scared?" Joshua took a deep breath, his shoulders tense.

"It might not end well this time," Joshua murmured. Bryan sighed, holding Joshua close as they walked. "For some reason, I think it's possible that we might just make it this time, Joshua. I feel tense and anxious about what might happen, but we are strong in our own ways," Bryan reassured him.

As the boys and Darcia kept their distance from Larry's group, Larry approached the front line of his coven, which had come to a halt. "Okay," he said, "if we split up into groups of eight—some going right, others left, and the rest staying in the center—we might be able to surround Gabriel and his group and launch a full attack. Gabriel is not as strong as he thinks he is. I took him down once before. Just because he managed to shape-shift into Caleb some time ago doesn't mean he's stronger than me," Larry declared. The other members nodded in agreement and dispersed in various directions. Larry stayed in the center with five of his members, waiting about twenty feet from the apartment complex where Amy was being held.

Gabriel, now closer, felt Amy's presence intensifying. *Amy, this is your father. I need you to do something for me,* Gabriel thought, trying to reach out to her telepathically. Amy, feeling the connection, focused her attention toward one of the windows in the apartment complex, but saw only darkness.

*Father, what should I do? I do not think I can escape with three babies in my arms. How can I get them all out as quickly as possible without appearing visible in my actions?* Amy thought. Gabriel crouched down outside of the apartment complex and saw some of the windows were open and some had the curtains closed.

Inside, Nathan saw Amy's gaze shift from the open window to him, her expression hardening. "What?" she snapped. "I'm just daydreaming about what I hope to do with my children someday, Nathan." Nathan scoffed in response. Amy turned her attention back to her three infants, sleeping peacefully on the floor.

Nathan got to his feet, but William remained seated. "Say, Amy," William said. "You have not answered my question. Will Caleb actually be the father to raise your children?" Amy looked over at William and shook her head.

"Why would he, William?" Amy asked. "Why would someone who never intended to be a father suddenly feel the need to become one?" William smirked at Amy's retort, prompting Amy to turn the question on him. "What about you? Do you have someone in your life to share an eternal bond with?"

William shook his head. "Not at the moment," he replied, "but that doesn't mean she's not out there." Amy shook her head in disbelief, as if questioning who would find William attractive. Meanwhile, Nathan glanced outside, saw nothing but darkness, trees, and other homes, and decided to close all the curtains before returning to the living room. Gabriel, on the other hand, reconvened with his group.

"She is in there, brothers, but she's worried about getting her children out," Gabriel shared. "What if we shape-shift into Caleb and Larry to trick those creatures, snatch the children from Amy's grasp, and then make our escape?"

Gabriel's brothers and Alistair nodded in agreement. "Okay, here's the plan: I'll transform back into Caleb, and Alistair, you shape-shift into Larry. Then, we'll take those children away from them," Gabriel laid out the strategy. Alistair, looking at Lucien and Daniel for reassurance, nodded in agreement.

"Okay, Gabriel. I hope this plan will work this time," Alistair said before he pictured himself as Larry and turned into him.

Gabriel and Alistair both walked over to the entrance of the apartment complex and rang the doorbell. Alistair, feeling uneasy about the unexpected plan, maintained his composure as Nathan opened the door. "Boys, what a surprise," Nathan exclaimed, gesturing for Gabriel and Alistair to enter. "Is Gabriel dead?"

Gabriel exchanged glances with Alistair and nudged him to respond. "Um…yes, father," Alistair said, feigning sorrow. "Gabriel is finally dead."

Just then, Buffy came out walking and Bianca came out from her own room. "Boys," Buffy said. "It is so wonderful to see you both back, again."

Amy, now feeling scared and uncertain, thought, *Father, what is going on? You can't be dead!* As Gabriel, now Caleb, approached, Amy stood her ground, baring her teeth. "Stay away from me, Caleb," Amy snapped. "You cannot have my children."

Without responding, Gabriel swiftly grabbed one baby while Alistair grabbed the other two. Amy lunged at Alistair but missed, slamming into the wall instead. Gabriel and Alistair dashed outside and into the bushes where Lucien, Daniel, Adrian, and Vladimir were waiting. Back inside, Amy, witnessing Buffy, William, Bianca, and Nathan laughing at her, felt defeated.

"What a foolish girl," Buffy laughed, the other ones wiping tears from their eyes.

Amy, gathering her strength, retorted, "This is not over," and headed toward the front door. William quickly grabbed her from behind, underestimating Amy's newfound strength. She threw him over her shoulder, and as Bianca attempted to tackle her, she was sent flying across the room by Amy's might. Buffy, now showing her true form, bared her teeth and extended her claws. Just then, the front door swung open, and Larry entered.

"Where are my children?" Amy demanded, grabbing Buffy in a headlock. "Release my children, or your mother gets it!"

Larry looked confused. "What are you talking about, Amy?" Larry asked in a bored tone. "I never took your children, except once to lure Gabriel into chasing us. However, it seems he has no intention of saving you." William, looking puzzled, turned to Larry.

"We saw you and Caleb take Amy's children away from here. That was you, was it not?" William asked.

Larry rolled his eyes and shook his head. "Perhaps Gabriel is here," Larry said. "We still have Amy as leverage," Larry said before he closed the door and locked it. "Quite a fierce fighter you are, Amy. Did your daddy teach you those moves?"

Amy, maintaining her grip on Buffy, dug her nails deeper into Buffy's flesh, eliciting a moan of pain. "One more comment or step, Larry, and your mother dies quickly," Amy threatened. Larry looked over at Amy with concern.

"You are not a killer, Amy," Larry said. "You are more of a mothering and caring type. You would not kill another woman, especially not one of your own gender, would you?"

Amy chuckled at Larry's expression and words. "What kind of game are you playing, Larry? I remember how charming and protective you were in Oregon, but then again, liars and con men often are," she retorted sharply.

Nathan, though capable of intervening, remained still, cautious of Amy's firm grip on Buffy's neck. "How about this: get your father to release Caleb, and you are free to go," Larry proposed. "Does that sound fair?"

Amy smirked and shook her head. "And then what? Allow you to go after me and my family again, Larry? I have no reason to agree to a prisoner swap. I want you gone forever, never to return to any of my family members. My babies will be scarred after today, and it's all your fault."

Larry smirked. "I never had any quarrel with you, Amy. If I ever showed any genuine feelings back in Oregon, they were real. I did enjoy being around you. You are strong, but now you are quite an emotional wreck. To go after my mother, Amy, shows you are not as kind as you seemed back in Oregon."

Amy shook her head. "It takes one to know one, Lawrence," she snapped back. "Your parents did a poor job raising you, especially with that big lie you were talking about—the part about how your parents were the first ones to hate Gabriel. Why didn't you ever mention that?" Amy demanded. Larry glanced at Nathan, who returned his look.

"Well, aside from that little interlude, Amy, I still think you should accept my offer with a prisoner swap and you shall not be harmed tonight. What do you say?" Larry asked.

Amy looked around, unaware that her father was outside with her children. Hesitantly, she loosened her grip on Buffy and let her go. "Good choice, Amy. Now, if you could call up your father with my cell phone and get him to release Caleb and ensure his safe return to us, you may then return to your pathetic castle," Larry said, handing Amy his phone.

Amy took the device, unsure of which number to call. She decided to try Alistair, the number she remembered. "Hello?" Alistair answered.

"It's me," Amy said in a hushed tone. "Is my father nearby?" she asked. Alistair, sensing the urgency, handed the device over to Gabriel.

"Amy," Gabriel said, relief apparent in his voice. "We are outside with your children. Try to find a way to escape the situation."

Amy rolled her eyes before she looked over at Larry. "Larry has proposed a prisoner swap. Is Caleb in the area?" Amy asked.

"No, Amy," Gabriel said. "He is back at the castle. We can resolve this without succumbing to Larry's deceitful offers, Amy. Is Larry there with you?" he asked. Larry gestured impatiently for Amy to wrap up the call.

"Yes," Amy whispered, "he is here." Larry then snatched the phone from Amy's hands, leaving a scratch from his sharp nails on her left hand before hanging up.

"What did your father say, Amy? He sounds quite skeptical of my plan. If he is indeed out there, Amy, I plan to put an end to him once and for all. We won't have any more shape-shifting patriarchs roaming this world." Amy took a step back and approached one of the windows, catching sight of Larry's group and their glowing red eyes.

*Father, what is the plan? I have a feeling that this might not go so well for any of us anymore. As long as my children are safe, I am okay with whatever will happen.* Amy remained still and then, when she squinted her eyes, she recognized Bryan and Darcia, approaching the house. If Gabriel and his brothers were indeed outside, Bryan might have some backup on taking down Larry's new younglings. Amy started to feel more confident and relaxed about the whole conflict and leaned against the window. Larry noticed Amy's smile and walked over to her. "Did you see anything of interest, Amy?" Larry asked.

Amy shrugged and looked outside again. "Oh nothing, Larry. I just need to know, how well trained are your friends anyway?" Amy asked.

Larry furrowed his brows in confusion. "Are you really eager to witness another bloodbath, Amy?"

Larry moved toward the front door and saw Bryan, Darcia, Raymond, Joshua, Silas, and Xavier in the distance. "Clever move, Amy. But even with your six friends and your father out there, you're still outnumbered. Just because you can toss my siblings around like ragdolls doesn't mean you stand a chance against me. I was practically created by your father, whereas you are merely his little girl," Larry taunted, his voice filled with laughter.

Amy bared her teeth and growled. "Oh yeah, how intimidating. Seeing a puppy like yourself making scary sounds," Larry snapped. Amy got into a crouching position while keeping her gaze on Nathan, Buffy, and the other two kids. Larry then walked outside and closed the door behind him. "Gabriel, wherever you may be, I concede and will let you win this battle. It is true that my group members may not be strong, but then again, I have no interest in fighting with you either," Larry said as he held his hands up.

Gabriel emerged from the bushes , approaching Larry with Lucien and Daniel following behind, and Adrian and Vladimir trailing after them. "You win, Gabriel Ambrose. You can have your precious daughter back. I do care about Caleb, you know, so if you could release him, you'll never have to deal with me again," Larry stated. Gabriel then put two fingers in his mouth and blew a loud whistle, signaling Alistair and Darcia, who appeared behind him with their sons.

"Bryan, could you fetch Amy for me?" Gabriel asked. Bryan nodded and walked over to the apartment complex. Amy approached Bryan and embraced him tightly, while Nathan, Buffy, William, and Bianca formed a protective square around them.

"What makes you think you two will survive the night?" Nathan asked. Amy and Bryan exchanged glances before they kissed each other.

Bryan swiftly lunged at Nathan, pinning him down, while William attempted to grab Bryan from behind. Amy acted quickly, grabbing William and tossing him across the room once again. Bianca attacked Amy from behind, scratching her shoulders with her nails. Buffy then put Amy in a headlock. As William returned to the fray, Bryan reached for him, twisting his neck forcefully. Nathan retaliated by scratching Bryan across the face with his nails, eliciting a shriek of pain from Bryan. Buffy intensified her grip on Amy, scratching her neck and causing blood to flow freely.

Hearing the chaos unfolding inside the apartment complex, Gabriel lunged at Larry, but missed and fell to the ground. Meanwhile, other members of Larry's group charged at Gabriel and his allies, igniting a new battle. Gabriel quickly regained his footing and landed a punch on Larry, knocking him backward. A female member of Larry's group grabbed Gabriel from behind, but he swiftly twisted her neck, sending her to the ground. Lucien, Daniel, Adrian, Vladimir, and Alistair engaged Larry's friends, enduring scratches, bites, and blows.

Gabriel , undeterred, lunged at Larry again, biting him fiercely on the neck. Two other members of Larry's group grabbed Gabriel, but they were no match for his strength, and he sent them flying across the street. Suddenly, lights from nearby homes flickered on, and screams of fear filled the air as residents witnessed the brutal fight. Realizing the commotion had attracted attention, Gabriel scanned the surroundings and noticed open windows in other homes. The fight momentarily ceased until Larry seized the opportunity, grabbing Gabriel's left wrist and biting off a chunk of flesh, eliciting a scream of agony from Gabriel.

Injured members of Larry's group seized the chance to flee into the darkness. Alistair quickly came to Gabriel's aid, pulling him away from Larry and offering his own wrist for Gabriel to feed and regenerate. Daniel, seizing the moment, grabbed Larry but failed to notice Katrina approaching from behind. She stabbed him in the heart with a sharp stick, causing him to fall to his knees before she twisted his neck, finishing him off.

Lucien, filled with rage, attacked Katrina, biting her viciously and draining her blood until she was lifeless. Adrian and Xavier rushed to Daniel's side. Meanwhile, Larry managed to get to his feet and disappeared into the darkness. Gabriel, overwhelmed by grief, cradled Daniel's lifeless body in his arms, breaking down in tears. Darcia, seizing the initiative, stormed into the apartment complex and dragged Buffy out, draining her completely. Raymond and Joshua pursued William, dismembering his body and remembering to bring a pack of matches this time to finish the job. Bianca, seizing the chaos as her opportunity, escaped by jumping out of a window and followed Larry into the darkness.

"Brother," Gabriel whimpered. "I am so sorry for this. You did an amazing job. You deserve to be in whatever heaven you wish to be in. I am so sorry," Gabriel said through tears. Lucien got to his knees, crying in Daniel's shoulder, and then Vladimir got to his knees as well.

Amy, hearing her babies cry from the shrubs, had Darcia and Bryan help her gather her children. "Mommy is here," she cooed soothingly, despite her body being covered in scratch marks and blood. Bryan cradled another baby in his arms, saying, "So is your father." Darcia, smiling at Bryan, held the third baby in her embrace.

Amy walked back to the grieving group and broke down next to her father. "Daniel is dead?" she asked. Gabriel, his face tear-stained, could only nod in response. Amy dropped to her knees, resting her head on Gabriel's shoulder. "This cannot end like this," she declared. "Larry will be ended forever."

Joshua, Raymond, Silas, and Xavier began setting the bodies ablaze. They then turned to Daniel, who lay there with an unresponsive, dead expression on his face.

Gabriel shook his head, stating firmly, "Daniel deserves a proper ceremony and burial. He cannot just be burned like that." The group waited, allowing everyone time to prepare for their return to the castle.

Back at the castle, Arabella and Ginger did their best to remain calm, while Hildegard compulsively cleaned every surface. "Please stop, Hildegard," Arabella implored. "I am sure everything is okay." Despite her laughter, nervousness edged Hildegard's voice, but she continued to spray chemicals and wipe down surfaces with a cotton towel.

Upon their return, Gabriel, carrying Daniel in his arms, walked into the living quarters to find Arabella and Ginger waiting, shock registering on their faces. "What happened?" Arabella gasped.

Gently placing Daniel on one of the sofas, Gabriel asked, "Where is Amelia?" Without hesitation, Arabella ran to fetch Amelia from the dining quarter, where she had been sipping from a glass.

Amelia rushed to the living quarters, her shock evident as she took in the sight before her. "No," she whispered, tears forming in her eyes. "I will try and bring him back," she declared, before running off to her sleeping quarters.

Gabriel, his mind numb, sat on another sofa, staring blankly at the wall across from him. "This went too far. This war with Larry will end, and I will make sure that his death is slow," he vowed. Ginger and Arabella, seeking to help, walked over to Bryan and Darcia to hold Amy's children.

Amelia returned, spellbook and herbs in hand, and knelt beside Daniel. Gabriel, his eyes dry and burning, watched as she began her ritual. Opening her herb bottles, she sprinkled dried leaves around Daniel's wound. Closing her eyes, she hovered her hands over the wound and began to mumble ancient words, the same Gabriel had heard when Arabella was on the brink of death.

Arabella wrapped her arms around Amy, offering comfort, while Ginger handed an open bottle of blood to Amy, positioning it near her lips. Amy, her focus solely on Amelia, felt no thirst at the moment.

Amelia's voice grew louder until, suddenly, she clapped her hands together and fell silent. The entire room followed suit, everyone's attention fixed intently on Amelia and Daniel. When Amelia opened her eyes, confusion clouded her features. "What did I do wrong?" she murmured to herself, perplexed. "These spells have worked before, so why are they not working on Daniel?"

Gabriel, overwhelmed with sadness once again, covered his eyes with his right hand, taking deep breaths in an attempt to compose himself. "I never wished for any of this to happen. I feel as though it is all my fault," he choked out. Lucien sat down next to Gabriel, placing a reassuring hand on his shoulder. "Death is inevitable, brother," Lucien said, his tone soothing. "It comes at different times for everyone, and it's never fair. No one is ever truly prepared for it."

Gabriel exhaled deeply and turned to face Lucien. "But we are already dead, brother," he whispered. "Our kind usually regenerates within moments. Look at Larry, for example. Bryan attacked him a while back, Alistair and Bryan dismembered him, and yet he came back. But one act of penetrating Daniel's body, and he is gone. It makes no sense, Lucien." Gabriel's gaze drifted back to Daniel's lifeless form.

Amelia rose to her feet, turning to face Gabriel. "I'm not sure what I'm doing wrong, Gabriel. I've tried different spells, but nothing is working to wake him up. Is there something in our library that might have more information on our kind?" she asked. Gabriel could only shrug in response, his attention returning once again to Daniel.

"Forgive me, brother," he murmured, rising to his feet only to kneel again, this time hovering over Daniel's body. He pulled Daniel into his arms, cradling him like a child as tears fell freely down his cheeks. The rest of the room remained still and silent, many of them also in tears.

Meanwhile, Larry returned to his family's apartment complex, tending to the wounds and blood on his body. Five of his group members, similarly injured, accompanied him. "Larry," said a brunette girl in torn cotton leisurewear and tennis shoes as she approached him. "What do we do now?"

Larry regarded her with disappointment. "I almost had Gabriel, but Katrina just had to go and get his brother killed instead. Now we're in for an even bigger, more problematic battle, soon, Bianca," he snapped. Guilt welled up inside Bianca as she watched the other four members—three guys and another girl—enter the apartment complex. Larry took a seat in the chair previously occupied by Amy, his gaze falling upon the lifeless bodies of his parents and William.

Bianca cradled William's body in her arms, her voice filled with desperation as she asked, "Is there a way to bring them back from the dead, brother?" Larry simply shrugged, his attention still on his sister. The other members settled into various seats around the room, all of them focused on Larry.

"Katrina got her wish finally. She got to die in the hands of those monsters," Larry said sarcastically.

Bianca looked up at him, confusion etched on her face. "Who is Katrina?" she asked. "Oh, you mean that blonde woman we met briefly?" Larry nodded in affirmation. "She was quite pretty. I loved her hair and nails." Larry could only roll his eyes at her comment.

"She was quite an emotional wreck, though. She was used and abused by Gabriel, given false promises with no inkling of the two girls in his life. And now, she's gone forever," Larry said with a sigh.

The other members kept their focus on Larry, their faces etched with fear and concern. Bianca looked over at them and smiled reassuringly. "Larry will be okay, my friends. Do we have any blood or something to eat here, Larry?" she asked. Larry pointed in the direction of the kitchen.

"There might be some blood packs in the refrigerator or something like that. Otherwise, it would give us a reason to go hunting," Larry said.

Bianca gently placed William back on the floor before standing up and heading to the kitchen area. She opened the refrigerator and found three regular blood packs. Grabbing several glasses and a tray, she brought everything out for everyone. Larry smiled at Bianca's return. "Is that all?" he asked. Bianca nodded as she set the tray down.

As Larry and Bianca attended to their friends, back at the castle, Gabriel stepped outside, finding solace in the courtyard. He lay down on a lawn bed, gazing up at the stars. Arabella joined him, sitting in the chair next to his. "I'm so sorry for your loss, Gabriel," she said softly. "Daniel was a wonderful man and a remarkable protector for our children."

Gabriel looked over and offered her a small smile, reaching for her hand. She took his right hand in both of hers and kissed the top of it gently.

"I've reconsidered the idea of potentially divorcing, and I'm going to put it on the back burner for now," Arabella stated. "The death of Daniel has changed everything for the time being, and I see no reason to leave." Gabriel smirked at that, gently pulling his hand from her grasp.

"How thoughtful of you, Arabella," Gabriel said, his voice laced with a hint of sarcasm. Arabella rolled her eyes before standing up and heading back inside.

Gabriel chose to remain outside, taking the moment to himself, while Lucien, Adrian, and Vladimir prepared for Daniel's cremation. When Arabella re-entered the castle, the three men looked up at her. "How is he?" Lucien asked. Arabella simply shrugged.

"This new phase in our life has hit us all hard," Lucien commented as he helped wrap Daniel's body in white sheets. "It's painful to lose a close family member, a brother, and a remarkable warrior for our family."

Arabella placed her left hand on Lucien's shoulder, offering her support. "I know, Lucien. I understand how much it hurts to lose a family member. I'm relieved that he will be in a beautiful realm, I suppose," she said, her voice trailing off into a chuckle, though it was clear her heart wasn't in it. Adrian and Vladimir exchanged confused glances.

"I understand that he was meant to be here right now," Arabella said softly.

Lucien nodded in agreement as the three brothers finished preparing Daniel's body. Just then, Gabriel re-entered the castle.

Lucien, Adrian, and Vladimir stepped aside, allowing Gabriel a moment to observe their work.

"Are we ready to give him a proper farewell?" Gabriel asked , his voice breaking. The three men and Arabella nodded in unison. "Daniel would have been the one to help me with the electronics... just like last time," Gabriel said, his voice trailing off as he succumbed to his grief, breaking down in tears.

Lucien enveloped Gabriel in a hug, cradling him against his body. "I understand, brother," Lucien murmured soothingly as he gently caressed Gabriel's back. "I know how much this hurts. But we three can manage these electronic devices, can't we brothers?" Lucien asked, looking toward Vladimir and Adrian, who both nodded in agreement. "Shall we inform the other coven members through their electronic devices?" Lucien inquired, and again, the two brothers nodded. Together, the three of them made their way to Gabriel's study.

Gabriel, meanwhile, stood silently in front of Daniel's corpse, Arabella beside him. Taking a deep breath, he relaxed his shoulders and then walked over to where Alistair and Darcia were with their sons. Upon entering the living quarters, Alistair immediately approached Gabriel and embraced him tightly. "We're so sorry, Gabriel," Alistair whispered. Darcia, too, stepped forward to hug Gabriel, saying, "He was a wonderful man in our family, Gabriel. We were so lucky and fortunate to have him."

Tears welled up in Gabriel's eyes as he took a seat next to Raymond on the sofa. Struggling to speak through his choked words, he addressed Joshua, "Was there any way to stop that moment? Could you see an alternative way out of this mess?" All eyes turned to Joshua, who suddenly felt like a deer caught in headlights. Darcia moved to sit beside him, offering support.

"No sir," Joshua responded softly. "As a matter of fact, I actually foresaw your death," he whispered. Confused, Gabriel furrowed his brow and asked, "What? How was I supposed to die? By throwing myself between Katrina and Daniel?"

Joshua shook his head, clarifying, "You were going to save Amy from her death, resulting in Larry killing you instead." Stunned, Gabriel rose to his feet.

"Were you ever going to mention that to me, Joshua?" Gabriel snapped, his voice strained with emotion. "When were you planning on telling me this? I feel like I should have been the one to die hours ago. I should have sacrificed myself. Daniel was innocent and such a wonderful guy. I loved him so much," Gabriel said, breaking down once again in tears.

Raymond stood up and moved to a different chair, giving Gabriel some space. Alistair moved to sit beside Gabriel, and the room fell into a heavy silence until Lucien entered, a proud look on his face. "Yes, brother?" Gabriel asked. "What is with the look?"

Lucien smiled, announcing, "It took us some time to figure out these electronic devices, but we managed to get the other coven members to come back here for Daniel's departure." Gabriel managed to dry his eyes and stood up, asking, "Okay. When will they be here?" Lucien glanced at his watch, replying, "Probably in less than twelve hours. The low-key traveling can be a bit complicated for some of them, so they will arrive at different times." Gabriel couldn't help but smile at Lucien and patted him on the shoulder before heading to the dining quarters to chug down an entire bottle of blood.

Darcia and Alistair stood up, curious to see where Arabella and Amelia were. They found them in the dining quarter, each sipping blood from their glasses. Darcia approached Arabella and glanced around to ensure Gabriel wasn't nearby before asking, "How is Gabriel doing anyway?" Arabella shrugged, responding, "Same old Gabriel. He will be suffering a lot this time, but probably not as much as when I had died, I think." Alistair looked around once more, ensuring they were still alone in their conversation.

"How are the girls doing?" Darcia inquired, her gaze shifting between Arabella and Amelia. Arabella offered a smile in response.

"They're doing okay. However, I am worried about Amy's children. Normally, human babies have no recollection of their birth, but these younglings aren't human, and they'll probably remember all of this chaos for the rest of their lives," Arabella shared. Amelia, on the other hand, shrugged off the concern.

"I am sure they will be okay, sweetie," she reassured Arabella. "What really baffles me is how Larry keeps escaping death so swiftly. It's almost as if he can reincarnate, even after being burned," Amelia pondered aloud before downing the last drops from her glass.

Arabella's expression turned concerned as she regarded Amelia. "Gabriel and I had a fight, and I told him that this Larry issue was his problem. I can't help but wonder if I played a part in Gabriel's first encounter with him, or if I might have inadvertently caused Audrey's death—Logan's daughter," Arabella confessed, her voice laden with guilt. "Something inside me feels like I might be the root cause of it all. If I hadn't pushed Gabriel into such an emotional state, none of this would have happened," she added, tears welling in her eyes.

Amelia was quick to envelop Arabella in a tight hug. "Arabella, stop thinking that way," she chided gently, her tone stern yet soothing. "Gabriel needs to learn to handle these conflicts better. It's not your fault that Daniel is dead. Okay? According to Joshua, it was Gabriel who was supposed to die, not Daniel, and yet here he is," Amelia tried to comfort her.

Arabella, however, scoffed at the attempted reassurance. "What does that have to do with anything, Amelia?" she snapped, frustration evident in her voice. "Is that supposed to make me feel better about the whole situation?"

Amelia sighed, realizing she needed to clarify her words. "What I meant, Arabella, is that you are not the cause of all this. These things sometimes happen without a clear reason. You died on the birthing table years ago because childbirth is inherently risky—not because of something you did. People die for unexpected reasons. Daniel died protecting Gabriel. It's tragic, but it could just as easily have been Gabriel lying on that table. He was lucky; he dodged death," Amelia explained. "Please excuse me; I'll go see if the others need any help."

With Amelia gone, Arabella recapped the bottle and placed it back in the cooler. After closing the door, she returned to the table to put the glasses in the sink. Darcia stayed put in the room, while

Alistair decided to check on the others. He entered Gabriel's study to find Lucien, Adrian, Vladimir, and Amelia gathered together.

"How's it going in here?" Alistair asked. Lucien raised a hand to hush him.

"Lucien is dealing with some of Gabriel's affairs. It's quite amusing to watch him fumble with the keyboard," Adrian teased. Lucien sighed but maintained his focus on the computer screen.

Meanwhile, Alistair turned his attention down the hallway, spotting Gabriel observing various paintings of himself and Daniel. When Gabriel heard Alistair approach, he turned around.

"Yes, Alistair?" Gabriel asked. Alistair shrugged, his gaze lingering on the portraits.

"I'm just trying to decide which portrait of Daniel to use for his cremation," he shared, a hint of sadness in his voice. Alistair then moved a bit closer to Gabriel, his eyes scanning the various paintings of the brothers and Amelia.

Gabriel maintained his attention on Daniel's first painting, noting the youthful appearance captured in it. "Have any of our guests arrived yet, Alistair?" he inquired. Alistair shook his head in response.

"Okay. They shall probably show up in a few hours. I'm having a hard time processing this whole moment, Alistair. I still can't believe it all happened. If I may ask," Gabriel continued, "how did Joshua actually see me getting killed when I had asked Bryan to go into that house to grab Amy?"

Alistair gave another shrug. "I don't understand my son's powers all too well at the moment, Gabriel. Sometimes I think I know what he's thinking or feeling, but then it turns out to be the opposite. I would have never known about any of their powers. I always raised them to keep their true selves under wraps and never to talk about it openly."

Gabriel nodded, appreciating the honesty. "I'm happy to have you with us, Gabriel. You've always been, and still are, the patriarch—the father figure, the protector. I just remember when I introduced you to Darcia for the first time and how you had me turn her," Alistair said with a chuckle.

Gabriel remained expressionless. "I'm glad that I chose her as my life mate. She has been wonderful to me and my sons."

Gabriel smiled, feeling a wave of sentimentality. "I understand how powerful love is, Alistair," he said, turning to face him. "I loved Katrina in my own way, but nothing could ever match my feelings for Arabella. I know she has mixed feelings about me, but I never gave up on bringing her back from the dead either. She was my muse, my euphoria. Her smile made all my worries and fears disappear," Gabriel expressed, feeling himself relax a bit.

Alistair enjoyed listening to Gabriel's heartfelt words. "She is a wonderful woman, Gabriel. I think we both lucked out in our choices, even if the circumstances were complicated," Alistair said, chuckling. Gabriel couldn't help but laugh along.

"The curse of the Ambrose family, I believe," Gabriel said, before his attention was drawn back to the paintings. "Oh, look," he said, pointing at a painting of Daniel in an evening suit.

Alistair walked over to examine the painting, noting Daniel's handsome appearance. "I think we should use this painting for his cremation ceremony," Gabriel suggested. "Could you help me with it?"

Alistair nodded in agreement. "Of course, Gabriel. I can even bring it up for you if you'd like," he offered.

"I appreciate that, Alistair," Gabriel said gratefully. He carefully took the painting off the hook and handed it to Alistair.

As Gabriel prepared to return to the main floor, he was caught by the sight of another painting—this one of Arabella in a white, wavy gown. He was struck by how young and angelic she looked, just as she had when they first met. His heart swelled with happiness at the memory of finding such a beautiful woman.

Lost in his thoughts, Gabriel didn't notice Arabella's approach. "Gabe?" she called softly. "What have you been up to?" Gabriel turned to her with a smile, his eyes flicking between her and the painting.

"Do you remember when I had this painting of you made? Do you remember what we did that evening?" he asked, his voice filled with nostalgia.

Arabella took a moment to reflect, then smiled warmly. "I remember how you showed me around Romania for the first time and how gentle you were with me. You even carried me in your arms, like a bride-to-be, and treated me to a fine meal, all the while sitting across from me with nothing but a glass of wine in your hand," she recalled.

Gabriel's face lit up at Arabella's recollection. "I know you have a sweet side, Gabriel. I know you didn't intentionally have me killed, but the fact remains that you did kill off my family, which is inexcusable. Nevertheless, we do have beautiful children and now grandchildren. We also have some wonderful family members who are very loving and supportive in our time of grief. Daniel was a wonderful man, Gabriel. And if what Darcia told me is true about Joshua seeing you killed instead, then for the sake of my love for you and for Amy and Ginger, I am glad you are still alive," Arabella expressed.

Gabriel turned to face Arabella and drew her close in an embrace. "Thank you, Arabella. I truly do want to be a better husband, leader, and father to all of you. I admit, I've chosen some wrong paths in the past, but I feel that with this awakening, we will all be okay again," he shared, his voice sincere and full of hope.

# The Funeral

As dusk approached, Dante, Logan, Kristjan, and Alarick's family all arrived at the castle, dressed in black dresses and suits. Gabriel stood beside Hildegard as she opened the door for each group, welcoming them in. They all embraced Gabriel, offering their condolences for his loss, including Logan, who had lost his daughter.

"I really want to see an end to that Larry creature," Logan said, his voice heavy with emotion. "My wife, Mackenzie, is still traumatized by the fighting, as am I, Gabriel," he admitted.

"I agree, brother," Gabriel responded, , his tone somber as everyone gathered in the living quarters. Amy and Ginger were present, looking as devastated as ever. Arabella stood between them, holding them close, as the entire shape-shifting family sat around, their expressions filled with sorrow. Gabriel then stepped forward, addressing the family.

"My dear and wonderful family," he began, his voice filled with emotion. "We have all endured great suffering. I have apologized in many ways for the whole situation, but I know I can't apologize forever. We have lost our dear brother, Daniel," Gabriel paused, turning away to dab at his eyes before facing the family again. Overwhelmed with grief, he found himself unable to continue speaking, but he was met with empathetic eyes from everyone around.

"We understand, Gabriel," Dante interjected, his voice compassionate. "Talking about such things can be incredibly hard.

What's the plan now? How does this creature manage to escape and regenerate each time?"

Gabriel took a deep breath, steadying himself before speaking again. "We have to murder him, dismember him, burn him, and perhaps add a death curse from our sorceress, Amelia Ambrose," he declared determinedly. "This time, we won't let any mistakes happen in our family. The hardest and most difficult mistakes often teach us the most important lessons. The loss of a family member helps us understand the true nature of pain."

Arabella looked over at Gabriel, offering him a warm smile, though she wondered if he was referencing the tragic loss of her own family. Catching her gaze, Gabriel returned the smile, "We are one strong family, and there's nothing in this world we can't handle together. Larry has managed to maintain his fighting and hunting skills, something I've somewhat neglected, never imagining we'd find ourselves in this situation. Hildegard, could you please fetch the fifty bottles of blood you've managed to gather from various hospitals and blood banks?"

Hildegard responded with a smile and a nod. "My pleasure, sir," she said before leaving to fulfill the request. Gabriel then turned his attention back to his family. "I know how challenging our first battle was, my dear family," he said. "But I promise you, we will be able to handle Larry and put an end to him once and for all." Everyone nodded in agreement.

"Um, Logan?" Gabriel queried, drawing Logan's attention. "Have you and your family already cremated your dear Audrey?" Logan shook his head in response. "We brought her over since you were planning a proper burial for Daniel. Perhaps it would be nice for them to be together, and it allows the whole family to say their goodbyes," Logan explained.

Gabriel nodded. "I think that's a good idea, Logan. We will have two separate ceremonies for our beloved family members." Logan and Mackenzie offered faint smiles. "The pain will never fully go away, and even my kind words can't erase the loss of someone so special. But remember, you all are always welcome to stay here with me for as long as you need," Gabriel reassured them.

Mackenzie, dabbing at her eyes with a tissue, managed to choke out, "I wish it had been me taken from the family, not my dear girl."

Logan wrapped his arm around her, offering comfort. "I know, my love. The pain feels like a dagger through our hearts," he whispered soothingly.

Lucien, overwhelmed by memories of Katrina's deadly attack on Daniel, felt tears welling up in his eyes. A heavy sadness hung in the air, palpable to everyone in the room.

Hildegard returned with ten bottles of blood and left again to fetch the rest. Gabriel, in the meantime, went to the dining quarter to get crystal wine glasses for everyone. He placed the tray on the living quarter table and began pouring the blood into the glasses.

Arabella joined him to help with pouring, and soon Helen and Ginger were at their side. Amy, feeling a profound sense of loss and confusion, looked around the room. She saw Alistair and Darcia, their faces etched with sorrow and fear, and then her eyes landed on Bryan, who looked angry.

Ginger handed Amy a glass of blood, and Amy, in turn, offered it to Bryan, but he shook his head. "You need it more, my sweet Amy," he said calmly. "You're feeding three children; you need all the nutrients you can get." Amy smiled and nodded in gratitude.

"Is there anything I can do to help, Bryan?" Amy asked. Bryan shook his head, indicating there was nothing she needed to worry about.

"There has been too much drama and too many problems in this family. I really wish we didn't have to suffer like this," Bryan said. Darcia put her left arm around Bryan's shoulders, drawing him close. Amy watched the motherly gesture from Darcia with a smile. She then turned her attention to Raymond, Silas, and Xavier, who all appeared depressed and angry. Joshua, however, looked neutral. Why would Joshua, the seeker of the future, remain so calm? Curious, Amy decided to approach him.

"How are you doing, Josh?" Amy asked. Joshua looked up at her and smiled.

"Average, I guess," Joshua said. "Why do you ask Amy?" Amy didn't reply immediately, instead focusing intently on his demeanor.

"Larry?" she asked sternly. Joshua's expression turned angry. "Did you shape-shift into Larry?"

Joshua shook his head. "What makes you think I'm Lawrence?" he retorted. "Just because my brothers aren't handling this well doesn't mean I should follow suit. If I were Larry, I wouldn't be standing this close in a crowd, Amy," he snapped.

Alistair walked over, placing a reassuring hand on Amy's shoulder. "That's enough, son," he said to Joshua. "We're all suffering greatly right now, so please try to keep any drama to yourself." Joshua fell silent, his attention now on his glass of blood, taking small sips.

Gabriel cleared his throat, drawing the attention of the room. "Tomorrow evening we shall have our family funeral. For now, feel free to rest, drink, and do whatever you need to prepare yourselves for tomorrow night's bonfire funeral," he announced. Everyone nodded in agreement, but Alistair and Darcia's sons suddenly realized that they would have to give up their bedrooms once again.

Bryan walked over to Alistair. "Where is the sleeping bag again, Father?" he asked. Alistair could not help, but chuckle at the way Bryan looked.

"I will take the floor this time, son. Don't worry about the dusty carpet," Alistair replied, his tone laced with sarcasm as he walked past Bryan. Bryan smiled at his father's remark and joined his brothers.

"Well, brothers, I am glad that we are still together and that we have not lost one of our own. I love you all so much and I really do care about you all, whether you believe me or not," Bryan said.

Joshua smiled and nodded. "As do I, brother. Gabriel seemed to be suffering a lot while he was speaking earlier. A brotherly bond is quite strong in our family. I think that's probably how Amy and Ginger feel," he commented. Bryan smiled in agreement.

"I just want to say this to you four. When Amy approached me earlier, suspecting I was Larry due to my neutral expression, I realized I've never felt close to Gabriel or his brothers," Joshua admitted.

Bryan nodded in understanding. "Daniel was quite provocative the last time we had a family gathering. I remember him questioning me about where I belonged and giving me stern looks whenever I answered," he shared. "I would never treat any of you like that, nor your future spouses or children."

Raymond smiled. "Me neither. If I may propose a toast," he said, raising his glass. "May we never break this brotherly bond and always stay together, no matter what." Bryan and the others raised their glasses, their glasses clinking together.

"To brothers," they all chimed in unison.

Amy watched Bryan and his brothers from a distance, taking small sips from her glass, before deciding to check on her babies who were sleeping in their crib. As she approached, Gabrielle opened her eyes.

"It's me, my darling children," Amy whispered gently. "Let me take care of you for now. Now that your grandfather has given his grand speech, it's my turn to take care of my children."

Just then, Ginger entered Amy's bedroom, quietly closing the door behind her. "Wow," she whispered, a hint of exhaustion in her voice. "I've never felt so tense in my body after these last few days, Ames. I feel so sick inside. That blood beverage didn't help either."

Amy nodded in understanding. "Could you help me with my children, though? Like, changing them, for example?" she asked. Without hesitation, Ginger picked up Maggie and took her to the bathroom.

Shortly after, Arabella arrived at Amy's room and saw her with Gabrielle in her arms. "Do you need any help, Amy?" Arabella asked.

Amy nodded.

"Shall I take Nathaniel and wash him up?"

"I would love that, Mother," Amy said. "Gabrielle is about ready for her bath, as well. Ginger is in the bathroom with Maggie."

Arabella carried Nathaniel, who had grown a bit bigger and whose light brown hair was getting long for a baby, to the bathroom. Amy followed, entering the bathroom just in time to see Ginger testing the bath water to ensure it wasn't too hot for the infants. The three women diligently attended to the babies, while the rest of the family members were scattered around the castle.

There was a knock on Amy's bedroom door. "Great," Amy said sarcastically. "Who could that be?"

Amy placed Gabrielle in the bath, which had about five inches of water and dried off her hands before she walked over to her bedroom door and opened it up to see Helen and Francesca.

"Is it a good time to see the younglings, Amy? I have been looking forward to meeting your children," Helen said.

Amy felt a bit awkward and shook her head. "Not right now, ladies," Amy said. "They are in the midst of getting washed up. Perhaps in an hour or so when they will be awake for a while," Amy said with a chuckle. "And I mean, a while, like hours, you know?"

Both Francesca and Helen chuckled at Amy's remark. "Okay," Helen said. "So, what did you name them by any chance?" Francesca asked. Amy moved her face closer to theirs.

"Maggie, after my ancestor, Gabrielle after my father, and Nathaniel, because of how angelic our family names have been," Amy whispered. Both women clapped their hands with glee.

"So beautiful, Amy," Helen said. Francesca smiled and nodded. "Well, we will let you get back to attending to your children."

After the women left, Amy walked back to the bathroom to see her three children looking up at her with smiles on their faces. "They are so precious, Amy. I think they are ready for their fluffy towels," Arabella said before she got to her feet to grab three separate towels for Amy's kids.

Ginger looked at the three children with bittersweet feeling. "I wonder if I will ever have a baby of my own," she murmured to herself.

Amy put her right hand on Ginger's shoulder. "You will, Ginger, if that is what you want," Amy said. "Your time will come, and it will be all the more precious, especially when you find the man of your dreams. I might have Bryan, I think," she added with a thoughtful tone. "I really do hope you find your Prince Charming and live happily ever after, surrounded by your little ones."

Ginger looked up at Amy and smiled. "I love you. I hope you know that, sister dear," Ginger said. "I really do care about you. Your bravery. Your caring nature. Just everything about you is so beautiful," Ginger said.

At that moment, Arabella entered the room, towels in hand. Each of the women took a baby, gently drying them off before dressing them in their pajamas. However, as Amy picked up Gabrielle, she suddenly saw a vision of her daughter as a young woman, fighting alongside her mother in a futuristic battle. Amy stood still, unresponsive, as Ginger and Arabella tried to shake her out of her trance. Eventually, she snapped back to reality.

"Goodness, Amy," Arabella exclaimed, concerned. "Are you okay? You looked like you had seen a ghost." Amy furrowed her brow, confusion etched across her face as she turned to face them.

"Did neither of you see that? I had some kind of vision from Gabrielle. Did you feel anything when you touched Maggie or Nathaniel?" Amy questioned urgently. Both Arabella and Ginger shook their heads, still confused. "Huh. Perhaps it was a gift from my side. Who knows," Amy pondered aloud.

She then placed Gabrielle on the bed, noticing how adorable she looked in her red polka-dotted onesie. Sitting beside her, Amy tried to make sense of what had just happened. She looked over at Gabrielle, who maintained a straight, neutral expression as she licked her lips. "Are you gifted, my child?" Amy asked, more to herself than to her daughter, who simply stared back at her. "Hmm. Perhaps it's all just a result of my lack of sleep," Amy murmured to herself.

Arabella and Ginger returned to the room, dressing Maggie in a purple polka-dotted onesie and Nathaniel in a green one. Arabella glanced at her watch, realizing it was nearing four o'clock in the morning. "Perhaps we should all try to get some rest," she suggested. "Tomorrow, we have Daniel's funeral to attend."

Ginger and Amy both nodded. They shared a group hug before Ginger and Arabella left Amy's room. Amy then turned her attention back to her children, tucking them in for the night. However, as she touched Maggie, she experienced another quick vision—this time of Maggie as a young woman, tearing into the flesh of another creature, her sharp teeth bared and blood splattered everywhere. The vision made Amy jump.

"My, my," Amy whispered to herself, trying to shake off the image. "This lack of sleep is really getting to me."

Lastly, she wondered what she might see if she touched Nathaniel. Hesitantly, she leaned down and gently stroked his forehead, only to see a vision of him and Bryan together, which brought a smile to her face. "Okay, that's probably enough for now, my children," Amy said softly before climbing into her own bed, turning off the light, and falling into a deep sleep.

In her dream, Amy found herself back in the same woods, pushing the same stroller as before. However, this time the sun was breaking through the trees. A sense of fear ran through her body as her babies began to cry when the sun touched them. "Oh, man," Amy exclaimed, her voice filled with urgency. "We need to get back to the castle." But as she turned around, she realized the castle had somehow disappeared, and the sun's rays intensified, its burning touch scalding her arms and scalp.

Amy hurried into the woods, pushing her stroller filled with her crying babies. She found a cooler spot and stopped to catch her breath, only to notice a woman crouched down, sobbing, her back turned to Amy. Amy instantly sensed that this woman was trouble. She began to back away slowly, but the woman stood up, still facing away. When she turned around, Amy saw it was Katrina, but with a horribly scorched face. Amy felt a stabbing fear in her gut, and she wanted to turn and run, but something about Katrina held her frozen in place. Katrina approached the stroller, peering down at the children. "I never got to have a baby," she moaned, before reaching down to pick up Maggie. In a panic, Amy lunged forward, and suddenly woke up on the floor next to her bedroom door, heart pounding.

"Oh goodness," Amy said as she looked around. "That dream was terrifyingly realistic. What is going on?" She glanced at her alarm clock; it was eight in the morning. The thought of getting back to sleep now seemed impossible. Right on cue, Gabrielle began to cry, quickly followed by Maggie and Nathaniel. Amy got up and went over to the crib to pick up each baby, preparing to feed them.

Downstairs, Arabella was stirring from her sleep in the basement, immediately feeling the emptiness beside her. Gabriel was in his living room quarters, in the same spot where he had first met Amy and Ginger. He was nursing a bottle of blood, staring blankly at the wall in front of him.

"Gabriel?" Arabella called softly, concern in her voice. "What are you doing up? Did you get any rest?"

Gabriel shook his head, his expression heavy. "I can't stop thinking about Daniel. I should have been the one to die, not him. I don't understand why Alistair pulled me aside, knowing I was Katrina's target," he confessed.

Arabella nodded, her heart aching for her husband. "I understand, my dear. I've been having trouble sleeping as well. The drama and challenges our family has faced...it does take its toll, doesn't it?"

"Yes, it does, my love," Gabriel agreed, his voice filled with sorrow. "In about ten hours, we'll have a feast prepared for the whole family. But sometimes...sometimes I wish it had been me instead of Daniel. I've done terrible things without thinking, driven by lust. I deserve to burn, not Daniel. He was beautiful, strong, innocent, and a pillar of support for our family. In many ways, he was far better than I ever was."

Arabella wrapped her right arm around his shoulders, pulling him close. "Amy and Ginger need you too, Gabriel. Don't forget about them. You're their father. If anything happened to you, they would be devastated. And Amy's children need their grandfather's support. You have so much wisdom to share about our kind, and you can teach Nathaniel what it means to be a strong male leader. They all need you, Gabriel Ambrose. Losing a family member is incredibly hard, but remember, you are not alone."

Gabriel looked at her and smiled, gratitude in his eyes. "You are such a beautiful soul, Arabella," he said sincerely. "You always know how to ease my pain. What can I do to make amends for my past actions? I'm willing to do anything to make you happy."

Arabella smiled and shook her head. "Gabriel, simply having the desire to improve and be there for your family is a crucial step. You don't need to repent for past actions; what's done is done. Learn from your mistakes and strive to better yourself in areas that need attention. Teach Amy's children how to control their lusts, be a supportive mentor for Amy and Ginger," she advised.

Gabriel nodded. "You're right," he said, a smirk playing on his lips. He took a moment to admire Arabella's beauty, his eyes filled with love, before they leaned in for a tender kiss.

Afterward, they joined the others on the main floor, where Alistair and Bryan were setting up Daniel's painting in the courtyard. Darcia, Helen, Francesca, and Mackenzie were arranging chairs, while Lucien, Adrian, and Vladimir prepared their speeches. Amy and Ginger remained in the background, helping Bryan and his brothers with flowers and stage setup.

Despite the bustle of activity, Gabriel felt a turmoil of unease and anger inside. He found he had no appetite for food or drink. Meanwhile, Alarick, Dante, and Logan were also working on their speeches. Logan, in particular, was struggling, overwhelmed with agony and sadness as he looked at his deceased daughter in her casket. He gently touched her cold, unresponsive cheek, tears welling in his eyes.

Mackenzie approached and wrapped her arms around him, offering a gentle hug. "You shouldn't feel pressured to speak, my love. I might say a few words, but I'm hurting too," she whispered.

Logan held onto Mackenzie for a few moments longer before reluctantly letting go. Meanwhile, Darcia was ensuring everything was set up perfectly and went over to the microphone to do a sound check.

Gabriel slowly made his way to the stage area, where Lucien, Adrian, and Vladimir were carrying Daniel's coffin. He looked down at Daniel's face, his heart heavy with guilt and anger. "Wherever you are now, dear brother, I hope you find peace and luxury. You deserve the finest meals, clothing, and sleeping quarters. I never wanted to see you like this, and I'm so sorry for everything, Daniel Ambrose. If it had to be someone, it should have been me," he murmured, his voice barely audible.

Alistair stepped onto the stage, maintaining a respectful distance from Gabriel until he noticed Gabriel's attention shift to him. "Whenever you're ready, Gabriel," Alistair said softly.

Gabriel nodded, gathering himself before stepping up to the microphone. The crowd settled into their chairs, their attention focused on him.

"This...this is probably the second hardest moment in my entire existence, spanning thousands of years. I lost my wife about twenty years ago, had to give up my children to the human world shortly after, and now...now I have lost two invaluable members of our coven," Gabriel began, his voice heavy with grief.

Helen, Francesca, and Mackenzie dabbed their eyes, while their husbands held their hands. "Death is part of life," Gabriel said. "For our kind, we never had to think of these moments because we are not human. I never had to contemplate death personally, but I have witnessed others suffering and dying. It made me rethink my approach to hunting in many ways. Humans do deserve their moments of happiness. That's why I have had Hildegard provide donated blood for my home rather than sourcing it from humans. I never understood what pain felt like until I lost my beloved wife, my soulmate, my world, years ago. That must have been akin to the excruciating pain Daniel felt before he passed. It's an unimaginable pain until you've experienced it yourself," Gabriel continued.

Everyone listened to Gabriel's speech with interest and acknowledgement. "I remember when I met Daniel. He was a beautiful man. A thoughtful gentleman to everyone when he was human. After I left Larry's situation, I traveled around Western Europe to find out more about my kind. I was in a hotel lobby outside of our home in Romania. He was a bartender at this hotel. He wore a white blouse, brown trousers, and a green gilet with a nametag. I remember how the drinks he served did not taste good to me, but I remember how he would listen to my stories of my traveling and all of the obstacles I had overcome. Daniel was quite an interesting man to listen to, as well. He came from an American background and he told me how he grew up. He told me how he chose to live in Romania, because of his fascination with vampires. Of course I thought that was quite amusing, because of how vampires are just fictional from what I have learned. I remember how he was quite attracted to me in the sense of how strong I seemed and how confident I was. He wanted to have a mentor in his life. He wanted to have someone who would teach him of many topics. I was quite honored to hear such words coming from him, but I was also worried that he would be scared of my true identity. I was worried he would have the law enforcement sent after me. Somehow, we met on various occasions. I would tell him the history of some countries and of philosophers," Gabriel said before he had to stop and exhale from exhaustion.

"I remember…" Gabriel began, his voice faltering as he struggled with his emotions. "I remember how much Daniel wished he could be part of this family, how I was like a father figure to him. He didn't care much for his own family but appreciated me for who I was. In all my years alive, living in solitude, I'd never met someone as kind as Daniel. I brought him to my home in Romania and showed him the country. He was the one who proposed staying with me. I felt uncertain about it—I wasn't sure he'd survive a single night until he found my unlabeled bottles and realized I was a blood drinker. His fascination with vampires made him think it'd be thrilling to become one. Of course, I'm not a vampire but a shapeshifter with an unknown origin. He was so adamant about joining my family, but I couldn't turn him. It wasn't until he ran into the city to tell others about me that I had to act quickly. I brought him back and turned him. Goodness, he could be quite the little brat, but I felt a connection to him, almost like a son," Gabriel shared.

The audience nodded in agreement, connecting with the sentiment. "Well, I have no more to say for now. If anyone wishes to speak about their memories of Daniel, please feel free. Lastly, we will take a moment for Audrey, Logan's child," Gabriel announced before stepping down from the stage. A respectful silence settled over the crowd until Lucien rose and approached the podium. He spoke of a bond with Gabriel similar to Daniel's, describing his initial impression of Daniel as a spoiled child, which evolved over time into a deep friendship. They had developed a brotherly bond, sharing interests and experiences.

Adrian followed with his tribute, and then Vladimir took the stage, speaking about Daniel with the affection one would for a brother and best friend. Each shared their stories of the strong bond they all held with one another.

After the brothers shared their stories, Alistair got to his feet and made his way to the stage. "Good evening, family members," Alistair began. "My family and I, probably like many of you, kept our distance from Gabriel and his household for quite some time. That was until we were summoned to care for Amy and Ginger. When we traveled from our home in France, where we had been relocated, to Romania, our hearts broke for Arabella upon our arrival. It was then I met Lucien, Daniel, Adrian, and Vladimir. The shock of Arabella's death and the sight of two infant girls in Lucien and Amelia's arms was overwhelming, but I couldn't help noticing how sharp you all looked in your suits. Gabriel had indeed turned you into remarkable individuals. I remember my first encounter with Gabriel fondly; he was fatherly and loving when I was turned. As for Daniel, I can't say much personally, but I recognize the fortune he—and all of you— had in having Gabriel in your lives. Thank you," Alistair concluded before he exited the stage.

Amelia was next to speak about Daniel. Looking down at Daniel's lifeless form, tears welled up in her eyes. "I can't believe this could happen, even to our kind. I thought we were immortal, but it took just one moment, one piercing stick to his flesh, and now he's gone, just like that," she whispered to herself. Gabriel nodded in acknowledgment of her words.

Approaching the microphone, Amelia cleared her throat. "Daniel was a beautiful and wonderful man, talented, especially with technology. He was probably the first among us to master those computer machines," she said with a light chuckle, prompting a ripple of laughter from the others. "He had his own brand of strength and power. Between you and me," she continued, her voice dropping to a more intimate tone, "I had hoped to be Daniel's life mate. I waited a long time to be his, but he always kept his distance when it came to partnerships and love." She paused, reflecting. "Sadly, I am not so certain about partnerships at the moment, either."

Gabriel mulled over Amelia's comments, pondering what support he could offer her. But his thoughts were pulled back as Amelia resumed her speech. "Aside from that, Daniel deserves the most beautiful resting place, where he can love, eat, hunt, and sleep to his heart's content. I will always miss you, Daniel," she finished, leaning down to embrace him one last time before stepping away from the casket.

Following Amelia, Dante spoke briefly about death and Daniel. Then Alarick, Helen, Francesca, and Mackenzie took turns to offer their words, each adding to the collective eulogy. Finally, it was Logan's turn to speak.

Lucien, Adrian, and Vladimir lowered Daniel's coffin and then joined Dante and Alarick to carry Audrey's. Logan stood silently, gazing into the grass for a long moment before speaking. "My wife, Mackenzie, told me it's okay not to give a speech, but what kind of father would I be if I couldn't honor my daughter's death? Here's my speech: Losing a child is incredibly hard. No parent should have to bear the loss of their child. I believe that all parents—or at least most—would wish to see their child find success and happiness in life," Logan said.

Gabriel furrowed his brow and rolled his eyes. Logan glanced at Gabriel, a questioning look on his face. "Where was I?" Logan murmured to himself. "Oh, right. The pain of losing a close family member is profound, but the agony of losing a child, as a parent, is indescribable. No words or gestures of comfort can fill the void. I remember Alarick saying to Gabriel about a month ago that he would rather sacrifice his own life than see the rest of us suffer," Logan continued.

Gabriel's anger began to rise until Arabella placed a calming hand on his shoulder and shook her head. "Siblings are painful enough to lose, but a child? A child is a part of you. When a child dies, a piece of the parents dies too. I'm not sure I can continue being a good husband to Mackenzie after today. I can't eat, drink, or even take pleasure in life anymore. I am sorry for the loss of Daniel, but my pain feels more consuming. Thank you," Logan finished, stepping down from the stage.

Gabriel rose to confront Logan. "What kind of speech was that, Logan? Was that a dig at me? As far as I knew, no one expected your child to be the one we'd lose. And I certainly didn't foresee my brother's death either. So, I'd appreciate it if you wouldn't diminish my grief at this time," Gabriel retorted sharply.

Mackenzie got to her feet and walked over to Gabriel. "How can you say that, Gabriel? Losing a child is an unbearable pain for us. Audrey was our little ray of sunshine. I understand it's hard to lose a brother, but Logan has every right to his grief," Mackenzie retorted.

Arabella rose, standing beside Gabriel. "I think we all need a moment to collect ourselves. Let's get a drink and take some time to reflect on our emotions."

Mackenzie scoffed. "Oh, the wife of the monster. Arabella, when did you start suffering from Stockholm syndrome? Remember the awful things Gabriel did to you? To your daughters?" Arabella met her gaze firmly.

"I won't engage in this. Everyone is in pain, and I refuse to argue," Arabella countered sharply before turning to her daughters. "Children, would you please come with me?" she asked.

Gabriel cleared his throat, regaining his composure. "We need to complete this ceremony. Brothers, please procure a source of fire, be it from a candle or a match. Logan, my apologies for my earlier outburst, and for your loss. Let's unite to give our loved ones a dignified farewell. Please, join us," Gabriel invited, his tone now more conciliatory. Logan nodded in agreement.

"I guess I could have kept my speech shorter and less angry," Logan admitted. Gabriel wrapped his arms around Logan in a comforting embrace.

"Audrey was a remarkable woman, Logan. Don't forget who she inherited that from," Gabriel reassured him as he held Logan close.

Logan took a deep breath and exhaled. "Thank you, Gabriel," he murmured. "I never imagined I'd be giving such a speech, or facing such a terrible loss." Gabriel nodded in understanding. Lucien handed Logan his silver lighter, while Vladimir and Adrian doused the body with gasoline. Mackenzie stood by Logan's side, crying softly. Logan felt a wave of anger and sorrow wash over him as he stood there, lighter in hand, hesitating to set flame to his child's remains. Gabriel watched and waited for Logan to make the move so that he could do the same for Daniel.

With a heavy breath, Logan dropped the lighter, igniting the pyre. Mackenzie let out a shrill cry, clinging to Logan, who felt constricted by his emotions, uttering a low growl. The onlookers shed tears, heads shaking in disbelief and sorrow. Once Audrey was reduced to ashes, Hildegard collected them into an urn and offered it to Logan or Mackenzie.

Lucien, Adrian, and Vladimir then prepared Daniel's body in the same manner, pouring gasoline. Gabriel, feeling a multitude of metaphorical stabs to the heart, remained silent. With a solemn gesture, he dropped the lighter and watched as Daniel's body was consumed by flames. In that moment, Gabriel felt as if a part of him had died; he was wounded and nauseated with grief. Turning away with a look of profound loss, he retreated to the back of the crowd.

Amy walked over to Gabriel and wrapped her arms around her father, feeling him stiff as a board. "I am sorry, Father," she whispered. Gabriel placed his hands on Amy's soft beautiful hair and stroked it gently. Amy released her grip and walked past him. Alistair walked over to Gabriel and wrapped his arms around him. Others then followed. Bryan, struck by the depth of Gabriel's grief, feared whether he could endure the loss of his own brothers in a similar way.

Brushing away tears, Bryan sought out Darcia, who stood with Alistair, apart from the group. "Mother," he said, "have you seen the look on Gabriel's face? I doubt I could bear such a burden," he confessed quietly. Darcia offered a comforting smile and placed her hand on Bryan's cheek.

"Death is a profound challenge for all of us, my son. The thought of losing any of you is unbearable to me as well. Logan and Mackenzie have shown remarkable strength in participating in this ceremony," Darcia spoke softly before she turned to walk inside the castle.

# New Beginnings

After everyone had gathered in the living quarters, each person laden with feelings of sadness, anger, hopelessness, and devastation from their losses, Gabriel retreated to his study and sat behind his desk, uncertain of his next steps. Arabella knocked on Gabriel's door, and upon his opening it, she entered at his gesture. "That was quite brave of you, Gabriel," she said. "Organizing a beautiful ceremony for Daniel and Audrey. You've shown a new side to yourself, and I have great respect for you."

Gabriel offered a fleeting smile before his face settled back into its neutral state. "Death is so hard, Arabella. When you died on that birthing table years ago, I felt compelled to join you and leave our children parentless. I never thought I'd be capable of remaining the patriarch of our family," he confessed. Arabella nodded. "My brothers and Amelia—they were so strong," Gabriel continued, his eyes welling up again. "I was blessed with such an amazing family then, as I am now."

Arabella nodded as she was wiping away some tears in her eyes. "We do have a wonderful family, Gabriel. I'm grateful you chose to stay with us. And I'm especially thankful for our strong, beautiful daughters," she said. Gabriel smiled genuinely this time.

"They'll be excellent matriarchs one day, Arabella. If they take after anyone, it's you," he said warmly. "You have a beautiful soul. I've been a monster, a horrid creature, but you—Arabella, you were my salvation. You gave me the strength and courage to face my demons," Gabriel admitted, his voice catching in his throat.

Arabella rose to hug Gabriel as he sat. "You are also strong, Gabriel Ambrose. Our daughters have your resilience as well. Despite your struggles and losses, you've become one of the most formidable men in the world, and within our family. You are deserving of honor in many respects, and I do love you," she confessed.

Gabriel released Arabella and looked up at her, startled. "What did you say?" he asked. Arabella smirked, then reiterated with emphasis, "I love you. Your speech about Daniel, the love and care you've shown—not just to the world, but especially as a provider and protector for Amy and Ginger—it's admirable. You should acknowledge your virtues as well."

A smile broke across Gabriel's face as he embraced Arabella again. "I know I've made mistakes, and I appreciate your kindness," he said. A knock at the door interrupted them, and Arabella opened it to reveal Amy and Ginger standing there. "Yes, my girls," Gabriel said, swiftly wiping his tears with the sleeve of his right arm.

"Some guests are preparing to leave for home. Did you want to say goodbye to them, Father?" Amy inquired. Gabriel nodded, rising to join the others in the living quarters. Alarick and Logan's family were the first to depart, while Dante and Kristjan chose to stay behind.

After Alarick and Logan's family had departed, Dante, Kristjan, Francesca, and Helen remained seated, awaiting Gabriel's presence. "Gabriel," Dante initiated, "we really need to devise a better strategy for dealing with this Larry entity." Gabriel nodded, casting a glance toward Kristjan.

"It appears no matter how meticulously I plan, Larry always manages to evade death. Last time, Alistair and Bryan dismembered him but neglected to burn the remains, which is crucial," Gabriel admitted. "I'll need your help and support as well."

Dante turned to Alistair with a puzzled expression. "Why didn't you burn the body?" he inquired. Alistair, visibly irritated with Gabriel, replied, "Caleb was with Darcia, and he got away. Where has Caleb been lately? Was he at the fight as well?"

Gabriel pondered for a moment, realizing he hadn't seen Caleb there. "Caleb is currently in our basement," he revealed. "Perhaps we should pay him a visit, don't you think?"

Together, they descended to the basement, finding Caleb behind bars, his gaze fixed on them. "Well, well, well," Caleb remarked sarcastically, mock applauding their arrival. "What brings you here today?" Gabriel disregarded Caleb's taunts, addressing his family instead.

"This is Caleb, Larry's associate," Gabriel introduced, prompting a growl from Caleb.

"Excuse me, Gabriel, I was under the impression I was your adoptive son. What became of that?" Caleb challenged, receiving no response from Gabriel.

"Larry and he abducted my daughter Amy and her children," Gabriel continued, to which Caleb scoffed.

"Ahem, you're mistaken, Gabe. I've been here all along. It was Larry and Katrina who abducted your darling angel and her brood. So, what do you want from me? Clearly, you need something, but I'm looking for a quid pro quo. What can I do for you?" Caleb bartered.

Gabriel turned with a smirk. "What are Larry's plans, Caleb? How does Lawrence Harrison intend to eliminate me this time?" Caleb scoffed again.

"I'm not certain," Caleb admitted with a chuckle. "He's not always the sharpest tactician—often led astray by his emotions. Who knows, he might even come for me next," he speculated.

Dante stepped closer to the bars, probing further. "You claim to be Gabriel's adoptive son. How does that work, Gabriel?" he inquired. "It seems you share little resemblance to him. Perhaps ten percent, but beyond that, the likeness is not apparent." Caleb glared at Dante, hissing in response.

"You're not the sharpest tool in the shed, are you? And your name was...?" Caleb sneered, misremembering Dante's name.

Ignoring the jibe, Dante retreated a few steps. Gabriel, arms folded, positioned himself in front of Dante. "Do you desire your freedom once more, Caleb?" Gabriel questioned.

Caleb did not respond immediately.

"If you're interested, I'm willing to release you from this dungeon, but there's a condition," Gabriel proposed. "You must divulge Larry's plans and assist us in putting an end to his machinations. I may be over a few thousand years old, but I'm not too weary to tackle some drama."

Caleb scoffed. "My freedom isn't enough, Gabriel. I need assurances, perhaps a deal. Your promises hold no weight with me anymore. You call me your son, yet you've never once mentioned your daughters to me. How do you reconcile that?" His voice was tinged with resentment. "How do you sleep at night, knowing all the harm you've caused?"

Gabriel sighed, his gaze dropping to the concrete floor. "It's a long story, Caleb. Not something I can distill into a few sentences. I'm tired of having to justify my actions, but I'll ask you once more, do you want your freedom?"

This time, Caleb nodded. "Fine. That's a step in the right direction. How do you personally view Larry? Does he treat you as an equal, or are you merely a pawn, a relic to him?" Gabriel inquired. Caleb remembered all the turmoil he'd experienced with Larry, his erratic scheming, and simply shrugged. "Regardless, if we can align our objectives, I'll grant you freedom and provide the assurance you need. However, I can't let Larry threaten my family anymore. You must aid me with this," Gabriel's voice softened.

Caleb's scoff turned into a head shake. "I find it hard to trust you, Gabriel. I need to be certain you're not spinning more lies, the kind that turned me from human to this... creature. I loathe these bars, but I'm also indifferent to the fighting. Fine, I'll help you," Caleb conceded. Gabriel nodded, his face a mask of somber determination.

Meanwhile, Larry was in his parents' apartment with Bianca when the doorbell echoed an hour later. He found Caleb at the door, disheveled, with dirt and pine needles in his hair. "Goodness, Caleb, where have you been?" Larry asked, amusement in his voice. Caleb strode past him, dusting off his black jean jacket.

"I managed to escape from that Darcia creature," Caleb said. "She's tough, but I slipped away from her grasp."

Larry chuckled, leading Caleb toward the other group members. "Caleb, you remember my sister, Bianca?" He gestured toward Bianca, who was seated on the sofa among other associates. Caleb nodded in acknowledgment. "Now that we're mostly assembled," Larry began, "it's worth noting we took down one of the Ambrose clan—Daniel, handsome yet repugnant in equal measure."

Caleb listened to Larry's monologue while taking sips from his glass of blood. "Why didn't you go after Gabriel?" Caleb inquired. "Taking out one of their key members was a solid move, but why stop there?" Larry sighed and settled into a living room chair.

"In the heat of battle, you aim for your target, but things can get redirected," Larry explained. "I had my sights on Gabriel, but Alistair intervened, and it was actually Katrina who finished off Daniel. Then, Alistair and Bryan, I believe, dealt with her rather... thoroughly. It all happened so quickly."

"So, what's the new plan?" Caleb prodded. "If we continue creating more of our kind and causing disturbances, we're going to attract unwanted attention, especially with all these missing persons notices. We need to be selective, target those who won't be missed—single, widowed, no ties. Otherwise, we risk drawing law enforcement to our doorstep, and we'd be forced to comply with their inquiries. We can't afford the spotlight that comes with preying on well-connected humans," Caleb advised.

Larry nodded, taking in Caleb's point. "You're right. I sometimes lose control, forgetting the cardinal rule of our kind: no spectacles. I've heard Gabriel lecturing his family on this very topic during my... visits to his home over the years," Larry admitted. The others in the room nodded in agreement.

Changing the subject, Larry queried, "Doesn't it bother you that Amy is raising your children, or are you indifferent?"

Caleb smirked. "Frankly, Larry, I don't see them as my own. Their existence serves Gabriel's desire for a 'perfect' bloodline. And as for Bryan, he's of no interest to me. At least Amy's offspring are appealing, unlike that... mongrel," he said, his tone souring.

Larry's smirk broadened. "You seem quite bitter about the situation, Caleb. Or am I misinterpreting your sentiment?"

Caleb glared at Larry, irritation evident. "What are you implying, Larry? I'm indifferent to the progeny out there. Fatherhood isn't for me. So yes, you're reading too much into it," Caleb retorted sharply.

Larry raised his hands in a mock gesture of surrender, stifling his emerging laughter. "Alright, Caleb. I was just trying to defuse some tension," he said, a chuckle coloring his voice. Caleb rolled his eyes and stood up.

"I question my reasons for returning to you, Larry. If anyone bears a grudge against Gabriel, it's your issue. I harbor my own resentment towards him, but I'd never target Amy's children. Using Amy as bait would've been sufficient to draw Gabriel out. Sometimes, Larry, your emotional responses are too much for me," Caleb stated.

Larry rose to his feet and crossed his arms defensively. "What's gotten into you? I make one light-hearted comment, and you're filled with animosity towards me. Why don't you go back to your adoptive family and see if they welcome you? Oh, but wait— Arabella despises you, so returning won't be simple for you. In fact, I'm starting to question whether I want you here at all. It seems to me that you're nothing but a pawn. Why else would you have gone back to Gabriel before, Caleb?" Larry challenged.

Caleb scoffed dismissively. "You see that? Right there," he said, pointing at Larry's face. "You're being emotional. That's why our plans keep failing. You're not a strategist; you're an emotional roller coaster, blindly hoping for a different outcome without changing the approach. Instead of contemplating sending me away because you found my criticism of your 'humorous' joke disrespectful and in poor taste, you get upset. I could easily walk away from this, Larry, but why would I? My hatred for Gabriel runs deep, but unlike you, my plans aren't clouded by emotion. If one tactic fails, we shouldn't repeat it—we should adapt. We are shape-shifters; we ought to be able to leverage our abilities, don't you think?" Caleb retorted.

Larry, visibly agitated by Caleb's relentless critique, cut him off. "I've had enough of this conversation, Caleb. You can either stay here and follow my lead, or you can take off and do as you please. I don't need your so-called advice, especially not from a weakling like you—always playing the victim and returning to your tormentor."

Caleb shook his head and sat down, his gaze shifting to Bianca, who remained passive and uninvolved. "If anyone here has issues with Larry's tactics, speak up. Don't wait until he's not around to voice your complaints. I shouldn't be the only one here capable of offering direct criticism and suggestions. Don't just conform and allow him to steer you towards the same fate as his past followers—speak your mind, or resign yourselves to his rule indefinitely," Caleb declared.

Larry's growl was a precursor to his fierce glare at Bianca and the rest of the group. "Well?" he snapped impatiently. "Does anyone else have a problem with my leadership? Let's discuss it."

Caleb shook his head in disbelief in disbelief. "There you go again—emotional, not strategic." At this, Bianca tentatively raised her hand.

"Larry, I believe you have the makings of a good leader, but perhaps we should re-evaluate our strategy for dealing with Gabriel. It appears they consistently anticipate and counteract our moves," Bianca suggested cautiously.

Larry scoffed and dismissively gestured to Bianca. "I once held you in high regard, Bianca, sister dear, but those words don't do us any good. If you believe my plans are inadequate, you're free to leave. I have been nothing but supportive and caring for our team members, and yes, it hurts to lose them, just as it pained me to lose my beloved fiancée, Viviana, that night at the tavern. I am willing to adjust my approach somewhat, but I won't tolerate anyone thinking they can plan better than I can. My survival over many years, having evaded death multiple times, should speak volumes about my strategy," Larry said, his tone easing.

Bianca smiled and nodded. "Fair point, brother dear, but perhaps instead of creating more people and indeed, if we do, go after certain people to avoid spectacles." Larry nodded in agreement.

"So, Bianca dear, what do you think we should do?" Larry asked. Under his expectant gaze, Bianca felt suddenly on the spot and uncomfortable. "I wish to hear from someone I feel comfortable with, not someone who relishes criticizing my methods," he added, shooting a glance at Caleb, who responded with a frown.

"Well," Bianca began, her tone betraying her nervousness, "let me think about it for a moment. I'm not much of a strategist myself, but I'm willing to learn as we go," she proposed hesitantly.

Larry nodded, his smile conveying approval of Bianca's willingness to contribute.

Meanwhile, Amy and Ginger were upstairs with Amy's three children, engaging them with rattles and bells. The children's squeals of delight and giggles filled the room.

Arabella and Amelia entered with extra blankets, laying them on Amy's bed. "How are the little ones?" Arabella inquired, watching the babies squirm and roll.

"They're doing much better now, Mother," Amy replied, her affection for each child evident. "I hope they never remember being taken by those horrible monsters. I never wished any of this upon them—or me."

Arabella enfolded Amy in a comforting embrace. "If they do remember, my dear child," she advised, running her fingers through Amy's hair, "it's best to be honest with them. Never lie to your children, ever. Don't replicate your father's mistakes."

Amy nodded, her agreement interrupted by a knock at the door. Arabella stepped back, allowing Amy to answer it. Hildegard entered, her attention immediately on the children. "Do they need another bath?" she inquired with a gentle smile.

Amy gestured for her to come in, and Hildegard picked up Gabrielle, remarking on the child's growth over the past week. "My, you are all getting strong," she cooed before taking Gabrielle to the bathroom.

Amy lifted Maggie, and Ginger took Nathaniel, following Hildegard. Left in the room, Arabella and Amelia settled on the edge of Amy's bed.

"The children are thriving, aren't they, Amelia?" Arabella observed.

"Indeed, they are becoming quite perfect little beings," Amelia replied. "I must admit a touch of envy for not being a grandmother myself, but I am genuinely happy for you, Arabella."

Arabella smiled at Amelia's comment. "In all honesty, Amelia," Arabella said. "I wish Amy had the chance to choose her own partner and create the family she wanted, not be saddled with raising Caleb's children. But then again, he isn't here, so hopefully, those children won't come to see him as their actual father."

Amelia nodded in agreement. "I certainly hope so. I do wonder about Caleb's dealings with Gabriel. I just can't bring myself to trust him." Arabella nodded, sharing the sentiment. Meanwhile, as the women attended to themselves and the children, Gabriel and his group gathered in the living quarters.

"Gabriel," Alistair began, "what do you expect Caleb to achieve by sending him to Larry again? Are you sure he'll hold up his end of the bargain and extract valuable information? What if Caleb doesn't return?"

Gabriel exhaled heavily. "If he fails to return, he'll die the next time we see him. He doesn't have Larry's age or experience, which gnaws at him since he's never felt equal in his entire life. I will not show mercy again, brothers and sisters," Gabriel declared, and Dante nodded in agreement.

"How did you even choose Caleb, Gabriel? Honestly, I don't find him attractive. I've seen many more handsome men. Gabriel, you could have set the bar higher, especially since he's the biological father of your grandchildren," Dante commented.

Gabriel looked over and shook his head in disbelief. "Beauty is in the eye of the beholder, Dante," Gabriel said. "Just remember that. I fell in love with Arabella, because of her beauty and found out later that she made a wonderful shape-shifter." Francesca snorted at that comment, which caused Gabriel to glare at her.

"What is it?" Gabriel asked.

Francesca shrugged with a smile on her face. "Oh, nothing. Just wondering, is a woman's appearance all that matters to you? Her skills and thoughts are secondary?" She challenged. "Dante found me attractive, sure, but he also loved me for my abilities, right, sweetheart?"

Dante smiled warmly, taking Francesca's hand and kissing it tenderly. "Absolutely, my dear. You're intelligent and beautiful in every way," he affirmed. Lucien, Adrian, and Vladimir exchanged knowing smiles at the tender exchange, while Gabriel looked at his brothers, slightly puzzled.

"Arabella is more than just a beauty to me. She's my rock, my anchor. Her words have a way of soothing me during stressful times," Gabriel defended.

Glancing at his watch, Gabriel noted Caleb's prolonged absence with concern. "I wonder where Caleb is," he murmured. "I hope you're wrong about him, Alistair, or else he might die by my hand."

Alistair shrugged, his expression neutral. "For his sake, I hope I'm mistaken."

Darcia then placed her right hand over Alistair's, her touch reassuring. "Caleb wouldn't foolishly risk his life or betray us," she assured Gabriel. "Sometimes the harshest lessons are the most instructive. You're not naive, Gabriel. Perhaps Caleb found a compelling reason to stay with Larry, something so crucial he couldn't leave."

Gabriel nodded. "Perhaps you both are right. I mean, why would he want to risk his life so soon?"

# First Light

Caleb recalled Gabriel's instructions before he was released from the dungeon. Larry sensed an odd tension in Caleb and maintained a cautious distance in the room. "Larry," Caleb began, "I believe that if we go after Gabriel, we should leave Amy and Ginger out of it. They don't pose any threat to me."

Larry furrowed his brow, eyeing Caleb with confusion. "Why, Caleb? Once their father is out of the picture, won't they seek revenge? It's safer to eliminate all potential threats now. Does that not make sense to you, or do you believe those two can stay neutral after their father's death? They felt betrayed by him because of his lies," Larry reasoned.

Caleb strove for composure, Gabriel's directive echoing in his head: distract Larry long enough for Gabriel to ambush him. Meanwhile, Larry grew increasingly restless, scratching at his neck, arms, and biting his nails, sensing that something was amiss.

"Caleb," Larry said with a feigned smile as he edged closer, "where did you say you came from? I noticed the pine needles and dirt. Did you bed down on the ground, or climb a tree, perhaps?"

Caleb stood, clearing his throat. "As I told you, Darcia confined me to her room, but I escaped through the woods and came here," he retorted sharply. Larry's stare lingered on Caleb, scrutinizing. "Are you accusing me of lying to you, Larry? I won't stand here and be interrogated," Caleb snapped before striding to the room where he could still sense Gabriel's lingering presence.

Left in the living room, Larry pondered with Bianca, while other members of their group were engrossed in TV shows, drinks, or books. Larry felt certain something was afoot, yet he couldn't pin down whether Caleb was being truthful. His gaze drifted to the open window, where he watched branches sway with the wind, his thoughts turning to Viviana—Gabriel's victim—and whether she could've been a shapeshifter. Gabriel hadn't fed her, but then, he hadn't fed Larry either. Could Viviana still be alive, hidden away in Romania? With a glance at his watch indicating one in the morning, Larry contemplated a visit to the old tavern where he'd last seen her, questioning whether it even still stood.

Larry decided to visit the tavern. He left the apartment complex, got into his father's Mercedes SUV, and headed to the city and area where he once lived. Bars and some restaurants were still buzzing past midnight. He drove by where he believed the tavern was, only to find it had been transformed into a gym, now closed. Parking the car, he glanced in the rearview mirror and saw nothing but the empty street behind him. Clutching the locket he had held onto since proposing to Viviana, he sighed at the memory of her beauty and purity. How deeply he had been in love with her. Then, as he prepared to drive away, a sudden draft caught his attention. He surveyed his surroundings; nothing. With his foot on the accelerator, he heard the sound of breaking glass—probably the revelry of inebriated humans.

Locking the car doors, a familiar voice from the back seat then caught him off guard. "Lawrence Harrison?" a feminine voice inquired. Larry spun around and through the rearview mirror, his gaze met with Viviana's visage. She wore a white flowy dress, her short blonde hair framing blue eyes that held a sinister glint. "My love?" he asked, incredulous.

The girl's smile revealed sharp teeth as she giggled. "What took you so long to find me?" Viviana asked, her voice teasing. "I was able to find you easily, but your senses are dulled, my sweet, beloved heart." Larry, filled with emotion, smiled back.

"Would you join me in the front?" he invited. Viviana glided through the car to the passenger seat. Larry quickly embraced her, tears streaming down his face. "Oh," she remarked, "such emotion." Larry gently pushed her back to look at her.

"How long have you been around, Viviana?" Larry asked. Viviana playfully counted on her fingers. "About five hundred years, my sweet Larry," she revealed. His look of compassion prompted her to query, "What? Is there something on my face?"

"No," Larry assured her. "You're beautiful. But what happened to you?" He remembered only that she had been attacked by the creature called Gabriel and that he had been left alone in the forest.

Viviana made a clicking sound with her tongue. "It was quick and painless, surprisingly," she recalled. "When I awoke, I was not myself. I remember the monstrous creature with red eyes attacking me. Before I could scream, I was pinned to the tavern's wooden floor."

Larry nodded solemnly. "Where have you been living? Have you found a new partner?"

Viviana smirked and looked over at Larry. "I drift from place to place," she said, a hint of sadness in her voice. "I have no home, no family, no friends. I am utterly alone."

Larry's smirk echoed her own. "Not anymore," he offered. "If you want, you can live with me at my parents' home."

Viviana rolled her eyes. "I saw you with that Katrina girl. Is she your new bride, Larry?" she inquired. "If she is, I'm not interested in sharing you with another woman."

Larry chuckled and shook his head. "Katrina passed away a few days ago, Viviana. We were never an item. She detested Gabriel as much as I did and decided to join me and my group in the hunt to bring down that monster."

Viviana nodded, considering his words. "Well, since you just mentioned that important factor, I wouldn't mind staying with you, if you're okay with it as well?" she asked. Larry's smile broadened as he took Viviana's right hand in his own.

"I would love that, my love," Larry whispered before planting a gentle kiss on the back of her hand. "Have you ever met my sister, Bianca?" he asked. Viviana furrowed her brow.

"No, I don't believe I've met any of your family," she replied. Larry let out a sigh.

"Well, sadly, they did not survive our last battle, so it is just me and Bianca left from my side of the family."

Viviana withdrew her hand and placed it on his shoulder, her touch tender. "I'm sorry to hear that, Larry. Dealing with death and loss is always tough." Larry nodded, patting her hand in gratitude. "So, are you going to take me to your place, or did you want to hang out here for a while?" Viviana queried. Larry glanced at his watch, noting it was nearing three in the morning.

"Perhaps we should plan something for tomorrow. It'll be sunrise soon, my sweet Viviana," he suggested. Viviana nodded. "Do you need to fetch any belongings?" She glanced down at her pink shirt and jeans.

"I should probably grab a few things," she conceded before stepping out of the car and heading toward her apartment. Left alone, Larry sat in the car, awash with a sense of unease. Viviana returned within moments, carrying two duffel bags. "Okay, that should cover my needs for now."

Larry started the car and drove to his parents' home. Stepping out, Viviana took in the surroundings. "Hm," she murmured, observing the quiet street bathed in the glow of streetlights. "So this is where you live? It seems cozy." Larry carried Viviana's bags to the front door. As they entered, they were met by Bianca, her eyes dark and teeth bared in aggression.

"Larry, who is this woman?" Bianca demanded, growling. Larry quickly stepped in front of Viviana, shielding her.

"This is my fiancée, Viviana," he introduced. "There's no need for concern, dear sister. She's a friend and poses no threat." Bianca's stance softened, and she reverted to her human demeanor. "Viviana, this is my sister, Bianca," Larry continued. Viviana offered a timid wave, staying close to Larry. "There's nothing to be afraid of, my sweet," he reassured.

"Who are you referring to, Larry? Me or her?" Bianca snapped back. Larry's smirk was teasing.

"Both," he replied playfully. "Now please, both of you are here, and there's no need for fear."

Bianca shook her head before walking away, heading to the dining room. There, she grabbed a blood pack and downed it in seconds, regaining her composure. She then retreated to her bedroom and closed the door behind her.

"Right," Larry said, turning his attention back to Viviana. "Your bedroom. We have about ten rooms in this place. Each of my members has their own, so you and I can either share a room like before, my sweet, or you can have your own bed with your own covers and pillows," he said with a smile.

Viviana smiled and walked over to the staircase. Larry showed her some of the rooms and brought her bags up to one of the spare rooms. "You can start off in here if you like, or you can join me in my room whenever you feel like it," he offered. Viviana nodded.

"I think I might stay here alone and see how that goes before I take any further steps," Viviana said. "How do these curtains work?" Larry walked over to the window and drew the curtains closed, plunging the room into darkness.

"Like that. Modern times," Viviana remarked. "Have a good night's sleep, Larry," she said.

Larry hugged her before he left the room and went to his own. He lay in bed fully clothed, staring at the ceiling. The situation with Viviana felt surreal. Was she truly alive, or was all this a dream? He lay there in the dark, sleep eluding him.

Meanwhile, at Gabriel's castle, Gabriel and Arabella were in their sleeping quarters. Arabella, dressed in her Victorian nightgown with her wavy hair cascading over her shoulders, broke the silence. "The last few days have been quite hectic, haven't they, Gabriel?" she mused. Gabriel chuckled in agreement.

"I sometimes wonder if we should take like a vacation somewhere. Just to get away from all our problems."

Gabriel sighed, turning to look at Arabella as she lay on her back. "Not with Larry on the loose, my dear wife," he whispered. "I won't be able to relax until he is gone for good." Arabella nodded in understanding.

"But still," she persisted, "a luxurious spa or a wellness resort would do us good, especially after the energy we expended on Daniel's funeral."

Gabriel felt a pang of sadness. "It's been exhausting, dealing with everything," he confessed. "I'm not sure how long I can keep up with the duties of being the patriarch, my sweet." Arabella sat up and embraced him.

"For now, just rest, my dear husband," she soothed. "You need to rejuvenate for any surprises that may come our way."

Gabriel donned his satin robe and leaned back against the mattress. "Sleep does sound good right about now," he admitted, and quickly drifted off. Arabella watched him, still as a statue, before she turned out the lights and joined him under the covers.

Upstairs in their bedroom, Alistair and Darcia were interrupted by a knock on the door. Joshua entered and closed the door behind him.

"I do not mean to disturb you both, but I just got another weird vision," Joshua whispered. Alistair and Darcia both propped themselves up against the headboard, eyeing Joshua with concern.

"What was it about, son?" Alistair inquired. Joshua walked over and sat on the edge of the bed. "Larry might have another ancient newcomer," Joshua stated.

Darcia and Alistair exchanged worried looks. "What do you mean, Joshua?" Darcia pressed. Joshua let out a sigh.

"I mean, there might be another creature, one from around the time when Larry was turned. Something about a girl, I think?" Joshua explained. Alistair sighed and shook his head.

"Alright. Thank you for telling us, son. Once Gabriel is awake, we will inform him. For now, try to get some rest," Alistair instructed before Joshua departed and returned to his room where Silas was sleeping.

Unable to sleep after Joshua's interruption, Alistair lay awake, Darcia beside him. "This conflict is wearing on me, my wife," Alistair whispered. Darcia nodded in agreement. "I'm thinking we should move to a warmer place where humans are oblivious to our existence, away from all this drama and conflict. The sight of Daniel in that coffin... it was so grim. Despite our history with hunting humans, maybe it's time we reconsider our sources of sustenance," he mused.

Darcia nodded. "I'll back you whatever you decide, Alistair. I want our family to be happy, healthy, and most importantly, alive," Darcia affirmed. Gradually, Alistair's eyelids grew heavy, and Darcia curled up beside him. They drifted off to sleep around five in the morning, later than their usual hour.

In his dreams, Gabriel found himself in the park where he had previously confronted Larry. Alone, with just minutes past midnight, he heard the rustling of leaves followed by a low growl. He prepared for an attack, baring his teeth, claws at the ready. The growling intensified, and then a redhead girl in a pink poodle skirt with two bowties in her hair appeared before him. He recognized her. "Gabrielle?" Gabriel questioned. The girl smiled. "Your hair— it's magnificent. I would've guessed you'd have brown hair, though our bloodline does have its redheads," Gabriel observed.

The girl smiled. "I do not want you to die, grandfather," the girl whispered. Gabriel, touched, stepped closer, but she retreated in fear, pointing behind him. Suddenly, Larry pounced toward Gabriel, startling him awake with a shout. Arabella screamed in response, jolted from her slumber. It was about eleven in the morning. Arabella tenderly cupped Gabriel's face.

"You're safe, Gabriel. There's nothing to fear," Arabella soothed. Gabriel's tension eased.

"My love, do you have redheads in your family?" Gabriel queried. Arabella considered for a moment, recalling her grandmother and great-grandmother's red locks. She nodded.

"I believe our little Gabrielle will be a redheaded gem," Gabriel murmured. Arabella beamed. "They may be rare in this world, but she will undoubtedly be a blessing to our family."

Arabella smiled. "They all are, my sweet Gabriel," Arabella whispered. "Are you able to go back to sleep, or do you need a drink?"

Gabriel shook his head. "I am okay. I may not be able to fall asleep just right now, but I am not energetic enough to go up to the main floor just yet either," Gabriel said. Arabella nodded before she turned around with her back to Gabriel. As dusk approached, Gabriel was still awake. He decided to walk over to Amy to see how she and her children were doing. Arabella was still asleep. When he approached Amy's door, it was quiet and dark. Gabriel opened up the door and saw her children slowly waking up, as well. Gabriel walked over to the crib to see them.

Suddenly, Amy woke up screaming. "Who are you?" she demanded. Gabriel quickly turned around.

"It's me, my child," Gabriel whispered. Amy, with anger flashing in her eyes, turned on the night lamp. "Forgive me, my sweet, but I had to see how your children were faring." Amy shook her head.

"It's only seven in the evening. I usually don't rise for another hour, until I hear my children cry. Now that we're all awake, thank you for this 'wonderful' wake-up call," Amy said, her voice dripping with sarcasm.

Gabriel approached Amy and sat on the edge of the bed. "I had a dream about Gabrielle," he murmured. Amy's expression softened into a smile. "She's going to be a rare redheaded beauty, my sweet child. Your mother has redheaded ancestors who shared the same vibrant hair." Amy smiled, touching the tips of her brunette hair.

"Sorry for disturbing you, Amy," Gabriel said as he stood and walked towards the door, leaving the room. He knew his intrusion was misguided. In the hallway, he encountered Ginger, her arms crossed.

"What was that about?" Ginger asked sharply. "I was afraid Larry had come back to kidnap her again." Gabriel gave a wry smile and approached Ginger, who glared at him.

"All is well, my sweet child," Gabriel reassured her before descending the staircase to the dining quarter. Lucien, Adrian, and Vladimir were just rousing themselves.

"Is everything okay, Gabriel?" Lucien asked, yawning. "I thought I heard Amy scream." Gabriel offered a dismissive chuckle.

"Everything is fine. I just felt compelled to visit my grandchildren. They are so precious, my brothers," Gabriel said.

Adrian smiled. "Heading to the dining quarter, Gabriel?" he inquired. Gabriel nodded. "Good. Perhaps we can share a brotherly moment. How is everyone coping with Daniel's absence? I'm not over it yet," Adrian confessed. Lucien nodded solemnly.

"Death and loss are irreplaceable, brother. You just have to accept the emptiness for a while or perhaps even forever. I remember how Gabriel felt about the loss of Arabella," Lucien said. Gabriel cleared his throat.

"Yes, we should always go back to that lovely memory. Arabella is alive and well, and I am happy she is back," Gabriel said. "From now on, please avoid that topic. It is and never was a fun memory. Please stop bringing that up." Lucien nodded.

"Understood, brother," Lucien said.

Gabriel grabbed a fresh, unopened bottle of blood while Lucien grabbed five glasses by accident, not thinking about how Daniel was gone from their lives. Realizing the mistake, he returned the extra glass to the cupboard before rejoining the group at the table. Gabriel poured a full glass for everyone and raised his in a salute. "To Daniel, one of our most beloved," Gabriel declared. The others joined in the toast and took a generous sip.

Amelia entered the room followed by Arabella. "What are you boys doing together?" Amelia inquired as she approached the cupboard, retrieved the glass Lucien had put away, and walked over to the table.

Gabriel looked at her and smiled. "We are drinking to Daniel. Sometimes, it is nicer to have an exclusive moment with our closest, rather than include everyone. After the mild drama with Logan, the atmosphere didn't seem right to honor Daniel's memory," Gabriel explained. "Dante and Kristjan's family are here, but since we were closer to Daniel, I wanted us to have our own moment. Forgive me for not including you or Arabella, but I didn't want to disturb you either."

Amelia smirked. "Of course not, Gabriel. I've missed Daniel terribly. It's been hard to sleep, always catching glimpses of him out of the corner of my eye." Gabriel wrapped his arms around Amelia, offering comfort. "Thank you, Gabriel," she whispered. "You do have a wonderful side, one that I've always known was there, despite your lust for hunting," she said with a chuckle.

Gabriel smiled. "I am glad to hear you say that. I sometimes question my own positivity," he admitted. "Is it true, what you said earlier about being in love with Daniel? He never indicated he felt anything from you. Or did you keep it to yourself?" Amelia shrugged.

"I've always kept my feelings to myself. I was taught to see emotions as a weakness and that love had no place or meaning for us shape-shifters."

Gabriel released Amelia, taking a step back. "Huh," he mused. "I hope I don't give off that impression, Amelia. I want all of you to feel free to express love, anger, sadness, and joy. If you did love Daniel," Gabriel continued with a note of firmness, "you should feel entitled to that emotion without the need to conceal it. Honesty is vital in this family. Though I'm not always the best example, I aspire to be a better patriarch. You can always come to me to talk or share anything. I want everyone to feel at ease with me, whatever your needs, desires, or secrets might be."

Arabella stood a few feet from the table, an amused smirk on her face. Noticing her, Gabriel turned. "Is something amiss, my wife?" he inquired. Arabella shook her head.

Arabella's voice carried a mix of acknowledgment and caution. "Trust isn't easily built after just a reassuring talk, Gabriel. You lied to Katrina and Caleb about everything, which was wrong. Trust is earned over time, from days to years, depending on when someone feels comfortable with you. I'm beginning to see your old self, the one who wooed me with lavish gifts and dinners. Yet, I see your vulnerable and honest side too," she said.

Gabriel's smirk was a mix of gratitude and introspection. "Hearing that from you means a lot, Arabella. I am indeed learning from my past errors, even as the patriarch. I want you to feel at ease with me, regardless of my faults." He nodded, accepting her stance.

"Is there enough for me as well?" Arabella asked, eyeing the half-full bottle. Gabriel retrieved an empty glass for her, filled it to the brim, and refilled Amelia's glass, which had quickly emptied.

While Gabriel and the others settled in the dining quarter, Amy was upstairs, watching her three children toddle and tumble on the carpet. She chuckled, reminiscing about her own childhood with Emma and Athan, wondering how the family dogs had reacted to her non-human nature. Yet, she reminded herself not to dwell on the past, which had little bearing on her present life.

A knock on Amy's door interrupted her musings. Opening it, she found Ginger with a look of concern. "Everything alright, Amy? I heard about our father's late visit. Are you okay?" Ginger inquired. Amy nodded reassuringly.

"Yes, it was unexpected, but it's better him than Larry seeking revenge," Amy responded. Ginger nodded in agreement.

"It's a relief to have you and your children safe again. It was tough, not knowing your state while trapped in this castle. But Mother always believed in your strength—a comforting thought," Ginger reflected.

Amy giggled at a lighter memory. "Like our mad dash through the Oregon airport? It's funny now, to think of how bizarre we looked, you using your powers on those college students. Remember?" she asked. Ginger's smile grew at the memory.

"I must have inherited that knack from our father unless Mother had a secret talent for getting her way," Ginger mused. Amy glanced back at her kids, now engrossed with their toys.

"Did you want to come in?" Amy offered. Ginger declined with a polite shake of her head.

"No, I just wanted to check on you. Your scream was quite alarming," Ginger explained. Amy's smile was warm with gratitude.

"Thank you for your concern, Ginger. I truly treasure you as the best sister in the world."

Ginger rolled her eyes and smirked. "Okay. Enough sweet-talking for now. Go and tend to your children, mother dearest," Ginger said teasingly before she left Amy. Ginger walked down the staircase toward the main floor. She heard her father, mother, and Amelia talking together. She just casually walked by them, nodding to them.

"So anyway," Gabriel resumed, "we should really rethink our strategy for dealing with Larry before he eludes us once more." Arabella, Amelia, Lucien, Adrian, and Vladimir all nodded in agreement.

Ginger paused mid-step. "What are you all discussing?" she inquired, feeling the collective gaze of the group.

"Oh, nothing of concern, my sweet child," Gabriel replied with a casual wave. "How is Amy? Is she still troubled by earlier events?" Ginger shook her head, but Arabella and Amelia exchanged concerned glances with Gabriel. "What happened with Amy?" Arabella pressed. "What did you do?"

Gabriel rolled his eyes dismissively. "I merely slipped into her room to see the children after a frightful nightmare about an encounter with Larry. I caught a glimpse of our granddaughter Gabrielle, with her blue eyes and wavy red hair. I wasn't aware our lineage carried the gene for red hair," Gabriel mused.

Arabella nodded. "Some of my ancestors had red hair, so it's likely she inherited it from them," she explained. "And given that she is officially Caleb's biological daughter," Arabella continued, only to be cut off by Gabriel's tense hiss through clenched teeth.

"Yes, since she is Caleb's daughter, and he was originally from Australia—Logan's son, right?" Arabella queried. Gabriel gave a reluctant nod. "Australia does have a notable red-haired population, so perhaps it's a trait from his side as well," Arabella conjectured.

Ginger chimed in, "Does my name have anything to do with that too?" Gabriel chuckled, shaking his head. "Your mother named you, Ginger. It had nothing to do with hair color," he said. Arabella playfully jabbed Gabriel's shoulder. "Ginger is a splendid name, and it suits you perfectly," she said before glancing at her watch. "It's still early for us—only ten in the evening. What's the plan for tonight?" she asked.

Gabriel surveyed his siblings and then Arabella. "We'll wait for Kristjan and Dante to awaken before we formulate plans for the upcoming final battle," he decided. Arabella nodded in agreement. "For now, you are all free to pursue your own interests. If you'll excuse me," Gabriel said, taking his leave. Alistair, Darcia, and Joshua descended the stairs, their faces etched with anxiety. Arabella's expression mirrored their concern.

"Is everything all right? Was it a troubling sleep or has something happened?" she inquired.

Alistair glanced toward her. "Is Gabriel nearby?" he asked. Arabella pointed toward Gabriel's study. "Thank you," he replied.

Upon reaching Gabriel's study, Alistair, Darcia, and Joshua waited for him to welcome them. "Alistair, Darcia, Joshua, what a surprise. Please, come in," Gabriel invited, motioning them inside. "What brings you to my study?"

Alistair nudged Joshua forward. "Well, sir," Joshua began, a tremor in his voice. "I've had another vision." Gabriel's attention sharpened, urging Joshua to continue. "It seems Larry has a girl in his life, a shape-shifter. Does the name Viviana ring any bells?" Joshua asked. A flicker of recognition crossed Gabriel's face as he recalled Larry's fiancée—the woman he believed he had killed.

"I believe so," Gabriel said, a hint of uncertainty creeping into his tone. "Is that all you saw, Joshua, or is there more?" Joshua shook his head.

"Nothing else, sir," Joshua replied in a flat voice. Gabriel nodded, leaning back in his chair.

"Okay, well, thank you for sharing that with me, Joshua. This certainly makes the situation more intriguing. You see," Gabriel whispered, motioning for Alistair and Darcia to come closer. "Viviana is Larry's fiancée—the woman he thought I had killed."

Alistair and Darcia exchanged confused glances. "Okay?" Alistiar said with uncertainty in his voice. "So, what should we be doing about that?" Gabriel leaned back against his chair again.

"Killing is a last resort, but perhaps we can gain Viviana's trust and see if she can deter Larry from his vendetta against us," Gabriel suggested, his own voice laced with doubt. "I have no desire to kill after what happened to Daniel and other humans, which is why I have my own blood source. If Larry persists in his attempt to have me killed, I will act in self-defense," Gabriel declared. "Now that his fiancée is back, he may lose interest in coming after me."

Alistair shrugged. "Maybe, but we can't read Larry's mind. We don't know if he's lurking outside with a weapon or just getting some air. Thankfully, we have Joshua, who can foresee events from afar," Alistair said, draping an arm around Joshua's shoulders. Gabriel smiled and nodded.

"A good son to have, indeed, Alistair," Gabriel said. "Otherwise I must continue with my planning, but if there is nothing else to be mentioned, go on ahead and do whatever you need to do. In case Dante or Kristjan wake up, feel free to let them take as much blood from the cooler as they desire. Hildegard will be making another run in a few days," Gabriel said.

Alistair, Darcia, and Joshua bid Gabriel farewell and left his study. "Well," Alistair said, relieved. "That went rather well. I was a bit uneasy because of how unpredictable Gabriel can be, but son, you handled yourself admirably. I'm quite impressed." Darcia patted Joshua gently on the back.

"As am I," Darcia affirmed. "Having a conversation with the patriarch is no small feat. It might have been nerve-wracking, but you did well." Joshua smiled, his tension easing.

"It was nerve-wracking, and I'm glad it's over for now. Whatever Larry has planned, we'll be ready," Joshua said before heading back to his room. Bryan and Raymond were in the hallway, observing the trio.

"Joshua was quite brave back there, my boys," Darcia commented as she walked past them to her room. "Gabriel can be a challenging personality to face, but your brother managed to convey confidence when explaining that Larry's fiancée is a shapeshifter."

Bryan scrunched his brow. "What? Since when? I thought Gabriel had killed her off, but now she is back from the dead? How is that even possible?" Bryan said as he felt his anger boiling inside of him. "How does she manage to survive, but Daniel is gone forever? Nothing makes sense," Bryan said. Alistair placed his right hand on Bryan's shoulder, trying to calm him.

"It is okay, Bryan," Alistair said soothingly. "Not everything makes sense to us, but that doesn't mean we should give up. Larry will probably come back for revenge, and this time, we'll be more than prepared for the final showdown, okay?" Alistair asked, his eyes stern. Bryan nodded in agreement. "Good. Now, in case you all are in need, feel free to take whatever you want from Gabriel's cooler in the dining quarter," Alistair said before he closed the door to his and Darcia's bedroom.

Joshua remained silent before he turned to Bryan and Raymond. "What?" Joshua asked. "That might have been the bravest thing I've ever done. Gabriel may have a loving smile, but deep down, he can be a real monster to his victims, you know?" The other boys nodded in acknowledgment.

"I remember how scary it was when Darcia and Alistair had their trial down in the living quarters. I remember hearing Darcia whimpering and breathing fast before they left the motel room to have their trial. Gabriel can be quite coldhearted when it comes to other people's lives, I guess," Bryan said. "Well, now you are here and all is well. What would you boys like to do for fun this evening? Should we check out some of the nightclubs or bars?"

Joshua looked intrigued and glanced at the other boys, who shrugged in response. "Okay. Which should we try first? I think nightclubs could be fun; maybe we'll meet some cute girls?" Bryan suggested. The others nodded in agreement. "Nice. Shall we go?" Bryan led his brothers out of the castle, and they walked over to a nightclub where modern pop music blared, seeing people dancing, drinking, and enjoying themselves. Bryan made his way to the center of the club until he caught the attention of a young girl with brown hair and blue eyes, who was sipping on a club soda.

"Good evening," Bryan greeted her with charm. The girl smiled back. "What brings you to such a loud and obnoxious place?" The girl giggled, looking over at a man behind the bar.

"My boyfriend," the girl said. "He owns this club. I actually find the ambiance quite fun, you know?" The girl said. "And you?"

Bryan smiled, but upon realizing she wasn't a potential target for the night, he turned to leave. The girl shouted after him, and as Bryan turned back with black eyes, she flinched and quickly walked away. Bryan noticed Raymond gesturing to his eyes from a distance; calming his mind and body, his eyes returned to their original color.

A guy looked at Bryan weird. "Narcotics," Bryan said. The guy smiled and continued dancing. Joshua was talking to a girl. Silas was trying to talk to a guy, and Xavier was scouting the area for a potential victim. Suddenly, a blonde hair girl bumped into Bryan and turned around apologetically.

"I am sorry, sir," the girl said. Bryan smiled and then the girl smiled. "I am Brittany," said the girl.

"Bryan. So Brittany, where is your boyfriend right now?" Bryan asked, a hint of playfulness in his tone. The girl looked confused.

"I don't have a boyfriend. I'm here spending time with my friends over there," Brittany said, pointing to two girls—one with brown hair and the other with silver-colored hair. Bryan smiled.

"Do you want to dance with us, Bryan?" Brittany invited. Bryan agreed and they merged with the rhythm of the music. Xavier approached the silver-haired girl with his charms. She giggled and joined in the dancing as well. As the night wore on, Bryan and Xavier escorted the three girls out of the club, where they found Raymond and Joshua with their victims.

"Have you all ever been to this park?" Bryan asked, leading the group towards a park where Larry was often seen. He nodded at Joshua before they all bared their fangs and launched a full attack on their victims in a secluded area of the park, where their screams went unheard. After their midnight feast, the brothers felt the strength of their bond more than ever.

Upon returning to the castle around two o'clock in the morning, Alistair and Darcia greeted them with concern. "Where have you boys been?" Darcia inquired. "I thought we had agreed to end all the hunting, yet you all reek of blood. What did you do?" Bryan shrugged nonchalantly.

"Just some brotherly bonding," Bryan replied quietly. "I mean, the blood from bottles is okay, but sometimes the original source is more... satisfying."

Alistair shook his head. "I'll forgive you this time, considering Joshua's service to us, but don't make a habit of this. Humans talk, and they distribute those missing persons flyers of their loved ones. We need to stay hidden from the human world as much as possible. Understand?" Alistair asked. The boys nodded. "Good. Now go on and do whatever you need to do."

# The Planning of the Future

Gabriel had finished his final paperwork for the strategy to take down Larry. He organized the papers into separate piles before stapling them together. Feeling weary and exhausted from it all, he contemplated abdicating his role as patriarch of the family. Once Larry was dealt with, he considered allowing Amy to take over as matriarch. Let her children then shape the future of all shape-shifters. Gabriel picked up one of his ink pens, twirling it in his hand, pondering his next move.

There was a knock on his study door. "Enter," Gabriel called out. The door opened and Lucien entered the room. "Brother, what can I do for you?" Gabriel asked. Lucien looked both uncertain and worried.

"Are you really thinking about stepping down as patriarch, Gabriel? Why not let me, Adrian, or even Vladimir take over? Are you sure someone like Amy, with her youth and lack of leadership experience, is ready to be queen?" Lucien questioned. Gabriel smirked, entertaining the thought.

"Are you suggesting that women aren't cut out for leadership, brother? As far as I'm concerned, Amy has faced enough hardships in her life to take on such an important role," Gabriel said.

Lucien sighed before sitting down. "Apart from that, do you have a new plan for finally defeating Larry?" he asked. Gabriel shrugged.

"I'm still thinking it over, dear brother. I'm not certain if I have a better plan yet. I'm waiting for Dante and Kristjan to recover from the past few days, but we'll devise a stronger, more strategic plan," Gabriel responded. Lucien nodded.

"I just do not want anything bad to happen to you, Gabriel. That is all. I am sure Amy and Ginger would be wonderful matriarchs, so please do not get me wrong about what I had said earlier," Lucien said.

Gabriel smiled and nodded. "No worries, dear brother. Growing up, I often questioned that myself, but seeing Arabella and Amelia as strong women in our lives changed my perspective." Lucien returned the smile, then stood and left the study. Gabriel rolled his eyes and shook his head.

"Well," Gabriel said to himself. "I think my work is done for now. I shall see what everyone else has planned for this tranquil evening." He stood up and walked over to the living quarters, where he found Adrian, Vladimir, and Amelia.

"Good evening, my dear family," Gabriel greeted. The others looked up with interest. "What are your plans for this beautiful evening?" Adrian and Vladimir shrugged. "I've been thinking about something. I'm not sure if Lucien mentioned it, but once our conflict with Larry is resolved, we'll need someone to step up as the next patriarch or matriarch," Gabriel explained. Adrian and Vladimir appeared confused.

"When did you start considering this, Gabriel?" Adrian inquired. "I've never really seen myself as a candidate. I thought Daniel or Lucien would be next in line. Has Lucien said anything?"

Gabriel shook his head. "He's just concerned about me. But honestly, there's no need for worry. I was in my office, looking at paperwork, and suddenly felt extremely tired. Becoming a grandfather recently made me think about the future," Gabriel shared.

Amelia felt sadness inside of her. "What does that mean for the rest of us, Gabriel? What are we supposed to be doing?" Amelia asked. Gabriel sighed, then embraced her.

"It's just a thought for now," he reassured her. "Sometimes I need a break from all the work and fighting." Adrian and Vladimir nodded in understanding.

"For now, I'll remain as your father figure for a few more years. This isn't about ending my position soon, but I felt the need to share it with you all," Gabriel explained.

Just then, Arabella entered the room, sensing the somber mood. "Is everything okay in here?" she asked. The others turned to her. "Gabe, what's happening?" As Gabriel released Amelia, he walked over to Arabella.

"Would you ever consider becoming queen or matriarch of the family, or perhaps see Amy or Ginger in that role?" Gabriel asked. Arabella frowned in thought.

"What brought that on, Gabriel?" she inquired. Gabriel shrugged.

"Old pop pop is getting tired, my wife," he said. "Sometimes, I wish I could just sleep for a few days without having to worry about everything."

Arabella smirked at this remark. "Oh? Since when did you start to feel that way? After my death or when I came back from the dead, Gabriel?" Arabella asked. Gabriel's face went serious. "Forever, my dear wife. I mean, the fact that I have been trying to understand my past and dealing with unnecessary problems in my life, it has made me feel weary and exhausted from everything," Gabriel said. "I mean, the fact that Larry was almost able to take me down is already a sign that someone else needs to take over the reins, at least for a while."

Arabella shook her head. "It's understandable to feel that way, given the exhaustion. But you're not finished with your role yet, Gabriel. Try to hold on a bit longer and stay as relaxed as possible before considering such drastic measures. I could remain queen for as long as I wish, but you need to keep going and not succumb to a depressed slumber. Is Daniel's absence affecting you? It sounds like you'd rather join him than be the dependable Gabriel we know," Arabella observed.

Ignoring her comment, Gabriel walked past Arabella to the dining area. Arabella looked confusedly at the others in the room. "What? Did I say something wrong?" Amelia shrugged and shook her head.

"Perhaps he's grieving Daniel's death but finds it difficult to discuss. I don't blame Gabriel for feeling this way. I'm over eight hundred years old, and sometimes I feel another five hundred years would be enough," Amelia said. Arabella nodded.

"Perhaps," Arabella said. "If I know Gabriel, he tends to be reserved. He expresses himself not through words but through actions, either by keeping his distance or staying busy," she added.

Adrian cleared his throat. "Workaholics often stay busy to avoid intimate interactions, which I think describes Gabriel. I respect everything he's done for us, but now that you mention it, I see that pattern more clearly," Adrian remarked. Arabella nodded.

"Well, if any of you are interested in leading our species, let me know. Despite being around a hundred years old in human terms, I'm still quite young for a shapeshifter," Arabella said before walking to the dining area. There, she found Gabriel sitting alone at the table with a glass and a full bottle of blood.

Meanwhile, Amy and Ginger were in Amy's room with the three children. Gabrielle, Maggie, and Nathaniel were now walking better after a week of crawling. "This is impressive," Ginger observed as she watched the children. "I wonder if Emma or Nathan ever found our growth spurts strange."

Amy nodded. "I agree. These kids are growing up quite fast. I wonder what the pediatricians thought of us during our medical checkups," Amy said with a chuckle, which caused Ginger to giggle. "I wonder if we were just as colicky as these children can be at night. Waking me up, wanting to be fed or changed. Goodness, the role of a parent is quite exhausting," Amy said, stretching out her body. Ginger smiled bittersweetly. "What?" Amy asked.

Ginger suddenly went serious. "This whole situation, you being pregnant, should never have happened, Amy. It's perverse, having children in your twenties not with the man of your dreams, but as an act of maintaining a healthy bloodline," Ginger remarked.

Amy felt a wave of sadness. She was aware of the wrongness of her situation, but knew dwelling on it would only lead to a dark mental state. She had to find happiness and light, not just storm clouds. "I understand, Ginger. I have to stay strong for these children, too. And Bryan has offered to help with them, which is a silver lining," Amy said.

Ginger nodded slightly. "Perhaps," she murmured. "They are beautiful children, though. I see so much of you in them – your nose, eyes, cheeks, and hands," Ginger observed. Amy looked at her hands and laughed. "What? You have strong, beautiful hands, Amy," Ginger said. Amy's laughter continued, realizing it might be a manic response to her troubles. Ginger joined in her laughter.

In their bedroom, Alistair and Darcia couldn't help but smile at Amy's laughter. "I'm glad the girls are finding positive aspects in all these horrible occurrences, my love," Darcia said, holding Alistair's hand. "And it seems everyone needs a break. I heard Gabriel might consider stepping down as patriarch, which feels bittersweet."

Alistair nodded. "I agree. Gabriel has been a central figure in our lives, and it won't be easy for anyone to fill his shoes." Darcia agreed.

"We deserve a break ourselves, especially once Larry is dealt with," Darcia said. "A long rest, relaxation, and no stress about our children's well-being, or yours, my dearest husband."

Alistair smiled and kissed Darcia's hand. "And yours too, my dearest wife," he replied. Just then, Joshua walked into the room without knocking, causing both Darcia and Alistair to sit up quickly. "What's wrong, son? Are you okay?" Alistair asked as Joshua closed the door and shook his head.

"What is this about Gabriel wanting to abdicate?" Joshua asked. "I think he's planning more than just replacing his position. It seems like he's trying to get himself killed. He might let Viviana take him down because he wants to disappear. Please tell me that's not true," he implored.

Alistair looked frightened. He quickly got to his feet and ran out to Gabriel's study, only to find it empty. He then headed to the living quarters, where he found Vladimir and Adrian sitting together. "Where's Gabriel?" Alistair demanded. Adrian glared at him. "Why the tone, Alistair?" he retorted. Alistair, frustrated, left the room and went to the dining quarter, where he found Gabriel sitting with Arabella.

"Gabriel, is it true? Are you planning to let yourself be killed?" Alistair asked, alarmed. Gabriel rolled his eyes in disappointment.

"Let me guess, Joshua figured it out?" Gabriel replied sarcastically. "Look, I'm tired. I've been around for about thirteen hundred years. I can decide to check out whenever I want without being judged by my family. I have rights, too," Gabriel asserted.

Alistair scoffed. "If you want someone else to lead, fine. But death, Gabriel? Are you that depressed over Daniel's death?" he asked, his voice laden with emotion. Gabriel's anger flared.

"So what if I am, Alistair? Yes, I'm depressed and exhausted. I didn't realize my strength was waning with each fight against Larry. Please, either sit and join us for a drink or leave me alone," Gabriel said, sitting back down.

Disheartened, Alistair shook his head and walked back towards the staircase, muttering, "Unbelievable." When he returned to the bedroom, Joshua and Darcia were still there. "What else have you seen in your visions, Joshua?" Alistair inquired. Joshua shrugged. "Nothing more, except how he plans to let Viviana and Larry kill him. It sounds quite narcissistic," Joshua commented.

Alistair shook his head. "This situation is getting worse. Darcia, if you want to leave this place forever, I'll support you. With Gabriel's death wish, Larry will come for us next," he said, troubled. Darcia looked at Alistair, then back at Joshua.

"Let's think about it tomorrow, husband. For now, why don't we rest?" Darcia suggested. Alistair sighed and sat at the edge of the bed, feeling hopeless.

"Joshua," Alistair said, "do your visions ever change?" Joshua pondered for a moment and nodded. "Okay, maybe this is just a vague vision," Alistair mused, lying back and allowing Darcia to snuggle close to him. "Perhaps it's just a thought, not yet set in stone," he said more calmly. Joshua then left the room and went back to his own, where he found Silas and Xavier watching television. He decided to join them but realized he was radiating stress.

Xavier looked over at Joshua with concern. "Is everything okay, brother?" he asked. Joshua nodded, but was not able to shake off the vision he had. Xavier turned back to the screen. Silas sighed, feeling tension building up.

"What's going on with our parents, Joshua?" Silas demanded. "You barged in without knocking, so clearly something's wrong. Is it guilt from the hunt at the club, or is there something else bothering you?"

Joshua sighed. "Gabriel is planning to let Larry kill him. I think this whole conflict is getting to him." Silas, confused, looked at Joshua.

"What does that mean for us? Our family?" Silas asked, standing up. "Where are Mom and Dad?" Joshua gestured towards the closed door in the hallway. Silas, deciding not to disturb them, stayed in the room. "Do Bryan and Raymond know about this? What about Amy and Ginger? Should we tell them?"

Joshua quickly closed the door. "We're not telling anyone about this. Okay, brother? Please, try to relax. You're getting worked up over nothing," Joshua urged. "Alistair said it's a vague vision, so it might not even happen. These could just be my concerns. But please, Silas, don't do anything drastic right now. We need to stay calm. Gabriel is still here. We're all still here. Nothing bad is going to happen. Okay?" he reassured.

Silas nodded, still shaken. "That news hit me like a ton of bricks, Joshua. Okay, I won't say or do anything drastic. I respect Gabriel, but he does intimidate me," he admitted.

"I understand, brother," Joshua replied, as Silas sat back down, visibly unsettled by the news. Bryan and Raymond then entered the room.

"What's all the drama about, brothers?" Bryan inquired. Raymond sat on the other side of Silas's bed. Silas shrugged, his attention seemingly on the television, but his mind clearly elsewhere.

Xavier rolled his eyes. "Joshua had a vision, but Dad says it could be vague. Never heard of that before, but what do I know? So, yeah, that's the drama," Xavier explained. Bryan furrowed his brow.

"What was the vision?" Bryan asked. Joshua's frustration bubbled over. "Gabriel might let himself be killed off," he snapped. Bryan rolled his eyes.

"Lovely," Bryan said sarcastically. "Remember how we were just living our own lives, before Alistair got the call from Gabriel regarding Amy and Ginger, how wonderful it was?" Bryan asked.

The other boys nodded. "I may feel somewhat obligated to help Amy with her kids, but let's be clear, I'm not the one who got her pregnant," Bryan added. Raymond turned to look at Bryan, his expression indicating there was more to discuss.

"Seriously, Bryan? Are you considering abandoning Amy when she has three children to care for? Why is there so much tension in this room? Look, we should all try to stay relaxed. Drama and emotions won't help us. Let's remember the happier times and be optimistic about the future," Raymond said before leaving the room to get a drink in the dining quarter.

Bryan shook his head. "I didn't mean I would abandon Amy. But, I also feel overwhelmed. It's not Amy's fault she's burdened with this responsibility, but it's not mine either. If Gabriel chooses to end his life, that's on him, but I blame him for creating this mess and not helping to resolve it. He shouldn't consider such a drastic step out of depression or anxiety unless he's suffering from an incurable chronic illness," Bryan said, not realizing his brothers were no longer paying attention. "Great, I'm pouring my heart out, and I'm being ignored. Just great," Bryan muttered before heading to the dining quarter to find Raymond sipping his drink.

Bryan poured himself a glass of blood and drank it down quickly. "Do you ever feel alone in this family, Raymond?" he asked. Raymond shrugged. "If you feel isolated, there's probably some truth to it. We might not always show our feelings or support openly. After seeing how Daniel and Gabriel reacted to the funeral, I believe we do support each other in different ways. Maybe it's just your perception," Raymond suggested.

Bryan nodded in acknowledgement. "I just can't see myself as a father figure to Amy's children right now, and it bothers me that I might have to step up, especially since Gabriel pushed me to help. I'm not cut out for fatherhood like Alistair was. I can't see myself in that role," Bryan admitted, finishing his drink.

Raymond chuckled. "Of course, Bryan. We're in the middle of a war. It's understandable to feel that way. Maybe after Larry is dealt with, you might change your mind," Raymond said. Just then, Silas, Xavier, and Joshua entered the dining quarter. "There's still some blood left in this bottle," Raymond announced. The others nodded and each grabbed a glass.

As the boys sipped their drinks, Gabriel was in his sleeping quarters' living room, the same place he had brought Amy and Ginger earlier. He looked and felt exhausted. Although he saw no reason to continue his life, he also knew Amy and Ginger were inexperienced leaders. Perhaps he could guide them to become future queens of his family, slowly helping them ascend to that position.

Arabella then came down to where he was sitting and walked past him. "Are you coming to our room, Gabriel, or will you stay here?" she asked. Gabriel smiled.

"I'll be there in a moment, Arabella," he replied. He watched her open their bedroom door and waited for her to close it. Not wanting to burden Arabella with his plans, he decided to wait until evening to seek Amelia's help and guidance. Entering the room, he saw Arabella in her nightgown, brushing her long dark brown hair. Taking the brush from her, Gabriel continued brushing her hair, admiring her beauty in the mirror.

"What prompted this tender moment?" Arabella inquired. Gabriel smiled, continuing to brush her hair. "Gabriel, what are you thinking? There's a sadness in you, like you'll miss our moments together, but why?" Gabriel kept brushing her hair, ignoring her question until Arabella placed her hand on his to make him stop.

"Arabella," Gabriel began, "I've been considering the future, guiding Amy and Ginger to become the family's future matriarchs. I didn't want to trouble you with the details, but I want to help them towards that future."

Arabella took Gabriel's hand with the brush and gently pushed him away before standing up. "So, you're really planning to end your life. Isn't that selfish, Gabriel? Your daughters are just starting to see you as a father, and now you want to give up? What about your brothers, Amelia, Alistair, and Darcia? Don't they matter to you? They cared for your children after you abandoned them, and now you want to give up? I disagree with that, Gabriel. I won't stop you, but I'll lose respect for you if you proceed," Arabella said sharply before walking to the bed and getting under the covers.

Gabriel sighed, looking at his reflection in the mirror, noticing his messy hair and glazed expression. "We'll talk about this when you're ready, Arabella. Perhaps this wasn't the right time," he said before changing into his satin pajamas and getting into bed, turning their backs to each other. When dusk fell upon the castle, Gabriel got dressed in his suit and went to the main floor to find Amelia. He went to her bedroom but found her asleep with an eye mask and earplugs. Returning to the main floor and the dining quarter, he found Arabella in her white satin robe, drinking blood.

"Good evening, Gabriel," Arabella said in a monotone voice. "I was hoping we could talk about what you said a few hours ago." Gabriel rolled his eyes.

"What about it, Arabella?" Gabriel asked. "I've already made my decision to have my children take over for me, and you're trying to stop me. I'm going to stop apologizing for my actions. It's done and over with, so please don't bring up my past failures as a father and husband. I'm doing my best to manage this family and provide the best life and protection for all of you," Gabriel said.

Arabella scoffed. "If you say so," she murmured. Gabriel grabbed his empty glass and slammed it on the table, startling Arabella. "Nice. Getting aggressive with me, are you?" Arabella snapped. Gabriel scoffed in response.

"I have no interest in dealing with your drama, Arabella. You should be glad I'd be out of your life forever. The girls will still have Darcia and Alistair as their real guardians, and they'll have you, the favored parent," Gabriel retorted. Arabella rolled her eyes. "Very mature," she said, as Gabriel grabbed his full glass of blood and walked over to the living quarter to light the fireplace.

Arabella followed him. "We're not done yet, Gabriel. I don't want to fight with you, but I also don't want to deal with your drama. If you want to die, why not let Larry kill you? I should never have intervened when you were last attacked. Then we wouldn't be in this situation," Arabella said, holding back tears. Gabriel sighed and shook his head.

"Arabella, I am sorry," Gabriel said softly. "I appreciate your protection back then, and I'm glad to have you as the mother of our children. Please understand that."

Arabella sighed and nodded. "I understand, Gabriel. I didn't mean to be harsh, but this news was unexpected. Please don't think I resent you. The children do need you, Gabriel, regardless of your age. Children always need their parents," Arabella said calmly. Gabriel nodded and smiled.

Meanwhile, Alistair and Darcia woke up from their slumber, overhearing the argument. "My love," Darcia said, "I'm not sure if Gabriel was serious about that plan, but I'm relieved Arabella might be persuading him against it." Alistair looked towards their closed door and sighed.

"I don't know what to think anymore, my sweet Darcia," Alistair said before getting out of bed and putting on his jeans and T-shirt. Darcia followed suit, dressing and brushing her light brown hair until it was soft and silky. "I know our sons were affected by Joshua's vision, my love," Darcia said. "I heard them arguing, but I'm thankful it hasn't escalated to them harming each other."

Alistair chuckled. "I believe we taught them well, my sweet wife," Alistair said. "I am glad about that, as well." Alistair and Darcia then walked out of their bedroom and saw Dante and Francesca walking over to the dining quarter. "Good evening, Dante…Francesca," Alistair said. Both of them smiled and nodded. "How are your bedrooms? Gabriel never gave us a tour of his castle, but I assume your rooms are quite nice?" Alistair asked.

"Yes, Alistair. I am sure they are nice for you and Darcia, as well?" Dante replied. Both Darcia and Alistair nodded. "Say, Alistair, I've sensed some planning I couldn't quite catch over the screams and cries of the other members, but is it true that Gabriel is considering stepping down as patriarch?" Dante asked.

Alistair frowned in confusion. "Um… yes?" he said uncertainly. "Why do you ask?" Dante shrugged.

"No particular reason. I'm just curious about what prompted his decision. He's an immortal shapeshifter, so why would he want to leave his position?" Dante wondered. Alistair nodded.

"I understand," Alistair said. "It was a shock to my boys, Darcia, and me too. Gabriel shouldn't relinquish his position. I can't imagine any of us taking over as leaders of our group," Alistair remarked.

Dante smirked and shrugged. "Maybe someone could handle the responsibility? I've always wondered what it would be like to lead our family," Dante said, grabbing an empty glass for himself and Francesca before heading to the cooler for a new bottle. Alistair felt a wave of discomfort. "Did you and your wife want some?" Dante offered. Alistair kept his distance from him and shook his head. "Oh well, more for us, Dante said.

Alistair took Darcia's wrist and led her to the front door of the castle. "I think Dante is plotting something, Darcia. I hope he's not planning to overthrow Gabriel," Alistair expressed his concern. Darcia shrugged.

"Perhaps you're overthinking it, my husband," Darcia suggested. "He might just be teasing you, thinking you're a potential threat." Alistair rolled his eyes.

"I do not think I gave off that type of vibe, my dear," Alistair said. "I only expressed mild concern, because Larry is still out there and Gabriel has not done anything too drastically at the moment," Alistair said. Darcia smiled and cupped Alistair's face with her hands.

"Of course not, so have no worry about Gabriel's plans right now," Darcia said. Alistair smiled and nodded. "Perhaps a wild hunt for just the two of us?" Alistair asked. Darcia smiled before they walked out of the castle, over to the same park Larry used to hang out at.

Back in Gabriel's study, Gabriel was pondering his strategy before he would share it with Dante and Kristjan. There was then a knock on his study door. "Enter," Gabriel said in a sternly. The door opened and Kristjan came into the room. "Yes, brother?" Gabriel asked.

"When did you say your human maid was going to buy more blood resources? I believe Dante and Francesca consumed the last bottle, but I am not certain," Kristjan said.

Gabriel frowned, got to his feet, and walked past Kristjan to the dining quarter and the cooler. Dante looked at Gabriel. "Gabriel, I need to ask you something important," he said. Gabriel briefly waved him off.

"One moment. I need to ask Hildegard to fetch more blood since it's been two weeks since the funeral, when we had plenty. We do go through our supply quite fast," Gabriel said before walking to Hildegard's bedroom, where he found her on her cellular device.

"Hildegard, could you make another blood run? We've run out of bottles, and one of our guests needs to feed," Gabriel requested. Hildegard nodded, quickly putting on her shoes and coat, and left the castle within minutes. Kristjan watched her departure with a hungry gaze. Gabriel placed his hand on Kristjan's shoulder, holding him back. "Not now, brother. She is my maid and must not be harmed," Gabriel instructed. Helen then entered the room.

"What's going on? Do we have any blood left, or do we need to hunt?" Helen inquired.

"Nobody is going anywhere," Gabriel snapped. Dante then raised his hand. "What is it, Dante?" Gabriel asked.

"I heard you might be stepping down as patriarch. Is that true?" Dante questioned. Helen and Kristjan looked at Gabriel, puzzled. Gabriel sighed and stepped back from Kristjan. "Well?" Dante pressed. Gabriel faced Dante sternly.

"Who told you that?" Gabriel asked. "As far as I am concerned, I am still the patriarch of the family and I have no interest at the moment to leave that position, so why do you ask, Dante? Do you aspire to be the patriarch?" Gabriel asked provocatively.

Dante rolled his eyes. "Why the tone, Gabriel? I was just inquiring about rumors I heard. I have no intention of overthrowing you, so I don't appreciate your accusatory tone," Dante retorted. Gabriel smirked and shook his head before leaving the dining quarter. Checking his watch, he noted it was past midnight. He returned to his study and sat down, contemplating. Perhaps abdicating wasn't wise after all. Maybe he should remain patriarch indefinitely. Giving up wasn't in his nature, especially since he still wanted his children to use their powers for him. Gabriel abandoned the idea of stepping down, feeling a resurgence of power.

Meanwhile, in Amy's room, she observed her children walking like typical youngsters, feeling a hint of fear. Why were they growing so rapidly? What was in their blood or milk that accelerated their growth? It baffled her. She recalled how Emma must have felt watching her and Ginger grow so quickly. Maybe her children would reach a certain size and remain that way. Still, it didn't ease Amy's anxiety about their future, including school and any plans her father might have for them. Overwhelmed with worry, she decided to find out her father's plans to distract herself from potential problems.

Amy left the room and hurried down to her father's study. She knocked on the door and waited for him to open it. "Amy, my child," Gabriel said. "What a surprise. What can I do for you? Please come in." Amy entered his study and waited for him to close the door before sitting down.

"I'm feeling anxious. My children are growing unusually fast, and it's only been four months since I gave birth. What should I do?" Amy asked.

Gabriel leaned forward, resting his elbows on the desk. "Right now, you don't need to do anything, dear Amy," he reassured. "Their development is normal for this phase. They'll learn a lot from your uncles, aunt, mother, Alistair's family, and me. They'll become skilled hunters and protectors for both their immediate and our extended family," Gabriel explained. Amy frowned, confused.

"What does that mean? Shouldn't we also teach them about the human world and let them integrate, or is that too dangerous?" Amy queried. Gabriel smiled and shrugged.

"As their mother, your input is vital, Amy," Gabriel said warmly. "Have you discussed this with your mother? She might offer some guidance on what's appropriate for your children. They'll learn various life lessons along their own path. I never attended public school like you did, Amy, yet I became an accomplished patriarch," he said with a chuckle, bringing a smile to Amy's face.

Amy acknowledged Gabriel's words. "I often wonder if I'm a good mother. Sometimes I just want to let them sleep while I enjoy life," she admitted. Gabriel took Amy's hands in his.

"You are an excellent mother, Amy Ambrose. You've cared for them wonderfully for four months, and you'll continue to do so. Caleb may not be involved, but Bryan could also be a great help. Stay calm and remember, you can always come to me for help, guidance, and support," Gabriel said, patting her hands before leaning back in his chair.

# The New Empire

In the living room of The New Empire, Larry paced back and forth, accompanied by a frustrated Bianca and a hungry Viviana. "Larry, what's the plan?" Bianca asked, trying to avoid Viviana's gaze. Larry sighed and shrugged.

"I'm not in a rush to go after Gabriel right now. Viviana is back, but sadly, we can't have children, something I hoped for after marrying her," Larry shared, glancing at Viviana.

Bianca rolled her eyes. "Who says it's impossible, Larry? Our parents had us, so why couldn't you and Viviana? Why not get married right away? There must be an evening chapel open for your wedding," Bianca suggested, smiling at Viviana. Viviana, feeling uncomfortable with Bianca's smile, sighed.

"I am in no rush to get married right now, Larry," Viviana said. "As creatures different from humans, I feel the desire to live larger than life. We deserve a nicer place than your parents' home, Larry and Bianca. Something bigger and more luxurious."

Bianca chuckled at Viviana's remark. "Oh really? Like what, Viviana? A mansion or a castle, like Gabriel's?" Bianca asked. Viviana rolled her eyes at Bianca. "What's your problem, Bianca? I didn't choose this life, and I don't appreciate your constant awkwardness around me. Larry, please say something," Viviana implored. Larry turned to Bianca sternly.

"Bianca, please be more accommodating. Viviana is here, practically against her will. I'm surprised no one noticed you were here, Viviana. How did you escape detection by Alistair and Darcia? They are skilled hunters and seekers, you know?" Larry said.

Viviana shrugged. "I kept mostly to myself, Larry," she explained. "I hunted birds and small rodents on the streets. Hunting humans seemed too risky, and I feared detection since I was alone. I had difficulty finding you, and I'm still unsure why you didn't come looking for me," Viviana added.

Bianca looked at Larry, puzzled. "What are your powers, Larry?" she inquired. Larry rolled his eyes.

"I'm not sure, beyond strength, speed, excellent hearing, and an intense thirst for blood. I can't read minds or do much else. You'd think Gabriel's attack might have transferred some of his abilities to me, but that doesn't seem to work for everyone," Larry explained.

Viviana sighed. "Bianca," she addressed, noticing Bianca's attention on her. "How does one conceive under these circumstances?" Viviana asked. Bianca shrugged. "If your parents were shapeshifters, does it work the same for humans?" Again, Bianca shrugged, turning back to Larry. "How were Amy and Ginger conceived, considering their parents?" Viviana inquired. Larry sighed.

"Arabella was human before she died and then was resurrected," Larry explained. Viviana looked at Larry, confused.

"How does that work? Is there magic involved in our world or is this some sort of science?" Viviana asked.

Bianca laughed at Viviana's question before standing up and walking to the kitchen to get a blood pack. "Larry, your sister dislikes me. I'm not sure if I want to stay here," Viviana said, heading towards the staircase to her bedroom. Larry quickly intercepted her.

"Wait. I'll talk to Bianca about this, but please don't leave me now. I was abandoned in the woods and left to die until I found the strength to hunt birds for survival. I wasn't sure if you were still alive, Viviana. When I tried to return for you, you were gone," Larry explained.

"Please, don't leave me right now. Bianca can be somewhat reserved, but she acts that way because she cares about me," Larry said.

Viviana scoffed. "Uh-huh," she remarked. "As far as I'm concerned, you've let her treat me poorly too, so why should I stay here with you, Lawrence Harrison? I thought I was your dream girl, but now I feel like I'm second to your sister," Viviana said, walking past Larry to her room to pack her bags.

Larry quickly approached Bianca, who had finished her drink and clipped the pack closed. "Bianca, could you start treating Viviana with some kindness and support?" Larry asked. Bianca frowned in thought. "She thinks you hate her, given how you've been acting. Please, tell her that's not true."

Bianca sighed before she walked over to Viviana's guest room. She knocked and waited for Viviana to open the door. "Yes?" Viviana asked. Bianca looked remorseful. "I don't hate you, Viviana. I'm just overly protective of my brother. I know women can sometimes be catty, but I want you to stay. I'll try to be more supportive. What do you say?" Bianca asked.

Viviana smiled and nodded. "Thank you, Bianca. It means a lot. I often feel alone in this world, and having people to rely on is comforting," Viviana said. Bianca nodded, then left and returned to the living room, joining the others so Larry could spend more time with Viviana.

Back at the castle, Gabriel was in his study when he heard a knock. "Enter," he called. Arabella entered and closed the door. "Wife?" Gabriel asked. Arabella smiled.

"So, how are your plans for Amy and Ginger's coronation going?" Arabella inquired. Gabriel smirked and shook his head.

"I've canceled those plans. There's no need to abdicate. The situation with Larry and his fiancée will soon resolve. However, I do need to know where Caleb is. He was supposed to report back to me," Gabriel said. In his mind, he called out, *Caleb, I need you to return to the castle.* Caleb, hearing this, looked up, prompting Bianca to notice.

"What?" Bianca asked. Caleb smiled and shrugged.

"Nothing," Caleb said. "I think I'll go for a drive to clear my mind. It's two in the morning, but I'll be back before dawn," he said, nodding at Viviana as well. As Caleb headed outside, Larry called out to him.

"Where are you going?" Larry inquired. Caleb shrugged.

"Just getting some fresh air. I'll return before sunrise," Caleb replied before leaving. Larry watched him go, a thoughtful look on his face.

"Did you two ever get acquainted?" Larry asked, looking between Caleb and Viviana. Caleb smiled and approached Viviana, extending his hand. Viviana took it, but suddenly released her grip with a shock, having experienced a vision of Caleb going to Gabriel.

"Viviana, are you all right?" Larry asked, turning a stern gaze toward Caleb. "What happened?" Viviana hurried back into the apartment complex, and Larry followed her inside, while Caleb headed toward the castle. "Viviana? What happened?" Larry inquired. Viviana stopped and turned to him.

"Did you see that?" Viviana asked, looking at her hand. "When I touched Caleb's hand, I had a vision of him at a castle," she explained. Larry furrowed his brow in confusion before realizing what had occurred.

"Oh," Larry said, understanding. "So, you have visions? I wonder if Gabriel has the same powers." He paused, then added, "You saw Caleb at a castle? I need to find out where he's going at this hour. Excuse me, Viviana. I'll return shortly, with or without Caleb," Larry said, anger evident in his voice. He left the apartment complex and followed Caleb's scent to the castle, staying out of sight. Larry watched from the woods as Caleb approached the castle and was greeted by an elderly woman, followed by Gabriel.

Feeling a sense of betrayal and growing anger, Larry stayed hidden, observing Caleb's interaction with Gabriel. When Caleb started to leave, Larry quickly transformed into a raven and flew back to the apartment complex, shifting back into his human form upon arrival. He found Viviana watching TV with the others. "Viviana, can we talk for a moment?" he asked. Viviana stood up and joined Larry in the kitchen. "What else did you see in your vision?" Larry asked. Viviana shrugged. "I tracked him, and he was talking to Gabriel," she said.

That doesn't seem right," Viviana commented. "What should we do, Larry?" she asked. Larry pondered for a moment, then heard the front door open. Caleb had returned to the apartment complex and locked the door behind him. Larry instructed Viviana to return to the living room while he waited for Caleb. Caleb entered with a casual demeanor.

"That was a short outing. I thought you would be back before the sun would rise, Caleb. Is everything okay?" Larry asked.

Caleb glanced at Larry and shrugged. "Nothing special, Larry. I just felt that a short outing is better than exhausting myself," Caleb said. Larry rolled his eyes, , contemplating his next move. Caleb retreated to his bedroom, trying to stay calm. There was a knock on his door. Larry stood there, glaring at him.

"Where did you go, Caleb? I believe we both know the answer to that," Larry snapped.

Caleb, feeling fearful yet trying to maintain confidence, replied, "Out in the woods?" He then sniffed Larry. "Did you go outside too, Larry? You smell like pine." Larry scoffed. "Maybe for some fresh air, but back to you, Caleb. Is there anything you'd like to share with me?" he pressed. Caleb shook his head. "Well, that makes things between us more awkward, doesn't it?"

Caleb rolled his eyes. "I'm quite tired, Larry. Can we continue our conversation tomorrow evening?" he requested. Larry smirked.

"I'm not sure about that, Caleb. I know where you've been, so either tell me the truth or leave this place forever," Larry demanded. "Where were you?"

Caleb glanced around and noticed the window in his room. As he moved toward it, Larry grabbed his wrist. "What did Gabriel tell you, Caleb? Are you spying for him? Are you working with the enemy?" Larry accused. Caleb pulled his wrist free and approached the window, only to realize it was nailed shut. "You can't escape without facing consequences, Caleb. How long have you been Gabriel's pawn?" Larry questioned.

Caleb, growing angry, bared his teeth and growled at Larry. "I told you to leave me alone, Larry, but you insist on bothering me. Leave me be, or face the consequences," Caleb warned. Larry laughed and walked away. Caleb, returning to his human form, decided to flee the apartment complex. He ran to the city outskirts, finding a motel with a vacancy sign. Approaching the reception desk, he realized he had no money. Waiting for the male receptionist to be distracted, Caleb quickly grabbed a key and bolted to the room to hide.

Back at the castle, Gabriel entered his sleeping quarters, finding Arabella under the covers. He got into bed and wrapped his arms around her. "So, you've decided not to abdicate as patriarch? What changed your mind?" Arabella inquired. Gabriel smiled.

"I think Dante was hoping something would happen to me, because he kept asking about it. The fact that Alarick would have me end my life, so the feud with Larry would end was another red flag," Gabriel said.

Arabella looked concerned. "Dante wants you dead? Does Francesca know about that? Should I talk to her about it?" she asked. Gabriel smiled and shook his head. "I do not feel safe knowing that they might be plotting against you, as well, Gabriel," Arabella said.

Gabriel sighed and closed his eyes. "I am quite tired, Arabella. From everything. Shall we continue on with this conversation tomorrow or perhaps end it?" Gabriel asked.

Arabella closed her eyes, but was not able to sleep. Gabriel , noticing her restlessness, opened his eyes again. "Are you alright, Arabella?" he asked. Arabella sat up in bed, her arms crossed. "Nothing is going to happen to me or any of us. If Dante wants to become patriarch, let him entertain those thoughts. I can't be overthrown that easily. Instead of worrying about such trifles, let's focus on nicer things like our children, grandchildren, and your aspirations in life," Gabriel suggested.

Arabella sighed, turned her back to Gabriel in bed, and closed her eyes. Still unable to sleep, she got up and walked to the living area outside their room, sitting on the sofa to ponder their next steps. Glancing at her wristwatch, she noted it was five in the morning, but sleep still eluded her. She wandered down to the main floor, where all the curtains were drawn, and decided to have a drink from the cooler, hoping it would help her relax.

Hildegard, dressed in her regular clothes, came downstairs and expressed surprise at seeing Arabella with a bottle and glass. "Milady, shouldn't you be asleep right now?" Hildegard asked. Arabella simply shrugged.

"Sometimes sleep escapes me, especially when I know some family members are plotting against us," Arabella revealed. Hildegard sat across from her at the table, concerned.

"What do you mean, milady?" Hildegard inquired. Arabella scoffed, then shared her thoughts with a focused gaze.

"Apparently, Gabriel changed his mind about abdicating as patriarch because some extended family members, whom I won't name, are aspiring to take over his position. That worries me, Hildegard," Arabella confided. Hildegard leaned back in her chair, understanding the gravity of the situation.

"I understand, milady," Hildegard sympathized. "Is there anything I can do to help, or do you think you have it under control?" she offered.

Arabella smiled reassuringly. "No need to worry on your part, dear Hildegard. Just continue being our loving and trustworthy human friend," she said.

Hildegard smiled and nodded. "Understood, milady. If you need anything, please don't hesitate to ask," she said. Rising, Hildegard noticed the cooler was stocked from her recent blood run and decided to take the day off for her own needs. Arabella returned the bottle to the cooler and went back to her bedroom, finding Gabriel sitting in the living area, his gaze fixed on Katrina's old room, a look of sadness on his face. Arabella passed him and entered their bedroom.

Gabriel followed her in and sat on the edge of the bed. "How are you feeling, Arabella?" he asked gently. Arabella turned to him and nodded.

"Fine for now. Perhaps an evening drink was just what I needed to help me sleep. And you?" Arabella asked. Gabriel, smiling, removed his satin robe and got into bed, quickly falling into a deep slumber. As the castle finally settled into peace, Caleb, staying in the motel room, found himself unable to sleep.

He was filled with fear and anger about how his fate had shifted from a life of opportunity to one of fear and uncertainty. The curtains in his room were drawn, yet he couldn't shake the fear of someone breaking in to harm him. Sitting in a chair facing the door, Caleb realized his throat was burning with hunger. He walked into the bathroom, splashed water on his face, and attempted to drink, but it only made him feel sick and nauseous. Panicking and screaming, he bit his own wrist, and the taste of his blood began to calm him. Looking in the mirror, he saw his disheveled hair, red and glassy eyes, and marble-like complexion, and broke down crying.

"What did I do to deserve this? How did I fall for false promises and cruel people—or monsters?" Caleb lamented through tears. "I was always good. I don't deserve any of this." Suddenly, there was a knock on the door. Caleb didn't respond. The knocking persisted but eventually ceased. Caleb then locked the bathroom door.

"Is someone in there?" asked the male receptionist from outside. Caleb answered through the door.

"Alistair booked this room for me, sir," he said. The receptionist stood outside the closed door. "I'm not decent right now, so please come back this evening," Caleb added. The receptionist walked away, leaving Caleb feeling a sense of relief and overwhelming fatigue. He eventually fell asleep on the motel bed.

When dusk arrived, the receptionist returned with his own key and knocked again. Caleb opened the door. "Alistair booked this room for me," he said, using his powers of persuasion. The receptionist nodded blankly. "Could you send any girl from the area to me? I need some company," Caleb requested, massaging his throat. The receptionist nodded again and walked away. Caleb closed the door, relieved that his powers worked on humans. He decided to make the best of his new situation for as long as necessary.

Back at the castle, Gabriel sat in his study again. *Caleb, what is going on? I am sensing that you are in some sort of trouble,* he thought. Glancing at his watch, he noted it was nine o'clock in the evening. He contemplated tracking Caleb down to discover the issue. If Caleb broke his promise and stayed with Larry, Gabriel would never offer him leniency again. Gabriel headed to the apartment complex where Larry's parents had lived, but it was dark inside, and he couldn't detect Caleb. Maybe Caleb wasn't with Larry, or perhaps they were out hunting. Considering all possible locations where Caleb might be, Gabriel found no leads and decided to return to the castle for a drink.

Upon entering the castle, Hildegard directed Gabriel to the living room television, where a news channel reported on dead women found in a motel room. The female newsreader suggested they might have been killed by their boyfriends. Gabriel shook his head, dismissing the motel room where Alistair and Darcia had stayed, and went to the crime scene. There, amidst photographers and interviewers, the motel clerk was visibly stressed and stuttering. Scanning the crowd, Gabriel couldn't find Caleb, so he moved to a wooded area nearby, noticing drops of blood on the ground. Deciding against investigating alone, as he had done with Larry, Gabriel was about to return to the castle when he heard a familiar voice.

"Wait," Caleb called out, hiding in the shrubs, his mouth and teeth bloodied. Gabriel sighed and slowly approached, ensuring they weren't observed.

"Did you do this, Caleb? Killing those girls? What were you thinking?" Gabriel demanded. Caleb, tears streaming down his face, crouched down. "Is Larry nearby?" Gabriel whistled to check for any response, but none came. He focused back on Caleb. "What happened, and why are you like this?" he asked sternly.

"Larry threw me out. I tried to hide, but he caught on quickly," Caleb explained. Gabriel couldn't help smirking at the thought of Caleb being ousted from Larry's group. "In desperation, I ran to the motel, stole a key, and influenced the clerk," Caleb admitted. Gabriel shook his head.

"Why didn't you return to the castle, Caleb? If I'd known you were in trouble, I would've provided a safe room. Or did you prefer the dungeon?" Gabriel asked sarcastically.

Caleb shook his head. "Please, Gabriel, I need your help. I'm lost. I might have exposed our kind. Those girls tasted good, but now they'll know we exist," Caleb said, breaking down in tears.

Gabriel sighed and nodded, extending his hand to Caleb, who took it up and stood up. "What do I need to do, Gabriel?" Caleb asked. Gabriel looked around.

"I think I can help you with this one. Follow my lead, Caleb," Gabriel said before he led the way over to the crowd. He decided to employ a method he had previously vowed against but deemed necessary. Standing beside the clerk, Gabriel drew the attention of the press. "*Buna seara*, ladies and gentlemen. I may have insight into what happened," Gabriel announced. "There could be wild animals, *animale salbatice*, in the area, or someone who might be responsible for these events," he suggested. Then, using a hypnotic trance on everyone, including those watching at home, he commanded, "You will not remember this moment," and snapped his fingers. The crowd snapped out of their trance, looking confused, and dispersed.

Gabriel took Caleb's hand and led him back to the castle. Once inside, he brought Caleb to the dungeon. "I can't trust you right now, Caleb, given your tears and fear. You'll stay here until Larry is dead. You'll be fed and safe from Larry if he's expelled you from his group," Gabriel explained before leaving for the main floor.

"Thank you, Gabriel," Caleb said.

Upon reaching the main floor, Gabriel was met by Lucien, Adrian, and Vladimir standing at the top of the stairs. "What happened, Gabriel? We saw you on television. Were you trying to provoke the humans into attacking you?" Lucien asked sharply. Gabriel exhaled deeply.

"That phase is over forever, dear brothers. I've decided to remain patriarch for a longer time. I wasn't able to contact Caleb, so I went looking for him," Gabriel explained.

"Alone?" Adrian interjected. "Gabe, remember what happened last time you went out alone? You nearly got defeated by that monster." Gabriel raised his voice.

"Enough! I don't appreciate being interrupted. Caleb nearly caused a scene, and I resolved it with my powers. No more questions or arguments for now. I need a drink," Gabriel said, brushing past his brothers towards the dining quarter where he opened a bottle. Alistair and Darcia descended the stairs, looking concerned.

"Is everything okay?" Alistair asked. Gabriel waved him off as he was drinking down the bottle. Lucien approached Alistair.

"Gabriel just averted a potential disaster of exposing our kind to the human world. Nothing more," Lucien explained. The three brothers, Lucien, Adrian, and Vladimir, left the scene, while Alistair and Darcia exchanged glances. Dante and Kristjan then walked into the dining quarter.

"Gabriel," Dante began, "is everything okay? We thought you were under attack. By the way, did you bring someone back with you?"

Gabriel smirked and nodded, acknowledging their concern but offering no further explanation.

Gabriel shrugged. "Yes, Caleb is back in the dungeon," he said. The others frowned in confusion. "I know it seems dangerous and problematic, but he was expelled from Larry's group. Maybe he can be rehabilitated. For now, he's in the dungeon and shouldn't be disturbed."

Francesca shook her head, taking Dante's hand, and they both left the area. Kristjan and Helen followed suit. Arabella then entered the room, holding Gabrielle. The child's reddish hair had grown, and her blue eyes mirrored Gabriel's. "May I?" Gabriel asked, and Arabella handed Gabrielle to her grandfather. Gabriel cradled her, and she gazed up at him, revealing tiny sharp teeth.

Gabriel chuckled at her development. "How are the other two doing?" Gabriel asked. Arabella looked behind her, seeing Ginger and Amy holding Maggie and Nathaniel in their arms. They approached Gabriel and the other two also showed their sharp teeth. "They are perfect," Gabriel whispered.

Arabella smiled. "What happened back there? It sounded like you were having a meltdown back there, Gabriel," Arabella said.

Gabriel smiled. ""Caleb has returned after being cast out by Larry," he explained. Arabella bared her teeth in frustration.

"Since when, and why didn't you consult me first?" Arabella questioned. Gabriel shrugged.

"It wasn't planned. Caleb was gathering information from Larry until he nearly exposed us, so I intervened," Gabriel said. "Please, don't be upset with me."

Arabella relaxed, finishing off a bottle of blood. Amy then interjected, "I was thinking about introducing our blood to my children. What do you think?" Gabriel smiled, opened a new bottle, and filled a syringe, carefully administering a few drops to each child. Gabrielle squirmed but then settled.

"Wow," Amy remarked, looking at Ginger with uncertainty. "Were we like this as children?" she asked.

Ginger, looking unsettled, said, "I'm not sure I want to witness this. It seems inappropriate," before handing Nathaniel to Arabella and walking away.

Gabriel then gave Nathaniel and Maggie a few drops each. They reacted similarly to Gabrielle. "It seems they've been weaned off milk. Maybe they take after me," Gabriel mused. He walked around the castle with Gabrielle, showing her paintings and pictures. In his study, he pointed out various items, contemplating bequeathing his possessions to her. As Gabrielle began to cry, Gabriel returned her to Amy.

"Is she being fussy right now, Father?" Amy asked. Gabriel nodded. He then pricked his index finger before placing it over Gabrielle's mouth, which shocked Amy. "Father! What are you doing? Some blood is enough for today, but stop trying to feed them more," Amy snapped, pulling Gabrielle away from him. Gabrielle licked her lips. "I want them to know about the respectful human world too, Father. I won't let them become hunters in this world, seeing humans only as food sources. Please leave," Amy insisted.

Gabriel left the room as Arabella and Ginger approached him. "Don't push too hard, Gabriel. Whatever these kids become, let them be," Arabella advised before entering Amy's room. Gabriel, realizing his mistake, headed to his study, feeling overwhelmed. The situation with Caleb's return, Larry still at large with his new partner, and his own actions with his granddaughter weighed heavily on him.

In the bathroom, Arabella helped Amy and Ginger bathe the children. The kids playfully splashed water around, and Amy introduced rubber ducks, which they immediately chewed on, growling. Amy gently removed the toys, causing the children to cry, then handed them back.

"Please tell me they're not becoming like my father," Amy said anxiously. "I don't recall being like this. The pictures Emma and Athan took of us didn't show this behavior." Arabella and Ginger exchanged worried looks.

"Don't panic, children," Arabella reassured. "We're all shapeshifters, and so are your kids, Amy. It's possible they take after your father since he's the patriarch, but that doesn't mean they'll be exactly like him," Arabella explained.

Amy stood to grab a towel and picked up Gabrielle, who then nipped at her shoulder. Amy yelped, dropping Gabrielle back into the tub, causing all three children to cry. "Ow!" Amy exclaimed, noticing the healing bite marks in the mirror. Arabella checked Gabrielle for injuries but found her unharmed.

Ginger stood up, breathing rapidly. "Amy, I'm not sure I can help you anymore. I don't want to get bitten," she said. Amy looked at her, disappointed. "What?"

"She just nipped me, Ginger. Maybe she's weaned off milk and needs blood. I wonder if I should contact Emma about this and see how she and Nathan are doing," Amy pondered.

After dabbing her shoulder with a white towel, Amy decided to call Emma. She paused, realizing it was probably morning for them, but dialed their number anyway. The phone rang until it went to voicemail. Amy stuttered and quickly hung up. Sighing, she returned to the bathroom, where the children were getting dried up and looking clean and beautiful. She picked up Gabrielle, who made a squeaky sound and curled up in Amy's embrace. "I have already forgiven you, my sweet child," Amy whispered, carrying her to the bed to put on her thick onesie pajamas. Arabella and Ginger brought over the other two children, laying them next to each other.

Suddenly, Amy's phone rang, startling both Amy and Ginger. Arabella noticed 'Emma' on the caller ID. "Why is she calling you, Amy?" Arabella inquired. Amy picked up the phone.

"Emma, what a surprise," Amy said, her voice tinged with panic. "How is everything?" Emma hesitated. "Amy, is that really you? I recognized your voice on the answering machine," Emma said. "Nathan and I are fine, but we had to say goodbye to the dogs. It reminded me of when we last saw each other. How have you been?"

Amy smiled, glancing at Arabella and Ginger before putting the call on speaker. "Quite well, Emma. I have a question. When Ginger and I were babies, did you notice anything unusual about us?" Amy asked. Emma hesitated again.

"You both were sensitive to light as babies. We kept the blinds down for meals," Emma recalled. "We thought about using candles, but they can be hazardous, you know?"

Amy nodded. "Yes," Amy said. "But what about our diets? Did we ever make a fuss about the food you and Nathan fed us, or were we acclimated to a human diet?" Amy probed. Emma pondered the question.

"Well, you both loved ground beef and pork, making meals manageable. Nathan might have fed you raw steaks a few times, which you seemed to enjoy. Other than that, nothing out of the ordinary. Why do you ask?" Emma inquired. Amy smiled.

"You won't believe this, Emma, but I have three children now," Amy said with a chuckle.

Emma gasped. "Oh, Amy, that's wonderful! How many and what genders?" she asked enthusiastically.

"Two daughters, Gabrielle and Maggie, and one son, Nathaniel," Amy revealed. Arabella gestured for Amy to end the call quickly. "Anyway, I need to go. It was nice catching up after all these years," Amy said.

"You too, Amy. Please give my love and regards to your sister, as well. Even though the time with you both was short, it was a beautiful part of my life," Emma said.

Amy smiled. "Yes, I know. Well, anyway, give our regards to Nathan as well," she said before hanging up and sighing.

"Well, that went well," Amy commented. She pondered for a moment, realizing that she and Nathan might also have been under Gabriel's influence, unaware of anything that could jeopardize his secret as an immortal shapeshifter.

# Final Details

As dawn approached the castle, Amy snuggled under her covers with her three children beside her in bed. She closed her eyes and dreamt of a future with her children, now much older. Nathaniel was strong-built with neck-length brown wavy hair; Maggie had light brown and blue eyes with chestnut hair; Gabrielle had reddish hair and blue eyes. They were in the same park where Larry often lingered. Caleb approached them from a green pasture. "You all look so beautiful, my loves," he said. Amy hugged Caleb tightly. "You too, my wife," he replied.

Holding hands, they walked together to a green pasture overlooking a beautiful lake, the children following. "You did an amazing job raising our children, wife," Caleb said. Amy smiled and giggled. "You look so cute when you do that," Caleb teased, making Amy chuckle.

"Those children are quite beautiful, Caleb. They've even taken to killing people. They make me so proud," Amy said. Caleb smiled and kissed her, waking Amy from her dream in shock.

"Caleb," Amy growled, remembering Gabriel mentioning Caleb was in the dungeon. She put on her robe and slippers, intending to sneak down to the dungeon, only to realize she didn't have the keys. Then she heard Caleb's voice from the other side of the door.

"Amy? Is that you?" Caleb asked. Amy hesitated before responding.

"Yes, Caleb, it's me," she replied. Caleb chuckled from behind the door.

"What brings you to the dungeons? Did your father send you here?" he teased.

"No," Amy replied sternly. "Why are you back here? I thought you and Larry had made a home together." Caleb sighed.

"I used to, but he cast me out for betraying him. Now I'm homeless. Your father took pity on me after I almost caused a spectacle. That's why I'm here," Caleb said, his voice tinged with sorrow.

Amy felt a mix of sympathy and resentment for Caleb, recalling how he had tricked her in the past, like shape-shifting into her ex-boyfriend at prom and ignoring her at the airport.

Caleb fell silent. "Why are you here, Amy? I'm not in the mood for taunting. I'm hungry, and your father promised to feed me, but he hasn't yet," he said. Amy rolled her eyes.

"Do you want some of our blood supply? I won't be hunting humans for you, Caleb," Amy stated.

"That's fine, Amy. I just need something for my throat and fatigue. I'm starving, like I could take down a dozen humans right now," Caleb said.

Amy nodded, walked to the main floor, grabbed her father's keys to the dungeon, and a fresh bottle from the cooler, then headed back down to the dungeon. She opened the door and instructed Caleb to step back so she could place the bottle on the floor before closing the door again.

"Thank you, Amy," Caleb said before quickly downing the entire bottle. "That feels much better."

Amy could not help but smile. "Well, I should head back to bed," she said.

"Wait," Caleb interjected. "Would you like to talk for a bit? I could use some company." Amy sighed and shook her head. "That might not be wise, Caleb. You know that," she replied. Caleb shrugged.

"How are the children, anyway? Since they're officially from my genes, how have they been?"

Amy smiled. "Wonderful creatures. They already have sharp teeth and have taken a liking to blood," she revealed. Caleb chuckled.

"I'm sure they're developing nicely," he said. "A taste for blood. Perhaps they take after me," he suggested provocatively. Amy turned and bared her teeth. "What? I'm just being honest. I'm sure they also resemble you, Amy."

Amy hissed at Caleb before she walked up towards the main floor to see Gabriel standing there in his black satin robe, arms crossed. "Father," Amy gasped. "I was just..." Gabriel raised his hand.

"What were you doing down there?" Gabriel asked. Amy felt uneasy. "We only feed our captive one cup a day to keep him alive, not an entire bottle, Amy. I should have informed you, but you also shouldn't have left your room during daylight."

Amy nodded. "I had a nightmare about him, Father," she explained. "I thought he cast a mental spell on me, so I had to check on him." Gabriel nodded and placed his hand on Amy's shoulder, guiding her gently towards the staircase.

"What was the nightmare about, Amy?" Gabriel inquired. Amy sighed.

"I dreamt Caleb and I were a couple, having a family outing. It made no sense. I know these children are biologically Caleb's, but I have no romantic feelings for him."

Gabriel stopped Amy and had her face him. "Try to get some sleep now. Nothing will harm you or our children. I promise," he assured her, kissing her forehead and nudging her forward. He watched Amy ascend the stairs before retiring to his sleeping quarters. Arabella, awake, saw Gabriel enter.

"Husband," Arabella said, "is everything okay? Is Amy okay?" Gabriel smiled and nodded.

"All is well, wife," he assured her before removing his robe and getting under the covers. "Amy had a nightmare but is now safely back in her room." Arabella smiled, and they both fell asleep beside each other.

As dusk fell over their home, Gabriel decided to check on Caleb. He walked to the dungeon and found Caleb asleep on the concrete bench. Opting not to wake him, Gabriel noticed the empty blood bottle. Picking it up, Caleb stirred and opened his eyes.

"Good evening, Gabriel," Caleb greeted, stretching. "Sleep well?"

Gabriel rolled his eyes, choosing to ignore the question. Caleb, teasingly, asked, "Did you have a nightmare too?" Gabriel continued to ignore him and headed towards the door. "When do I get my next feeding? That bottle was good for the day, but I could use some more," Caleb inquired.

"Soon, Caleb," Gabriel said. "You will not die on my watch, so in a few hours or so." Caleb nodded and sat up against the concrete wall, watching Gabriel leave him.

Upon reaching the main floor, Gabriel went to the dining quarter to place the empty bottle on the rack. He then grabbed a new bottle from the cooler and a glass from the cupboard, downing half of the bottle. Amy, in her white satin robe and slippers, came downstairs. Gabriel, surprised, greeted her. "Good evening, Amy. How are you? Were you able to get back to sleep?"

Amy shook her head. "No, Father. The children slept well, but the dream about Caleb really unsettled me," she said. Gabriel walked over and hugged her tightly. "Thank you," Amy murmured. After a few minutes, Gabriel released her.

"Would you like to join me for a walk outside, to clear our minds?" Gabriel suggested. Amy smiled and nodded. "Let me know when you're ready." She returned to her room to change into regular clothes, then came back to join Gabriel, who opened the sliding doors to the courtyard.

"I feel we don't spend enough time together, Amy. As a father, I should be more present in my daughters' lives. If you want to talk, I'm here to listen. Or we can walk in silence," Gabriel said. Amy nodded, choosing silence for a while. They walked to a park bench near a beautiful fountain, sitting quietly under the bright stars.

"How would you like to be queen someday, Amy?" Gabriel asked. Amy chuckled at first, then noticed Gabriel's serious expression. "No joke, Amy. How about taking over the family in a few years, once your children are teenagers?" he proposed. Amy quickly stood up.

"Is this why you wanted to spend time with me? Father, please. I can't think about that right now. What about Ginger? She's the older one," Amy countered.

Gabriel sighed. "That is true, which is why this is only a question. Nothing more," Gabriel said while he remained on the bench. "Please sit back down. I did not mean t scare you." Amy reluctantly sat back down but faced Gabriel.

"Father, are you dying?" Amy asked with concern in her voice. Gabriel smiled and shook his head.

"No, my child. I just wanted to see how you would feel about becoming the matriarch of our family. I am sure you will do well. Your sister would also be a matriarch, like Lucien and my other brothers who are patriarchs beneath me. If something were to happen to me, they would quickly take over until a new plan is devised. Amy, I think you have the potential to be a queen. You've proven in many ways that you're capable of handling everything," Gabriel said.

Amy nodded and gave a small smile. "Okay," Amy said in a monotone voice. "Perhaps that was just an unexpected question. Father, maybe Ginger might be a better choice since she doesn't have the added stress of children. I'm honored to be considered, but I don't feel ready for such a responsibility right now," Amy said. "Of course, my child," Gabriel said. "This wouldn't happen for another decade or so, but it's something I needed to mention. This isn't about dying, but I thought you might be interested." Amy suddenly felt a wave of sadness.

"Why bring this up now, father? I've heard disturbing rumors about you wanting to end your life, hence my panic," Amy said. "You can't die now, father. Please don't mention this again, at least for a while."

Gabriel smiled and nodded. "Of course, my child. I'm not going anywhere, but I still can't comprehend how someone like Daniel died. Am I the only immortal one in our family? Just one sharp stick, and he's gone. I've never experienced that, but if it's true, we aren't immortal. That your mother returned to us with magic was also new to me, Amy," Gabriel said, gazing at the fountain.

Amy looked at Gabriel, fear evident in her eyes. "Goodness," she said. "I don't know what to think or feel anymore, Father. Everything feels so strange and uncertain," Amy said. Gabriel looked at her.

"What? Nothing makes sense anymore, Father. I wish we were just regular humans with regular problems, not our kind with our problems," Amy said. Gabriel nodded.

"I understand, my sweet Amy. I know what it is like to have such uncertainties thrown at you. I was alone for many years in my life not knowing much about anything," Gabriel said.

Amy felt tears welling up. "Does it get better, father? Will we be okay?" she asked, her voice choked with emotion. Gabriel, feeling tears himself, nodded.

"You will, Amy. You and Ginger will excel in whatever you plan," Gabriel said.

Meanwhile, Arabella was in the dining quarter, pouring herself some opened bottle of blood, sipping from it. Amelia joined her, grabbing a glass. They sat together in silence. Then Lucien, Adrian, and Vladimir entered, joining the women for a drink. "Is it true Caleb is back in the dungeon?" Amelia asked. Lucien glanced at Arabella, who nodded.

"That is true. Gabriel mentioned Caleb was thrown out of his group and almost exposed our kind, so he's back where he belongs now," Arabella said. Amelia chuckled, prompting the men to laugh along. "Where's Gabriel, by the way?" Arabella inquired. Lucien gestured outside.

"I believe he's with Amy," Lucien said. Arabella looked concerned. "I'm sure they're both fine. I haven't sensed Larry or anyone else for a while. Maybe there won't be a battle or war," Lucien suggested.

Amelia smiled. "I hope so. We have lost some of our kind and that does hurt," Amelia said. Arabella nodded before she took another sip. "Well, since there's not much required of us today, it might be nice to get some fresh air. Maybe explore parts of the city we usually overlook. As long as we're well-fed, we should be fine," Amelia proposed.

Adrian smiled. "I am not sure if I am ready to face humans right now, Amelia. I mean, just because I feel sated right now does not mean the hunger might creep up on me in an hour or so. Humans have no purpose for me," Adrian said. Amelia smiled and felt sadness inside of her.

"Daniel used to talk like that. I remember how he enjoyed hunting when we were younger," Amelia said. Adrian's mood shifted to anger.

"I really hate Larry. Even though Katrina was decent, I can't forgive her for killing our brother," Adrian declared.

Vladimir nodded. "Losing someone special is irreplaceable, and words can't heal the wounds and scars. I hope this Larry character meets his end soon," he said, finishing his glass. Just then, Gabriel and Amy re-entered through the sliding doors.

"Oh," Gabriel said as he saw everyone looking somber. "Are we interrupting?" Everyone shook their head. "Is this about Daniel?" Gabriel asked. Then they all nodded. "I know the feeling. I love you all, but the fact that one of our own members is missing does hurt," Gabriel said.

Arabella noticed Amy had been crying. "My child," she said gently. "Are you okay?" Amy nodded. "If you ever need company or someone to talk to, you can always come to me. Remember that, Amy," Arabella offered. Amy nodded again before heading toward the staircase. Ginger was descending the stairs.

"Amy, are you okay?" Ginger asked. Amy shook her head, tears streaming down her face. Ginger rushed over, embracing her.

"What happened? Did Father do something?" Amy shook her head. "Mother?" Ginger queried. Amy shook her head again.

"No," Amy said. "Father is considering sacrificing himself. He asked if we were ready to become queens and matriarchs of the family. It's all happening so fast, Ginger," Amy confided. Ginger held Amy, comforting her with her embrace.

"Breathe, Amy," Ginger urged. "It's going to be okay. Just try to stay as relaxed as possible. You're having a panic attack. There's no point in getting scared now. Mother and father will be fine, and so will we. If and when the time comes for us to become matriarchs, we'll be ready. For now, try to breathe in and out," Ginger said, using her powers to calm Amy. Following Ginger's instructions, Amy soon found herself relaxing.

"Good," Ginger said soothingly. "Now, your children are hungry and need you. Do you need anything to feed them?" Amy pondered for a moment.

"Well," Amy replied, "they do seem to enjoy drinking blood. Maybe I should ask father where the syringe is so I can feed them blood again." Ginger rolled her eyes.

"Okay, I'll leave you to handle that. I still can't get over the fact that you're feeding children blood," Ginger said, walking towards the dining quarter.

"Good evening, Ginger," Gabriel said. "Is everything okay?" Ginger nodded, noticing Amy re-entering the dining quarter. "Amy, what can I do for you?" Gabriel asked. Amy looked around.

"Do you still have that syringe and a fresh bottle of blood?" Gabriel smiled and stood up. "My children have developed a taste for blood," Amy informed the others.

Lucien chuckled, prompting laughter from everyone. "They're growing up fast, aren't they?" Lucien asked. Amy joined in the laughter.

"Yes, they are," Amy said, taking the syringe and bottle of blood from Gabriel. She sat down, crossed her legs, and let Gabrielle sit with her back to Amy. Amy drew some blood into the syringe and gently squirted it into Gabrielle's mouth until she grabbed the syringe, sucking on it until it was empty. "Wow," Amy exclaimed. "That was strange."

Gabrielle then began to whimper, causing the other two children to want some. "Okay, just a moment, my sweets," Amy said, distributing the blood to Maggie and Nathaniel, then back to Gabrielle, who eagerly consumed it. "Holy moly," Amy whispered. "You're all growing up so fast."

There was a knock at the door. "Come in," Amy said. Arabella entered the room. "Mother, what a surprise," Amy remarked. Arabella smiled.

"I just wanted to check on how you're doing, Amy," Arabella said. "Wow, your children have grown quickly. Is it because of the blood?"

Amy shrugged. "I'm not sure. I'm not sure about anything anymore, mother. Nothing makes sense," Amy said sharply, rising to her feet and walking to the window.

"Is everything okay, Amy?" Arabella asked. Amy shook her head. "What is going on? What happened?" Amy turned around and sighed.

"Is Father planning on having himself killed off, Mother? I mean, he asked if I was ready to become matriarch of the family," Amy said with anger in her voice. "Why does nobody ever tell me about these things?" Arabella nodded.

"I understand, Amy. I was never told of anything either. I never had a say in any decisions. Your father was the one who took care of everything, including having you both sent away and returned. That was quite a surprise to me. Even being brought back from the dead was also unexpected," Arabella said.

"What should I do, Mother? I need you all to support me. I am not sure I can handle anything right now," Amy said. Arabella nodded.

"Well, for now, just take it one day at a time. Don't overburden yourself with too many tasks. Focus on your own needs and desires. Take good care of your children. Nothing urgent is happening. We're all alive and healthy. You'll be okay," Arabella advised, kissing Amy's forehead.

Amy nodded, clinging to her mother. "Please, don't leave me right now. Stay with me for a little longer. I feel like this panic attack isn't over yet," Amy said.

Arabella wrapped her arms around Amy, offering comfort. "Of course, my sweet Amy. I'll stay as long as you need. I'm sorry if this is our first real moment of mother-daughter bonding. I've been preoccupied with other issues, but I promise to be more present in your life. You're never alone. Remember, you have your sister, father, aunts, uncles, and me. You're never alone," Arabella reassured.

Amy slowly let go, feeling a bit better. "Thank you, mother. Sometimes it all gets too overwhelming, and I feel a bit crazy. I just want to do well, but fear catches me off guard," Amy said. Arabella nodded.

"You're not alone in feeling that way. Everyone experiences moments of calm, then suddenly, stress and anxiety hit," Arabella said with a light chuckle. Amy giggled and released her embrace.

"Do not worry about anything right now, Amy. Your father is just looking out for our best interests. If he trusts you with such an important role, just consider it. There are no immediate steps or coronations, but he believes these discussions are important. Just think about it, nothing more," Arabella advised. Amy smiled. "So, are you okay now?" Arabella asked. Amy nodded. "Good. I'll go see what everyone else is up to," Arabella said, leaving the room.

Gabriel then transformed back into his original form. Arabella approached him, but Gabriel motioned for her to wait. "Just a moment, Arabella," he whispered. "I just spoke with Amy, and she's doing well. She wants some time alone."

"Well, okay, I guess," Arabella said, sounding uncertain but allowing Gabriel to lead her back to the staircase. Left alone, Amy pondered her potential future. Would she make a good queen of her kind? Would Ginger feel jealous if she became queen?

Ginger walked over to Amy's room and closed the door. "Say, Amy, how are you feeling? I heard that our mother was calming you down, but for what reason?" Ginger asked. Amy sensed a hint of anger in her voice, but tried to remain as calm as possible.

"It's nothing major, Ginger. Just a wave of anxiety with everything happening. I haven't been sleeping well and had this awful dream about Caleb being my husband. It felt so real that I went to see him," Amy explained.

"What?" Ginger interrupted sharply. Amy frowned, pausing for a few seconds before continuing.

"As I was saying before you rudely interrupted, Ginger, I went to see Caleb to check if he was casting a spell on me. But when I saw him, I didn't notice anything unusual," Amy said. Ginger rolled her eyes and crossed her arms.

"And?" Amy prompted. Ginger shrugged. "Did Father talk about ending his life?" she asked. Amy's eyes widened.

"Yes," Amy confirmed. "I've also heard rumors that he's changed his mind and now wants to do it. It's all so absurd. Is there something you need, Ginger?" Amy asked. Ginger shrugged again. "Would you like to spend time with your nieces and nephew?" Ginger offered a small smile.

"Perhaps another time," Ginger said. "I think I will see what our father is up to for today," Ginger said before she walked out of the room.

Amy sighed, relieved yet troubled. She wondered if Ginger knew about Gabriel's plans. The secrecy and lack of honesty within the family were starting to weigh on her. Amy had assumed Lucien would be the next patriarch, not her becoming queen, a role she wasn't eager to embrace.

Deciding to find Gabriel, Amy went to the main floor of the castle. She found Amelia, Lucien, Adrian, and Vladimir in the living quarters, but Arabella was absent. Guessing that Gabriel and Ginger might be in the study, Amy headed there and saw Ginger and Arabella standing before Gabriel. As Amy approached, Ginger turned with a look of anger.

"Well, well, well," Ginger said, clapping her hands sarcastically. "Isn't this the future queen?" Arabella placed a hand on Ginger's shoulder, attempting to soothe her.

"No, Mother. Why should Amy be the queen of our family? Why not you or Amelia?" Ginger demanded.

Gabriel rose and beckoned Amy into his study, indicating she should close the door. "Girls," he began, only to be interrupted by Arabella clearing her throat.

"I am not a girl, Gabriel," Arabella said sharply. Gabriel sighed and shook his head.

"I wasn't referring to you, Arabella. I meant our daughters. I know you're a woman, but they'll always be my little ones, regardless of their age," Gabriel responded.

Arabella struggled to control her emotions, trying not to get angry at Gabriel. "So, nobody is being appointed queen of this family. That was merely a fleeting thought. As I've already mentioned twice, I will continue as the patriarch of this family. Is that understood?" Gabriel said firmly. Ginger glanced at Amy and shook her head.

"Father," Amy interjected. "What's all this about? Why are you acting like this, and when did you start thinking this way?" she asked. Gabriel leaned back in his chair.

"It began when Larry almost defeated me. It made me reconsider our whole situation and conflict. Your mother was right; this conflict is my responsibility. I tried to resolve it, but it ended badly," Gabriel explained. Ginger scoffed, drawing a confused look from Gabriel. "Yes, Ginger? Did you want to add something?" he asked. Ginger shook her head.

"Who will be the next heir or heiress of our family, father?" Amy inquired. Gabriel turned to Arabella.

"Your mother," Ginger interjected. "My sweets, I considered having one or both of you as queens of our family, but Arabella is my wife and the rightful queen. Larry wouldn't dare go after her, unless he wanted to make her his queen. And your mother is strong and capable of handling any threats," Gabriel explained.

Amy shook her head and stormed off. "This is ridiculous," she snapped, drawing attention as she passed. "This family is despicable and dangerous. I have no desire to stay here anymore." Gabriel followed Amy to her bedroom and closed the door behind him. "Please, Father, don't try to fix this now. I can't handle any more lies, deception, and responsibilities. It's too much," Amy said, her voice breaking.

Gabriel raised his hands in a gesture of surrender. "Amy," he began, "I'm sorry for everything you and your sister have endured. I regret bringing you into this world, but at the same time, I don't. You both are precious jewels in my crown, strong and beautiful women. My intentions were good, but it led you both down a dangerous path. Please don't give up on this family or on me. Despite the occasional drama, we're doing well," Gabriel pleaded.

Amy sighed and sat on the edge of her bed, dabbing her eyes. "I just wanted a normal life without these problems," she said. Gabriel knelt in front of her.

"The human world has its challenges, too, Amy. Remember Heather?" Gabriel asked. Amy looked up at him, frightened. "Too soon?" he asked. Amy shook her head.

"How do you know about Heather, Father?" Amy asked as she slowly moved away from him.

Gabriel sighed. "Alistair told me about her. She was not entirely cruel as a girl, but she did make your life a bit harder. Now we have our family drama and we do love each other despite these situations. I do care about you and will always care. I mean, I was so worried and scared when Larry kidnapped you. I love you, Amy Ambrose. You are my light. Both you and Ginger are the lights in my darkened life and heart. You both are my jewels to my crown. Nothing or anyone will ever replace you," Gabriel said with a smile on his face.

Amy sighed. "I love you too, Father. I just want to have some positivity in my life, you know?" Amy said. Gabriel nodded. "I want my children to have a beautiful future, filled with everything they desire," Amy added. Gabriel nodded again.

"And they will," Gabriel said. "I had to come up here and let you know that you are loved, Amy." Amy nodded and stood up.

"Thank you, Father," Amy said. "I will be okay. You do not have to worry about me right now."

Gabriel smiled, stood up, kissed her on the forehead, and left the room. Exhausted from everything, Amy lay down on her bed to rest. Meanwhile, Alistair and Darcia, accompanied by their sons, decided to take a walk outside the castle. "That was quite something, wasn't it?" Darcia commented as they walked ahead of their sons. Alistair nodded.

"I do hope that this Larry character will soon be out of the picture. We could use a vacation, just the seven of us, like before," Alistair said. Darcia agreed.

Walking silently beside Raymond, Bryan mused, "So, if Amy becomes queen of our kind someday, what would that make me?

Would I be king, or is there only one queen or king per lifetime?" Alistair smirked and turned around.

"I wouldn't be so sure about becoming a future king, Bryan," Alistair replied. "First, enjoy your own life before considering such a significant responsibility." Bryan rolled his eyes.

"Why not, father?" Bryan challenged. "Do you doubt my ability to be a potential ruler of this family?"

Darcia looked at Alistair. "I think he would make an excellent ruler, my dear husband," she said as they continued their stroll, observing humans dining at restaurants and bars.

# Darkest Time

In the darkest time, Larry remained at his parents' apartment complex with Viviana and Darcia, who were growing closer. Noticing his group's lackluster mood, Larry decided to treat them to a fancy meal, proposing a group hunt.

"What say you?" Larry asked as he looked at the other members, just lounging around looking bored. The other members nodded. "Good. We leave now," Larry said.

After locking the door, Larry led the way to the city area. However, his nose detected a familiar scent. "Alistair," he muttered through clenched teeth. Bianca, confused, looked at him. "He and his family are out for a walk," Larry whispered. Viviana tapped Bianca on the shoulder.

"Who is Alistair?" Viviana asked. Bianca shrugged. "Is he dangerous?" Larry smiled and pulled Viviana closer to him.

"Of course not. However, his sons, especially Bryan, might be a potential threat," Larry said, recalling how Bryan had nearly killed him. Larry considered Bryan as a possible next target after dealing with Gabriel.

As Alistair walked with his family, he suddenly stopped. "I think we've gone far enough," Alistair whispered, sensing an ominous presence. As Alistair and Darcia turned to leave, they noticed humans staring at them oddly. Alistair smiled faintly and urged his sons to move faster ahead.

Larry, sensing Alistair's fear and anxiety, quickened his pace. Then, he halted, realizing Gabriel would retaliate if Alistair were harmed. He remembered Amy's ability to overpower his brother William and defeat his parents in their last battle. Larry raised his hand, signaling his group to stop. "Let's head to a different part of the city," he suggested. "Maybe we can find a hospital to obtain resources." The group then headed toward a hospital.

Alistair felt the chilling sensation fade and regained his composure. "What was that about, Alistair?" Darcia inquired. Alistair nodded.

"Larry was nearby," Alistair whispered. Darcia's eyes widened in fear. "It's okay. He's no longer near us, but I wanted to avoid any confrontation."

"Why?" Bryan asked. "What if we could have ended Larry once and for all? We could finally be free from all this drama and leave the family behind."

Alistair dismissed Bryan's remark. "What?" Bryan snapped. "It feels like we're just waiting for things to happen. Why not take control? Why wait for trouble to come to us?" Alistair sighed.

"Bryan, I can't afford to lose any of you...ever," Alistair said. "After seeing Daniel's lifeless body, I couldn't stop thinking about if that were one of you or Darcia. Caleb hurt Darcia, but what if he had killed her in that motel room?"

Bryan shook his head. "Nothing would have happened to Darcia, Father. We are immortal, remember? Larry keeps coming back from the dead, but what happened to Daniel? I am not sure about if he truly is dead. I mean, why did Gabriel not have Amelia try harder with her spells?" Bryan said. Alistair held Bryan in his arms. "What are you doing?"

"Holding you, my son," Alistair whispered. "I know how hard it was to be at that funeral service, but you all did wonderful."

Bryan nodded. "Thanks, I guess," Bryan murmured. Alistair gently stroked Bryan's cheek.

"I do not consider myself weak. I prefer to be cautious before facing new challenges," Alistair whispered. Darcia embraced Alistair, holding him tightly. "I can't bear the thought of losing any of you," he said.

Darcia looked at Bryan. "Neither can I," she agreed. "You all are too precious to me." Raymond, Silas, Joshua, and Xavier all nodded in agreement.

"Should we head back to the castle now?" Bryan asked. Alistair surveyed the darkness around them.

"Well," Alistair considered, "maybe we could do it the old-fashioned way. Hunt some animals for a change."

Bryan sighed, shaking his head. "What about a club, like you taught me, Alistair?" he asked. Alistair smiled and nodded.

"You remember?" Alistair asked. Bryan couldn't help but smile back. He nodded.

"I do, Father. I remember my first female victim was this petite brunette girl. How sweet and soft she tasted," Bryan said as he remembered that first moment. "I remember what you told me to do and I was quite skeptical at first, but once it worked, I was convinced about my powers," Bryan said.

"Well then," Alistair said, "how about we visit a nightclub and dance our troubles away?" They arrived at a nightclub bustling with attractive men and women. Bryan wandered around until he spotted a beautiful redhead with green eyes, reminding him of Gabrielle's blue eyes. Overwhelmed with sadness, he rushed outside, feeling nauseous. Some humans approached him, but he waved them away.

"I'm okay," Bryan insisted, turning to see Alistair joining him, dismissing the concerned onlookers.

"What happened back there, Bryan?" Alistair inquired. "Are you alright? Did you drink too much?" Bryan shook his head.

"No, Father, but I saw someone who looked like she could be an adult Gabrielle," Bryan said. "I could not do it, Father. I could not go after her. She looked so sweet and beautiful, but I could not claim her as my victim. If someone looked at Gabrielle that way, I'd destroy them if they ever targeted those kids," he said, wiping his eyes.

Alistair placed a hand on Bryan's shoulder, nodding. "Since I've shown you your powers, Bryan, I believe you could be a great patriarch. You'll be a strong protector for those children, and they'll love you," Alistair affirmed. They waited for Darcia and the other boys to emerge with their victims.

"Well," Alistair remarked, eyeing the four girls and one guy leaving the club, "we have a special treat for you all." He led them to a secluded, wooded area for the attack. The scene was interrupted by an elderly woman walking her dog, witnessing the horror and fleeing in panic. Alistair watched her go, regretting the disturbance.

"Bryan, would you like to take her?" Alistair asked, gesturing toward the woman. Bryan looked at him, confused. "Or I can handle it," Alistair offered. Bryan nodded in agreement. Alistair approached the woman, whose dog barked fiercely, and cupped her face gently.

"You saw nothing tonight. You and your dog were just enjoying a pleasant evening, and then you went straight home to bed," Alistair said, using his powers to influence her. The woman nodded blankly and walked away.

Alistair returned to his group and saw them disposing of the bodies. "Alistair," Darcia said, her voice tinged with fear. "Is everything okay?" Alistair nodded. "Everything's fine. We should be more cautious with our hunting," he advised. Darcia and the boys nodded in agreement. Bryan crossed his arms, stepping back.

"Son, are you alright?" Darcia inquired. Alistair glanced at Bryan and smiled. "What?"

"I believe Bryan will be an excellent father figure to Amy's children," Alistair said. Darcia looked puzzled. "Bryan saw a girl resembling Gabrielle and felt a protective instinct, right?" Bryan nodded, wiping his eyes.

"I'm a monster," Bryan lamented, looking at the remnants of their hunt. "I can't keep doing this, but my instincts crave humans."

Darcia offered a comforting smile. "If you all want a break from hunting, I understand," she said, placing a hand on Bryan's shoulder. "Let's head back to the castle." Alistair led them back, and everyone retired to their rooms. Alistair and Darcia entered their own room and closed the door.

"Alistair, do you think our son will stick to blood donors for his sustenance?" Darcia asked.

Alistair shrugged. "Perhaps, my sweet," he said, removing his shoes. "Perhaps we could rely on hospital donor blood for a while?" Darcia nodded in agreement.

"It's heartening to see Bryan wanting to change," Darcia reflected. "I recall how difficult it was for me to transition from hospital blood to humans. Our first hunt together was memorable," she said with a smile.

Alistair smiled back. "It was intense, but I was impressed with your development," he said. Darcia took his hand and kissed it.

"Returning to blood donors will be challenging, but we'll manage," Darcia said. "Gabriel's blood supply is adequate, but it doesn't satisfy like human blood. We can try a different source for a while." They then snuggled under the covers and turned off the light.

Amy tucked her children in when a knock sounded at her door. "Yes?" she asked, a bit unsure. Bryan entered and gently closed the door.

"How are the little ones?" Bryan asked. Amy smiled and nodded. "Wow," Bryan whispered. "They have grown quite fast, have they not, Amy?" Bryan asked. Amy nodded.

"They have taken a liking to our blood source, Bryan," Amy whispered with a giggle. Bryan chuckled and looked at each of them. Then his focus went back to Gabrielle.

"I was out with my family tonight, our last hunt for a while," Bryan whispered. "At a dance club, I saw a girl with red hair and green eyes, similar to Gabrielle."

"Gabrielle has blue eyes," Amy corrected, looking at her daughter. Bryan nodded.

"I know, Amy," he whispered. "That's why I said 'similar.' Seeing her made me reconsider our hunting. I'd hate for these children to be viewed as potential prey."

Amy nodded in understanding. "I know the feeling, Bryan. Larry and Katrina kidnapped me and my children, which I hope won't traumatize them forever," she said. Bryan nodded sympathetically. "Sometimes, I wonder if I'm in over my head being a parent. I was raised by a human mother whom I loved deeply. Then I find out I have a biological mother who came back from the dead. That's been traumatizing for me, Bryan," Amy confided.

Bryan nodded and wrapped his arms around Amy. "I understand, Amy. If you need to cry, I'm here for you. If you need comfort, just let me know," he whispered. Amy nodded and hugged him back.

"Thank you, Bryan," Amy whispered softly. "You're truly an amazing person, you know?"

Bryan smiled, holding Amy for a few more minutes, waiting for her to decide when to release the embrace. "What would you like, Amy? Do you want a sleeping companion, or would you prefer to be alone?" he asked. Amy smiled and nodded.

"It would be nice to have someone here with me," Amy said. Bryan smiled and nodded before he took his jacket and shoes off before getting into the other side of Amy's bed.

"Do you need proper sleepwear, Bryan?" Amy asked, noticing him in his outdoor clothes. Bryan shook his head. "I could check if my father has spare pajamas?" Bryan shook his head again. "Well, okay. Sleep well, Bryan." They both fell asleep in each other's arms.

In his quarters, Gabriel, dressed in satin pajamas and a robe, wasn't feeling tired. Arabella looked over at him before turning to drift off to sleep.

Gabriel pondered how to convince Amy to become the next heiress of his group. How did Ginger learn about his plan? Did Amy mention it? He reminded himself not to overthink. Perhaps Ginger had some unknown powers, or maybe Amy did talk about becoming matriarch. Either way, it wasn't a significant issue. The challenge was persuading Amy to accept the position without using his powers, which he reserved for emergencies.

Leaving his bed, Gabriel walked to his lounge and then entered Katrina's old bedroom. It was small but cozy, with a red duvet decorated with roses and paintings of cottages and mountains. He felt remorseful about her fate, realizing he no longer wanted to create new members. Everything he had hoped for and done had turned out contrary to his expectations. He was overwhelmed with guilt, recalling how Katrina once saw him as her prince charming, but it all ended tragically.

He thought about Caleb, remembering how young and naive he was when they first met. Gabriel had promised him a wonderful life, but now Caleb had been ostracized by his friends and was confined in the dungeon of Gabriel's castle. Gabriel recognized he had overstepped in many ways, yet he was curious about the girl named Viviana. Glancing at his watch, he saw it was approaching seven in the morning. He planned to wait until evening to take a walk to Larry's residence and learn more about her.

Gabriel attempted to rest, but his mind was restless. He kept going back to the moment he saw Larry and attacked Viviana and him. The memory kept replaying like a broken record. Arabella, sensing his unease, opened her eyes but remained still. "Gabriel, are you alright?" she asked. Gabriel sat up to find Arabella gazing at him. "Can't you sleep?" she inquired. Gabriel shook his head.

"I'm conflicted about my plans, Arabella. Should I let myself die so you can become queen of our family?" he asked.

Arabella rolled her eyes and then closed them again. "Try to get some sleep, Gabriel. It might help," she suggested before falling silent. Gabriel, still restless, put on his suit. It was now midday, and he had a few more hours before his investigation into Larry and Viviana's plans.

Meanwhile, Larry lay in his bedroom, contemplating how to execute his plan against Gabriel and Bryan. He considered using Viviana as bait to lure Gabriel, but he knew she might resent being used in such a way. It was a complex situation, finding the right strategy to draw Gabriel closer. Moreover, his fiancée was back in his life, but she hadn't shown interest in advancing their wedding plans. Confused and unsettled, he closed his eyes, drifting into sleep.

In his dream, Larry found himself back at the castle, with Amy standing at the top of the stairs, sharpening her nails. "If you're here for my children, you'll have to get through me," Amy snapped. Larry raised his hands in surrender and knelt.

"I want to apologize for my actions over the past years, Amy," he said. Amy paused her nail filing but kept her gaze fixed on him. "I know I've made your life difficult, and I understand if you can't forgive me."

Amy slowly descended the stairs. "Oh, Larry, hearing those words from you means so much to me," she said, opening her arms. As he moved closer, expecting an embrace, she suddenly bit down hard on his neck, blood spurting out. Larry growled and screamed until Gabriel appeared, biting into the other side of his neck near his shoulder. Startled awake, Larry jolted up in shock from the vivid nightmare.

"Gabriel must die, and soon!" Larry exclaimed in his room. Bianca hurried in.

"Brother, are you okay?" Bianca asked. Larry looked at her , then fell back onto the mattress. "Do you need anything?" Larry shook his head and sat up again.

"I can't stand knowing Gabriel is still alive out there, Bianca. He must be eliminated. No matter how many attempts we make, he will eventually die in this life," Larry asserted.

Bianca nodded sympathetically. "And so it will be, dear brother," she said softly. "I'll return to my room, but if you need me, please call." Larry nodded but found himself unable to sleep again, the dream having deeply disturbed him. He contemplated a different approach to Gabriel, maybe a friendlier gesture, perhaps offering a human or a bouquet of flowers. Whatever the plan, he knew it needed to be executed swiftly.

As dusk fell on the castle, Gabriel, dressed in his usual black suit, brushed his long black hair, and checked his teeth for any bloodstains. He left the castle and headed towards Larry's apartment complex. Just as he arrived, he saw Larry leaving the building. Gabriel quickly hid behind a nearby tree to observe Larry's movements. Larry stopped, sniffing the air.

"Gabriel? Is that you?" Larry called out, standing a few feet from Gabriel's hiding spot. Gabriel reluctantly emerged, noticing Larry wasn't in an aggressive stance. "What brings you here alone?" Larry inquired.

Gabriel nodded. "I'm not here to fight, Larry," he said. "I came because a family member saw that your fiancée is alive again. I'm glad to hear it," Gabriel explained.

Larry eyed Gabriel suspiciously. "How did your family member find out, Gabriel? She hasn't been around here much, so that confuses me," Larry questioned, his tone sharp. Gabriel raised his hands in a gesture of peace.

"We each have different abilities, Larry, does that make sense?" Gabriel asked. Larry shrugged. "I can't see the future, but someone in my family can. They saw Viviana. How is she? Was it my doing, turning her?" Gabriel inquired.

Larry nodded absentmindedly. "Yes, Gabriel," he said. "She's one of us now, a shapeshifter. Does that please you?" Gabriel shook his head.

"In all honesty, Larry, nothing makes me happy. Never has and never will," Gabriel said. Larry smirked at Gabriel.

"So, what, you're here for a psychological session to discuss your life's grievances?" Larry asked sarcastically. Gabriel shook his head.

"No, Larry. I just wanted to confirm if Viviana is indeed back in your life."

At that moment, Bianca and Viviana stepped out, both glaring at Gabriel and baring their teeth. "Larry, should I call for backup?" Bianca asked. Larry raised his hand, signaling no.

"Maybe not this time," Larry said. Gabriel looked up and saw Viviana, the same woman he had once violently attacked. He fixated on her until Larry snapped his fingers, redirecting Gabriel's attention.

"Focus here," Larry commanded, pointing his fingers at his own eyes. "Stop staring at her." Gabriel nodded in acknowledgment.

"Apologies," Gabriel said. "I regret what happened, but I have nothing more to add." He then turned to leave.

"Wait, Gabriel. Maybe we can find closure to our feud," Larry suggested. Gabriel paused, intrigued. "What if you didn't have to die at all? What if we end this feud with apologies, maybe some financial compensation? Interested?" Larry proposed.

Gabriel, sensing danger, began to back away. "If you have more to say about this deal, you know where to find me," Larry said, watching Gabriel head back to his castle. "What a coward," Larry muttered, returning to Bianca and Viviana. "I hoped to exploit his vulnerability, but it seems he saw through me."

Viviana offered, "Maybe I can act as bait for Gabriel. I could win his trust and lure him here for a surprise attack." She noticed Gabriel's gaze earlier. "He looked at me with such love and devotion," she said teasingly. Larry hissed playfully.

"Gabriel is undeniably handsome, Viviana. Just don't fall for his charm," Larry cautioned. Viviana smiled wryly.

"He did look good in a suit, but I know the monster he is," she stated firmly. Larry then left to replenish their blood supply, leaving the women alone.

"So, using seduction to gain Gabriel's trust," Bianca mused with a sneer. "Maybe you could pretend to be a babysitter or a housemaid?" she suggested. Viviana agreed.

"I'll play any role if it means ending that monster's life," Viviana declared. "He may be handsome, but inside, he's repulsive. I can't imagine how many people he's consumed to stay strong and youthful. It's heartbreaking."

Bianca smiled and gently cupped Viviana's face with both hands. "I have complete faith that you will be excellent as bait for Gabriel Ambrose," Bianca said before she released Viviana. Observing Viviana's tomboyish attire, Bianca asked, "Have you ever worn a dress, Viviana?" Viviana nodded regretfully.

"All my dresses are gone," Viviana admitted. Bianca then led her to her bedroom and showcased a variety of outfits, ranging from jeans and suits to dresses. "My mother wore lots of dresses before she switched to jeans," Viviana noted.

Bianca picked out a black dress adorned with a floral pattern. "Try this. It'll make you more appealing to Gabriel," she suggested. Viviana emerged from the bathroom transformed. Bianca was pleased.

"Do you use makeup? What colors suit you?" Bianca inquired. Viviana confirmed she did. "Given your blonde hair, I think pink and peach shades would suit you. May I do your makeup?" Viviana agreed.

While Bianca prepared Viviana for her new role, Gabriel returned to the castle, visibly distressed. Hildegard quickly fetched a bottle of blood and handed it to him. "What happened, Master Gabriel?" she asked. Lucien, Adrian, Vladimir, and Amelia gathered around in concern.

"Nothing much, but Larry almost made a deal with me. It felt off, and I saw his fiancée again, now a shapeshifter," Gabriel explained. Lucien was intrigued.

"So Joshua's visions were accurate?" he asked. Gabriel nodded.

"Indeed," Lucien mused. "What did Larry want to bargain for?" Gabriel shrugged.

"It didn't feel right, so I fled before he could attack," Gabriel said, slowly regaining his composure. "He's planning something. Maybe Joshua can provide more insight."

# Epilogue

Bianca had successfully transformed Viviana from a street girl into a beautiful nanny candidate for Amy's children. Admiring her work, she said, "I think you're ready for your first job, Viviana. How do you feel?" Viviana shrugged nervously.

"Nervous. I feel like I'm being sent to my death. Why couldn't you be the nanny?" she asked.

Bianca shook her head. "The way Gabriel looked at you, I saw how much he's captivated by you, Viviana. You might even become the queen of that castle someday. What do you think?" she asked playfully. Viviana laughed at the idea and shook her head.

"Me, a queen? I'm more of a housewife type," Viviana said modestly. Bianca shrugged, acknowledging her perspective.

"You never know, right?" Bianca asked. Viviana nodded. "Well, let's head over there, and we'll see if they'll invite you inside," Bianca said, grabbing their jackets and opening the door to their apartment complex.

As they approached the castle, Bianca stopped a block away. "This is where we part ways. Act like a girl in desperate need of a job. If Gabriel is as I expect, he'll probably take pity on you," Bianca advised. Viviana hugged her tightly, surprising Bianca.

"Oh, a hug," Bianca reacted. "Good luck out there, Viviana." Viviana seemed uncertain. "Should we keep in touch, or should I try to escape?" she asked. Bianca, realizing the importance of staying connected, handed over her phone.

"Here is my phone. Call our home if you have questions or concerns," Bianca said, letting Viviana take it. "Good luck, Viviana. We'll keep in touch," she added, then turned back toward the apartment complex.

Viviana walked toward the castle, feeling anxious with every chirp and rustle. "Relax, Viviana," she whispered to herself. "There's no immediate danger."

Back at the castle, Joshua and his brothers were watching TV when Joshua suddenly had a vision of Viviana approaching, looking stunning. He stood up abruptly. "Viviana," he whispered, drawing teasing comments from the others. Realizing the gravity of the situation, Joshua rushed to find Alistair.

"Father, Viviana is coming here," Joshua said urgently. Alistair sat up in bed.

"We should inform Gabriel. Did you see anything else?" Alistair asked. Joshua shook his head. "Thanks for the heads-up. I'll check on Gabriel," Alistair said.

The doorbell rang just then. Hildegard answered the door. "Yes, dear, how can I help you?" she asked.

"I'm here to see Gabriel Ambrose. Is he available?" Viviana asked. Gabriel arrived at the door, greeted by Viviana's seductive smile.

"Gabriel, I'm Viviana, in need of work. Do you need a nanny or a housekeeper?" she inquired. Gabriel smiled warmly.

"Welcome, Viviana. This is Hildegard, our housekeeper and nanny. But tell me about your qualifications," Gabriel said, inviting her in.

Meanwhile, back at the apartment, Larry returned with a box of blood packs, setting it on the dining table. "So, our plan is in motion?" he asked. Bianca nodded with a smile.

"Yes, brother. I gave Viviana my phone so she can contact us," she confirmed.

Larry smiled, pleased. "Excellent," he said, and they both laughed, reveling in their scheme.

Back at the castle, Joshua hurried down the stairs. "Gabriel, I need to talk to you," he said, but paused when he saw Viviana looking up at him with a grin.

"What is it, Joshua?" Gabriel asked. Viviana smiled seductively at Joshua, which caused Joshua to forget what he was about to say.

"Oh nothing Gabriel. I just heard we had a visitor," Joshua replied, forcing a smile.

Gabriel nodded. "She would be interested in becoming our new nanny and help Amy out with her kids. She even brought what the humans call, a resume," Gabriel said. Joshua smiled and chuckled.

"Did she? I am Joshua and who might you be?" Joshua asked. Viviana got to her feet, extending her hand.

"Viviana. Gabriel had made me many years ago, but I have forgiven him for his actions. He gave me a new and more beautiful life," Viviana said. Joshua smiled.

"Of course, he did," Joshua said.

Gabriel could not help, but laugh at Joshua's expression. "So, Viviana. When would you like to start?" Gabriel asked. Viviana shrugged seductively.

"Whenever you need me, Master Gabriel," Viviana said with her seductive voice and eyes. Gabriel smiled and nodded.

"I shall go over to see my daughter Amy and see how she is doing," Gabriel said before he left. Suddenly his head hurt and he felt blood returning back to his brain. What was he going to do?

Then, Amy appeared with Gabrielle in her arms. "Father, good to see you. The children need more blood. Is there some in the dining quarter?" Gabriel confirmed there was. "Thank you," Amy said, heading to the dining quarter. When she entered, her gaze met Viviana's bright blue eyes, and she instantly felt a sense of dislike.

"And who might you be?" Amy asked, holding Gabrielle securely.

Viviana smiled warmly. "I'm Viviana, and I hope to become the new nanny for this family," she introduced herself.